THE BLOODSTONE PAPERS

THE BLOODSTONE PAPERS

Glen Duncan

Scribner

First published in Great Britain by Scribner, 2006
An imprint of Simon & Schuster UK Ltd
A CBS COMPANY

Copyright © Glen Duncan, 2006

Scribner and design are trademarks of Macmillan Library Reference
USA, Inc., used under licence by Simon & Schuster, the publisher of
this work.

1 3 5 7 9 10 8 6 4 2

Simon & Schuster UK Ltd
Africa House
64–78 Kingsway
London WC2B 6AH

www.simonsays.co.uk

Simon & Schuster Australia
Sydney

A CIP catalogue record for this book is available from the British Library

Hardback ISBN: 0-7432-5229-2
Hardback EAN: 9780743252294
Trade paperback ISBN: 0-7432-9543-9
Trade paperback EAN: 9780743295437

Typeset in Bembo by M Rules
Printed and bound in Great Britain by
Mackays of Chatham plc

For my mum and dad,
with love

ACKNOWLEDGEMENTS

Daily, during the writing of this book, I've been reminded of how fortunate I am in my family and friends, all of whom, in different ways, have helped me see *The Bloodstone Papers* through to its end. Therefore my sincerest thanks to: Kim Teasdale, Louise Maker, Mark Duncan, Marina Hardiman, Edgar Duncan, Stephen Coates, Nicola Stewart, Jonathan Field, Vicky Hutchinson, Sarah Forest, Peter Sollett, Eva Vives, Andrea Freeman, Mike Loteryman, Gavin Butt, John Cairns, Nicola Harwood, Jeremy Woodhouse and Isobel Haydon. Thanks to Lydia Hardiman for The Beige Moment.

My agent, Jonny Geller, and my editor, Ben Ball, have between them guided me through six novels with a diligence, sensitivity and loyalty that leaves me profoundly in their debt. Thanks too to Rochelle Venables, Hannah Corbett, Helen Simpson, Carol Anderson and all at Simon & Schuster.

The following titles have been especially useful:

Allen, C. (editor) (1975), *Plain Tales From the Raj*, London, Andre Deutsch Ltd
Anthony, F. (1969), *Britain's Betrayal in India: the Story of the Anglo-Indian Community*, Bombay, Allied Publishers

Brennan, J. (2000), *Curries and Bugles*, Tuttle Publishing, Periplus Editions, North Clarendon, VT

Caplan, L. (2001), *Children of Colonialism*, Berg, Oxford, New York

French, P. (1997), *Liberty or Death*, London, Flmingo

Lonely Planet (Singh, Barkordarian, Beech, Bindloss, Derby, Ham, Harding, Hole, Horton, Pundyk Vidgen) (2003), *India*, Lonely Planet Publications, Melbourne, Oakland, London, Paris

Singh, K. (1974), *India, an Introduction*, HarperCollins Publishers India/The India Today Group, New Delhi, London

Westwood, J. N. (1974), *Railways of India*, David & Charles, Newton Abbot, London, North Pomfret (VT), Vancouver

Lastly, it's not an exaggeration to say that this book would have been impossible without the love, support, faith, tireless story-telling and inimitable cuisine of my mum and dad. Throughout this work – throughout my *life* – they have been, and continue to be, the lights by which I steer.

CONTENTS

CHAPTER ONE

nowadays

(Bolton and London, 2004)

We don't remember everything. Just enough to make it difficult.

'You know the story,' Pasha says, not seeing the problem. 'So what is there to tell it? You start at the beginning, go through the middle, then get to the end.'

The two of us sit whisky-loosened in opposite armchairs after Sunday lunch in the retirement flat in Bolton. I make my pilgrimage there once a month bearing Johnnie Walker Black Label (my dad's switched from Bushmills) and an increasingly unconvincing air of being happy and in control of my life in London, land of *News at Ten* and, by extension, imminent terrorist attack. My mum's in the kitchen, 'getting the washing-up ready' for me, since I, dutiful son, insist on doing it, which consists of her doing the washing-up, then pretending she hasn't. For her that's part of the order of things, along with the pizzazz of Gene Kelly, the unimpeachability of Marks & Spencer and the vandalization of Bolton by its own smoking, swearing and spitting infant yobs, who before we know it will be beating pensioners to death for three pounds forty-seven because they're not one *bit* frightened of jail. I used to throw my hands up at such mantras, patiently and with self-congratulation bring forth undergraduate liberal arguments like exquisite bits of origami. She loved it, that education had worked. I used to romance her with reasoning; it kept us in mutually flirtatious cahoots. These days – paying tax, flagging halfway through novels, sleeping with a claw-hammer under the pillow – I make a flaccid noncommittal face and let it go. This, as much as anything, tips her off that All is Not Well with Her Son.

It's been a good day. Eleven o'clock mass (my monthly faithless gesture for them; there's a shift in their aura come Communion but I remain empewed and kneeling, face averted), then back to the flat for gold and ruby booze: three wets of Black Label for me and the old man, a long Sandeman's port and lemon for my mum, drinks accompanied by the moreish nibbles of my parents' lost past – gathia, choora and seo – followed by a lunch of korma (the dry South Indian version, not the curry house's coconut jism) with pepper-water and plain Dehra Dun rice. Fresh Pakistani sucking mangos – velvety ovoids in flamy yellows and reds that always look extraterrestrial to me – with Walls soft scoop vanilla ice cream to round off. (I've come home to sublime wifely vanilla after years of whoring with mint choc chip and rum and raisin. In all sorts of ways I'm accepting my youth has gone.) Eating temporarily over, the Black Label's out again.

The air indoors holds its ghosts of chilli and tamarind, but the window's open, letting in the exhalation of mown lawns from the tiny council-house gardens across the road, as well as the Boltonian base note of exhaust fumes and old brick. They're built in war zones, these Sheltered Housing schemes. Cheap land. Retirees get to spend their Autumn Years marooned in a sea of paupers, drunks, hookers and thugs. Last month, walking back after midnight from a depressing get-together with an old St Cuthbert's schoolmate (miserably divorced and mercilessly alimonied, looking straight into a nicotine future of brightly lit pubs and quality porn), I was hello loved on Barrow Lane by a bleach blonde prostitute in a purple vinyl mac and white stilettos. She was fat-calved, with a thick porous face and lashes mascara'd up into tarantulas. Lust began its scurry like a match catching – my loins are of an age and jadedness to be ignited by the poor, the half ugly, the too young, the too old – then checked: these are the streets my parents walk. Chastened, I shook my head in furious refusal and trudged on, disappointed that she didn't persist.

The old man and I are discussing, for the umpteenth time, The Book. There is the other thing to discuss, our Secret Business, but the drink's made him forget. I'll have to find a way of reminding him before I go, or there will be hushed clandestine calls from the downstairs communal payphone, the recent digital-ization of which confounds him. My train leaves Manchester at seven; we have only a couple of hours.

'You know the story,' he says again. 'You know all the stories.'

'Yes, but it's not just a question of knowing the stories.'

'Thenwhat?'

Quite. Thenwhat. In the Anglo-Indian – or Eurasian or East Indian or Half-caste or Mongrel or Pariah or Cheechee or Chutney Mary, depending on your angle – idiom, which is to say *our* idiom, this 'Thenwhat?' means: then tell me in what way it's not just a question of knowing the stories, dunderhead. I, when it comes to the business of The Book, am the dunderhead. They were born before The Camps, The Bomb, The Moon, The Ozone, The Internet, The End of History. For them the big things don't change: God, Fate, Love, Time, Beginnings, Endings. Good and Evil. Therefore my difficulty. The Book is to be their story. I've toyed with *The Big Things Don't Change* as an ironic title. Also, since I share Keri Hume's weakness for portent, *The Beige People*. Pasha, who likes to get to the indelicate quick of things, prefers *Mixed Blood*. I can't quite bring myself to reveal the latest working title, *The Cheechee Papers*.

'Whatall do you need to know? Ask me. I remember every-thing.' He claims I've inherited my superhuman memory from him. (It's been a lifelong problem for me, remembering every-thing. *What* restaurant in Manchester? Maude or Melissa or Carl will ask. The one with the Chinese waiter with the Hitler tash. Christ, you can't possibly have forgotten. But they have. My sis-ters, my brother, even Mater and Pater. If I relied on their powers of recollection I'd end up convinced half the details of my past were dreams or imaginings.)

Wearily, I get out my notebook, a Moleskine, since like thou-sands of others (including, the marketing tells me, Earnest Hemmingway and Bruce Chatwin) I've succumbed to the writerly pretensions of this product. I start with some details. 'What year did the Great India Peninsula Railway become the Central Railway?' I ask. I've tried to explain: it's not what I need to know, it's that there's so much I'll *never* know. They want a story with a beginning, a middle and an end. I've told them: every beginning is fraudulent, every middle arbitrary, every ending an illusion. It's the ending that bothers me most. These days I don't even like the sound of the word. *Ending.*

My father leans back in his armchair, points his toes until his ankles crack, narrows his eyes, allows his tongue the run of his proudly not false front teeth. He looks good for seventy-nine, a brown man with a side-parted quiff of thin white hair. The right eye's lost its pep under a blue-grey caul of glaucoma, but the left's shiny hazel, resolutely feisty. He'd suit a thin white moustache, I keep telling him, go the Douglas Fairbanks route. I'm invested in his looks, naturally. Girls I've brought home have flirted with him, surprised at themselves but incapable of ignoring the saltily weathered male flag that'll still rattle and snap in the right oestral breeze. 'Nineteen fifty,' he says. 'Or pos-sibly fifty-one. Actually it could've been fifty-two. Wait. I got my demob papers in . . . nineteen forty-five . . . Or was it . . . Wait. Bleddy hell . . .'

Anglo-Indian accents, the old man's in particular, present a problem. He says 'shot pants' for short pants, 'parr' for power, '*look*hyur' for look here, and 'bleddy', as above, for bloody. Years ago my sister Maude and I secretly tape-recorded him. 'Cheh' was his response when we played it back. 'I sound like a bleddy Indian bugger.'

'And you fought Docherty when you were, what, seventeen?'

'Eighteen. I'd have been . . . Yes. Eighteen. He was a wiry bugger with a bleddy ridiculous handlebar moustache. And I'd given away a stone in weight. You should've seen their faces, my God.'

'Which would have been . . .' I calculate, make a note. 'Nineteen forty-three.'

'Forty-three. Yes. Got him with a straight right, one *kutack* dead on the point.'

And so it goes. After an hour's interrogation (with much side-tracking, many tangents, my dull gentle insistence on dates and places) I've filled three Moleskine pages.

'He'll be asleep in a minute,' my mum says, when I trade places with her at the kitchen sink. 'Fascinating afternoons for me, watching him blow spit bubbles there in the corner.'

I wash the dishes and do yesterday's *Sun* crossword with her. I've given up fighting them about the *Sun*, too (they both tut and shake their heads at the daily Asylum Seeker fictions: What is this country *coming* to, I ask you?), a fight which was in any case hypocritical since I've always found its cartoon news, topless girls and apocalyptic soccer headlines irresistible and infallibly laxative. The flat is at peace, hyperclean salmon shag pile throughout making its contented presence felt, the window sill's carriage clock clucking, visible brass innards hypnotically shuffling and reshuffling fragments of caught light. My mum and I eat Marks & Sparks seedless grapes. This is part of the pattern, our quiet couple of hours while Pasha sails his archipelago of kips. It's where we come into our best alignment. She stops worrying about whether I'm bored.

Sometimes we talk about her lost childhood, for The Book. Occasionally something astonishing surfaces (I remember the afternoon she told me about The Deal with God), but not today. Out of character, Bolton offers a baked afternoon of street stasis and monotonous sunlight, a shaft of which falls on my dad's armchair, that winged and antimacassar'd throne of taupe velour, where he reclines post-prandially unbuttoned, paunch liberated, tartan-socked feet crossed on the pouffe. The hot-pot or kedgeree of our genes is a much revisited subject, but at seventy-nine his body has settled in favour of Indian old man type, short and slim-limbed, with redoubtable belly. It's not the European gut, beer-distended, pendulous, but a planetary curve, a drum-tight convexity from sternum to pubes. I've got the beginnings of one myself, held in check only by my being single and desperately on the pull. With millions of other men I feel a draft of death every time Brad Pitt takes his shirt off on screen.

'I wish I could sleep like that,' my mum says, legs tucked under her, arms folded. Her knees make me feel tender, since they seemed so huge when I was small. When I'd had enough of shopping I'd wrap my arms round them to make her stand still. Palliative odour of Nivea or nylon, chilled skin against my lips. She looks tired. Back pain and the old man's violent dreams ruin her nights. She haunts the small hours, knows the kitchen's four a.m. murmur, the micro's LCD glow, the nocturnal personalities of things. 'You'd think he'd spend his nights wide awake, the amount he sleeps during the day.'

Pasha is indeed unequivocally out of it, tumbler still clutched. ('Pasha', by the way, has been, second only to 'Dearie' [pronounced 'D'yurie'], my mum's nickname for him as long as I can remember. I've grown up assuming it means 'father' in Hindi. In fact it's Turkish, and means 'governor' or 'high official'. God only knows how my mum acquired it. There's no Turkish in our family. Indian, Scottish, English, French – no Turkish, although these days one's loth to rule anything out. She applies it ironically, along with 'Squire' and 'Bwana'.) I find myself studying his hands, snuff-brown, thin, crazily inscribed, a knot of urgent veins – but elegant. *Cool*, as his granddaughter says: Grampy, your hands are cool. That's twenty-year-old Elspeth, my sister Maude's daughter. (Elspeth tickles him pink. She's *nowadays*. Look, Grampy, she says, lifting her T-shirt, I've had my belly-button done. This is last month. He drops the evening paper, foreheads his specs, leans forward, peers. Did it hurt? Yeah, a bit. Looks groovy, though, doesn't it? He inspects more closely, face screwed up, me in the background not sure about Elspeth's nutmeg-brown and newly jewelled midriff being flashed Saloméishly about like this. I'm The Uncle, after all, he's The Granddad. But the old man chuckles. Whatall things nowadays, eh? Looks nice, my girl. Have to learn the belly-dance now. At which Elspeth cackles; he tickles *her* pink. Then specs resettled and attention returned to the *Bolton Evening News*, of which he hasn't missed an edition in forty years.)

'Is everything all right, Sweetheart?' my mum wants to know. She means my life. Specifically my love life. I'm Sweetheart. Melissa is Angel and Carl is Darling or Carling. Maude is Baby because there wasn't supposed to *be* another baby after her. Then ten years later, when the name had already stuck, *me*, Owen Grant Monroe, wrecking nomenclature, economy, faith in the rhythm method.

'Everything's fine, Ma. I'm just knackered.'

'You're yawning away.'

'I'll sleep on the train.'

We look at each other for a moment in which is all her love and I know and it doesn't matter what and I know Mum but don't ask just now I'm not going mad or going to kill myself or anything like that and yes you were a good mother. I imagine her thinking of my life as a large house through which she's being selectively tour-guided by me: What's in that room? Can't go in there, Ma. Oh. What about this one? Sorry, off limits. Oh. Well what about in here? No, Ma, that's not part of the tour. Deep down she knows: Scarlet left me useless for anyone else. She knows, I know, she knows I know she knows. Thinking of Scarlet, my scalp contracts and blood warms my head as under the heat of a spot lamp. I take another grape.

'What happened with that waitress you were seeing?'

'Didn't work out.'

'No?'

'Nah.'

She pauses – details? No, Mum, no details – tuts and rolls her eyes, then looks away out of the window into the ether of all the world's failed affairs. 'I always said you'd never get married,' she says, with a smile of complacent wistfulness. In this soft late light she looks frail and glamorous. Hair colours have come and gone since my unplanned conception turned her grey almost forty years ago but for the last decade or so she's availed herself of a pale blonde L'Oréal semi-permanent. Because you're worth it, Ma, I tell her, in line with the current ad campaign. With this, her papyrus-coloured skin and the very light pink lipstick she has a golden, Angie Dickinsonish look. That's another of mine: Mum, you look like Angie Dickinson, the *Police Woman* years. She blushes, shakes her head, dismisses, enjoys it.

'Well, never mind,' she says, taking another grape. 'There's time.'

Hair sticking up all wrong but punctually awake for his four o'clock cuppa, Pasha intercepts me in the hall on my way back from the loo. We're flanked in the gloom by my mum's crime thrillers and what amounts to a gallery of framed family photos. He has of course remembered (horrified that he forgot: Bleddy *mem*ri these days my son I tell you) the other thing we need to discuss. Our Secret Business.

'So?' he whispers. 'Anything?'

'Not much,' I whisper back, lying. 'He worked for the Gas Board in Croydon for a while, but he left in nineteen sixty-nine. He could be anywhere.'

His shoulders sag. 'Oh,' he says.

I can't bring myself to tell him what I've discovered. But I can't stand his disappointment, either. 'There's one old guy there might remember him, apparently, but he's away on holiday for two weeks.'

'Who's this bugger?'

'Healy,' I invent. 'Eddie Healy.'

'Oh-*ho*.' The alertness returns.

'Look, I'll contact him when he gets back, okay?'

'Okay. What's his name again?'

'Eddie Healy.'

'What are you whispering about?' my mum calls from the lounge. I give my dad a conspiratorial shoulder-squeeze as I pass him. He's making a note of the name in his own little black book, also a Moleskine, bought by me, satirically. It was decided at the outset that this would be our secret, mine and his. No point in worrying your mother. Maybe not, but of late I'm doing enough worrying for the three of us. I know I should tell him what I've got, what I've by sheer chance discovered, but the instinct to buy time is overwhelming. When I'm *certain*, I tell myself. When I know for sure . . .

The last hour melts away. God only knows how, but I eat a chocolate choux bun. Choux buns, Viennese Whirls, potato cakes, crumpets, Heinz Toast Toppers. My mum holds my child-hood prisoner in the larder. Tastes and flavours explode the past, leave me with the aerated feeling of all the distance between then and now, all the ways I've betrayed my earlier selves. I look at photos of myself as a child and think, Christ, I'm so *sorry*.

We go downstairs to the lobby to say our goodbyes. A few other residents or Old People (upper-cased by me and my siblings because we don't think of Mater and Pater in the same bracket) are depressingly visible in the communal lounge. These Old People have my mum and dad pegged as Indian (they *come* from India, after all) or Pakistani, or Portuguese, or Spanish or Italian or

Greek, or indeed Turkish. One lady asked my mum if my dad was a *Red* Indian. Whatever you are, I've told them, you're not *white*, which means the rest is just conversation.

The lobby smells of industrial carpet and excessively used Pledge. My nose hunts for an undernote of urine (I tell myself it'll be the last straw if the place ever starts to smell of piss, although what that last straw will precipitate is unclear), but gets only a trace of mothballs and Windolene. I feel a surge of love for the cleaners, inwardly bless them and the distant inventors of conti-pads. My mum, as usual, sheds a few tears.

'For God's sake, Ma, I'll be back in a month.'

'It's so quiet when you go.'

'But I'll be coming back.'

'I know, I know.'

It's not enough. What if I don't come back? In my arms she's small, never lets go first. Once it was just the two of us. *Watch With Mother.* Now hugging her calls up in me remorseless Latin. Scapulae, vertebrae, humerus, cranium. When she dies the world will contain no one who will love me unconditionally. That's quite a shift. I'm nowhere near ready for it.

'Ma, you smell nice.'

She sniffles. 'It's Dune.' This is me buttering her up to soften the leaving, we both know, though with her terrible weakness for good perfume she does smell nice, always. She rests her forehead against my shoulder, sighs and holds on to my elbows. 'Aunty Sheila brought it back from Australia,' she says. 'Duty-free.' Another sniffle. 'When will we see you again?'

At the door my dad tries to give me twenty quid but I fend him off. I've left a twenty of my own upstairs, half under the coffee jar. It's a routine. I shoulder my bag and begin to walk away, carrying the guilt of every grown-up son from the beginning of time, the guilt of knowing it's my world, now, not theirs. If they'd been younger when they had me there would have been a period – me in my mid-twenties, say, them in their mid-forties – when the world was ours, together. But by the time I was twenty-five they had already retired.

My first look back at them (there'll be several before I turn the corner at the end of the street) shows him standing behind her, right hand on her shoulder. She waves, holds a hanky crushed under her nose. The old man gives an upward jerk of his head to remind me of our Secret Business. Don't forget. Talk to that Gas Board bugger. Keep me posted.

I stop at the corner and wave. Bolton's gloom-gravity has drawn clouds. The air is lagged. There will be a storm, which is good; they like the big weather, God losing patience. They'll turn the lights out, stand and watch at the window, listening to the thunder, remembering the first berry-sized droplets of the monsoon darkening the dust, stunned for the thousandth time to think that here they are on the other side of the world, the four kids grown and gone, grandchildren, great-grandchildren, all the past rolled out behind them like the flotsam of a lost liner.

The seven o'clock Virgin train to Euston is crowded, brightly lit, draughty and a-jabber with mobile phone conversation. Only the smell of hot coffee from the buffet offers romance, says this is, after all, a journey through twilit land. My reading options sit on the tray-table: *Rabbit Redux*; *Britain's Betrayal in India*; *The Collected Poems of Gillian Clark*. I don't open them. Instead, I sit mentally holding the perennial half-dozen things to feel bad about like a shit hand of cards. A couple have been added. I'm never going to write The Book. I don't know what it means to be an Anglo-Indian. I don't *care* what it means to be an Anglo-Indian. I should have told my dad about Skinner. I should have told my mum about Scarlet. In a month I'll be thirty-nine. I've stopped bothering to look words up and I can't stop thinking about death.

CHAPTER TWO

❦

The Boy and the Ring

(*The Cheechee Papers*: Bhusawal, Jabalpur, Bombay,
Lahore, 1932–42)

I don't like beginning my father's story with the bloodstone ring.
Ring beginnings imply ring endings. Lost rings are found, stolen
rings recovered; cursed rings detonate their evil, lucky rings work
their charm. Rings have mythic baggage, the whiff of Tolkien,
implicit narrative tilt. (Except in real life. I wore a few in adoles-
cence, my faux Navajo or Apache incarnation. For at least a year,
ajangle with beads and bracelets I told girls at parties I was
Geronimo's great-great-great grandson – efficaciously on two or
three occasions, since it got me into their pants. The rings – a
turquoise nugget, a Celtic silver band, an abalone crescent moon,
a skull and crossbones with tiny obsidian eyes – were part of this
teen fiction but none of them *meant* anything, and now they're
gone.) So I repeat: I don't like beginning my father's story with
something as plottish as a ring, but it's inescapable. There was a
ring, it did begin something.

Ending something is another matter, and it's the business of
endings – I must also repeat – that gives me the willies.

However.

As a child my father, Ross Douglas Aloysius Monroe, youngest of ten siblings, was fascinated by his mother's bloodstone ring. The jewel, green chalcedony with blood-like spots of jasper, had been given to her, Beatrice, by her first beau, Raymond Varney, who'd broken her heart (*only* her heart, she stressed, mantrically, with raised index) by abandoning her for 'a life of adventure on the oceans of the world'. As she recited this her eyes teared and looked far off, relishing the fierceness of the wound. (Ross's father, Louis Archibald Monroe, had his own version of the story, namely that Raymond had run off with a Polish prostitute treasured amongst the Bhusawal railwaymen for her apparently miraculous immunity from the clap. Blessed Olga of the Holy Crotch. It delighted my grandfather to repeat this. When he did Beatrice turned her face away and breathed superiorly through her babyish round nostrils.)

She didn't wear the bloodstone (Ross was drawn as much by the red thud and mineral rasp of the word – *bloodstone* – as by its object) but kept it in a lacquered trinket box on her dresser. You remind me so *much* of him, you know, she would incant, taking her youngest's face between her hands while the boy turned the jewel in the light. 'Him' was lost love Raymond Varney, and had it not been for chronological impossibility Ross might have suspected himself the man's child. When you come of age, my son, Beatrice would murmur, this ring will be yours. She was a small, restive woman with a penchant for ominous utterances. In her mind unrelated things were force-married into mysterious meaning; in this case Ross and the legendary Raymond, but she could make grist of anything – a simple bazaar purchase could be imbued with Fate. Child at that *very moment* this teapot caught my eye, you know? There was no *question*. Certain things . . . She'd leave the rest unsaid, lean back, suck her teeth, *chit*, turn down her mouth-corners in satisfied submission and look away into the great web of Destiny.

'But *when* will I come of age, Mumma?' Ross asked her one morning, holding the ring up to the window's ferocious light in which the jewel's red, gold and green throbbed with apparent sentience. Mother and son were in Beatrice's bedroom at the Bazaar Road house in Bhusawal. In a week Ross was to go up to Jabalpur to begin boarding school. His brothers, seasoned pupils, had spent hours telling him what a fucking *place* it was, extreme punishments for *little*ornothing. There couldn't, he knew, be many of these moments with his mother left.

Beatrice closed her eyes and lifted her chin, broad little face crinkling with arcane knowledge. 'My son, these things cannot be *speci*fied like that,' she said. 'The time comes when the time comes. You will know and I, too, will know. God will give us a sign.'

'But *how* will we know?' Ross persisted, slipping the ring on to his thumb, still years too small for it.

'Bus,' Beatrice said, holding up her hand. 'Trust me. Your mother will know, God willing she lives long enough, with that maniac trying to murder her.' 'That maniac' was Ross's father: sober, a genial and witty man; drunk, apocalyptically violent. Boozing segued into lashings out, belts across the face, kicks up the arse, cracks on the head with anything that came to hand. The whole household suffered, wife, kids, servants, dogs. Ross loved him but in the face of the rages had built up a charge of anger, a violence of his own with as yet nowhere to go.

'Enough now,' Beatrice said, taking the ring from him and putting it back in the box. 'Go and comb your hair before you go with Agnes.'

At the mention of his sister's name Ross's spirits sank. For weeks his brothers had been warning him – cryptically, with a sickening lack of detail – that this time must come. The interlude with the bloodstone had been the latest in a long line of flimsy distractions. Now, like an outreaching tentacle of Fate, the moment had found him.

★

Agnes was the oldest Monroe girl, a nurse at the Bhusawal
Railway Hospital. Today Ross was to accompany her there for
purposes unknown to him. He'd managed to extract a promise
that it wasn't for injections or dentistry, that it wasn't going to *hurt*,
but there was no fooling his deeper instinct. Mother and daughter had gone into quiet confab that morning on the veranda,
fine-tuning this, whatever it was. Whatever it was, he knew he
wasn't going to enjoy it. It wasn't going to be a *treat*.

'Don't be such a baby,' Agnes said, as they crossed the hospital
compound and Ross quailed with the first inhalation of the building's ammoniacal stink. 'All your brothers have done this before
you. There's absolutely nothing to be afraid of.'

She ushered him into Reception, through swing doors, down
a newly plastered corridor and into a low-ceilinged screen-
dimmed room with a dozen beds, all occupied. The atmosphere
was close, wettish, and though in one corner a glistening punka-
wallah somnambulistically pulled, the air sat still and hummed
with flies. A smell of runny shit from somewhere, the fruit-sour of
diarrhoea. Agnes's hand between his shoulders pushed him ahead
of her. This was the way your legs moved in nightmares, Ross
thought, as if space was quicksand. He'd had this nightmare, hadn't
he? Himself being forced towards something terrible?

Agnes, fierily alive, brought them to a halt by a bed in which a
man Ross didn't know sat with knees drawn up and parted, covered only by a single cotton sheet. He was thin, with
rough-chopped greying hair and a long-chinned coffee-coloured
face set in a look of feeble misery. An open pyjama jacket of
maroon and cream stripes revealed an emaciated, hairless chest
glistening with sweat. His hands gripped his kneecaps as if pre-
venting their detonation. He looked to Ross as if he was about to
burst into tears.

'Now, Mr Carruthers, as we agreed if you don't mind.'

In the bed opposite a man sat up, summoned phlegm, spat it –
tunk – into a tin can kept nearby, cleared his throat, then lay down

again. Ross pressed back against his sister, felt with his head through the starched uniform skirt the hard of her hip and soft of her thigh. Warm. He'd seen all his sisters naked at one time or another; dark hair triangles down there, burgeoning or full-blown breasts, brown nipples. He didn't know why he thought of it now, nor from where it popped into his head that Agnes was supposed to have gone into the convent, but hadn't.

'Mr Carruthers?' Agnes said. 'Come along now.'

Another patient in a bed by the window moaned, falsetto. The moan resolved into a whimper, then ended with 'Jesus *Christ* have mercy.'

'Oh, nurse,' Mr Carruthers said. 'Nurse . . .' He shook his head and began to sob, tearlessly.

Agnes leaned forward and placed her right hand over Carruthers's left, big-knuckled round his bent knee. 'Think,' she said. 'All I ask you to do is *think* of the good this will do in the world.'

'Sweet black cunting *hell*,' the man by the window said, carefully.

'Stop that, Mr Blanchet,' Agnes said, raising her voice but not turning her head. 'I have my young brother here.'

Silence from the window bed. Every muscle in Ross's body pleaded for permission to take him elsewhere.

'I want you to look at what I show you now and remember it,' Agnes said, her little green eyes triumphal. 'Remember it as long as you live.'

Mr Carruthers shook his head again, without conviction. His hands left his kneecaps and went up to cover his face as Agnes drew back the sheet.

The shock of what Ross saw was still with him when he left for Jabalpur the following week.

'It's so we don't get VD,' his brother Hector told him, as the train pulled out of Bhusawal station. The four Monroe boys,

Ross, Gilbert, Alfie and Hector were travelling up to St Aloysius together. 'You see a fellow's tullu like that, covered in sores—'

'*Weeping* sores,' Gilbert amended.

'Weeping sores, and you'll think twice about any bleddy hanky-panky.'

'What hanky-panky?' Ross said, snivelling.

'"What hanky-panky?"' Gilbert scoffed. 'What a *baby* you are, men.'

'Leave him alone,' Alfie said. 'He's too young. He doesn't know about hanky-panky.'

Ross didn't, and deeply did. 'Do you know that house with the yellow and red balcony behind the bazaar?' Agnes had asked him. (He'd turned his face away from the sight of those ravaged Carruthers genitals but with coconut-scented hands his sister had forced it back, while the patient had murmured, Oh, my boy, my boy, look at my condition and think, for God's sake only *think* in your years ahead.) Agnes's grip on his face had tightened. 'That place where men go in and come out and don't look at you when they pass?' Ross nodded. He knew the house, its gravity. His Bhusawal gang periodically surrendered to its pull, sniggered, conjectured, understood precious little except that men went there, that there were women inside, that it was dirty. *Whoreshop*, Edward Mendez had said, and the word had entered with a vague insinuation. Something like *worship*. Once, when Ross had sneaked there alone to spy, a young nose-ringed Indian woman with eyes glittering amid excessive kohl had caught sight of him from an open upper window. She'd made a strange face, wide-eyed and showing teeth like a tiger – then lipstickishly laughed and waved at him, bangles jingling. He'd skedaddled. It was as if she'd touched his essential self. 'Men go and pay money so that they can have sexual relations with the women in there,' Agnes had said, holding his face between her hands while Carruthers looked down at his poor parts and made a face like the Tragedy mask. 'But those women are kept as slaves and they are *diseased*.

Do you understand?' Ross had gone home from the hospital queasy. He had thought that this exposure to horror might have constituted the coming of age his mother had alluded to, that now, having endured initiation, the bloodstone would be delivered to him. But though he'd hung around the lacquered box conspicuously for his remaining days, Beatrice had said nothing more about it.

''Course, you're the last to go, you see,' Hector said to Ross. Bhusawal was behind them. The carriage windows gave on to sunblasted dry open land dotted with scrub and thorn trees under a bleached sky with one mountainous white cloud reaching up from the horizon like an iceberg. 'Now there are no more of us left at home with her, Puppa's going to give her merry hell. No doubt about it, you leaving for school is breaking her heart.'

'Ripping her heart *out*,' Gilbert corrected, seeing that Ross was somehow still holding himself together. 'I wouldn't be surprised if this *finishes* her.'

It finished Ross, who wept, on and off, the whole three hundred miles to Jabalpur.

The Monroe boys had exaggerated about St Aloysius (that the school name was one of Ross's own had been seized by his mother as evidence in the case for Fate) but not by much. In his first weeks there he saw pupils routinely bashed, clobbered, kicked, punched, belted and thrashed. Many of the masters were psychotic, but the priests (English-speaking European Jesuits, one or two Indian Christians, a Goan) were artists of pain who'd had years to refine their cruelties. Canings were administered not on the spot but after swimming, with trunks and therefore backsides still sodden. Bedwetters were thrashed and made to walk about in the compound at breaktime wearing their soiled sheets over their heads like cowls. A boy who attempted to run away was captured, thrashed, and had his head shaved completely bald. In Ross's geography class an unnaturally small boy, Jerry

Valentine, failed to identify the three crosses that made up the
Union Jack. He was sent outside for two handfuls of gravel upon
which, back in the classroom, he was made to kneel upright
with his arms stretched out in front of him. A thick book was
placed on the palm of each hand. Father Venanglers (whose nickname, not surprisingly, was Danglers) continued the lesson in his
preferred manner, strolling between the desks, but every time he
passed Jerry and noticed his hands dropping under their load
administered to them (with a look of mild pleasant surprise) two
sharp cracks with the cane.

Confession was a twice-weekly obligation. Have you been
doing anything dirty down there? This was Danglers's chief area of
interest. Ross only half understood. No, Father. Ah yes, but I
know you boys. Make a good Act of Contrition now and leave off
those filthy pollutions. Christ died for your sins, my son. You
know that, don't you? Suffered torment and death for your sake?
Ross thought not of his own meagre stash of sins but of Father
Galliano, or Gurru (from 'Gorilla', so named by the Aloysians for
his frantic body hair), who came into the dorm after lights out and
manhandled certain boys. These boys were known as Gurru's
BCs, Gurru's Bum Chums. The phonetics had a juicy value, like
a brand of chewy sweets: Gurru's Bum Chums.

Ross slogged through his first two years and felt disproportionately older at the end of them. He was growing into a quick, wiry,
muscular boy, small and scruffy but naturally athletic. Maths, geography and biology he could do without effort; the rest of academia
was a matter of indifference to him. He had a big-eyed, bony face
and sticking-out ears considered parodically available for tweaking
and flicking by the priests. He took his share of thrashings but
escaped the attentions of Gurru, whose pederasty was reserved for
more androgynous Aloysians. He made no mention to his mother
of the school atrocities on visits home, and surprised her (ripping
out, he imagined, with a cold thrill, the last shreds of her heart) by
being baroquely indifferent to their old intimacy. He never asked

to see the bloodstone ring. She brought it out, slightly desperate. Try it on, try it on, let's see if it fits yet. It didn't. His fingers were still too small, which despite the grand aloofness galled him. Maybe next year, Beatrice said, eyes filling up. Or you could give it to Hector, Ross said, meanly. I'm sure it'll fit *him*.

Then, at the beginning of his third year at St Aloysius, everything changed.

One Wednesday morning after mass Ross and twenty other boys, having most of them turned twelve years old, were lined up by the gymnasium's weathered boxing ring. They'd all, in their first two PE years (limited to gymnastics, cricket, football, hockey, track and field), known this moment must come, had watched older pupils' bouts, seen the burst noses, split lips, cracked teeth, black eyes, had accepted, some with hunger, some with dread, that legitimate masculinity, truth, *life* couldn't really begin until they climbed between the ropes and let the ring show what they were made of.

When his turn came (paired with Tully, a thin but enrageable boy with a slight walleye) Ross stepped up with neither fear nor bravado. Until the moment his feet touched the canvas he was aware only of a strange, pleasurable tautening of his being, as if all the disparate flickering flames of his consciousness were drawing together into a single steady blaze. The damp heat and weight of the gloves felt familiar, though he'd never worn them before. Facing Tully, arms moving up into the guard position, he felt, suddenly, on the brink of an enormous, essential memory.

Then, at the command 'Box!' something extraordinary happened.

'Bleddy *hell*, men, how did you do that?' Gilbert wanted to know, having watched Ross knock down five opponents (the first three his own age, the fourth and fifth pulled from a group of fifteen-year-olds who were practising vaults at the other end of the gym) in as many rounds. The eldest Monroe boy, one of the vaulting group, had observed his brother's performance with first astonishment, then creeping unease, lest he, Gilbert, be selected as Ross's next victim. 'I mean who the bleddy hell taught you to *do* that?'

Ross shrugged. The answer was: no one. Prodigious talent had sprung fully formed, like Athena from Zeus's forehead, the minute he put the gloves on and climbed into the ring. His body knew what to do, that was all. Popping out his first three left jabs (each snapping Tully's shocked head back on its neck) and stinging right cross (which floored Tully halfway through his hissed What the fu—) had been, as far as Ross was concerned, effortless. It was as if he had done it thousands of times before. The thought that he might get hit himself hadn't entered his head, and in the contests that followed that day he took at most three or four blows.

Over the following weeks word of his impromptu masterclass spread through the school.

'I'm telling you this, now, Monroe, because it's the truth and as an educator I am in the service of the truth.' This was Naughton, senior sports master, Rockballs Naughton, as he was known to the boys. His professional credentials were uncertain but under him the school had won the Catholic Cup (football; Ross had also distinguished himself on the soccer pitch as a suicidally committed centre half) and the State Inter-Schools Cup (boxing) three years running. He was a tall, lean-muscled and incomprehensibly strong Britisher in his early forties, with faded nautical tattoos and a plump, nicotined moustache that looked too big for his face. See this? he would ask the terrified pupils, holding up his right fist. Most of the time this is flesh and blood and bone and nerves. When I hold a pen or stroke my cat, for example. (None of the boys liked this image of Rockballs stroking his cat, if such a creature even existed.) But when I *throw* it, when I really *throw* it at a fellow's head in the ring because that fellow has had the effrontery, the impertinence, to come and fight me – to come and fight *me*, for God's sake: what is he a mental defective? – then, *then*, this is not flesh and blood and bone and nerves. *Then* this is a lump of

Cumbrian granite. Do you understand? Yes, sir. What is it? Cumbrian *granite*, sir. That's right, you marionettes. Now, you, Wilson, and you, Tully, get in the ring. 'I'm telling you, Monroe, you've got talent. Train hard, focus, you could fight for money. Go to America and get paid. Do you know how much they made on tickets when Dempsey fought Tunney the second time?' Ross didn't. 'More than two million dollars,' Rockballs said. 'Think about it.'

Ross fought on. The ring was an arena of curious intimacy and beautiful mathematics: the molecular vividness of the other boy's face just before your punch landed; the punch itself describing an arc that glowed like a suddenly visible detail of God's original blueprint. Then the detonation, the bubble of stopped time like a glass ball surrounding you, silencing everything, leaving you perfected, angelic, stripped of need and desire, purely and absolutely yourself. He felt unfairly advantaged, as if he had come into an unearned inheritance. Gilbert's question – 'How did you do that?' – remained unanswerable, at least by Ross. The ring – canvas-bounce, rosin scent, rope burn – was home; every step, duck and punch was casually inevitable. He found it difficult not to laugh, seeing the giant gaps in his opponents' defences. At the same time he knew this was a grace period, the first rapturous statement of what he was: a fighter. God stamped the imprimatur of potential heavily at the outset so you wouldn't be in any doubt. Then you must work to fulfil it. It would, he knew, get harder.

'Your problem is focus, Monroe,' Rockballs told him. 'I know you. You want an easy life. You're distracted by pleasure.' This was true. Childhood as his mother's favourite had left him lazily expectant of the world's sensuous wealth. 'Three things wreck a boxer: booze, gambling and skirt. *Skirt*, understand?' Ross was fourteen. During cricket, of late, the thing had been to hit the ball over the wall, across the street, over the opposite wall and into the compound of St Joseph's Convent School for Girls. Once every three or four overs bowler would give batsman the wink. The girls would be ready with their giggles and whispers and billets doux. Skirt. Ross understood. 'But you focus,' Rockballs said, 'no booze, no gambling, skirt only when strictly necessary, and you can go anywhere. Olympics. England. America. You're laughing. Retire at thirty-five and have all the sweet pussy you want. Don't repeat that.'

Ross, by seventeen a confirmed Bantamweight, trained hard (but not as hard as he might), captained the boxing team in his final year, won all his bouts and carried the school to a record eighth consecutive victory in the Inters. When he left St Aloysius Rockballs gave him a frown and a handshake that was a single ferocious squeeze. 'Focus, Monroe,' he repeated. 'Never forget. *Focus.*'

The bloodstone was not, as Ross had half expected it would be, presented to him when he finished school and went home to Bhusawal. He had passed his Senior Cambridge Certificate and made an Aloysian legend of himself in the ring. 'A good lad, who has worked diligently and been a sporting credit to the school. He has a great boxing career ahead of him, if he wants it!' The testimonial was recited with manifest pride by his father at dinner, but Beatrice was quiet, depressed, clipped with the servants, elaborately barely touching her food. Ross went to her later in her room, where she sat unpinning the coils of her thin grey bun. 'What's wrong, Mumma?' he asked, putting his hand on her shoulder, shocked, rather, at its boniness; was she ill? It had never occurred to him that his parents would one day die; the thought sent an effervescence of excitement and panic through him. Beatrice's eyes were moist, her mouth a quivering pout. She looked old; the skin of her broad-boned little face had loosened and begun to shrivel. For a few moments she said nothing. Then put her left hand up to cover his. Squeezed.

'You grew up so *fast*, my son,' she said. 'To your mother it seems like only yesterday you were . . . you were just . . .' She closed her eyes and bowed her head. A tear or two fell on to her blouse. Ross swallowed, shocked again, this time by the realization that while there was no doubt a kernel of sadness in her she was exaggerating it for her own gratification. Suddenly he saw she'd always been this way, genuine feelings wrapped in layers of ungenuine performance, saw too that his older siblings had all, in their own ways, made the same discovery and drawn away from her into privacy. Not very long ago he would have dropped to his knees and put his head in her lap. Now he felt the thrilling, cold power of disinterested analysis. This, presumably, was coming of age: even your mother was revealed as just another person, riddled with flaws. He bent and gave the top of her skull a kiss, smelling the frail, waxy skin of her scalp. Beatrice, well aware of the discrepancy between this gesture and the one she wanted, sniffed, mightily, and wiped her nose with a hanky. 'Next thing you know,' she said, 'you'll be finding some girl and getting married.'

Ross forced a laugh. 'Don't be crazy,' he said. 'I'm going to fight. I've got no time for all that rubbish.'

Beatrice smiled and shook her head, as with torturous wisdom. 'You say that, my son, but always the sword of sorrow pierces the mother's heart. I know. I know how it is. They all leave. They must. It's the way of the world.'

The bloodstone remained unmentioned.

Ross's plan wasn't a plan but the default for any educated Anglo-Indian boy: to follow in his father's footsteps. Railways, Post and Telegraph Office, Civil Service, arenas in which His Majesty's Government had found employees who were neither British nor Indian indispensable. Louis Archibald Monroe was a mail driver, therefore Ross went up to the GIPR driver training school in Bombay. Boxing was the big picture but the railways were a natural way in; the industry was obsessed with inter-divisional sport.

A good fighter, cricketer, hockey-player or footballer could spend half his working year away on full salary in the annual tournaments. Ross had been too young (and not ready, not *ready*, you glistening *pup*, Rockballs had said) for the Berlin Games in '36, and now there was a war on; but it wouldn't last for ever. The Olympic Selection Committees (it had been made clear to him he could box for India; less clear whether he was — what? *fair* enough? — to box for Britain) had two reservoirs of talent to draw from: the military and the railways. Since Ross had no desire to spend his days having orders barked at him, the choice was no choice at all.

Or so he thought.

'Driver training' was a euphemism. All new candidates started as apprentice firemen, and Ross's superior in his first weeks was Mr Goodrich, a fair-skinned chain-smoking Anglo–Indian in his late forties with oiled wavy hair and a permanent sneer on his moist, pockmarked face. All his actions, the rolling of a cigarette, the scratching of an eyebrow, the tapping of a pressure gauge, languidly expressed contempt.

'Too bleddy *slow*, you fuckwit,' he said, no matter Ross's work rate with the shovel. 'Speed you're going you wouldn't get a *wheel*barrow moving.'

After the first few days Ross understood. His boxing prowess had reached Goodrich through the grapevine (courtesy of boastful Monroe senior, no doubt); therefore the Goodrich agenda was to provoke him into violence. Initially the insight enlarged Ross's tolerance; he hates me, he thought, because he knows I'm better than him. He's a bitter man whose life has disappointed him, abuses me because he's weak and filled with self-loathing. There was comfort in it, a dim intimation of the Christly heights such understanding might allow one to scale. Less dim and considerably more satisfying was the knowledge that in keeping his temper he was driving Goodrich crazy, though Goodrich showed it only by wiping his hands very slowly or rolling a cigarette with particular meticulousness. 'You're a fucking *weak*ling, Monroe. What are you?'

'A fucking weakling, sir.'

It might have lasted had it not been for a simple accident. The night before it happened Ross and another trainee, Lenny O'Gorman, got drunk and in the small hours went idiotically to the training school's gym to settle a slurred bet over who could bench-press the greater weight. Lenny left a loose clip on the end of the bar and at the third or fourth changeover a 15lb iron slipped free and crashed on to Ross's left foot. Grog-anaesthetized, Ross hobbled back to the dorms, laughing, one arm over Lenny's shoulder, but the following morning woke to nauseous pain. 'If you're walking on it it's not broken,' the doctor told him. 'Most likely a chipped bone. You can go for an X-ray tomorrow if you want, but they won't thank me for it. Up to you.'

Disgusted with the doctor and himself, Ross reported to Goodrich later that day. Goodrich looked hungover too. 'Well, look who it is,' he said. 'So pleased you could drop by. Would you like to do any work today or shall we sit down and have bleddy tea and crumpets instead?'

As the afternoon wore on Ross felt his reservoir of tolerance emptying. He tried (surprised at his Christian willing and depth) to keep in mind the image of Christ staggering up the road to Calvary, flogged, spat on, buckling under the weight of the Cross; to, as Beatrice was always suggesting, *offer up* his suffering to God. But in Ross's version Christ kept stopping in His tracks, turning and smashing the Cross into the nearest centurion's head.

When the crisis came, it was a relief. Ross was exhausted. His smashed foot throbbed. The engine's heat was a soft, murderous bulk on him.

'No no no no no *no*,' Goodrich said, 'the gauge on the *left*, you stupid sonofabitch.' He'd never touched Ross, had known it would constitute a failure. But in that moment (curiously, Ross had an acute sense of some particular new misery in the instructor's

scheme of things, as if perhaps his wife had left him or he'd been
cut out of a will) an occult mental line was crossed. Goodrich
stepped up to his apprentice and gave him a demeaning knuckle-
tap on the back of the head.

Which insult alone might have sufficed even if he hadn't trodden on Ross's bad foot.

When Beatrice tracked her son down two months later it was at
the air force training base in Walton, just outside Lahore, a thousand miles north of where he should have been. He was in
uniform, with a new severe haircut.

'Always the favourite breaks the mother's heart,' Beatrice
said, taking his hands in hers. 'I deserve it, I know.' They stood
face to face in Reception. She was barely five feet tall. (Agnes's
green eyes were from her, as were the small, thin-lipped mouth
and prominent brow. All the Monroe girls had inherited her
broad face, high cheekbones and deep eye sockets; all of them,
if they lost too much weight, were in danger of looking
skullish.) Ross was surprised by how much his mother's out-of-
placeness here – Reception hung about with squadron
photographs and Indian Air Force insignia, him shamefully in
uniform – made him ache for home. A smell of burned engine
oil came in through the open window. Visible beyond the
window the concrete expanse where the recruits day in day out
square-bashed, for Britain, for Democracy, for the War. (Oh aye,
the Tommies ribbed them, we want all you black buggers
fightin for freedom and democracy; just not your own.) Past that
a half-mile of stony scrub dotted with banyan trees. Heat rip-
pled the distance. At a desk across the room a British drill
sergeant stood scrutinizing something on a clipboard while the
Indian clerk stutteringly typed.

'God punishes a mother for loving one child more than the
rest,' Beatrice said, delighted. 'Oh, my son, how could you *do* a
thing like that? Your father I could understand because of the

violent streak, don't I know. But you . . .' Another version of the lowered mouth-corners, this time with eyes looking down and head shaking slowly no, no, no. He was *crucifying* her. He had Run Away And Joined The Forces. She was rosy with pleasure.

To buy time Ross went across to the canteen and returned with two cups of tea and a couple of buttered puris.

'Tell me how you came to *do* such a thing?'

'Mumma, I lost my temper. How did you know I was here?'

'The letter, my son, the letter. Merciful God guides our hands.' Beatrice closed her eyes, beatified: her will to martyrdom had been given this legitimacy; her favourite son had broken her heart. For this she had come hundreds of miles. 'Tell me from the beginning,' she said. 'Come, sit next to me. Are these cups even *clean* my God? How your mother's legs are *pain*ing after so long on the train. I had only one scrambled egg and toast but it wasn't good. Now, tell me what happened.'

So, though manifestly she knew already, he told her. Beatrice nodded, slowly, with closed eyes and widened nostrils: Goodrich: The Villain. More deep satisfaction. Son and thereby mother had been brutalized by the forces of evil, driven to extremis, desperate flight, intrigue that had brought them back into precarious cahoots. The Beatrice universe was as it should be. 'Anyway, I snapped,' Ross said. 'I don't know why that day of all days' – he'd left out the boozing, the dropped weight, the hangover, the injured foot – 'but that was the moment. He gave me a tap on my head, you know, not a proper hit or anything but he shouldn't have done it. My blood boiled and I just went for the bugger.'

'How many times haven't I told your father?' Beatrice said. 'Don't tap on the head. It's humiliating to a child.'

'Anyway, I slogged him,' Ross said; he was used to her dragging the old man into everything. 'It was a split-second thing.'

He'd given Goodrich a hard straight left and followed it with a clean right hook. A euphoric little liberation. The instructor staggered, crashed to the engine floor, collapsed backwards and third–degree–burned his shoulders on the furnace door. His *hair* caught fire briefly. He screamed and flailed, spastically.

'Shouting for the bleddy pol*ice* and whatall,' Ross said. 'I panicked.'

More delighted shaking of the Beatrice head. 'My son, my son.' Her hand closed over his again. Tears of joy welled and fell.

'So I took off for Richie's place. I couldn't think of anything except getting out of town.' Richie Pinto was a school friend from St Aloysius who had failed his Senior Cambridge Certificate and gone back home to Bombay to work in his father's photography business. 'But when I got to Richie's there was no one at home. What to do, Mumma?'

'What to do, my son?'

At a pause in the clerk's typing a bird went past the open window with a soft whirr. The British drill sergeant put the clipboard down on the desk, turned and walked out of the room. 'So I packed my bag and cleared out,' Ross said. 'Went to the recruiting office and joined up. They sent me up here for basic.'

'And you wrote the letters where?'

'In the post office at VT.' Before boarding the train for Lahore at Victoria Terminus Ross had dashed off two letters, one to Richie Pinto, telling the story of the Goodrich assault, one to Beatrice, telling her everything was fine.

Beatrice, shaking her head, brushing away a tear, smiling, handed him the letter. Richie's letter, which in his panic he'd put in the envelope addressed to her.

'Oh, my son, what *troubles* you bring on your mother,' Beatrice said, squeezing his hand.

She stayed in Lahore only two days, at a small hotel where nothing – not one *single* thing, my son – was clean, and at their parting on the train platform handed Ross a small package. 'Don't open it now,' she said. 'But when you do, remember that your mother is thinking of you, far away, and that when you need her, when*ever* you need her, she'll be there.'

He opened the package once the train was out of sight. This, he understood, was what she'd been waiting for, an opportunity to reaffirm that his primary allegiance should be to her, that her love, in a world of accidents and villains and flight from the Law, was the only thing he could rely on. It depressed him, measured precisely the limits of her power in such a world, the vast discrepancy between his future and their shared shrinking past.

The package contained two new pairs of underpants, a comb, a pot of guava jelly, and a twenty-rupee note wrapped round Raymond Varney's bloodstone ring. Apparently, he had come of age.

CHAPTER THREE

headlines

(London, 2004)

London is no longer interested in me. Its attention when I arrived twenty years ago reminded me of God's in my childhood, an eye under scrutiny of which I mattered, cosmically. That's long gone. The capital gave me enough to get me hooked, then turned its back. Gorgeous cruel whore, I used to think (trying to matter at least romantically), but it's ages since it was even that. The city has no personality, sexual or otherwise. It's been reduced beyond personification; or rather, I'm reduced beyond personifying it. With London as with God: it was me all along.

It's after ten by the time I get back to the flat. Vince, my flat-mate, my tenant, is out, most likely risking life and limb in the world of casual outdoor gay sex. The train has bullied me, with buzzing fluorescents and the woeful grammar of its announcements, into sobriety, and though I know a second drunkenness will make me feel terrible I open a bottle of Wolf Blass shiraz and drink a glass, quickly, standing up in the kitchen.

With only me in it my flat speaks through its angles and

furniture of a dull and deflated life. In the corner above the fridge–
freezer a faint brown–edged area of damp the map–shape more or
less of India says: time love loss death nothing. Later to be dismissed as maudlin melodrama, but this is now. A cat knocks
something over in the back garden and scarpers with a cartoon
yowl. I take the bottle down the hall to my bedroom.

There was a time a couple of decades ago when with only a
little help or luck a single working person could afford to buy a
cramped or dilapidated flat in London. I had both help and luck.
Help to the tune of five thousand pounds (a loan, but one which
took me so long to pay back at 0 per cent interest we might as
well call it a gift) from Melissa, whose demonically entrepreneur-
ial second husband, Ted, got rich (steam cleaning, industrial
coatings) under Mrs Thatcher's glacial squint. And luck in the
form of a full-time lecturing position at University College
London only six months after I'd finished my MA. Back then central London never bothered with things much south of Clapham.
Tooting, Brixton, Balham, Collier's Wood; it was all a glamourless
blur down there. Now more than a little luck or help is required.
The young white laptopped middle classes have come to Balham
with their artful casuals and polite terror of the remaining browns
and blacks. Little men with designer spectacles and media-
industry hairdos push ergonomic prams or cradle babies in
Bauhaus slings, praying their bolshy aerobic women won't draw
any big black male attention. I'm not dark enough either to scare
the honkies or to expect solidarity from the brothers. Even the
Asians know at a glance there's something, as Tarantino would say,
rotten in Denmark. 'And what colour is *Owen*?' my mum once
asked a very young Elspeth, having done sky, lemons, the rug, the
three-piece suite. My niece considered a moment, head at a pre-
cocious tilt. 'Beige,' she said, eventually. 'Like Hovis.'

My kitchen's India-shaped damp patch is anomalous; the flat
everywhere else is well kept, clean, tidy. I'm not normally slack in
my maintenance. I know what a shield against the universe's

Godless howl domestic order can be. Last year my upstairs neighbours and I had the building repointed. The boiler's only two
years old. My windows are double-glazed, my floors are stripped,
my period features (circa 1900) are nicely preserved. The flue's
open, and for the last few years my solo winter evenings have had,
courtesy of a real fire, at least the appearance of contented solitude
if not its reality. Ted, who has more favours to call in than the
Devil, has sent my way builders, plumbers, electricians and join-
ers (Turks, Poles, Jamaicans, Greeks, Malaysians, of late a plethora
of haggard East Europeans who work with a silent intensity that
suggests survived torture. Regardless of their race they all get
round to the question of mine: You Iranian, boss? Italian? Little
Afghan in you? No? You sure?) and incrementally the shit-hole of
twenty years ago has become the twenty-first-century monstros-
ity of conservative middle-class pretension I and my lodger inhabit
today. Everyone, absolutely everyone, with the exception of
Vince, keeps telling me to sell. Sell now. Make money.

I'm not averse to making money, but I am congenitally lazy.
Also, what will change do except remind me of brevity, ephemera,
death? Endings. Vince's rent pays the mortgage. I teach three and
a half days a week at the Arbuthnot College in Wimbledon. I
write two pornographic novels a year under the name Millicent
Nash for Sheer Pleasure, the erotica imprint of Dyer & Haskell
Publishers (a letter from whom, which I've been dreading, was
among my post gathered and left outside my door by Vince).
And, out of I'm not sure what perverseness (I told myself initially
it would facilitate meeting women), I work one evening a week in
a bar, Neon Hallelujah, just down the road in Balham. A bitty
existence, my sisters think. The patchwork life seems ungrown-up
to both of them, as does my professional apathy. I squeezed a
dozen or so articles out in my first few years, and published one
dismal, floundering book, *Artists of the Holy Blood* about the
Catholic literary imagination, then took a series of institutional
sidesteps at first calculated to keep myself in the liminal zone of

academia, later because I was stuck there whether I liked it or not. Eventually I downgraded to A levels. From time to time at the Arbuthnot College my position wobbles, so far not violently enough for me to do anything about it. Leave the poor bugger alone, my brother Carl says, from the safe distance of Arizona, where he works at some impenetrably abstruse level of information technology. Leave him alone and let him do his thing. What thing? Maude wants to know. He doesn't *have* a thing. Three and a half days a week? How is he *living*? I've kept quiet about the Sheer Pleasure sideline, naturally, and the bar. My mum and dad would equate Millicent Nash with the loss of my soul and my sisters would equate Neon Hallelujah with financial ruin. I'm doing something, I keep telling them. I'm writing The Book. It sounds unconvincing even to me.

I drink another glass in four gulps and pick up the letter from Sheer Pleasure.

Louisa Wexford
Sheer Pleasure
Dyer & Haskell
48 Margolis Street
London W1 6AG
September 26th 2004

Dear Owen

A *bit* worried that you haven't returned my calls since the new Millicent Nash's delivery date passed a week ago. Could you get in touch ASAP? Just to reassure me that something hasn't happened to you?

All best,
Louisa

Adrenalin buzzes through the booze. I pick up the cordless and dial Louisa's direct line. After the first ring I have to fight the impulse to hang up. What if she's there? Can't be; it's Sunday night. It rings again. Butterflies. Two more times. Then, plummily, Hi, you've reached Louisa Wexford at Dyer & Haskell. I can't take your call just now, but if you leave your name and number I'll get back to you as soon as I can. Thanks.

'Louisa, hi, it's Owen. Monroe. Got your letter. Listen, sorry I've been so crap getting back. I know you must think there's some dire problem but actually it's just been a bit hectic because there's been a shake-up at work. I'm not *quite* finished with the manuscript but I'm probably just being a wuss. I'll email it in the next day or two. Hope that's okay? Okay. Speak to you soon. Bye.'

I put the phone down.

Vince gets in after midnight, by which time I've finished the Wolf Blass and opened a bottle of Ernest & Julio Gallo's Turning Leaf cabernet sauvignon. I join him in the kitchen.

'So?' I ask, eyebrows raised.

He gives me the look.

'Oh God. How old?'

'Late thirties. South American, at a guess. Hard to say. It was dark. As indeed was his formidable chorizo.'

'You're going to get your genitals knifed one of these days.'

'I daresay, but not by a spic faggot. Can I have a glass of that?'

'If you've washed your hands.'

I pour, we clink, with our habitual silent grim shudder in honour of loveless existence. Swallow. He looks tired underneath the rain-cooled post-coital blush.

'How were Mater and Pater?' he asks.

'Fantastical. My dad went out with two left shoes on the other day.'

He sips, closes his eyes, smiles, relishes.

'Spent the whole morning with a vague feeling of something being wrong. It was only when he sat down in the bus shelter – with his string bag, his bananas, his Fruit and Nut – that he noticed. They weren't even the same colour.'

Vince lets one ripe berry of a laugh out.

'I read this line in Updike the other day,' I say.

Smile-residue morphs into preparatory wince.

'"We move forward into darkness, and darkness closes behind us."'

He closes his eyes again. Vince and I are in a state such that any-thing, no matter how glancing or tawdry its representation of or allusion to death or love or loss, has the power to reduce us to tears. Soap operas, TV commercials, birthday cards, home-makeover shows. Self-pity and latent sadism. The Nazis, he keeps telling me, were incurably sentimental, filling up over their fat-faced, leder-hosen'd, beaming blond thug-infants after a hard day's work at the crematoria. None the less my voice wobbles over that second 'dark-ness'. Vince, swallowing, keeps his mouth clamped tight.

'Well, thanks very much,' he says. 'Now. A huge spliff, don't you think?'

Vince has missed, narrowly, he claims, whatever opportunity there might have been in the past for his life hitting its stride. He got a two-one in history from Bristol and never did anything with it. My cog never bit, he says, with the over-articulated lip movements of a Lancashire granny confiding a sexual secret. Now, at thirty-five, he's in marketing for an academic publisher, on insufficient money to get out of the rental circle of Hell.

'I've got to go to bed.'

It's two thirty in the morning. Vince and I are each occupying one of the lounge's two aubergine couches. They're arranged at right-angles to each other, with a large, intricately patterned kilim rug of maroon and gold covering half the stripped wood floor between them. Opposite me the two alcoves are floor-to-ceiling books I never open any more, since they don't help with death, with ending. Two faux Moroccan table lamps with bases of what looks like beaten pewter, one on top of the telly, one on a side table, creamily low-light the room. It's clean, warm, faintly jas-mine-incense-scented, comfortable. Meticulously tidied. Game's up, Vince has said, you're being outed by your own flat. We've watched our recorded backlog of shows. *Friends, Frasier, Sex and the City.* American television. The great guilty pleasure of escape to a world where everything comes right in the end. However, my adulthood can be switched off only so long: I'm teaching at ten. Yeats. 'The Second Coming'.

'Wait,' Vince says. 'Have you logged on today?'

'No.'

'Hang on.'

He pulls a crumpled scrap of paper from his pocket and unfolds it. '"Iraq captors kill American hostage",' he reads. '"Fear grows for Briton after second hostage beheaded. *Plus*: Kylie's prim new look."'

'Fuck off.'

'Go and check if you like.'

Every morning on AOL's welcome page the News window contains two headlines. A while back Vince and I started collecting the most provocative pairings. We began in the Byronic *and if I laugh/'tis that I may not weep* manner. Sometimes we still do laugh. Mainly, though, we find ourselves without anything to say, dumbly annoyed not by the inane equalizations but by our still bothering to notice. Neither Vince nor I has ever cared, nor do we care now, about the world, though we go through phases of thinking we do. There's one of these phases in the offing, I suspect. Recently Vince bought a book by Noam Chomsky called *Hegemony or Survival: America's Quest for Global Dominance.* I know he hasn't started it yet because when he does it'll be left around the house, tented to mark his page. I don't want him to start it because *I* don't want to start it.

'Guess which one I double-clicked?' he calls, when I get to the door.

Mummy-shuffling down the hall to my room, I ruminate on the likelihood of Kylie enjoying sex. It seems remote. She's acquired that bright deadness. Can someone who refers to herself in the third person ever be alone? Can someone who is never alone have an imagination? Can someone without an imagination enjoy sex?

This is your mind, I think, aware also of a slight catarrhal wheeze; this is your life.

The video footage of Ken Bigley shows him dressed in an approximation of Guántanamo orange. These are my times. This year is turning out to be quite a year. The most powerful nation on the planet is breaking international law. By degrees the planet is assimilating the new situation (which is the old situation, the necessary situation), that the most powerful nation on the planet *is* international law. *The best lack all conviction.* I'm not thinking of America, I'm thinking of myself – then immediately remember that I long ago realized that I wasn't and never would be one of the best. Not taking responsibility for the world means you forfeit your right to complain when the world breaks into your home and rapes your wife and murders your children or imprisons you without charge. Very well. I will not complain. In the meantime leave me alone. No one's on the Anglo-Indians' side, I've told Vince, because there aren't enough of us to *constitute* a side. You need a fucking ethnographic microscope to see us.

These are my stoned circles and drifts, not infrequently – as now – without warning interrupted by paralysing intimations of mortality. Getting into bed (after writing a Post-it and sticking it to my satchel: 'Ring Dolmen Publishing re: Skinner') I'm suddenly caught and held by a physical sensation of the certainty of my own death. I feel the centre of myself opening and closing like a huge fish mouth. Either in reality or in my imagination I clutch at my chest. A vast bent wall or tidal wave of deep space, icy and star-filled, is suddenly there in my room; you're sucked in and in a last grasping second – you did nothing, *nothing* and now – know it's as simple as blowing out a match. Ending. I really will one day really die. The guarantee of the planet's indifferent continuance after my death throbs around me. The collective spirit or personality of television leers in and says, Oh yes, I'll still be going on: *EastEnders*, *The Sky at Night*, *Who Wants to Be a Millionaire?* This is the horror, the endurance of other things, each ignorant not just of your absence but of your ever having been there in the first place.

The fear passes. It always does. Your death's like the sun: you can't look straight at it for longer than a second or two. The looming-up momentarily annihilates everything else (like coming), then (like coming) lets it all back in. I drift. Sleep. Kylie's prim new bum. Beheadings on the net. Nowadays. We move forward into darkness, and darkness closes behind us. Tomorrow I must organize *The Cheechee Papers*. But first dreams. First Scarlet. Tomorrow I must do better. At everything.

CHAPTER FOUR

❧

The Girl and the Gold

(*The Cheechee Papers*: Lahore, 1942)

The gods and goddesses of romance make their inaugural demands. So do certain matters of fact. The first time he set eyes on my mother my father was, as a matter of fact, on wallet guard duty at a corner table in Ho Fun's Chinese restaurant, eating egg custards and waiting for his three friends to finish getting laid. The custards were anomalous on an otherwise predictable menu (predictably mistranslated, too: small prawn balls of dumpling dip fry in atrocious chilli) but my father was hooked. He was just finishing his second when my mother walked past the window. It wasn't love at first sight, but it was something. Until that moment, syphilis, courtesy of Agnes's shock tactics, had been much on his mind.

This was Lahore, 1942, five years before the carve-up that would drop it into bloodily newborn Pakistan's lap; like all cities, nooked and crannied with vice if you knew where to look. Shahi Mohulla or Hira Mandi (literally if now euphemistically 'diamond market') in the north-west corner of the Walled City had housed the courtesans of the Muslim middle classes in the glory days of the Mughals. Time had stripped an ornamented transaction to its essence: courtesans had become whores; what used to be exclusive to middle-class Muslim men had opened to anyone whose conscience and purse could cope. The sons of Islam had had to make way for the uncircumcised in every shade from blue-black to cadaver. Ho Fun's – archly or serendipitously named and positioned – sat opposite Mrs Naicker's Place (also known as the Lotus House, also known as the Mission, also known – courtesy of the obscure poetry of debauch – as the Ginger Rogers), brothel of choice for young men down from the air force training base at Walton. These *were* young men. Ross had only just turned eighteen, and of his three fellows enwhored across the street – Stan Ramsay, Dick Mills and Eugene Drake – only Stan was over twenty-one. But India, thanks to the imperious pronouncement of Viscount Linlithgow three years earlier, was at war with Germany *et al.*, and young Anglo-Indian men, mellifluous, Brylcreemed and natty in Oxford bags and bush-shirts, had enlisted. Some, certainly, out of tortured patriotism, some, as in Ross's case, because they were in trouble and needed to disappear, but many – Stan, Dick and Eugene, for example – with the same breezy expectation they brought to everything under the admittedly up-and-down parasol of imperial endeavour: that it would be a harmless lark from which they'd emerge unscathed with a hatful of damn good yarns. Hitler, if the photos and newsreels were to be believed, was a dwarfish toilet attendant who couldn't stop shouting in German.

In theory the Mrs Naicker's routine was this: Stan, Dick and Eugene entered with just enough cash for one trip to paradise while Ross sat in Ho Fun's and kept their wallets and passbooks safe – both from Mrs Naicker's light-fingered ladies and from Stan, Dick and Eugene's weak wills, which, unchecked, would continue shelling out until they were drunk, broke, miserable and raw of phallus. That was the theory. In practice, Stan, Dick and

Eugene kept coming out for more money (furnace-blast of heat and light between brothel porch and restaurant was God, to be agonizingly withstood by post-coital Catholic boys), then going back in, until they were drunk, broke, miserable and raw of phallus, and on each return to the restaurant tried to persuade him to join them. Eugene, who was never long about his business and was known to the girls at Mrs Naicker's as Quickprick or Sprintfinish, had already been over once.

'Why don't you give it a try, men?' he'd asked Ross.

'No fear.'

'Why not?'

'It's not for me.'

'Come *on*.'

'Not with them.'

'There's nothing wrong with them.'

'Look here, you want to go, you go. But don't say I didn't warn you when your bleddy *lund* turns green and drops off, okay?'

Eugene had plucked a leaf of mint off the side of Ross's plate and popped it into his mouth, Ross speculating where hand and mouth had been. 'Just give me another twenty,' Eugene said, chewing, hands back in pockets. He had pale hazel eyes and an olive-skinned chimpish face, sandy hair severely centre-parted. Added to which, shirt wrongly buttoned and carmine lipstick smudge on his left cheek. Give Eugene a lottery win or a clean-up on the Cotton Figures, Ross thought, and he'd quickly, quietly and with that same chimpish look of contented resignation, whore himself into the grave. 'One more and that's it, absolutely,' Eugene said. Then, in a guttural whisper, 'Seriously, there's one girl in there will do *what*all I don't know.'

That had been ten minutes ago. Stan would be out next, hot-faced, eyes pickled, dragging on a Craven A, conscious as the oldest of having a dissolute image to keep up. In expectation of this Ross took the last mouthful of dessert and raised his head to look out.

Just as my mother went past. Unignorable fusion, girl and taste.
Lovely bare neck and arms, flare of light off dress-hip, chilled egg
custard, fresh mint, cinnamon, nutmeg, then an intense whiff of
sizzling ginger from the kitchen. Her shadow crossed the restaurant's concrete floor and sleeping Persian cat. Sunlit womanly
shoulder and the heavy swing of curled-under dark hair. *Anglo.
Got colour*, Ross thought. Young. Walking fast. Calf muscles.
Nervous. One backward glance as if she might be being tailed.
Nasty-looking scratch on her cheek. Why here? Dress print was
what? Poppies?

Anglo. You knew straight off. As did the Britishers. Tommies
eyed-up Anglo-Indian girls with the look of disgusted entitlement. Chutney Mary. *Teen pau* pussy. Toilet graffiti and
overhearings. Told her it would lighten her skin and she was on
her back before you could say Churchill. 'She thinks she's the
bleddy cat's whiskers as it is,' his mother used to say of Mrs
Lorrimer, her arch-rival in the matter of Sunday hats. 'God only
knows what she'd be like if she had colour.' Having colour was
being fair-skinned, a semantic inversion. There was thinking to be
done about this, he knew, but the knowledge irritated him. He
was eighteen. His circuits of desire were live and reliable: knock
about, drink, box, play football, get clean girls, make the
Olympics when the war was over. Those were the pulses that took
him through the hours and days. Thinking would get in the way.
Politics was a disturbance on his peripheral vision.

'Nah one?' the waiter quacked.

'What?' Ross said. He'd leaned back on his chair to track my
mother through the window.

'Nah egg cussah?' the waiter said, pointing to the empty plate.

She'd disappeared into a clutter of rickshaws, leaving the street
vivified: one coral-pink wall; a conical pile of yellow sand; a splat
of betel in the bone-white dust as if someone had been gunned
down and whisked away. For a moment he could hear time
passing, a quiet hiss of evaporation: your life, *now*. Something

rattlecrashed beyond the serving hatch, followed by a jangling diatribe in Chinese. He shivered, a little current of pleasure. Fear of syphilis notwithstanding, he opened to life when it knocked; fierce forces ambushed or seduced and he went under aflame or dreaming. Technically, he reminded himself, he was still on the run from the bleddy *law*.

He snatched up the wallets, dropped four annas on the table, got woozily to his feet.

'Tell my friends to wait here,' he said, then hurried out into the blinding light.

The street was a stripe of sunlight with a margin of shadow a yard wide. His eyes stung. Pickled. They'd passed a half-pint of country liquor back and forth in the truck on the way to Ho Fun's. He'd drunk water in the restaurant but the grog in his blood had made short work of it. Now his mouth was thick and dry again. Neat country liquor with lime cordial. Jesus Mary and Joseph never again. The heat was an incessant scream. Excremental odours came and went. Nausea for a moment – a quiver of egg custard – then control. He felt better. He looked down the street. Red poppies on a white dress. Who scratched her face like that? She'd disappeared into the gaggle of rickshaws.

Stuffing wallets and passbooks into his jacket pockets (Eugene's and Dick's still had their two standard-issue condoms tucked into the back flap – madmen!), he set off at a run.

His shins hurt. Bits of the street flashed past. A paan shop, a trio of dhoti'd Hindus, one with a homemade purple eye-patch. A squatting black-toenailed sadhu messily fingering up rice from begging bowl to bearded mouth. A boy in filthy half-mast pyjamas staring at the ground next to his white-nosed and long-eyelashed donkey. A bullockless bullock cart tipped forward on its shafts. A post office, burned out, boarded up after the riots, *Jai Hind!* daubed in yellow on its façade. Outside it two men in Gandhi caps followed him with their eyes. Anglo in uniform. Indian Air Force. Khaki drill and buttons that weren't brass. They won't want you here when we clear out. A lone Tommy (*Royal* Air Force, double the pay, buttons that *were* brass) came over to the IAF canteen now and again to talk politics with Stan, who took a cynical interest in what was going on. 'They hate you just as much as they hate us. More, actually. At least we can go home. Where the fuck are you lot going to go?' In the riots protestors had had Gandhi caps whipped off and set fire to by the police. 'And who are the bloody police?' Stan's friend had asked, rhetorically. 'That's *you* lot, isn't it? The bloody Auxiliary Force, the bloody 'arf-castes.'

Ross ran on. The pain in his shins receded. Sunlight was sheer, all blades and planes. *Jai Hind!* Free India. Let them get on with it, then. That wasn't life. Life was something else, the feeling of significance you got at odd moments, the whore tigerishly grinning from the balcony, or that evening swimming alone in the Taptee, looked down on by a wafer-thin blue-etched moon; once a little lift of consciousness in the middle of a crowded street, with horns beeping and people shouting, as if for an instant you were given a glimpse of . . . he didn't know what. Inclusion in God's generous cunning. The pattern. Destiny. 'Sooner or later the niggers'll kick you out,' Stan's RAF friend insisted. So what? He, Ross, would go somewhere else. Wherever he went there would be the strength of his own two hands and cold water to drink and the dawn sunlight unfolding the trees' delicate shadows and the piercing conviction under God's somewhat scornful eye of his own significance. Wherever he went he could, for Christ's sake, box.

Still, *sooner or later* niggled. 'Storm's comin,' Stan's friend liked to say, with ghoulish relish, legs crossed, cup and saucer held just under his chin. He was a Mancunian (Mancunians, Liverpudlians, they sounded like creatures out of *Gulliver's Travels*), cadaverous, with watery blue eyes and tarnished horsy teeth. 'We pull out, you buggers are going to be up shit creek wi'out a paddle. Then what?'

This was the thinking to be done. Ross hated the obligation. The very words Legislative Assembly made him drowsy. People forming leagues, committees, parties, movements. He wanted to be left alone. Life was in the moments. You saw a girl and got up and followed her while God watched how you handled it. Which meant that how you handled it mattered. 'Don't see any fun in it,' Stan's friend had said of Catholicism. 'God spyin on you while you're avin a shite.' They'd laughed, Stan and Dick with guilty flashbacks to the hours at Mrs Naicker's, but Ross with a sudden intimation of how cold and meaningless he would feel *without* God's eye on him from time to time. Imagine that: the world, the universe, everything barrelling along unwatched, no one keeping score, the whole thing a giant accident. He'd laughed with the others, but the thought had led him to an abyss into which he'd looked down, vertiginously, then recoiled. This was the core of his faith, such as it was, that God was there, that things happened for a reason, though there was no guarantee of happiness in this world or the next, only the guarantee of some kind of story, your own.

A ripple went through the sunlit drivers who in the brash light seemed all teeth and eye-whites and fingertips. Rickshaw, sahib? Tonga-taxi? Rickshaw? It was as if he'd disturbed a flock of geese. You sat on your arse and they burned their bodies' energy getting you from A to B, the translation of what your legs wouldn't do into what theirs would, did, had to. If he called to one of the drivers, the man's response would be commercial delight, no sign of dread at what it would cost him, the horrible inroad it would make into his body's fuel. Ross thought of the fuel, a couple of parathas or chapattis, a handful of dhal, the disproportion between this and the exertions into which it must be transformed. It was impossible, and they did it, millions of them, day in, day out, while you sat on your arse and didn't give it a thought because all there was was the moment of slightly disgusting commercial delight then the man receded into his inhuman function. *Jai Hind!* An image formed of a crowd of rickshaw drivers taking their ease in a golden field, drinking tea, smoking, some of them wearing bits and pieces of left-behind British gear: a solar topee; riding boots; a lady's veiled hat. Suddenly a whole country abandoned, the curious quiet glee of kids left with the run of a house. Would it be like that for them? Was that what they were waiting for?

He had these thoughts from time to time but they didn't stick. They slid from him, oiled by the will to pleasure. Waving the drivers away, he rounded the corner at the end of the street. The girl was twenty yards ahead, hurrying. Towards Roshnai Gate, he assumed. What was she doing out here? She looked back over her shoulder, didn't see him. Too young. Sixteen? But the body had arrived, unequivocally, breasts and hips, those dancer's calves. No make-up. He slowed, followed more cautiously. This was the excitement a murderer would feel. Sex was God-shadowed, garlanded with warnings. His childhood image of Adam and Eve was printed for life, the pathetic bare bottoms and downturned mouths, the after, never the during. He imagined a smudge of Edenic mud on Eve's white (naturally, white) buttock, the earth dutifully telling its tale. Adam's face would have been tender with shame.

She ducked behind a newsstand and disappeared. He followed.

'Sahib?'

From a doorstep to his left. He looked down. His pursuit had brought him into a street that disappeared into a maze of covered market stalls.

'Sahib, is that yours?'

The man asking was young and tatty, sitting hunched forward, knees up, smoking a bidi with one hand, shading his eyes with the other. Crumpled kurta pyjamas and a light coat of dust on the blue-black waves of his hair. His mouth remained unnecessarily open, revealing betel-stained teeth too widely spaced. Ross imagined him lying on a bare bunk fantasizing about making a bundle and cracking the whip. A pinstripe suit, a gun, a lipsticked and sulky moll.

'What?'

'There, sahib, by your foot.'

Ross looked down. Next to his left foot was a dirty khaki handkerchief, scrunched up and tied with a bit of leather thong.

'No, that's not mine.'

The poppy-dressed girl reappeared from behind a fruit stall, briefly entered a shaft of sun, paused, aura'd in brilliant motes, then turned right and headed up the market's main aisle. Not so anxious now, Ross thought. Got her bearings. Holds her shoulders differently. Swimmer's legs, maybe. He saw her underwater, scissor-kicking for the bottom, eyes squinting, hard thighs slicing the water's buttery bulk.

'Sorry, sahib, I thought you must have dropped it.'

Ross was already moving away. He glanced back to see the man on the doorstep grin and sketchily salute him. The liquor had worn off. Drunk, he would have read the salute as sarcasm. Drunk, all those 'sahib's would have added up to the insolence of deliberate overuse. They won't want you here when we're gone. Drunk, he would have slipped with relief into outrage, felt its deep calm hardening in his head and fists. That was the other purity. When you fought, God didn't watch, He came into you.

No. That was a lie. Drunk, it was the Devil who took possession, the two of you in lip-licking collusion. God was for the ring. Transcendence there was sober, a clean flowing out into the infinite; you looked down with angelic innocence at the knocked-out man on the canvas and found you had to struggle back into time, causation, the physics and maths of how you'd done it. Feinted, drew his right, and caught the bugger with a solid counter, straight on the point. You could make a post hoc story out of it but it always felt false. It was a miracle, you wanted to say. God took me for a moment, that's all.

He was dehydrated. The market was busy and loud. A gorgeous cacophonous stall of caged bulbuls, mynahs and parakeets to his left, a tiny wrinkled matron to his right, shrilly haggling with a young fruit seller whose cheekbones shone like polished mahogany. A foxy dog the colour of wheat lay on its side in the shade of a striped awning, eyes slits, wet muzzle up as if in ecstasy. Dogs were everywhere, wet-nosed, lovely-eyed, with that tender, arresting way they had of sniffing each other's anuses. In his father's *Anglo-Indian Quarterly* years ago it had said, 'We may as well face it: to both the British and the Indians we Anglos are a pariah race.' He'd been a boy when he'd read that. Pariah dogs were mongrels. He hadn't understood.

Smells changed every few paces: dry-roasting mustard seeds; scalded coffee; frangipani incense; cow dung. A fat green-sari'd woman thickly musk-perfumed went past him. Glimpse of her midriff rolls and blood-red toenails. The city was sexy, Lahore, the *whore* sound in it. At St Aloysius' history had been history of the British Empire – the Spinning Jenny, American independence, the East India Company – the notion of India's history before the Raj barely occurred to the boys, but Danglers let the odd thing drop, that Lahore, for example was a much-looted city, Aryans, Mughals. Which must have given it this rich, tired feel of experience, like a woman long since used to every stripe of fornication.

Fornication. Woman. Just the words and your scrotum tingled. Burping, he tasted liquor and lime, shuddered. The morning's drunkenness sheet-lightninged from a distance. The girl had stopped a few yards ahead at a stall selling used books and magazines, Conan Doyles and *Photoplays*. Mental rehearsal so far hadn't got him past Excuse me . . .

An overweight perspiring Sikh in a sand-coloured suit, who, on the edge of Ross's awareness, had been creating a flap in a small crowd, spun out of it and bumped into him.

'Oh. Sorry.' They looked at each other. The Sikh grabbed Ross plump-fingeredly by the elbow. 'I've lost something,' he said. No 'sahib' this time. Ross was taken by the eyes, as large and black-lashed as a showgirl's. The beard was a fat pelt, oiled and silver-streaked. 'It's a matter of . . .' Suddenly the Sikh's face contorted, a grimace, almost tears, then righted itself. He squeezed his jaws together, an effort against psychic collapse that made his face shudder. Ross, embarrassed, looked past him. The girl had turned a corner and disappeared. 'My friend,' the Sikh said, opening his eyes. 'I've dropped, somewhere in this market, a little . . . frankly, a handkerchief, tied round something. Have you seen it?'

'Yes, back there on the pavement—'

The Sikh's head jerked away as if he'd been swung at, though the boneless fingers remained locked on Ross's elbow. '*What!* Where exactly?'

'Just back there next to the pawnshop. Fellow sitting on the doorstep asked me if I'd dropped it.'

For a second it was as if they'd fallen in love. Then the Sikh without a word tore himself away and ran.

So now instead of Excuse me he would say, I've just made a complete stranger very happy. The confidence to dispense with preliminaries would get her attention. He pictured Stan, Dick and Eugene back at Ho Fun's, stewing in their own guilt and calling piteously for chai or lassi – on tick, since he was holding the cash. No more Mrs Naicker's for them today. They had fucked their last. In mysterious ways you did God's work. He went on.

But at the next junction, aisles going left, right and straight on, there was no sign of her. The market floor was peppered with trodden scraps of food. Each person shopped intently, as if he or she were the only customer there, breaking reverie only to ask or argue a price. Hard to believe the din broke down to these utterances.

He went left, then right at a sweetmeats stall. Five minutes lefting and righting on instinct. Ten. No sign. He'd lost her. He stopped and bought a glass of lukewarm tea from a chai wallah, drank it standing up. Shouldn't have waited. Idiot. Her womanhood had come early, ambushed hips, breasts and thighs with rousing prematurity; embarrassment just beneath her surface because she knew men held her body's advertisements accountable. She hadn't wanted it, hadn't been ready, needed another year at least. If he had spoken to her she would have blushed, gone hot in the armpits. In the uniform he would have seemed older, impressive.

Useless hypotheticals. Missed moments like that subtracted something from your heart.

A barefoot beggarly boy of about nine or ten in ragged, filthy shorts shuffled past. He had the khaki handkerchief bundle in his hands, and was picking at the knotted leather thong.

Ross waited until the knots had brought the boy to a standstill under a nearby archway before approaching him with, in quiet Hindi, 'I don't think that's yours, is it?'

The boy looked up, frowning, as if he'd been inconsiderately disturbed. Everything in the dirty young face was all right except for one misangled canine, which poked out from under his top lip. There was a smudge of grease on his left cheek. Ross imagined a thieved samosa, wolfed down. 'You found that, didn't you?' he said.

The boy's frown became a scowl. He put his lips together in an enormous crooked pout.

'Let's have a look and see what it is.'

The boy shook his head violently.

'Come on,' Ross said, reaching out towards the bundle. 'I'll help you untie—'

The boy cringed and screamed as if he'd been burned. Heads turned.

'Shshsh!' Ross said. 'I'm only saying let me un*tie* it at least and we'll see what's in there—'

Again scream and cringe. More heads turning, the first ripple of collective censure.

'You won't handle him like that,' a voice said. Ross turned. A young Britisher, a little older than him, perhaps twenty, had come up alongside them. 'Bit simple,' he said quietly. 'But not so simple he doesn't know how to use it.' Then in flawless Hindi to the boy, 'We'll trade, Ram, okay?'

Ram, with renewed effortful pouting, shook his head: no.

'Yes, we will. Come on. You don't even know what you've got in there, do you?'

'You know him?' Ross asked.

The Britisher – English, the accent said – nodded with fond disapproval. He was shinily clean-shaven with a dramatically cleft chin; blue eyes that said not a trick missed, slicked-back blond hair. 'Local character,' he said. 'He's known on the market.' The voice had education, evoked for Ross lawns, frothily dressed white women, grand houses, but something alert and commercial, too. The tone and quick glance said: I'm not pulling anything on you, age, race, class. Just trust me. It excited Ross. He was used to every degree of British assumed superiority from abuse to painstaking condescension. Occasionally someone's burning Christlike fraternity, of which he was mere functional object. Something else going on here. He couldn't quite see it – then could: the young man was crooked. For a second he'd thought homosexual. Even now he didn't rule it out; but if it was there it was secondary. The communiqué was that they, the men, had an opportunity. A chance for profit. Amazing how quickly you could sound each other out. The Devil's shorthand.

The Englishman reached into his inside pocket (linen blazer, single-breasted, palest khaki) and pulled out an expensive-looking fountain pen. His hand movements were gracefully authoritative. Under the jacket he wore a pink cheesecloth shirt. 'Here,' he said, offering the pen to the boy. 'You hold this while I untie the knots, yes?'

Apparently a new angle of pain for Ram: dilemma. He screwed his face into a snarl.

'Come on, just while we open it up.' Then in English to Ross. 'Obsessed with fountain pens. Loves them. Any idea what's in there?'

'There was a Sikh fellow looking for it.'

'Fat chap. Gobind Singh.'

'You know him as well?'

'I know him; he's a crook.'

Ram snatched at the pen. The Englishman fluidly moved it away, shaking his head. 'Ram, listen to me. Give me the bundle and I'll let you hold the pen. Come on. Don't be silly.'

By painful degrees Ram delivered the tied handkerchief into the white left hand while receiving the fountain pen from the right. The Englishman looked at Ross: with your permission? Ross nodded. The man had an up-to-the-minute aliveness about him, an effect that made Ross feel that his experience of time, the present, the modern world, had until this moment been missing something. The market had got louder, as if everyone was debating at once. Ram inked a line on the back of his hand, then realized his lapse and forced himself to watch the unwrapping.

'Heavy,' the Englishman said. His clean-nailed fingers worked at the knotted thong. Spotless pink shirt cuffs, a yellow-faced wristwatch on a brown leather strap. 'Without making it obvious,' he said, not looking up, 'is anyone watching us?'

If Ross had smoked he'd have scanned the market under cover of lighting up. As it was he put his hands in his pockets, raised his eyebrows and looked up with fake boredom.

The girl appeared from behind a fabric stall, in front of which a chipped mannequin crookedly modelled a purple and gold sari. She'd bought a bag of pistachios. For a second he wondered if she, too, were simple; the anxiety had been replaced by a look of dreamily not caring. Then she lifted her head again, to her left, as if suddenly reminded that she might be being followed. Clean features, fine eyebrows and quick animal eyes. She wasn't mad. It was something else, Ross thought – then in a leap: she wasn't afraid of death. With a disgusted flourish the moustached stall-holder flung a roll of pink silk open in front of her, then immediately turned to talk to another customer. Some vendors were like that, as if the notion they might need to sell you anything was beneath their contempt. Others whined and babbled as if their children's lives depended on it.

'Please react in the manner of somone barely interested,' the Englishman said.

Ross just managed not to say 'What?', though he'd heard perfectly.

'I don't think we're much interested in these, do you?' the Englishman said in Hindi, holding out the unwrapped handkerchief, in which were four small, slender gold bars.

Ross stared, said nothing. Felt the tip of the Englishman's shoe touching his own, once, twice. 'No,' he said. He cleared his throat, then repeated, 'No.'

The Englishman snorted, hurriedly rewrapped the ingots and held them out to Ram. 'You can keep these,' he said. 'But you won't be able to trade them.'

Ram, sweatily gripping the fountain pen, narrowed his eyes as if trying to see something remotely distant. 'Gold,' he said.

'Ye-es,' the Englishman said, making two syllables out of one and forcing Ram's filthy fingers round the bundle, 'it is gold. But it's Gobind Singh's gold, which he lost today. Everyone knows he's looking for it. Who do you think will trade with you? Gobind is looking for it *right now*. Already this soldier sahib and I know you've got it. How long before everyone knows?'

The girl lifted the pink to look at a roll of orange chiffon underneath. The world was strewn with rights and wrongs; you passed through them as through the market's stinks and perfumes. There was an irresistible weave of wrongs around these gold bars. (And the girl?) He knew he was going to do the wrong thing, that God was going to watch and at some later time pay him back in proportional suffering. He considered, as he always did at such moments, refusing, walking away, confounding Heaven. But even as he thought it he imagined God grinning and shaking His head: we both know you're not going to do *that*.

Meanwhile the Englishman had been in quiet negotiation with Ram, who not infrequently writhed and made a great show of being unfairly stymied. Presumably the thought that the sahibs would be in the same position as him should they acquire the treasure hadn't entered his head, along with much else that hadn't entered his head, such as the absurdity of Gobind Singh's walking about telling everyone he'd lost four gold bars.

'What do you think?' the Englishman said.

'What?' Ross had drifted, was shocked back. The Englishman had pulled out a pack of Woodbines and was offering him one. Ram, now in an elaborate depression, had walked a few feet away and slumped to his buttocks. He sat with his knees up and his chin resting on them.

'No thanks, I don't,' Ross said, meaning the smoke. Then, 'It's incredible.'

The Englishman slipped a cigarette into his thin mouth, rolled his head through a slow left to right arc and back again as to relieve stiffness, then lit up from a matchbook. Ross observed the first needful drag and majestic exhalation. Smoking looked good; it was remarkable he'd never taken it up. 'Do you have any idea what those are worth?' the Englishman said, repocketing the matchbook.

'Not really. A lot.'

'Quite a bit, I should think. Possibly four or five hundred apiece. Have you any money on you?'

'Not much. About fifty rupees.'

'Are you willing to let me handle things?'

'Yes.'

'Okay. Give me twenty.'

The girl turned from the stall, looked around, saw Ross, slightly noticed him, then turned and walked away. Now or never. A dark bare-chested young man, wirily muscled, went past carrying in one hand a wire coop with two enormous chickens, in the other a basket of shiny brinjals. In the time it took for him to pass, the choice was made. Ross followed the Englishman towards Ram. The girl disappeared.

'As I said: simple, but awkwardly so.'

'Parents?'

'Around, somewhere. You know.'

They veered from the subject. Build a picture and you gave your conscience more to work with. It was good, the fluency between them. Every Britisher could've been this way and the whole country would've been different. Ross almost hoped the Englishman *was* homosexual; it would mean that in spite even of that you could fleetingly align in understanding.

The Englishman's fountain pen and cufflinks plus thirty-five Ross Monroe (or rather Ross Monroe and associates, since fifteen of the thirty-five came from Stan, Dick and Eugene's whore-house allowance) rupees secured two of the four bars. But bargaining appeared to work Ram up. He became truculent over the second pair. It was a careful balance. He'd get riled and shriek with impatience, which had two effects: first, it reminded him, Ross saw, that it was in his own interest not to draw attention (which might well become the attention of Gobind Singh) to himself; second, it filled Ross with fear of the crowd's attention. The Englishman put up the watch for a third bar, but the remaining cash, twenty rupees, wouldn't budge the boy on the last.

'I'll take that one ring also,' Ram said, with the stubborn little head-waggle and averted eyes.

You could see why people didn't bother with negotiation, Ross thought, just went straight to force. Once you got your soul out of the picture, it was simple economics.

'That one ring' was the bloodstone on his right index finger. The Englishman saw his hesitation. 'Up to you,' he said. 'But unless it's worth five hundred, I'd let it go.'

'Sentimental value,' Ross said. 'My mother gave it to me.'

Ringless but richer by perhaps a thousand rupees, Ross went over the scene in the cart on the way back to Walton.

He'd have to think of something to tell Beatrice when the time came, or replace the ring with a copy. The betrayal had left

a dirty aftertaste, as if her blood was on his tongue, old and iro-
nish. Becoming a man was of necessity murdering a little of your
mother. Ross had felt his skin warming with shame. But a thousand rupees! Every time he thought of it (the phrase unravelled
heraldically in his head, *a thousand rupees*) a thrill tightened his
balls. Undischarged lust maybe, the unvisited whores, the poppy-
dressed girl. He could make intuitive mental leaps. Sex-energy
was malleable, would find its way into something if not the act.
Lucifer, Danglers was fond of saying, is like molten metal, like
lava: he can trickle into any shape, and once he's there, once he's
there, my boys, he hardens for good.

Ross pinched between his eyes then pressed outwards round
their sockets. His father's gesture against the unreasonable load he
had to carry. He shouldn't have done it. His mother's bloodstone
ring. Well, he'd done what he'd done. Pilate, Danglers told them,
had said, *Quod scripsi, scripsi*. What I have written, I have written.
It had become for the St Aloysians a playground saw, to be produced whenever one was caught out in wrongdoing. You stole
that bleddy pot of guava jelly from my trunk, you thieving sonofabitch. A shrug: *Quod scripsi, scripsi*. Ross chuckled at the
memory. The day had gathered in him, given peace to his limbs,
the morning's liquor and lime, the egg custards, the grog-thirst
and the heat like an angel wrapped round him as he tailed the girl,
the Englishman's handshake, their mutual visibility and shared
shame. Two each, yes? It was as if they'd molested the boy
together. There was a knack to reaching out and taking life's
wealth, letting it accumulate in you, feeling the filthy enrich-
ment. He stretched, leaned back and put his feet up on the seat in
front of him, where in silhouette Stan and Dick sat sluggish, irritable, glutted.

'Are you sure we haven't had this bugger before?' Eugene whispered, leaning close. He smelled of Mrs Naicker's: incense and
perfume, cigarette smoke, his own cooled bittersweet sweat. His
breath was louche with booze and the brothel's greasy snacks.

'I'm sure.'

'How can you be sure, men?'

'Well he *took* us, didn't he?'

'He' was the cart driver, an inscrutable leathery Pathan, white-moustached, ropy with muscle. They were less than a mile from the base. Ross knew the moment couldn't be put off much longer. He didn't feel up to it. Just here the road was lined with and scented by cinnamon trees. It was a clear night. Stars when he tipped his head back and bared his throat to the current of night air. All these pleasures free if you knew how to take them.

'Listen, I don't think it's fair you using our money like that,' Eugene said. 'I mean, we should be in for a share.'

'You'll *get* a share,' Ross said, bringing his head forward again. 'I told you. Proportional.'

'Why not equal shares?' Dick said.

'Because it's not an equal bleddy investment, is it? See that?' Ross held up his right hand, missing its bloodstone. 'Did you part with your mother's ring? No.'

Stan leaned forward, smiling. 'Just remember you owe me fifteen rupees.' He had laughed, sceptically, when Ross told the story and produced an ingot. (No need for them to know there were two.) Stan had laughed, patiently, as on behalf of the entire jaded world and Ross had hated him for it. Coward's laugh: expect nothing and you don't need the courage to hope, nor the strength to withstand disappointment when nothing comes.

'It's time,' Eugene said quietly. Even saying this couldn't quite bring them to it. Another minute passed. The nag's clopping and the wheels' occasional judder. Bats kept shadowily just missing them.

'Stop!' Dick called. 'Driver, hold on! Stop!'

The driver looked over his shoulder, saw Dick and Eugene trying to get up from their seats, drew rein and halted the cart. The horse snorted, shook its huge head – tinkle of bridle bells and harness gewgaws – then settled. The driver turned in his seat to observe. Only the wet stone gleam of his eyes and two white twists of his moustache showed in the dark. He said something in Pushtu, a polite question. None of the passengers answered. Out of initial silence cicada-riot swelled around them. Pale flowers in the roadside darkness were fairyish presences, watching.

'Wallet,' Eugene said loudly, jumping down from the cart. 'I dropped my wallet.' Dick followed Eugene. Ross got up and stretched, stayed put for a moment, then dropped down on to the road. Terrible contained smash of blood in his soles from sitting too long. For all the free pleasures, your body kept reminding you it was blood and meat, destined for rot. Stan slowly and as if yet another unreasonable demand was being placed on an already exhausted man slouched down last. The Pathan watched without comment. Stan elaborately pantomimed searching his pockets and made the finger rubbing against thumb money gesture. Wallet. Dropped on road. We look. You wait. The driver nodded, once, almost a formal bow, then busied himself lighting a bidi. Scrutinizing the ground, the four men in uniform inched back down the cart's tracks, spreading out as they went.

'Enough?' Eugene whispered. Two minutes later they had regrouped, bent, hands in pockets, peering, as if at something discovered on the ground.

Ross shrugged. 'Okay.' The shrug was an effort, as if each shoulder carried a heavy bag. He was supposed to be getting himself ready. Very definitely didn't feel up to it. The day's residue that had been calm and golden and warm in his limbs was turning or had turned to mild disgust. This shift always came sooner or later; suddenly the casual delight went and it wasn't a game. For a while God jollily observed you mucking yourself up with sin, but always at some point let the jovial mask fall, became grown-up, left you with the stink of yourself and all the dismal consequences lined up.

'Driver!' Stan called. 'Come here and look at this.'

Gesticulation was needed. They spoke no Pushtu and the

driver's English was restricted to fares and destinations. Stan and Dick went part-way back to the cart and persuaded him to come and see.

'You know these Pathan buggers,' Eugene whispered to Ross as the driver approached. 'They never forget a wrong. They're bleddy *tribal*, men. You insult one of their women, they'll *kill* you.'

Ross said nothing. This was Eugene's shamed masochistic routine, after the whores.

'Seriously,' Eugene said, laughing. 'They're known to cut a fellow's guts out and wrap them round his *head*.'

Ross ignored him. The disgust had thickened. Presumably the way they felt after Mrs Naicker's. Ram's shift of interest from gold to fountain pen, wristwatch, rupees. They'd shaken hands with him, like gentlemen.

'Move,' he said to Eugene.

'Don't make a balls-up of it now.'

'Give me room.'

As kids in Bhusawal Ross and his gang used to waylay Indian farmers' boys moving donkeys between grazing grounds. A little terror-posse of Anglo-Indians with catapults and sticks. Hey, we're taking these donkeys. Even boys older than them offered little resistance. Him and his gang were brown sahibs. They took the animals home sometimes, kept them for a while, got bored, turned them loose. Ross remembered his mother asking, having discovered the bemused animal, 'Where's this thing come from?' and not batting an eyelid when he told her. Just a tut and a dismissive wave. 'Tie it up in the compound, then.' Entitlement. Immunity.

'I'm telling you I don't like the look of this bugger,' Eugene said. 'You better get it right first time.'

The driver, flanked by shamefaced Dick and smirking Stan, approached. Ross glance-checked: no weapons. He wondered if the man was married, had children, suffered a vivid mental image of him hoisting a giggling bright-clothed Pathan infant up on to his shoulders. Some of those kids had jewel eyes of emerald or winter blue. Beautiful.

He wasn't ready. Normally he'd be drunk. Drunk, it was easy. The man stood and looked at him. There was a moment in which Ross was aware of himself trying to use the disgust, haul it up into his shoulders. Then he *was* using it. He'd opened his mouth to say look forget it I'll get money from Robbie when we get back and pay this poor bugger. But instead of saying it he'd felt his hands coming up (curious the way the boxing stance asserted itself even here) and his weight shifting. A right cross started as a certainty in the left big toe. The power of God (or was it the Devil?) there, suddenly. Your father I can understand because of the violent streak, don't I know? We do good business, the Englishman had said to Ram, shaking his hand, and the boy's head waggling, okay, okay, sahib. Someone said, 'Hurry up,' quietly, just as the driver's eyes understood. Then Ross hit him.

CHAPTER FIVE

papers

(London, 2004)

Another Monday over with. I'm alone in my bedroom. It's after eleven. Vince is out. I was supposed, according to my own manful resolution, to ask Tara Kilcoyne the art teacher out today. Spent most of 'The Second Coming' inwardly rehearsing, then when I had her alone in the staff room couldn't do it. The moment came, the moment passed. No one's responded to my *Guardian* personal ad yet, either. I must do better, I keep telling myself. At everything.

My bedroom's heart isn't the bed, which says only *bad dreams, fear, masturbation, loneliness, ending*, but an old oak desk Melissa gave me when I moved in. From its brass-knobbed top drawer I remove three buff envelope files, the first marked in my dad's aggressively ornate hand 'Skinner', the second, in my own atrophied italics, '*The Cheechee Papers*', the third not marked at all. I take them and a freshened glass of shiraz with me on to the bed.

Pasha turned the Skinner file over to me secretly four years ago. Secretly because five years before that he'd promised my mum he'd destroyed it. 'You're seventy years old,' she said to him. 'It's utterly ridiculous and it's got to stop. I mean it. I can't stand it any more. I don't know what you think you'd do if you did ever find him. Apart from give yourself a *stroke*.' My dad had woken from one of his Night Horrors and she caught him, he later claimed, in a weak moment.

(A word about the old man's dreams: they're uniformly violent and absurd. 'My son, I was being attacked by a bleddy *gi*raffe. And you know what I had to defend myself with? A sandwich.' You may laugh, but I've heard the noises he makes in his sleep, the mewls and whimpers, the ghost-wails, the falsetto moans. You go into the bedroom and he's sitting up, traumatized. 'This tiger had cottold of my pant and I'm trying *like hell* to get away . . .' My mother has a dismal back-catalogue of injuries he's inflicted defending himself against the animals, terrorists, psychopaths and burglars of the unconscious realm. Three or four times he's hoofed her entirely out of bed. Wildlife programmes are a no-no. Action films. Horror films. Football. Boxing, naturally, since all his youth's uppercuts and hooks and jabs and crosses are still there, waiting for sleep's neural liberation. Elspeth's theory is that he's planning to murder my mum: he'll throttle her in the night, then cite the long, exonerating history of nocturnal hallucination to which his family cannot but testify. This strikes a grim chord with my mum, who devours crime fiction by the ton. I'm counting on you, she's said to Elspeth. I'm counting on you to *expose* him, darling, if he does it.)

Weak moment or not, Skinner is now a father & son Secret Business and not a word to Mater. My rationalization is that if I hadn't taken the file (the challenge, my son, the torch, the sword) the old man would have carried on in secret himself; mishap would have been inevitable. I did consider fabricating, maybe even after a few months producing a photocopy of a bogus death certificate to lay the miserable fucker to rest once and for all. I couldn't, when it came down to it. This is my father's past. This is my father. Sometimes, through finding out what I can't do to my parents, I discover I'm not the man I think I am.

Now, dear God, there is *Raj Rogue*, by Nelson Edwards.

The bulk of the Skinner file is my dad's work or the work of those he's hired down the years. Oh yes, private detectives. We were all surprised to find they existed off television. Not that they ever lasted more than a couple of weeks; the prohibitive cost, certainly, but chiefly their failure to inspire Pater's confidence. Cheh! Detective. All he's got is a bleddy *hat*. Maude once dangerously suggested the old man set up his *own* detective agency. My mother's eyes closed for a couple of seconds, then opened again. Maude didn't see it. 'The first *Anglo-Indian* detective agency,' she added. We were in the Brewer Street living room. I don't know exactly how old my dad was at time, early fifties, I suppose. He looked out of the window, snorted, let the expression of resignation to fate that to us was like a cloud covering the sun appear on his face. I remember a stab of guilt because the silence that followed mapped the restricted dimensions of his life, said there was no room for anything risky and new. My fault. I was the child born ten years after they should have been in the clear. All in a moment the possibility of sharing the fraternity of Kojak, Ironside, McCloud and indeed the great Columbo blossomed and wilted. The silence hung. 'What?' Maude said. 'Well, we *could*, couldn't we?'

But the file. Notes, hypotheses, telephone numbers, private dick reports carbon copied from the days before computers. All of which is of secondary importance if Nelson Edwards, author of the 1972 novel *Raj Rogue*, a flaking and yellowed copy of which has recently been added to the file, is in fact none other than George Edward Nelson Skinner, formerly of Wandsworth, Camden Town, Mile End, Delhi, Bombay, Lahore, Bhusawal, Poona, Wormwood Scrubs and for all I know Timbuktu, the man my father's been obsessed with for the better part of fifty years.

I found it in a second-hand bookshop near work a week ago, not looking for it, not looking for anything. *See?* Pasha would say. Doesn't that prove it to you? By 'it' he'd mean Purpose, Design, ultimately God, a narrative intelligence at work. I ought to be grateful. It ought to make writing the book easier.

Like all synchronicities my pulling *Raj Rogue* from the shelf had its twitch of déjà vu or resonance, an instant in which the world looked like an only partly occluded web of meaning. My mother and father, strangers to each other, unknowingly cross paths in Lahore in 1942. I, Owen Grant Monroe, their last child, pull a book off a shelf in a shop in Wimbledon in 2004. Moments more than half a century and half a planet apart connect. Someone with an insatiable appetite for story, a plot junkie, surely, is doing this. The hairs on the back of my neck stood up. Nelson Edwards. Aliases hint at identity. My own Sheer Pleasure moniker, Millicent Nash, combines my mother's middle name with my paternal grandmother's maiden name. Ego tags every pseudonym with a clue. By which reasoning this was hardly a stretch. George Edward Nelson Skinner. Nelson Edwards. Pores and scalp prickling, I paid the twenty-five pence and put the paperback in my jacket pocket. Twenty-five pence. The cover price was only forty-five pence. A Trident Paperback, 1972.

The biographical note is neither here nor there: 'Nelson Edwards was born in 1922. He has spent many years travelling widely in Asia, and now lives in London.' There is, however, the author photograph, a poorly executed passport-size black-and-white headshot on the back cover. Fifty-year-old 'Nelson' has a bony face (overexposed, its subtleties lost) and a slim, nondescriptly balding head. Moreover, a slight spectacle-lens reflection complicates his eyes. The cleft chin is pure Skinner. But (until I place it in front of Pasha's scrutiny) the only pure Skinner against which it can be gauged is a grainy photocopy of the mug-shot from his one arrest and conviction for fraud in 1958, with hair, sans specs. He did eighteen months of a three-year sentence, got out, disappeared.

My week's research has yielded two facts: *Raj Rogue* went out of print a year after it was published, and Trident, paperback imprint of Dolmen Publishing, was discontinued in 1978. Mercifully out of print, I should have said. Tosh and titillation in execrable prose, a sort of X-rated criminal Bond of the Raj, Clive with sex and drugs. In fact, Clive just moved on a couple of centuries. The appositeness isn't lost on me, Nelson Edwards, *Raj Rogue* and Trident being the decaf precursors of Millicent Nash, *An Adult Education* and Sheer Pleasure, but God's going to have to do a lot better than that to win me over. The cover is a colour photograph of a gratuitously oiled and deeply cleavaged brown dolly bird in a sari (incredibly, it looks like a white girl fakely browned-up — is that possible?), down on her packed haunches looking into a carpet bag of cash. At the door in the background is a pale-suited out-of-focus man with a gun. Lots of Carl's Brewer Street paperbacks had covers like *Raj Rogue*'s, girls with moistly heaving chests or belly-chained midriffs tokenly backdropped by or accoutremented with something suggesting genre or plot: a desert island, a laboratory, a cowboy hat, a machine-gun. My favourite (I spent, cumulatively, years in there) was a dark-haired girl in a partly unzipped black wetsuit top and pink bikini briefs, with her eye make-up running. The cover cut her off just under the plump bulge of her mons. Though I've never tried it, scuba diving has since had a profound erotic appeal. As would saris and carpet bags, had Carl owned a copy of *Raj Rogue*. (Christ, it's possible Carl *did* have a copy. Should I phone him and check? Imagine if that were true, Skinner all those years under our very noses . . .)

There are leads. Dolmen Publishing, first, since it still exists. If Skinner lives and is not yet vegetable, a letter to compose. Ingratiation, fake research project, personal contact, invitation to his home . . . And then what? What is going to happen if Nelson Edwards *is* Skinner, if he's alive, traceable, if, by whatever chicanery it takes, I bring him face to face with my father? What in

God's name is the old man going to do? Pasha's no cabbage but he's not the bantamweight he used to be. I took him to see the Ali–Frazier biopic *When We Were Kings* at a multiplex in Manchester. Returning from the kiosk I spotted him asking directions for the gents. Unfortunately, he was asking the foyer's cardboard *Men in Black* cut-outs of Will Smith and Tommy Lee Jones. Granted this was before the removable cataract had been removed, granted the lights were low; but, as I pointed out to him, each figure was at least eight feet tall and holding a science fiction weapon. What, I ask myself for the umpteenth time, is he going to be capable of? (Spike Lee more than the fight haunted me after the film, by the way, trivially for mispronouncing the word 'articulate' as 'artikulint', but chiefly for his diagnosis of our historical ignorance: 'Today's young generation, they don't know anything. Something happened last year, they know nothing about it. These great great great stories, great historic events . . . And I'm talking about— I'm not talking about 1850s stuff, you know, they don't know who Malcolm X is, they don't know who JFK is . . . and it's scary . . .')

Rain announces itself in soft *pits* on the window. I look up as if I've been shyly addressed. I still have intimations of the planet's aliveness, occasionally, until my educated self steps in and in a moment quietly re-murders the world. Dead. How can you *say* that? my dad demands, when I tell him the universe is Godless, accidental, finite, curved. After everything you know . . . it's madness. Think of me and your mother . . . the *fate* of the thing. If we weren't meant to meet . . . I don't know what. How else can you explain it?

Chance, I've told him. The need to see only the parts of a life that make it a story. He just laughs. Even my mum has to smile, the shy admission of her faith in The Plot. I worry about my genes.

I set the Skinner file aside and top up my tumbler.

(Wolf Blass shiraz is £7.49 at Safeways. If the philistine's zero and the buff's ten I'm about two. It's enough. The gnat's-piss days are behind me but I'm never going to talk about peppery base notes. It was only a couple of years ago I asked for a kitchen wine rack for Christmas. Buying a case still ignites my armpits, conjures for a Western second or two the ranks of famine kids, fly-eyed, balloon-bellied.)

The *Cheechee Papers* file bulges. Of course it does. Just imagining its contents – the notes, the drafts, the photographs, the certificates, the tickets, the stamps, all the papery memorabilia I've gathered to the cause of The Book – releases that brand of paralysing adrenalin peculiar to knowing you can't do the thing you must do. Fractions in Class Ten, for example. Or getting involved in making the world a better place. I take out a sheet of notes at random.

1687 – Letter from EIC (East India Company) Court of Directors to their officials in Madras: '. . . *the marriage of our soldiers to native women is a matter of such consequence to posterity that we shall be content to encourage it with some expense and have been thinking for the future to appoint a Pagoda to be paid to the mother of any child that shall hereafter be born, of any such future marriage, upon the day the child be christened, if you think this small encouragement will increase the number of such marriages . . .*' Pagoda = then 8 or 9 shillings. So deal was loads young Brit. men must fuck. Absence white women (too delicate for voyage & conditions) so native women. Control mixed-blood pop. via marriage, legit. etc. EIC recog. use of mulatto pop. Buffer between colonial pop. and native Indian pop. White cock brown pussy. (Poss title, ha ha.)

My note-taking hasn't changed much since undergraduate days, retains its sometimes violent poetry. Twenty years in even liminal academia has made me an orderly collator, too, but you wouldn't know it from these files. There are pages that might have been arranged by a schizophrenic, by Scarlet's mother, Dinah, for example. The handwritten sheets are a mess. On the same page as the EIC letter is a big red ring with inside it: MEANING OF 'CHEECHEE'??? followed by the *Collins* definition: '*n, pl* **cheechees** (In India, formerly) **a** a person of mixed British and Indian descent; Anglo-Indian. **b** (*as modifier*): *a cheechee accent.* **[C18**: perhaps from Hindi *chhi-chhi*, literally: dirt, or perhaps imitative of their singsong speech]' and another filled with the smallest version of my handwriting (I have several different styles and flit between them, a habit picked up from Scarlet) I can manage:

> '*Anglo-Indian parents commonly indoctrinated their children with attitudes of superiority over Indians and endeavoured to isolate them from intimate association with Indian children . . .*' (see Gist & Wright p. 39) NB: Dad stole boys' donkeys. Find place for this.

While a green circle contains:

> 1920s: '*In countless representations to the authorities urging more favourable treatment for their people, Anglo-Indian spokesmen lost no opportunity to remind the colonial rulers that during the "Mutiny" Eurasians played an important role in maintaining control of communications and transport, and thus of Britain's military lifeline . . .*' (see Caplan *Children of Colonialism*: 98 & Gidney 1934: 29) Wog-bashing kiss-arsers knew where bread buttered except wasn't and soon no bread.

A handful of yellow Post-its (and one pink) are stuck to the bottom of this page:

> '*The most pathetic of India's minority groups are the mixed-bloods. They were formerly called Eurasians . . . They always wear European clothes . . . They are ostracized by both English and Indians . . . They always speak of England as "home" though many have never*

been there.' (Williams cited in Hedin's 'The Anglo-Indian Community', *American Journal of Sociology* 40:2 Sept 1934)

The pink one, I see at second glance, has been inexplicably misfiled:

> SCHIZOPHRENIA: *A severe mental disorder in which there is a loss of a sense of reality and an inability to function socially. No single cause of schizophrenia has been identified, but genetic factors are known to play a part. A person who is closely related to someone with schizophrenia has a significantly increased risk of developing the disorder. Schizophrenia tends to develop in men during their teens or early twenties, but the onset in women may be 10–20 years later.*

What the hell is *this* doing here? I remember (naturally) its origin. I copied it out of a BMA *Encylopaedia of Family Health*, having discovered that Scarlet had underlined it.

The memory justifies another gulp of shiraz before I detach the Post-it and put it to one side.

Here's another yellow:

> '*Possessing no advantage of birth, breeding or education, it is no surprise that [Anglo-Indians] should be found lacking in moral stamina. With the exception of their lissom bodies and dark flashing eyes, they have little else to their credit . . .'* (Henry Bruce, novelist – year??? And by the way, 'Eurasian' = pun: 'you're Asian' – no one but me seems to have noticed this)

And one that used to make me laugh, before—

> '*That there is a deficiency of vitality among this community may be gathered from the fact, that while among other races in India, lunacy appears in many forms, among this community it invariably takes the form of melancholia.'* (Macrae 'Social Conditions in Calcutta:

The Problem for Charity Among the Anglo-Indian Community', *The Calcutta Review* No. 271 Jan 1913: 85)

Ho ho ho. Ho ho *ho* ho. Deficient in vitality, I swallow the last of glass three, pour and embark upon glass four. Ageing reveals peculiar pleasures. Sitting getting drunk among these papers is one. Moving quietly around my flat with the curtains closed is another. Lying foetally on the bathroom floor. Resting my head on my desk. Feeling the first shivers of flu. Browsing the Yellow Pages without purpose. There's so much to *do* – but it's no use. The pink Post-it throbs in my peripheral vision. With a feeling of shameful indulgence I open the third envelope file.

The biggest photograph is Scarlet's headshot from the aspirant acting phase, which was also the actual pole-dancing phase. Boyishly short messily wet-gelled hair, too much eye make-up, too much make-up full stop. The photographer went for gothic – doomed to fail with a beige person, doubly doomed with a beige person in black and white. The beige look terrible in black and white unless they're deliberately under- or over-exposed, nudged artificially North or South, or unless they're stunning. Scarlet wasn't. But she did have, especially without make-up, that very rare look of someone whose sexual self is distant, difficult, offering you nothing, worth working at and waiting for. It's a cold look of no promise few attractive women have. Catherine Deneuve, Barbara Parkins, Jennifer Connolly, oddly enough Hillary Clinton. The women I end up sleeping with these days (when I'm lucky enough to arrive at such an ending-up) are always those with a fizzing surface froth of sexuality – intimations, tips, hints, concessions, maybes, okays, come-ons – and a predictably flat drink beneath. The flatness of pretended enjoyment, desperation, misery, neurosis, or most often just boredom. (I don't blame them, since I'm guilty of all the same myself as well as having an unimpressive penis and post-Scarlet nil generosity between the sheets.) Anyway, though Scarlet had it the cretin photographer didn't see it. He saw large dark eyes and a wide, narrow-lipped mouth, so made a meal of those. She wore my leather jacket for the shoot, collar turned up à la Elvis. She looked ridiculous, like someone who has absolutely no idea that she has no chance of becoming famous. That was the photograph's second betrayal, because Scarlet did, actually, have what it takes.

I met her for the second time (ten years on, after our first great Brewer Street love, after Dinah, after Wally Da-Da and the Burned Girl, after what *happened*) at UCL when we were both eighteen. The freshman weeks had contained, yes, freshman anxiety, the vertiginous sense of being one's own boss, the thrill of brand-new books, the first intimations of the scale of the human effort at thinking and the first worrying notes of one's own finiteness and negligibility – all that but chiefly a sequence of nights with her like a necklace of beautiful dirty jewels. When we set eyes on each other in the student bar there was neither hesitation nor surprise. Destiny, like truth, never really surprises; some Chomskyan grammar is there to receive it. Our superficial selves manufactured the behaviour of surprise – Jesus Christ, I can't be*lieve* it's you – but our essences merely looked, recognized, delighted, accepted, *began*. We got drunk and went back to her room. And, in the manner of the Old Testament, Saw that it was Good. Taking each other's clothes off was especially good. I was fatless in those days, no beef, admittedly, but the wiriness and I thought charm of a poorly fed dog; it was an additional treat that our bodies had known each other before, an erotic tremulation for me to see and feel her grown-woman ribs and hips and the dove-soft firm breasts where before there had been a sexless little sternum. With a new body you get, granted, newness, but with someone not seen since childhood you get the body's full rich history of its becoming, all the genes' languidly delivered gifts, a profane (it seems) sense of the flesh and blood's packed and urgent adventures from then till now. It added a whiff of (what? paedophilic?) sin which we when our eyes met conceded without a word, took our time over, a decadent entitlement that gave us a vague revenge on the world. It's you. Yes. And it's *you*. They didn't know, did they, darling? No, my love, they didn't understand.

Afterwards soreness and the candlelit room looking as if burglars had rifled it. She said, 'I've been waiting to meet you again. Don't think I'm being cosmic or anything but I knew it would only be a matter of time.' Her warm dark soft golden leg lay across my chest, bent; I should have taken so much more time behind her knee, up the back of her thigh, everywhere. Never mind, there was tomorrow. Life had a plot after all.

There are other photographs, all from university and the London period, the Finsbury Park attic, the Limelight, the hungover Sundays in Camden. In any showing the two of us together, it's manifest that she's everything to me and I'm not everything to her.

There were never supposed to be any Scarlet Papers. It surprises me how many there are. The file bulges. Are these pages breeding? Not just what I've written. When she quit UCL she threw all her notes away. I fished them out of the bin, stashed them. Foresightedly, I now think: fragments to shore against . . . well, not *my ruin*; my average loneliness. There's a photostat of Browning's 'Love Among the Ruins' here, in fact, covered in her minute handwriting: '. . . *another of B's kiss-me-quick narrators; the girl supplants the ruins (Love displaces History) in the poem's structure. The romantic insistence is a self-curtailment: he can think past last line's 'Love is best!' but* <u>*won't*</u>. *It's what you like about B at first, then what makes you gag . . .*'

Papers papers papers. You know the story, Pasha said. So what is there to tell it? You start at the beginning, go through the middle, then get to the end.

I should have told my mum about Scarlet, I wrote earlier. But what should I have told her? She knows what there is to know, that there was love, that it was lost. There *isn't* anything to tell her about Scarlet. Except that of late she fills all the empty moments, invades my dreams, wakes me with hurting heart in the small hours.

When Scarlet's mother died in a car accident on the M4 (according to Scarlet, a madwoman suicide) she, Scarlet, said she didn't feel anything. She said not feeling anything had always been her problem. We were three weeks into our final year at UCL. You don't understand, she kept telling me, they could come and take you away and torture you and I wouldn't feel anything. You think I'm making it up. I'm not. You think this is just some sort of post-traumatic stress disorder. I've *always* been like this. I'm not saying you're *not* like this, I said. But you're like a lot of other things as well. For example, a girl who loves me. The one doesn't cancel out the other. With effort I was capable of these frail calm analyses, resting them just above the seething panic of my guts and heart because she was bigger than me, moving faster, expanding, leaving me behind. Listen to me, she said. They could scourge you, poke out your eyes, cut off your lips. I wouldn't feel anything. I'd just calmly move on to the next thing, whatever it was. She was calm, too. Another person might be experimenting, giving herself a thrill. Scarlet was reporting. Not without compassion. Her love for me at those moments was an object of measurable dimensions with around it all the dark, away-stretching space of herself. I told her I didn't believe her.

That's just you forcing yourself because you don't want it to be true, she said. Inside me there's an absolutely cold centre. It's the centre of myself. It's *me*. Exasperated, I told her I'd consider myself warned.

Not long afterwards she quit her studies and took a job behind the bar at the Limelight. Not long after *that* the bar job swapped for the pole-dancing job. I told myself the thing was to stay cool and go along with everything. Enlightened parents said of rebelling children: It's a phase. Give them room. Let them play it out. So I did. She had her hair cut short, with a fringe and little

feathery wings about the nape and ears. One of many estrangement rehearsals. I told her she looked like a thirteen-year-old boy
who'd just discovered rock music and was now, with shy defiance,
Growing His Hair. It was only a hairstyle, but of course it was
more than that. We were both aware of her head's different out-
line now when we made love in the attic dark, her astride me,
silhouetted by the thin-curtained window's ingot of light. It was
a small, bitterly arousing betrayal, a third presence with us, waiting for Scarlet to go away with it. I became a fixture at the club,
Miserable Owen, had a regular table opposite the neon-lined
stage from which I watched the world that wasn't me beat against
her in waves of strangers. The fucking call of the fucking wild, I
told myself, with maudlin spleen, sinking drink after drink and
still month after month giving Scarlet, so to speak, her head.
Then, one night, watching her black lingeried performance, I
realized that I'd been for years imagining one day having a child
with her. For a minute or two I avoided looking at her face.
When I did, between two of her head-flung-to-the-side-as-if-
belted-or-yanked-on-a-rein moves, she saw me, our eyes met.
There was a second of recognition: yes, it's me and I know it's you
and I'm— then the invisible hand turned her head with a slap and
in the time the look had taken I knew the ending – the long business of false notes and almost-endings and ravenous doomed
rapprochements and silences and strange calm afternoons of coldly
delivered truths (hers about me: that I wasn't, if we were being
honest, big or dangerous or potentially schizophrenic enough for
her) – had really begun.

The Scarlet file has done what it always does, left me, as Macrae
of the yellow Post-it would say, deficient in vitality.

There's a tentative knock on my bedroom door. My response is
a feeble indeterminate sound. Vince pushes it open, puts his head
round and discovers me lying on the floor halfway through the
second bottle, surrounded by papers. *The* papers. All of them.

'What is it with you, you fucking idiot?' he says. A standard Vince opener.

'What is it with what?'

'This. All this.'

He means the papers. The Book. The Dunderhead life. He means why am I not out doing what he's just done, namely looking for and – the pulse in his aura gives it away – finding, sex.

'Shut up,' I say. 'That's what's with this.'

He comes in and sits on the edge of my unmade bed. 'I mean,' he says, 'get out of this. Stop. Give it up. You're living a . . . a . . .'

'This is why I'm the writer, not you.'

'Yeah. How much have you written?'

I raise my glass.

'You're living a *half*-life, for Christ's sake,' he says.

'It helps with the fear.'

'What fear?'

'You know what fear.'

'Oh, don't be so melodramatic. You're not dying. No more than the rest of us.'

He's drunk. Perversely, my staying in and going through this makes him worry he's pissing his time away, makes him worry he should be doing something more.

'It makes you small,' he says. 'You know that, don't you?'

Small means anti-life. Small is what Vince is determined not to be. 'I *am* small,' I tell him, struggling on to my left elbow and topping up my glass. 'I was born small and I've been made smaller.'

'Bollocks.'

'It's not bollocks. If you end up surrounded by big people, you get smaller. Imagine if you were in the showers and all the blokes had massive knobs.'

'Are you serious?'

'You know what I mean. I mean . . . I don't have to explain myself to you, anyway, do I? You're the fucking *lodger*.'

He gets up off the bed and stands at the edge of my paper slew, looking down. 'That her?' he asks. The Scarlet headshot.

'Yeah, that's her.'

Vince bends, picks up the photograph, studies it. Gently returns it to its place. 'Well, I don't know why you don't just fuck off into the world and find her, if she's giving you all this trouble.'

Neither do I.

'Because I'm too small,' I say. 'She's too big. Well, she *was* too big. Maybe she's shrunk.'

Vince is waiting for me to ask about his evening but the truth is I don't want to hear it. The truth is I'm not in the mood. The truth is I want to get back to drinking and kidding myself that I'm writing The Book.

'I'm going for a humungously large bifter,' he says, shuffling over to the door.

'You're too late,' I tell him. 'I've already smoked it.'

CHAPTER SIX

The Valuation

(The Cheechee Papers: Lahore, 1942)

En route back into Lahore the following evening to have the gold valued, Ross took out the certificate he'd been awarded earlier that day.

THE LAHORE
YMCA OPEN AMATEUR BOXING TOURNAMENT
(AFFILIATED TO THE PUNJAB AMATEUR
BOXING ASSOCIATION.)

CERTIFICATE OF HONOUR

This Certificate is awarded to R. D. Monroe *of* RAF Walton,
winner in the
BANTAMWEIGHT
Class: OPEN
Competition, in the tournament held at Lahore *in 1942*

There followed three illegible YMCA signatures, president, general secretary and tournament secretary. They'd given it to him half an hour after he'd won, his hair still wet from the shower. He'd knocked out his opponent, a bulldog-faced Tommy he'd fought and beaten twice before (he knew what he had, rage and power, a murderous left hook, no science), in the second round despite the right hand, bruised from clean connection with last night's Pathan. (One night months before they'd taken a cart back to base and realized they had no money left to pay for it. Therefore, drunk, Ross had tapped the driver on the shoulder and knocked him out. It hadn't become a tradition, exactly, but it had become something. Certain nights, some group psychic recipe having been unwittingly followed, their collective will demanded it. The deal was Ross [and only Ross] got one punch. If the man didn't go down first time, they apologized and paid him double. So far they'd never paid.)

Sun came green-canvas-filtered into the stewed back of the truck. You felt, in the fishtank light, with the smell of engine oil and tyres in your nose, with the jolts and the men around you smoking and dropping in and out of reverie, that you were, actually, *in the war*, though without a Japanese invasion or air attack on the base there was a risible limit to the action any air mechanic was going to see. Eugene was saying something about Mrs Naicker's but Ross wasn't paying attention. When they gave him the certificate he'd folded it up and shoved it in his pocket, embarrassed. Now at the niggle of ego he'd got it out to look at again. 'R. D. Monroe of RAF Walton.' Lies. He wasn't in the RAF. This wasn't the first time such misdesignation had occurred. Two other tournament victories had attached him, in their certificates, to the wrong air force. On both occasions he'd requested a corrected document. One body, after much humming and hawing, had simply scratched out 'RAF' and written above, 'IAF'. Another had ignored the request altogether. He was the best bantamweight on the base, in light of which the boundary separating the two forces revealed a curious diffuseness. You listen to me, his father had told him, years ago, when it suits the bastards you're one of them, when it doesn't you're just another nigger. Eugene liked to tell the story of what happened when he, Eugene, had gone to the Bombay recruitment office to join up. The technical officer taking his particulars had stopped him when he'd answered 'Anglo-Indian', and said he should enter himself 'European' on the enrolment declaration. I must have looked at this bugger like an idiot, Eugene told them. He sighs and rolls his eyes and says, Look, son, it's up to you but your name's Drake and you can pass, you know what I mean? And Joe Soap here didn't have a bleddy clue what he was talking about. But I'm Anglo-Indian, I said. So he holds up his hand and says, Fine, fine, have it your way you silly fucker. They'd laughed. Eugene always delivered the last line in what was supposed to be a cockney accent, which he couldn't do, along with all other accents he couldn't do. And *now* look, Eugene said. I'm stuck in here with you black buggers when I could have been living it up in the bleddy RAF. It was true. Since joining up, Ross (who, dark enough not to tempt anyone into suggesting he enrol as 'European', hadn't been given the RAF option) had heard dozens of similar stories. In his own unit there was Freddie Holmes, whose fairer brother Malcolm was RAF, in quarters just across the compound. If you were light-skinned you could lie, and if you lied you were rewarded. It wasn't just the extra pay. Take the truck they were sitting in. Capacity: BOR (British other ranks, or non-officers) 12; IAF (Indian Air Force) 20. The magical ability of Indian forces to take up less room in a truck than their British counterparts. Ditto the mess, the dorms, the bogs.

R. D. Monroe of RAF Walton. Certificate of honour. At St Aloysius, Danglers would stop mid-sentence at an emotive word, '. . . for General Wolfe it was a point of honour—' and throw the chalk, 'You, da Souza, give me a definition of *honour*.' Da Souza, who hadn't been paying attention, floundered. Being of good character, sir. Rubbish! Too vague. Harris, define *honour*.

And so on. Wolfe of Canada unravelled into a semantics debate. Eventually, in ornate exasperation, Danglers had read to them from the dictionary.

Honour. Noun **1**. personal integrity; allegiance to moral principles. **2a**. fame or glory. **2b**. a person or thing that wins this for another: *he is an honour to the school*. **3**. great respect, esteem, etc., or an outward sign of this. **4**. high or noble rank. **5**. a privilege or pleasure: *it is an honour to serve you*. **6**. a woman's virtue or chastity.

At a woman's virtue or chastity Danglers's confidence had wobbled and he'd slammed the book shut. Personal integrity. Fame or glory. An honour to serve you. Honour.

'This driver's bleddy drunk or what?' Eugene said. The truck had dipped and lurched into and out of a pothole in the road. Ross didn't answer.

'What's the matter with you, men?'

'Nothing.'

'You got hurt in the ring or what?'

'No.'

'Thenwhat?'

'Nothing.'

Eugene's twinkle faltered. He had a core uncertainty about himself and a fear of the world against which perpetual excitable jollity was the only protection. He gravitated to the strong; seeing one of them troubled was like tasting the raw earth of the grave on his tongue. He turned away to cadge a cigarette off the private sitting next to him.

The truck rattled, jounced them, reminded them they were, underneath the packed flesh and blood, skeletons. Earlier they'd seen out of the open back a group of skinny children gathered at the roadside round a dead bandicoot the size of a small dog. One of the boys was stabbing the corpse with a stick; he'd found a nerve which when pressed made a leg twitch. All the other youngsters stood around, rapt. 'Bleddy kids,' someone had said, with lying lightness.

Ross knew how Eugene worked, what he needed, but couldn't shake his own mood. His muscles were irritated. You did something wrong and your body knew. Honour. This afternoon he'd been tempted to let the Tommy catch him with one of the wild hooks (he'd been caught once – once was enough – in their earlier bout, the glove like a wet medicine ball, a head-sound like the smash of cymbals) for penance. In the ring there were moments like glass spheres into which you could step to consider things. He'd considered losing the fight as an offering to God. Bouncing on the balls of his feet while the other man's round-houses hurtled past like planets, he raised his inner eyes to Heaven in query. Not enough, God had said. Robbing a boy. Hitting an innocent man. You know that's not enough. He had known, of course, and so tattooed the Tommy with stinging jabs until he saw his hands drop, then knocked him out with a perfect right cross. God, as if to underline his point, sent a shot of pain through the bruise from the night before, and Ross felt in his knees and scalp the shame of watching the Pathan go down, while before his eyes the Tommy went down the same way, one with honour, the other without.

Eugene was talking to him again, off the back of laughter in the truck. 'Did you hear that?'

'What?'

'The latest from Cawnpore. There are Quit India *women* demonstrating there. The British don't want pictures of policemen walloping women in the streets, so they ran a recruitment drive to hire other women to deal with them – and only the prostitutes applied for the job!'

The other men in the truck laughed again. Eugene held his hand round an imaginary truncheon. 'Well, they're used to the feel of a solid lathi in their hand, eh?' More laughter.

Ross smiled, still with his mind elsewhere. He'd dreamed of the girl last night, but only as an occasional vivid presence (the poppy-print dress, the light skin, the curve of dark hair tucked behind her ear) in a clogged mix. The market, Ram's greasily swiped face, his own father, drunk, lashing out at the Indian cook with a steel ladle and catching him on the back of the head. Whatever the details, the dream's flavour had been shame. He'd woken with the usual importunate erection but also with his face hot. Shame. As if someone had stripped you, like in those other dreams where you were naked in a public place. He hadn't forgotten the thrill of how quietly and calmly and collusively the Englishman had spoken to him, as if they'd known each other for years. Without making it obvious, is anyone watching? Certificate of honour.

'You need a drink,' Eugene said, grabbing his shoulder and squeezing, which did in separate innocence ease the muscle's knot.

'Yeah, maybe,' Ross said. He could have done without the mention of Quit India. At St Aloysius in the last years Indian boys whose parents could afford it had been admitted as day scholars. Hindus, Muslims, Jains, Sikhs, it made no difference to the Jesuits, who dragged everyone regardless of colour or creed or the 1935 Government of India Act to mass every morning, made sure they learned the responses, crossed themselves, sang the hymns. I believe in one Holy Catholic Apostolic Church. Only at Holy Communion was the line drawn, a rite from which enthusiastic non-Christian boys had invariably to be turned back, always with a look of scowling injury. Storm's comin, Stan's friend had said, horsy gnashers gleefully on display over his cup and saucer. We pull out, you buggers are goin to be up shit creek wi'out a paddle.

'Come on, men, relax,' Eugene said. Then in an undertone, 'We're going to be *rich*, remember?'

It was a soft, warm evening. The truck dropped them at the Delhi Gate and they went through into the Old City. In the Kashmiri

Bazaar half the main street was in shadow. Rickety multi-balconied buildings went up crookedly on either side like precariously stacked dominoes. Between the roofs a clear blue avenue of sky. (These northern skies were a hard, precious puri-fied blue, nothing of the haze or milk you got further south.) Ross loved the bazaar's jazz of scents and jabbering crowds, the way in spite of chaos details singled you out for fierce, brief intimacy: an old man in long quality white sucked hollow-cheeked on a hookah in a black doorway, his eyes met yours, asked something vague: Is this life? What have you seen? Will we die? Then because such nakedness was unbearable an argument would explode at a paan stall, or pigeons would rattle overhead, or a waiter would upset a tray to a smatter of applause.

'It's hereabouts,' Eugene said. 'I'm sure it's around here.'

Was it unbearable? The way the Englishman looked at him had been as intimate as if they *were* a pair of homosexuals. In the seconds before the blow the Pathan's eyes had understood, wearily. These moments of pure contact were unbearable, but they were what life was for, until you were ready to go after God in the desert. Which he was not. The girl all hips and breasts in the poppy dress, the clean right cross, Eugene's slaked chimp face between whores; the key pieces of his life were already set, suffi-cient, inadequate.

He and Eugene moved through the crowds, elbows, someone's mouth of huge teeth, laughing, a legless beggar on a trolley, his face with the predictable look of mild constipation. In shafts of sunlight dust languidly spiralled. The three domes of the Golden Mosque were a soft, fiery presence half a mile to the west. Gold spoke to gold; the ingots in his top pocket murmured above his heart.

'Got the bugger,' Eugene said.

The shop, squashed between a bakery and a supplier of wed-ding saris, was more junk than jewels, stuffed birds, garrulous wind-chimes, grandfather clocks, rugs, a central glass counter with beneath it a mind-boggling morass of watch parts, some with mechanisms still tinily in motion, making Ross think of remote creatures on the sea bed, the extraordinary fact of all the little lives that had nothing to do with us. The jeweller was a bald, corpulent, perfumed and much-moled Malaysian, known to Eugene from the reception room at Mrs Naicker's. It took him less than half a minute to make his determination.

'Brass,' he said. 'Plain brass.'

They looked at him in silence.

'Worthless,' he said, with a full-lipped smile.

Ross felt objection rise up in a wave, then subside. You didn't discover truth, you recognized it. Brass. Of course. Ross felt the tension stringing his muscles snap and die away, loosening him at last. Brass. He wanted to laugh, would have laughed had the secondary realization not at that moment dawned. The Englishman was in on it. They all were. As he stood there listening to Eugene – 'What do you mean, *brass*? We paid bleddy cash *money* for this, men' – he saw the beauty of the operation like a woman's robe slipping from her to reveal her whole naked body, the lovely necessary structure. The fellow on the doorstep. Sahib, is that yours? The plantain fingers of Gobind Singh. (Hadn't there been dishonesty in that touch? Hadn't each fingertip pressed a little lie? Your body told you these things but you ignored it.) Not so simple Ram. And the last rotten perfection: the Englishman. For a terrible mad moment Ross wondered if even the girl . . . But no. She had nothing to do with it. Except as God's offer, testimony to free will. Instead of going after her he'd followed the Englishman.

'What the Christ are you laughing at?' Eugene said.

But Ross couldn't for a moment get himself under control. The Malaysian, used to the queer relief of the duped, smiled also. His skin was big-pored, mocha, overlaid with large purplish patches. Something anciently saurian in the heavy jowls and bagged eyelids with their flecks of mole, a pleased patience with human greed, since it was his livelihood.

'You have I'm afraid been very nicely counterfeited,' he said, with a chuckle. 'I don't like to ask to the tune of how much.' He gave them mint tea and dry cakes in exchange for the story. The scent of the beverage cut through the shop's fug of old incense and camphor.

Eugene, devastated, took up the jeweller's offer of a loan. 'You can't get yourself worked up to the thing and then not go and do it,' he carped. 'It's impossible.' The night of excess premised on the proceeds of the gold, he meant. The Malaysian's rates were extortionate but Eugene was enjoying the profligacy of hopelessness. 'What do I care how many per cent?' he said. 'I'm damned if I'm going back tonight like a bleddy *monk*.'

It was cooler in the bazaar. Ross had no appetite for custards at Ho Fun's, and so meandered west through the old city, skirting the southern flank of the fort, then up through Hazuri Bagh. People in all shades of brown, bony arms and muscled legs and jabbering mouths. There were all these lives.

The evening faithful were gathering at Badshahi Mosque. Ross liked the building, paprika-red stone against the northern blue sky, those pearly domes. A sensuous pregnancy to the Mughal domes, marble dollops of female flesh, the breasts of houris, Allah jadedly reaching down to fondle.

He crossed the Circular Road and went up into Minto Park, where the smell of the lawns was soothing. A young family, father, mother, two small children and a baby in a pram, strolled along a few yards ahead of him. A breeze ruffled their loose clothes, his kurta, her salwar kameez. Two years ago the Muslim Leaguers had met here and passed the Lahore Resolution; even he, still at school in Jabalpur, hadn't been able to avoid talk of it. That bleddy pin-stripe stick insect, his father had said of Jinnah. You mark my words, that bugger will cause more trouble than Gandhi. Ross had only half listened. All the big chaps went to England, Jinnah, Gandhi, Nehru, got educated, came back with the ideas. Democracy.

He could go to England. The thought slowed his steps, the realization he'd been carrying it for a long time, ever since Rockballs had said, Olympics, America, anywhere. Anywhere had reduced to England. 'At least we can go home,' Stan's friend had said. 'Where the fuck are you lot going to go?' An image of England had sprung up in his mind at the time, derived he now realized from a colour illustration of the cliffs of Dover in a geography book at St Aloysius. The picture showed a white crenellated coast and a hurrying whitecapped sea. Grey seagulls with legs dangling. A blue fishing boat. Everything about it said *cold*.

The idea of cold was exciting, rain without the monsoon weight and warmth, something that bent in the wind. Was that his destiny? He slowed his pace further. It was a particular pleasure, not quite to stop walking while the idea thickened. Suddenly it seemed that everything that had happened over the last two days had happened to lead him to this conclusion: he would go to England. Plenty of Anglo-Indians already had, whether Stan's friend knew it or not. But you needed money. Box. Focus, Monroe, and you can go anywhere. All the sweet pussy you want. Don't repeat that. The rumour about Rockballs was that he was dying, knew it, carried on as normal, something British about that, carrying on making dry, deadpan jokes. There had been an article in *The Anglo-Indian Review*: 'If You're Going, Go Now'. 'How long do we think it's going to be before Britain starts tightening its immigration belt?' the writer wanted to know. 'Anglos who can provide documentary proof of British lineage on their fathers' side are currently applying for and getting British passports. This, in the author's opinion, *cannot last*. Let the community beware: our Fatherland's arms will not remain open for ever, and the arms of our Motherland are more likely to crush than to embrace . . .'

Ahead of him the young mother had stopped a few paces behind her husband to wait for the lagging toddler. She had a coltish face with liquescent black eyes. All the thick, dark hair tied loosely back with a few wavy locks lifted in the breeze. A low shaft of evening sunlight passed through the billowing yellow chiffon dupatta. The child, with nappied bow-legged steps of immense concentration, caught up, took her outstretched hand. She said something to him, melodiously intoned in Urdu, then turned and rejoined her husband.

Ross walked on, very slowly, in the dawdling family's wake. The laughter had settled his muscles and joints into peaceful omnipotence. It was all there, the limitless potential. He could do anything, leap off the ground into flight.

But a counter-thought was there, too: that God was above, gently stirring the world, that you were free to do anything except escape your destiny, that the story of your life would find you, that you would see it all in the end before death rolled out behind you like an extraordinary tapestry. This, secretly, was his grudging faith.

He would wait and see. And box.

CHAPTER SEVEN

personals

(London, 2004)

Depressing fucked-up ex-Catholic Anglo-Indian M, short, politically ignorant, ethically failed, part-time pornographer, still carrying torch for Scarlet, seeks soulful anal-friendly ex-Catholic Anglo-Indian F, or in other words Scarlet. Send photo.

According to Martin Amis suicide notes are like poems in that all of us flirt with writing one sooner or later. Ditto I say the personal ad. The one above didn't appear in the *Guardian*. One full of lies did.

'I don't think he knows how to look at me, because his wife's my friend and now he's my boss. I don't mean look at me in *that* way, obviously—'

'Maybe not but it sounds interesting. *Does* he look at you in that way?'

Though it's not sufficiently warm — an autumn breeze stiff enough to gooseflesh her bare shoulders and make the cloth napkins flap – we're at an outdoor table at Tiggi's in Clerkenwell (her choice, as was meeting for breakfast, which she presumably considers less a declaration of desperate availability than lunch or dinner) and this is my umpteenth attempt at sexing-up the conversation. I've decided, by my second coffee, that I will, given the opportunity, sleep with her, which really says nothing because I'll sleep with practically any woman these days. I don't need much in the way of looks and I don't need personality at all. Wondering if doing it they'll look the way I've imagined them looking is more than enough motivation. This woman, Stacy, has thick, wavy, hippyish dark hair, green eyes slightly too close together and a nose that has made me think, not disastrously, of a baby courgette.

'Hmm,' she says, lips pursed, pantomiming traditional female weariness with men who must get everything round to sex, '*aimee-way* . . . It's a case of damned if you do and damned if you don't.'

I have absolutely no idea what she's talking about. I haven't had for most of the meal, except that all of it's been about her. Once or twice she's caught herself, remembered me, asked me something about myself with such manifest absence of interest it's been hard for me to keep a straight face (and in any case I've lied, since the objective is to get her into bed and keep having sex with her as long as I can or want to, in which case the truth is of no service), but these have been glitches in an otherwise flawless ninety-minute demonstration of self-obsession.

On the Tube to work (at the end of breakfast I said, 'Shall I call you?' and she little-girlishly smiled and wrinkled up her baby courgette nose and shook her head: no. It was supposed to look impish and lovable in spite of being no, but in fact I could probably have shot her in the face) I take out the letter that arrived this morning from Nelson Edwards's daughter.

> Dear Mr Monroe
>   Thank you for your letter of the 15th, which I'm answering on my father's behalf. I'm afraid, however, that

he isn't well enough to be of help. Good luck with your
research.

Regards,

Janet Marsh

Dolmen dropped fiction years ago and now specializes in cookery,
computing, DIY and arts & crafts. After fifteen minutes being
transferred around the organization's departments I got a redundantly intelligent, bored, entry-level assistant who was happy to go
off on a quest through Paper Records, a joke zone in the bowels
of the building, soon to be converted into a directors' gym. No
no, she said, honestly, this is rain in the desert. Tell me more. By
the end of the afternoon, having fallen telephonically in love with
her, I asked her out for a drink. She said she didn't think her
boyfriend would appreciate it. (Everyone's taken, Vince says. You
look around and there seem to be millions. But every one of
those fuckers is *taken*.) The best she could offer was to forward my
enquiry. *Moral Exotica: Race in Pulp Fiction, 1945–2000*. Hmm,
she said. Yeah I know, I said, thrilling. But what do you want? I'm
an academic. I've got to publish. You don't have to tell me, she
said, my ex wrote his PhD thesis on tantric positions in *Lady
Chatterley's Lover*. Are you sure your boyfriend wouldn't appreciate me taking you out? It was hard for me; she had a flirtatious RP
voice which conceded with every phoneme that her current
boyfriend was temporary, annoying, *wrong*. Email me the letter,
she said. I'll print it out and pass it on. Won't even charge you for
the stamp.

The reply's on business paper. IMS (Information Management
Services), Rathbone Street, which if memory serves is somewhere up between Goodge Street and the electronics emporia of
Tottenham Court Road. Janet Marsh, Director. Phone, fax and
email options. Marsh. So if it is Skinner a.k.a. Edwards, his
daughter's married. But directing a company. Divorced seems
more likely, or more appealing. All this while the Tube rocks and

screeches (as it did presumably in Japan in the seconds before the
sarin nerve gas attack; you can't dwell) and Tiggi's continental
breakfast of buttery croissants and silty coffee sits not entirely
comfortably in my gut. I'm excited, far more by the letter than I
was by breakfast. That courgette-nosed woman's small, inacces-
sible promise. (The days of women's infinite promise are over.
Now their promise is of an exhaustible, finite kind. I meet a
woman and think: in about three nights/six weeks/eight
months/two years I'll have had what there is to be had. Which is
of course better than not having it. The upside of a life as dull as
mine is that something as little as this letter is a thrill. Obviously
I'll phone her. Janet Marsh, I mean. Two hundred miles north in
Bolton, Pasha knows nothing of this latest development. Which
is pleasurable, undeniably, perhaps in the way that holding in its
shit is pleasurable to a child, if Freud's right about shit being
money or money being shit or whichever way round it is. I
imagine the old man's face when I tell him: Listen, Dad, I've
tracked down the daughter. Compared to the fools' gold we've
had in the past this is a whopping genuine nugget. Information
Management Services, I'll tell him. What the bleddy hell is that?
Never mind. She says Skinner's a sick man. He'll lean back in his
winged chair, fold his hands over his paunch. Oh-ho, he'll say,
with raised eyebrows. Oh-*ho*, eh?

But here's the Tube pulling into Liverpool Street, where ranks
of worried-faced total strangers wait to get on. Everyone looks
funereal and sweaty. The world is full of people, billions, all connected if we only knew which threads to follow. Connected not
by the gods and goddesses of romance but by meaningless matters
of fact. I put my hand out to the top of *Raj Rogue*'s flaking spine
and with index finger alone tilted it and a terrible joke meaning-
fulness into my life. I see it now as in one of those films where,
trapped in the library, someone (the clown of the group, to show
ironic resignation) pulls a book from the shelf only to discover it's
the one that opens a secret panel, and there, suddenly (what were

the odds!), is a torchlit passage and a whole new possibility of escape . . .

The Arbuthnot College (prior to shut-down and sell-off, the Fine Art unit of the South London College of Art and Design) is a dwarfish neo-Gothic redbrick building just west of Wimbledon Common. The corridors' disinfectant evokes, queasily if I'm hung over or close to the reality of my own death, St Thomas's, my Bolton primary school. At all other times being able to experience this smell without nausea or fear fills me with quiet triumph; something formerly alien and dictatorial has let me in, revealed its mystery, made me a part of it. They're all fee-payers here, to the tune of ten thousand a year. The staff divides: lefties skulking under a cloud of guilt and right-wingers with shoulders back and faces lifted to the sunshine of private enterprise. Former state teachers with socialist sympathies are the most pitiful. They used to do the right thing, but doing the right thing nearly killed them. Now they sit in the staff room like shell-shocked soldiers brought home from the front, not quite daring to believe they don't have to go back. There are flapjacks, there is cafetière coffee; their eyes are wet with tears. It's all one to me, Mr Apolitical I'm the only non-white teacher here (but obviously not non-white enough not to have been taken on) but the snitty looks I get are mainly from the cleaning staff, all of whom are sufficiently non-white to guarantee only being taken on as cleaners. Aside from these I get irritated interrogation from the Indian and Pakistani students, of whom there are a handful. Two cheeky pretty Indian girls, Krishna (the daughter of a gynaecological consultant) and Sujartha (of corporate-law mother, divorced, single) regularly grill me, vacuously flirting.

'So your dad's English, then.'

'No, Anglo-Indian.'

'But your name's Monroe.'

'Actually, Monroe's Scottish. There's Scottish blood on my father's side, mixed with English, a little French, a lot of Indian.'

'Indian from your mum?'

'Well, my mum's Anglo-Indian, too, although her granddad was born and bred in Lancashire.'

They look at each other. They don't actually rotate their index fingers at their temples to indicate *screw loose*, but they might as well. 'Where were your parents *born*?' Sujartha says, as if addressing a simpleton with the last gram of her patience.

'India. Well my mother was born in Sukkur – that used to be India but now it's Pakistan. The fact is both my parents are Anglo-Indian. Both of them – and my paternal grandparents, and my great- and great-great-grandparents and possibly all the ancestors as far back as the seventeenth century – have mixed Indian and European blood. The Anglo-Indians are a *race*, albeit a relatively young one.'

They look at each other again. Krishna raises her lovely eyebrows at her friend. Clearly, I don't know what on earth I'm talking about.

'Yeah, okay, Mr Monroe,' lip-glossed Sujartha says, taking Krishna's arm and backing away, hamming gentle retreat from potentially dangerous crazy person. 'Whatever you say, Mr Monroe.'

Off they go, tittering, looking back over their shoulders.

Sujartha has a perfect glossy shoulder-length bob, hips packed in user-friendly flesh, large, firm, proudly carried breasts. She's aware of the money behind her, knows she's never going to have to take shit from anyone. It's freed her to swank with her impressive boobs. Krishna is high-cheekboned, willowy, gold-earringed and -bangled, with the Indian girl's impossibly long, thick plait tied with a wispy bit of purple ribbon. When I imagine her naked this wisp of ribbon rests halfway down the dark crack of her flawless young bottom.

(This is a new thing for me, fantasizing about Indian girls.

Presumably some last gauzy vestige of Eurasian snobbery is wearing away. It only occurred to me in my university days that black and Asian women were exempt from my imagination's attention. I confessed it to Scarlet. Oh come *on*, she said, wearily. Black and Asian women aren't your enemies. We were in bed one Sunday morning. For men, she said, *yawn*, fucking is an act of aggression. Fucking a white woman directs aggression at the enemy. What you really want is to fuck white men, but that's unacceptable to your heterosexual male ego, so you fuck white women instead. Where in God's name do you get all this shite? It's not shite. Or rather it is, but it's the sort of shite we've plumped for. Do you actually *read* anything? Every time you fuck a white woman you're engaged in an act of counter-colonization. For *really* black men there must be nothing like it. Okay, I said, why do I fuck you? *You're* not a white woman. You're the same colour as me. You're a *beige* woman. She shrugged. That's no mystery, either. Firstly, I'm a woman, and to men all women, whatever their colour, are the enemy eventually – have no illusions: you'd jolly soon get around to brown girls if the white ones vanished; and second, it's a sublimated incestuous desire for your sisters, with whom you've clearly been in love since infancy. Or alternatively, I said, maybe I love and fancy you. Either way, she said, I need you to do it to me again right now. When I got hold of her and we kissed she said, Lust is so nice, so horrible, so nice . . . Now it seems I've got round to the brown girls even without the disappearance of the white ones. I know what she'd say to that, too: Because after all these years you finally feel white *enough*, Mr Monroe. English Literature? No wonder you're ashamed of yourself.)

Janet Marsh's letter has had a strange effect on me, its tug towards intrigue like the first twitch of arousal in the phallic blood. I feel emboldened by it, that I've impinged on her consciousness (and who knows, perhaps on the consciousness of Skinner himself!). This, plus the vacuousness of my breakfast blind date, has called forth in me a new erotic determination: I *will* ask Tara the art teacher out. Today. This very afternoon. The minute I get her alone.

'Okay,' I say, 'Winston works in Records in the Ministry of Information. What does the Ministry do? What's its role in the Oceania set-up?'

Before I can get to Tara, however, there's my Friday three o'clock lot, sadly not including Krishna and Sujartha. There are others. There are always others. (I must be the only male academic who's never slept with nor had the opportunity of sleeping with one of his female students. [Not that you'd know it from Millicent Nash's *An Adult Education*.] *Male* students, Vince says, just give them a *chance*, you homophobe.) You'd think Orwell was a safe bet. Wrong. Orwell gets on their nerves. Literature gets on their nerves. I've tried 'They fuck you up, your mum and dad'. I've tried Wendy Cope. In desperation I've tried Roger McGough. They just go Yeah yeah yeah, whatever. 'Why are you studying English Literature?' I keep asking them, mystified. So far not one of them has answered with anything other than a shrug, or a tut, or an exasperated eye-roll. *Language* gets on their nerves, apparently. This is my experience of twenty-first-century teenagers: they don't want to talk about anything unless it's not worth talking about. Then they'll go on for hours. Who can blame them, if life is meaningless, ironic, finite, material and bent?

'Er, could it be . . . ?' Daniel Flynn says, with laboured sarcasm. 'I'm not sure about this but could it be . . . to do the *opposite* of providing information?'

We've got a little thing going, me and Daniel. He knows he's the flower in my desert. He's not sure what to do with his intelligence, keeps his cynic on more or less perpetual guard duty.

'Well, thank you very much, Daniel,' I say. 'Yes, I believe you're right. Let's think about this in relation, as I keep saying, to the present. Any novel – or film – that looks into the future is always really looking at the present and extending logically or quasi-logically from there. Yes?'

Daniel looks at me and smiles, shaking his head. Quasi-logically? Give *up*. No one *cares*. I look back at him, jaws clamped. *You* care, mister, and we both know it. I can still get him to look away first (out of the window in this instance) but the time is coming when he'll butch me out: no, I don't care, or at least I'm not going to. I'm going to get money and fuck women and do drugs and die without having fallen for the mug's game of thinking there's anything more to it than that.

'What do we think about what Winston's saying about the Oceanian media? How do today's media hold up in comparison?'

Heads go down, there are sighs. Time passes.

'I hate this shite,' Isobel Rolly says. A long time ago, years, decades, it seems, I told them I didn't care if they swore occasionally as long as it was because they were worked up – and willing to make a critical case for *why* they were worked up – about the text in question. I know why I did that. It was because more than anything else I wanted them to like me. It's what I always want, from anyone, anywhere, more than anything else. Only highly attractive women are exempt. What I want more than anything from them is that they let me fuck them. There was a time when it helped, libidinally, if they *didn't* like me, but that, like many other misogynistic kinks, has been relaxed. Moot, in any case, since I never get anywhere near the sort of highly attractive women to whom the exemption would apply.

'You hate this shite *why*, Isobel?'

'I don't see what all the fuss is about. The world we live in's nothing *like* 1984. This book's supposed to be so prophetic. I don't get it.'

'Is it like he's saying . . .' This is Dawn Edge, who'll sometimes have a tentative go, get me excited; then someone'll crack a joke and I'll lose her. 'Like he's saying, you know, if you can change the facts of the past, then . . .' Because of something Kate Stubbs has just said to her Jessica Aldridge snorts, then clamps her hand over her mouth, then giggles in silence. Which is Dawn's precious thread lost. 'Actually, no. I don't . . . I mean, what *is* he saying?'

I glance over at Daniel, who's sitting with his arms folded and his eyes closed and a nirvanic smile on his lips. His hair's dark and thick and artfully hacked. He's not good-looking, but he has cold, dark eyes and a face of interesting hollows and knobs. I pray there's a smart, not-too-good-looking girl out there for him somewhere who'll stop him turning into the poisonous capitalist misogynist his tender, terrified soul might otherwise force him to become.

'I think what Orwell's getting at here,' I say, with a glare at Jessica, who looks at me as if to say, No, this was *really* funny, 'is that our sanity, our ability to think, largely depends on our ability to remember. We need a repository, we need a history we can trust, so that when someone comes along on Friday and says x is the case and has always been the case, we can check the record to see what he was saying on Monday. It might turn out that the record shows he was saying y was the case on Monday.'

'*What*?' Isobel says.

'That's the worst explanation of anything I've ever heard,' Daniel says.

This happens to me increasingly of late. My mind slips out of gear. 'You're absolutely right, Daniel,' I say. 'Why don't you supply us with a better one?'

'Nah, you're all right.'

'Come on.'

'Nah, cheers.'

'Come *on*.'

Daniel closes his eyes again and makes a hurried, tension-relieving gesture with his head and neck. 'This is such a Jesus Christing *yawn*,' he says. Then, with sarcastic mellifluousness, 'Monday: Weapons of mass destruction in forty-five minutes. Tuesday: no weapons of mass destruction and simply *hours* if they had them. The difference is we can call Tony Blair a liar because we've still got him saying it in the *Guardian* or wherever, whereas the poor sods in Oceania have had their *Guardian*s reprinted so there's no way of proving he ever said anything in the first place.'

'That was Daniel Paxman,' Louise Bell says, 'reporting from the dark side of his brain.'

Two or three of the girls are attracted to Daniel's intelligence. Pretty, slim and pert-boobed Louise is one of them, but her superficial self won't stand for it; there's a quota of cool, good-looking brainless types to be got through before she's allowed any of *that* nonsense. My optimistic bet is that Daniel pricks the gorgeous with occasional reminders of their mortality. The certainty of ending.

'Which is all fine and jim-dandy,' Daniel says, still with children's TV presenter melodiousness, 'but the fact is it wouldn't matter to us if we had all our newspapers rewritten and all our archives re-shot. It wouldn't matter to us – that is, *us* – because we're all too busy watching who wants to be patronized by a fucking millionaire or I'm a fucking nobody get me an ad contract out of here. In case anyone's too retarded to have noticed, Big Brother doesn't need to watch us because we're all watching *Big Brother*.'

'Have another shandy, Daniel,' Kate says.

'Nobody *cares* if Tony Blair's a liar,' Daniel says. 'It's not news that *any* politician's a liar. I don't know why they don't just put that as the definition in the dictionary. Politician: liar. We all know that's what it means and we're all okay with it.'

'So you're okay with liars running the world?' I ask him.

'As long as it means *I* don't have to, yeah.'

When the bell rings I try to get a quiet word with Daniel – Listen I think you should keep these ideas in mind when you come to the exam, disinformation versus apathy – but he just says, 'Sorry, got to dash,' and hurries away down the polished and disinfected corridor, rolling a fag as he goes. It hurts. Not Daniel specifically, just the tingling electric aura all their young lives have that my life doesn't. They have a Friday night to go to, parties, drugs, sex. There is for each of them the absolute certainty of his or her centrality in the universe. They don't even need love yet. The adult realization of your own radical non-centrality is bearable if love arrives. Love is being the centre of someone else's universe and having them as the centre of your own, in which case *the* universe, whether it's owned by God or physics or Ronald fucking McDonald, can take a hike. But as I watch them go – the boys with a rubbery testosteronal lope, the girls in two groups, Louise's sashay, Kate's hunched shoulders, fat Rachel's laboured swivel (she's at her universe's centre, its miserable centre) – I see that they're still running on childhood's myth, that their lives matter, superlatively, objectively, that if not God at least their eager, significant Future is watching, waiting for them to reach it and fully blossom, even if it be the terrible glamorous blossom of suicide. What couldn't they be, in the future? What adventures in ecstasy and despair aren't they destined to have? The idea that their lives will be more or less bearable like more or less everyone else's is to them intuitively absurd. I remember what that was like and it's not like that any more.

This, I concede for the umpteenth time, dispensing myself a hot chocolate from the corridor's vending machine (something comfortingly pathetic about vending machines, as if they've secretly got so much more to offer, personality, if we'd just give them a chance; this unpatronized one at the end of the corridor and I are in mutual sympathy), is the platitudinous core of my condition. I'm leadenly soaked in its ordinariness, by the weight of my unexceptional heartaches, by, yes, the commonness of the disease of remembering the way things once were. (We're doing the Romantics. '*It is not now as it hath been of yore;*— /*Turn where-soe'er I may,* /*By night or day,* /*The things which I have seen I now can see no more.*' 'What do we make of this?' I asked them. Daniel said, wearily, 'When you're a kid everything's great, then you grow up and it sucks.' 'Unless you were abused,' Isobel said, 'in which case

it sucked from the start.' 'In which case *you* sucked from the start,'
Kate Stubbs said. 'In which case big deal,' Jessica said. 'Welcome to
the world.') The joke on me is the joke on everyone: youth makes
life mythic; then leaves. If you're lucky, first love comes along and
makes it mythic again. Then leaves. For a few God, the fit having
inexplicably taken Him, steps in and makes life mythic again. Then
most likely leaves. For the rest only death – the mother's funeral, the
aftershaved doctor and the test results – retains the heft to make life
mythic again, and that's an awfully high price to pay.

I've finished for the day but I go to the staff room in the hope
that Tara might be there. She's twenty-seven, tall, milky white,
wears green dresses and knee-boots, has a tiny grapelike pot belly
and a lovely pearly throat which comes out of her green V and
unmans you with its softness and faint blue veins. Lacklustre blonde
shoulder-length bob and narrow, lively eyes which might be hazel
or green or blue for all I can recall but which in my fantasies are
always looking collusively up (or down) at me while her long white
and no doubt faintly blue-veined legs part and wave around in
gentle ellipses like the antennae of a disorientated insect.

I don't want to go home. At home *The Cheechee Papers* remains
a mess. Through Dyer & Haskell I not long ago got a lunch with
an editor, Nick Gough, from Gecko Publishing, an opportunity
to pitch The Book. 'What interests me,' I told him, over devilled
quail and roasted asparagus in a Covent Garden restaurant of
headachy frosted glass and halogens, 'is the connection between
tiny racial minority and political engagement.' He chewed and
frowned at the tablecloth, not, I thought, very interested. He was
in his forties, masculinely built, with the sort of heavy, dark,
hawkish good looks that by the time he's seventy will have
become sinister, with eyebrows owlishly curling and a bushel of
black hair up each nostril like David Lodge. He had the meaty,
open-pored skin and slaked look of a man who's been eating
complex lunches and dinners for years and for years hearing what
other people think are terrific original ideas but which he's heard

dozens of times before. Hard to enthuse, touched by his aura of boredom.

'Part of being an Anglo-Indian,' I told him, 'is being a member of a race which to all intents and purposes simply doesn't register, historically. Too few of us, you see. We're invisible. What I'm thinking is that this invisibility creates at best a kind of unconcern for the world – since as far as the world's concerned we're not here, never were, so it's not, realistically, "our" world at all – and at worst a ring-of-Gyges relationship to morality.' He chewed languidly for a few seconds with large, muscled jaws and though he was staring at me I couldn't shake the conviction that his mind was elsewhere, on Gecko's receptionist, perhaps, a gingery girl who'd overseen me with occasional tight smiles while I waited for him.

But after swallowing, slowly running his tongue under his top lip and closed-mouthedly burping, he surprised me: 'I won't lie to you,' he said. 'The market's in love with mixed race just now, but the market gets bored quickly. How soon before you'd have something?' I must have looked vague. 'My sense is you want a deviant protagonist. Ring-of-Gyges, you said. Deviant but nothing too sexual. What you want is: Anglo-Indians – who are they? What are they like? But you do it through the burglar or the bent detective. There's a crime and mixed-race vein no one's tapped yet. That's your best ticket. Unless you want to do the straight historical thing, but that's limited.'

I went home and pored over the mess of *The Cheechee Papers*, feeling winded and fraudulent. There are gaps in my historical knowledge, I'd told him. Very large gaps. It's worse than that: there are gaps in my *feelings*. I have visions of post-publication interviews: So what does it mean, to *you*, being an Anglo-Indian? The microphone waits. My head wears the studio lights' heat like a tight-fitting cap. I open and close my mouth. A technician pinches a sneeze to preserve the silence. All I can think of is my mother and father saying, But it wasn't *like* that, Sweetheart . . .

The staff room's empty. It looks terminally empty, as if people have fled in a hurry because a tidal wave or comet is coming. There's a half-drunk cup of coffee on the table and a raincoat on the floor, a knocked-over stack of magazines, a *Times* with all the downs of its crossword filled in. The two ceiling lights are on. Like the vending machine the room is sad, as if what it's been offering all these years – oh, not *much* of a personality, but *something* – has gone unnoticed and now it's too late. I must stop this, I tell myself, this whatever-it-is, anthropomorphism or pathetic fallacying, the juvenilization of my experience. The lights being on makes me think with a small colonic thrill of the fast-approaching winter afternoons, dark early, the building's smell of wet woollens and radiators, outside car headlights probing the fog, the female staff coming in with damp hair and raw nostrils. Childhood's deep calendar says Halloween, Bonfire Night, snow, Christmas. The empty room itself is exciting, to my latent pointless snoop (I *have* always thought I might have been a detective); I want to go through the coat pockets, identify the coffee drinker from the lip ring, rootle a handbag or rucksack. It feels good knowing Janet Marsh's letter is there in my inside pocket. I'm dawdling here partly because I haven't decided yet how I'll handle the call. Will I call her tonight, even?

Tara comes in, bringing the world with her. She's been out for a Marlboro Light and smells of smoke and playground air and the extra-strong mint her tongue clacks against her teeth. Our eyes meet, then she looks away. 'Niptastic out there,' she says, vigorously rubbing her upper arms. She's not wearing a green dress today but a charcoal pinstripe pencil skirt and a close-fitting pink pure wool sweater. Not the knee-boots, either; instead, a pair of dark grey Forties high heels that come all the way up to the capable bare ankle. The look's Chandleresque, Marlowe's secretary or the femme fatale's sensible younger sis. She resumes her seat, her coffee. 'How's it been?' she asks. She hasn't decided if she's going to play a round of our game.

'Usual torture,' I say, taking a seat opposite her and stretching my legs. 'Flynn's just told me we don't need Orwell's Ministry of Information because we've got popular entertainment instead.'

There's a pause long enough for me to regret assumed reading. But she closes her eyes and tilts her head back, mentally searching. The white throat's unignorably there with its matrix of veins, giving me a tingle of vampiric pleasure that makes me shiver, though I muscularly conceal it. 'Orwell,' she says. '*1984*, Ministry of . . . They change history to suit the present and no one's any the wiser.'

'Exactly. Whereas, as Daniel will tell you, it's easier to provide non-stop entertainment so we don't care *what* history was like.'

She yawns, and is tardy getting her hand over her mouth so that I'm treated to a glimpse of black-filled lower molars and diminished extra-strong mint on her tense wet tongue before the white fingers arrive with half-hearted ladylike cover. The yawn makes her eyes fill up. For a couple of seconds after it she stares at me through a film of water as if she has no idea who I am or where she is. It's a glimpse of her stripped of any strategy or art, the sort of silent raw essence out of which she might say anything, like, My God you disgust me you miserable fuck, or You and I are both really going to die one day and be rotten meat in the ground. 'Yeah, well,' she says, blinking herself out of it, 'he's probably right. I started reading this book not long ago because I didn't know anything about the whole Israeli–Palestinian thing and I got sick of hearing about it on the news and not understanding it. It was a Beginner's Guide.' She leans back in the chair and crosses her legs, tucks her hands under her bum. I imagine the soft suck of the Forties shoe coming off her broad foot, the little release of warmth. 'Couldn't follow it,' she says. 'I put it down after about fifty pages and thought, No, amazing though it is, I'm actually too thick for this. I need a Thick Beginner's Guide. You don't do anything with your brain, it turns to mush.'

Even without all there is tacitly going on between me and

Miss Kilcoyne there are a lot of exchanges like this at the Arbuthnot, not quite talking at cross-purposes, but not quite connecting, either. The bulk of staff-room conversation falls prey to slight digression which expands with a fascinating fractal inevitability away from the point. Five minutes is enough to take you to a galaxy far, far away.

'You don't want to do anything until you understand what's going on, do you?' I say. 'I mean, if you don't know the history of the thing how can you know who's right or what to vote for or whatever?'

'Unless it's Bush,' she says. 'You've only got to watch him for five seconds to know he shouldn't be in charge of an ice-cream van let alone America. It's harder with Blair because he's not so obviously a moron.' Underneath the *Times* there's a two-day-old *Independent* open at a page showing a frowning Colonel Gadaffi caught mid-harangue. 'Gadaffi Appeals for Bigley's Release', the headline reads. Tara's right leg is crossed over her left, its long white calf muscle softly spread. Her foot goes up and down above the picture as if on an invisible bass drum pedal. I try to remember if the Americans are still bombing Libya. Can't. My memory isn't, I'm forced to concede, what it used to be.

'And this thing,' I say, nodding at the paper.

She moves her leg, looks down past it, reads. 'Oh God, I know. It's disgusting. Did you see his mum on telly?'

'I know, I know.'

'We just . . .'

I look at her, waiting, but she closes her eyes and slowly, with uglily tightened mouth, shakes her head. Superficially this is her rendered speechless by the horror of the story but in fact it's a retreat from her own lack of feeling about it and a pause in which she's weighing up, as she does every time I'm alone with her, what exactly if anything she wants to do about me. I'm not in her league (not laughably not in it, but still, not in it) but her chap ran off with someone else and she's taking affirmation where she can find it at the moment. She knows all this as well as I do. We're mutually visible in these encounters.

'What're you up to this weekend?' I ask, tonally letting her know the embarrassing subject of Ken Bigley and the World and being too thick for a Beginner's Guide is closed.

She opens her eyes and puts her head on one side, like a perplexed dog, then stretches the pose to ease those irresistible mastoids. 'I'm not sure. My sister wants to go to that Sixties photographs thing at the Tate.'

Her eyes, I now notice and fix for future fantasy, are yellowy brown, surprisingly thin on lashes, though this is what gives them their bald, arousing meanness. There are days when she wears her thin hair up, barretted or stabbed through with chopsticks. On such days you get the neck's full erotic clout and the lobeless silver-hooped ears going red from the central heating and the pink of her scalp under the lights. She's annoyed with her man for leaving her. She was waiting for someone better to come along. Now she's waiting on her own, and in a madwoman way considering – remotely – doing things like having a fling with me. It would have going for it the ease of no illusions. She and I know she'd be doing it as an act of self-disgust, to rub her nose in her misjudgement of him, to give herself a good, sensible slap across the chops. She's aware, now, at twenty-seven, that life is pretty much doing lots of lousy things you never thought you'd do. Getting to the grave without poverty or psychic fracture is just a case of showing your conscience who's boss.

She gets up quickly and goes to the sink to wash her cup, and I can tell from her shoulders that the moment to ask her out has passed and that she would have said no in any case.

CHAPTER EIGHT

❧

The Mother Country

(*The Cheechee Papers*: Quetta, Bhusawal, Bombay
and Lahore, 1935–42)

Unlike my father, my mother, Katherine Marie Millicent Lyle –
Kathy, Katie, Kit, Kitty, but most often Kate – has kept the mystery
of her past. Her sections of *The Cheechee Papers* are busy with
question marks, hypotheses, crossings out, ellipses, gaps. While Pasha
relies (for sanity, one assumes) on the meticulous retelling of the
events of his life, the causal chain that leads from his Then to his
Now, the *story*, my mother dismisses her own vast antecedent tracts
with a smile and a shrug.

'But, Ma, are you seriously saying you have no memories of
your life before you were seven or eight years old?'

This will be after lunch in Bolton. The old man will have
walked me through Ho Fun's or the bloodstone or Rockballs or Goodrich for the thousandth time, me furiously
scribbling in the Moleskine, while Mater, still nursing the
single afternoon port and lemon I bully her into, will be sitting embroidering or doing the crossword or watching *Columbo*
with the sound down low. At some point I'll have switched

my note-taking attention to her. 'I mean, what about birthdays?'

'Not that I can remember.'

'Christmases? A particular present? Your first day at school?'

She'll lean back in her chair, consider, shake her head. 'No, not really.' It doesn't appear to bother her.

'I remember *my* first day at school,' Pasha will jump in. 'I got such a bleddy crack on the head from Danglers. First *day*, even.'

Mater and I will roll our eyes, hers very lightly eye-shadowed and mascara'd. She can still carry it off, the faint dusting of cosmetics. (Other old ladies, it seems to me, apply their make-up like toddlers who've raided their mother's dressing table.) The girl in her has got more not less visible as she's aged. Granted her small face (two satiny pouches are burgeoning under her eyes) has its soft cross-hatching and the thin-skinned backs of her hands their thickened veins, but for a woman at the end of her seventies she's astonishingly well preserved.

'So you're saying the first thing you can really remember is your father's death? Nothing before that?'

'Nothing,' she'll say, eyes prettily moist. She feels sorry for me, with my notebook, my files, my *agenda*. In my childhood there was no peace like the peace of her touch, the cool hands with their silvery-pink nails and ghost of Nivea. Her voice is soft, to her Boltonian contemporaries maddeningly posh.

'See, Sweetheart, my life began when I met your father and got married and had children. I know that sounds silly to you, but that's the truth. I didn't care about anything else.'

In a way it is the truth: wifehood and motherhood revealed themselves to her as boxing revealed itself to my dad, as the identity that had been waiting for her to come and claim it; and if that was all there was to her story it would leave me (and *The Cheechee Papers*) stymied.

But that isn't all there was to it. There's the other thing. The monolithic thing. The thing that keeps me up in the small hours, chopping and changing and filling in the goddamned gaps to get it right. Her story – the Mother material – is turning the book into a nightmare of delicacy and analysis.

'You don't mind me writing all this stuff, do you, Ma?'

I've asked her umpteen times. No amount of reassurance is enough.

'About my childhood and everything?'

'Well, yeah . . .' I hesitate. Tread carefully. 'I mean the other thing.'

'About me deciding to kill Uncle Cyril?'

'Yeah. That.'

She looks away, out of the window. It's the parental look away, into the past, the foreign country. My father's version of this look comes with a fruity smile. My mother's is different, evinces triumphal serenity, the deep, humbling peace of realizing that against all the odds she's survived to have the life she wanted. Then the smile comes, not for herself but for me, the smarty-pants, hopelessly rummaging in ancient history, bothered about it, under its spell.

'I don't need to worry about the past. That's your father's mania.'

And yours, she doesn't need to add. But there's a little undercurrent of sadness. These conversations, the note-taking, the endless retelling, this penetration into the past, this project of the bloody Book reminds her that she has nothing of her parents' to remember them by. The orphan in her resurfaces, testifies in her eyes when the old man and I are deep into it. His side of the family clinks and rustles with legendary rings and wristwatches, photographs, diaries, letters, fractured certificates of birth and death. My mother has no such talismans, no links to take her back down the chain of her life before marriage and children.

'You write what you want, Sweetheart,' she says. 'None of that can touch me now.'

Write what you want. The permission appals, rushes me to the edge of a nauseous drop. I always step back. It's true her memory's no match for Pasha's or mine. It's true there are fogs, holes, blind alleys. It's true I don't know, as the old man would say, the whole bleddy *yarn*.

But I know enough.

'What have I told you about locking this door?' This is Uncle Cyril's bungalow in Bhusawal, his bathroom door, his fist pounding – *thab-thab-thab* – his voice lowered. 'Open it, I said. *Now*.'

Kate, fifteen, closes her eyes, feels her chest constrict. Lately he does this, pretends to go out, sneaks back, corners her. The sound of his voice in the first instant shocks and in the next deadens her.

'Did you hear me or not?'

She'd planned a quiet hour in the bath (more precisely the Japanned Travelling Tub, Army & Navy Co-op, a luxury from the days of her grandfather's prosperity) to go over her escape plan, but the day's earlier events have intruded. This morning at the sodden train station there was a demonstration, British big shot supposed to be going through en route from Calcutta; damp homemade banners – *Jai Hind! British Quit Now!* – perhaps a hundred people, station staff trying to make cordons, eventually the police turning up and walloping left, right and centre. The male faces had gone ugly in the fight, grimacing and cringeing, made her think of Hell, the indiscriminate wrestling of the damned. One man cradled his broken left arm in his right. Another bent to spit a stretched gobbet of blood and mucus into a puddle. One man with blood streaming down his face walked towards her with both upheld hands (fingers as if holding a pinch of salt) repeating an elaborate *why?* gesture, directed, it seemed, at her. It had astonished her that Bhusawal had this capacity, that ordinary people could gather and roar and punch the air in unison, make the familiar station platform unfamiliar. 'Best get out of here, girlie,' a coffee-breathed Anglo-Indian guard had said, suddenly close in her ear. She'd been standing transfixed, having spotted in the middle of the crowd Kalia, Uncle Cyril's servant boy. His mouth shouting the slogans had looked enlarged. 'Go on, pretty miss,' the guard said, giving her arm a squeeze, 'rain's coming again now.' She'd backed away as the first berry-big drops began to fall and burst. Twenty steps and it was coming down with a sound like raging fire. The dispersing crowd slithered and slipped. A policeman chasing a demonstrator went over flat on his face, got up and lashed out at a snack-seller who was standing nearby looking in the opposite direction. Budgias and pakoras from the vendor's tray went flying. The policeman hit two, three, four times more, until the vendor was down on the ground, knees up, arms curled round his head, tray twisted on its strap so that it was round his back, savouries squished into the mud. Kate had come home drenched.

Thab-thab-thab. '*Now*, I said.'

The monsoon is past its peak. Tomorrow she'll be back at Jesus and Mary in Bombay. The other girls will be miserable whereas it's all she can do not to drop to her knees and kiss the polished steps. You're crazy, Eleanor Silvers said. This is like coming back to *jail* for God's sake. In the next mid-term break Eleanor's older sister is getting married up north in Lahore. Eleanor is allowed to bring one friend from school on provision of a letter signed by the friend's parents. Kate's parents are dead. For the last seven years she's been under the guardianship of her grandfather and Uncle Cyril. She's written the letter herself, in disguised handwriting. Her grandfather has to sign it. *Has* to. She'll go up to Lahore. She'll never come back. She'll disappear. Freedom, at whatever the cost. For weeks now the plan has been growing in her like a delicious fever.

'I'm *warning* you.'

Kate wraps a pink towel round herself and unlocks the door, which Cyril steps through and slams behind him. He stands in front of her with his hands on his hips. Hair oil, cigarette smoke, old sweat and sandalwood cologne. She feels the change in her radius as if her outflowing life is being reversed and forced back into her, imagines tiny specks of light that should have gone from her into the world being pushed instead up through her nerves towards her heart and brain, where they gather in glowing tumorous clumps.

'I've told you *not* to lock the bleddy door. What if I want to come in here and shave?'

Always some transparent rationale, some argument. She says nothing because her saying nothing is what he hates. He wants her to argue, to help him get where he needs to get. It interests the detached, analytical part of her that he still has to go through the motions, however farcical or absurd, of justifying himself, that he still lacks the . . . what? guts? . . . to walk in and start on her without pantomime. It's satisfying that her silence leaves him flailing, gives her a height from which to look down at him.

'Who do you think you are?' he says, looking everywhere but at Kate. 'The bleddy Queen of Sheba or what?' He's not tall but he's taller than her, dark-skinned with a long, bony face, Brylcreemed widow's peak and an apeish outward curve to his mouth. 'It's all nakra,' he says. 'All bleddy airs and graces.' He turns away from her and puts his shaving bag down next to the basin. Underneath her anger there's boredom with his creeping towards his full capability. She knows him, that his denial has mileage yet to run. But that it will run, eventually, is like the weight of another body she's had to carry on top of her own.

Not for much longer. In her locker at Jesus and Mary there's a small cache of tinned and dried foods; under a loose bit of skirting in the dorm thirty rupees she's scraped and hoarded from Christmases and birthdays. It's nothing, but nothing will have to be enough.

She makes a move towards the door but Cyril turns and grabs the towel where it's tucked in on itself over her breasts. There's a second before he pulls it, a bubble of time between them when she looks him in the eye (This is what you are) and his face shows a wobble of horror. Then he yanks. The towel doesn't come away cleanly but pulls her off balance, towards him. He yanks again (sidestepping, as if her touch would be repugnant), his fingernail scratching her, a distinct, separate little hurt. 'Don't be stupid,' he says, turning away, as if her nakedness is a matter of indifference. 'Your hair's full of soap.' He drops the towel on the floor and goes over to the washstand, begins lathering his chin, watching her in the mirror. His tone lightens. 'Can't go like that, all soap in your hair like that. Madness.'

Very slowly Kate gets down on her haunches and retrieves the towel, rises and wraps it around herself. The reflex is to minimize movement, as if there's an invisible delicate shell surrounding her she mustn't disturb. The bathroom's one small window of frosted glass holds a lozenge of the day's between-rains sunlight. This hour alone would have been a private sacrament. The smell of Wright's Coal Tar soap, the warm tin against her back, the softness of the towel. One by one he's contaminated the small sensory pleasures of her world.

'I don't know why you have to give me such a bleddy headache, you know,' he says. 'I mean, this is my house after all.' Tone lighter still, beginning to cajole. He'll be jovial in a minute. Without a word she walks round to the far side of the tub, bends, dunks her head hairline-deep, holds it, hears the soap dissolve. She tries to focus on something else; the dress for the wedding (for flight, for freedom), white with a print of red poppies, used to be her mother's. (Everything else that belonged to her mother has gone, quietly, via Cyril to his sister, Kate's Aunty Sellie. Jewellery, dancing trophies, clothes, a gold wristwatch, an amber rosary. Aunty Sellie never looks Kate quite in the eye.) The spot where his nail nicked burns. She lifts her head from the water. Parts of her — armpits, throat, wrists, scalp — send little pulsing signals of their own unique vulnerabilities; they're like children she, Kate, the grown-up, must stop panicking. Shshsh. Cyril wipes steam from the mirror and draws the cutthroat upwards

over his lathered gullet with a rasp. Slashed throat gushing blood
eyes wide fingers opening and closing dying. She used to shut
such images out.

'This is my house and all I'm asking for is a bit of bleddy . . .'
Rasp, flick, splat, rinse . . . 'a bit of bleddy thisthing . . .' *Respect*,
he was going to say but she knows certain words die in his mouth.
He's contaminated his own vocabulary, too, lost bits of language
like rotten teeth. Without him seeing, she washes the place where
his hand met her skin under the towel. She twists her hair into a
short rope, squeezes the moisture from it, stands.

He wipes steam off the mirror, looks, sees she's staring at him.
This is what you are.

'Go on, then,' he says, making a dismissive gesture with the
razor, from which a wad of lather takes flight and detonates on the
door. 'I don't know what you're standing there gawping for.'

★

Kate's parents died within six months of each other in 1934 in
Quetta, her father of a heart attack, her mother of . . .

(Well, it's unclear. She went into hospital with tuberculosis. But
there were, mysteriously, 'abscesses', some medical impasse: If we
operate the anaesthetic will kill her, If we don't she'll die anyway.
My mum's fragmented recollection. She remembers a visit, her
mother saying, 'You've got so tall now . . .' Which turned out to
be the last words between them.)

I know this is hard for you, my child, Father Collins told Kate,
after her mother's funeral service. It's the hardest thing anyone has
to bear. But you must understand: there's a reason for everything
that happens. God knows *every*thing, you see? He knows the
reason why even painful things or sad things must happen to us
sometimes. I know you're very sad and upset because your
mummy's been called to heaven, but just think: she's with God
and the angels now, and she'll be happy for ever and ever. It's all
right to miss her and to wish she was still here, but always in the

end remember she's gone to a much better place – the very best place you can imagine!

He'd said the same thing at her father's funeral.

At New Year celebrations there was always someone dressed as an old man to represent the departing year being playfully chased out by a young woman dressed to represent the approaching new one. Kate had imagined God to be something like this old man, white-bearded and touchingly frail-kneed, eccentrically benevolent, with an aura of sadness, distant, aware of you and your prayers but only as one speck in a upwardly drifting swarm of millions. The familial relationship was with Jesus, Mary, the angels, all the interceding martyrs and saints; they knew you, Kate Lyle, personally, and were up on the current events of your life, delighted by your good acts and terribly hurt by your sins. Now, with the deaths of her parents, it was as if God, the *real* God, was addressing her with the full intensity of His gaze, not old and kindly but timeless and impenetrable (she imagined a giant dark gaseous face in the night sky frosted with constellations), coldly, patiently interested in her. It was a shock, but it gave her a feeling of recognition, too, as if she'd known this – Him – long ago but for years forgotten.

A curious duality followed: she continued, in church, in her night prayers, superficially addressing Jesus, Mary, the saints and martyrs, the white-bearded, octogenarian version of God the Father. They were all still there, legitimate, real, comforting. But simultaneously she was alive to (and enjoyed a bald dialogue in an idiom of equals with) this newly revealed essence. He was the core round which all the other aspects of Himself hung, needed no prayers, saw you, didn't love you or hate you but held you under perpetual icy observation.

After Kate's parents died she was looked after by their neighbours, the Haweses, Edwin and Margot, who were childless and made a strangling fuss of her. She expected her mother back, naturally. One lunchtime, one evening, or more likely one early morning after having been out dancing, smelling of cigarette smoke and night air and perfume. She'd stand on one leg and pull her shoe off with a wince, then the other leg, the other shoe. That was the trick the dead played on you, of making you expect them home again, some silly but ultimately believable explanation for where they'd been all this time.

She'd been told her grandfather was coming to Quetta for her and that she was going to live with him in Bhusawal, but didn't take the idea very seriously. Then, at the end of May, there was a knock on her bedroom door.

'Kate?' Margot said, peeping in. 'There's someone here to see you.'

The door opened wider and a tall old man with a flat-topped head of swept-forward grey hair stepped inside. Margot left them alone. (Kate's bags and trunk had been packed the night before. In with the clothes had gone as many of her mother's cups and trophies for dancing as could fit, the rest to be sent on. A separate vanity case held all her mother's jewellery. She, Kate's mother, had had a passion for it and Kate's father had loved indulging her: *Here, Magpie, look what I've brought you.* The only thing of Kate's father's going with her was a big book of Renaissance paintings, the water-buckled pages of which he and Kate used to pore over in the evenings in silence, only at a very deep level conscious of each other. It was one of the things she'd thought at the funeral, how few words she'd exchanged with him.) She sat on the bed, swinging her legs.

Her grandfather put his hands in his pockets. 'Hello, love,' he said. 'D'you know who I am?'

'My granddad.'

'Aye. And you're Kitty.'

Silence. He took a bar of Tarzan chocolate from his pocket. Didn't offer it to her, just looked at it. 'Daft in't it,' he said. 'Thought I'd give you this to say hello, so you wouldn't think badly of me.'

Daft in't it. Her mother had said: 'Your granddad's an Englishman, you know. He talks funny.' Kate's interest was piqued.

He hadn't, so far, been able to meet her stare. Now he looked out at her from under his brows. He didn't know what to do, she could tell, was trying, awkwardly, to make friends with her. She looked away, not knowing what to do herself. She hadn't thought about what this would be like, hadn't believed in it, but here it was. Now the thought of leaving Edwin and Margot, whom she'd known all her life, was a little globe of pain in her chest.

'Come on for a walk,' the old man said. 'You can show me where your daddy used to work.'

He put out his hand. Embarrassed, not looking at him, she slid down off the bed and took it.

It was a long journey south-east to Bhusawal, a night and a day and a night. Kate had grown up around trains but never travelled in a sleeper. The upper bunks folded down out of the wall and a porter came with crisp sheets and bedding. First Class, this was, with fat-tassled curtains and heraldically monogrammed cushions, NWR until they got to Jabalpur, then GIPR. Her first taste of milky sweet coffee. Eating on the move made every meal an adventure: eggs on toast, ball curry, mangos, mulligatawny soup. Her grandfather bought hot snacks from hawkers on the blinding platforms, samosas and budgias and oppers and stuffed naan. Food was an opportunity for them to be in collusion, which Kate first coldly saw that he wanted, then found herself slipping into in spite of herself. He went with her wandering up and down the train. Third Class was a cramped throng of beggarly Indians, all of whom looked depressed or harassed. There was a smell of feet and sweat and food. Kate and her grandfather poked their heads in, looked, withdrew. The journey seemed endless to her. All the windows were down on the carriage doors; at night, dark land and stars rolled past, sometimes the outlines of villages, tufts of fire. During the day, fields, distant hills, mile after mile of featureless

scrub. She had no idea where she was. The notion of getting off
the train receded. They could go on like this for ever, the sun and
stars rolling round, and when you stuck your head out the heroic
burnished flank of the engine taking a bend up ahead.

'Will I go to school?' she asked her grandfather.

'Oh, aye, that's been sorted. You're to go to school in Bombay.'

'Where's that?'

'That's a great big place by the sea with marble buildings an' all
that. Gateway to India.'

They had these pockets of conversation. To Kate they might as
well have been discussing an imaginary world. Yet there was
something she felt him (and herself) skirting. They both knew
and acknowledged in the code of all the other conversation that
there was this something else. It was avoidable, temporarily; but
Kate could feel him tensing the further into the journey they
went. He looked more out of the window, talked less.

'Bhusawal! Next stop Bhusawal!'

'How big is your house, Granddad?' Kate asked.

'Where we live?' he said, looking out of the window. 'Well, it's
a decent enough sized place.' Then, after a pause in which she
realized they'd come to the end of avoiding it: 'It's not *my* house,
any road. It's your Uncle Cyril's.'

He was on the sun-blasted platform to meet them. Kate's first
sight of the long face with its outward-curving mouth like a
monkey's, the gold ring and white cigarette. He wore silver-
rimmed black sunglasses and a heavy watch on a steel strap, a tight
white singlet and baggy khaki slacks.

'What then – have you heard?' he said to Kate's grandfather,
before hello, before anything.

'What?' the old man said. The platform was jittery with the
train's arrival. Around them passengers were struggling with
trunks and cases. Snack-sellers were up against the windows, fluttering passenger hands coming out for the quick exchange. The

train hissed, quietly, and Kate thought of how she'd kidded herself that she'd never have to get off it. Now it was going on without her, like a horse she'd loved but had to let go.

'Blaardy *hell*,' Uncle Cyril said. 'They've had an earthquake in Quetta, big one, God knows how many killed.'

'What?' Kate's granddad said, squinting. 'Rubbish. When?'

'Day after you left there! I've been bleddy marking time here, I can tell you, in case you missed the train.'

'Jalgaon!' the conductor shouted, strolling past. 'Pachora, Chalisgaon, Manmad, Deolali, Kalyan and Bombay Victoria Terminus! All aboard!'

'Who says?' her granddad said.

'Came through on the wire this morning. Blaardy *hell*, I tell you God only knows.'

The train whistled. Mournfully to Kate. Her heart hurt. The heat here made your body a transparent, negligible thing. Earthquakes were Acts of God. He could do things simultaneously, talk to you quietly in one part of the world and heave the land up and swallow houses in another. Kate looked up into the milky blue burning sky, behind which, she knew, the implacable face was watching.

'Anyway, come on come on, I'll tell you about it on the way. Is that her trunk?'

They took a tonga pulled by a grey horse with a knotted dusty mane and wet black eyes. The thin sunlit driver was the same deep leathery dark brown as the sunlit bridle and reins. When he smiled at Kate she saw that all his front teeth were missing.

'Forty Blocks,' Uncle Cyril told him, and after a tap with the long stick the grey horse pulled away. It looked effortful to Kate, as if the hooves were too heavy, the big sad head going slowly up and down.

In the following days news of the earthquake came down from the north. Estimates said twenty thousand dead. All but the cantonment area had been destroyed. Kate wondered about her mother's and father's graves, imagined them torn open, the coffins pushed up, splintered, a brief glimpse of bodies, then another black heave and them swallowed again.

'You know what I think?' her grandfather said to her. Four days had passed since her arrival. Nights, she slept on a fold-out camp bed in his room, which smelled of tobacco and leather and serge and aftershave.

'What, Granddad?' She knew he meant the earthquake, couldn't keep away from the subject. Thirty thousand, some reports were saying now. The papers liked it the more bodies were found.

'I think it's God can't meck is mind up. Shakin things about an turnin everythin topsy bloody turvy. Earthquakes and volcanoes and whatnot. Tidal waves. D'you know what a tidal wave is?'

'No.' She didn't know what topsy bloody turvy was, either.

'It's an enormous ruddy great wave that rises up from the sea, 'undreds of feet high, and blots out the sun, and comes slowly nearer and then crashes on t'land and destroys everythin underneath it. Now, you tell me what the point o' that is. You can't, can you?'

'No.'

'On t'uther and,' he said, lowering his voice, 'look at me an thee. Here. *Alive.*' In small ways he'd made it known to her that his power in the household was limited. She could count on him for low-voiced allegiance against Cyril, but for what beyond that remained unclear. 'I mean,' he continued, 'if things hadn't happened as they did *you* wouldn't be alive here today, would you? If your mother hadn't passed away I wouldn't have come for you. Or think if I'd come a day later. One *day* later. We'd a been swallered up wi' all them other poor buggers! That's destiny, that is. Ruddy *des*tiny.'

★

Kate comes out on to the rear veranda and finds Kalia down on his haunches, Brasso and yellow soft cloth in hand, meticulously cleaning the chrome on Uncle Cyril's motorbike. There's a stone-flagged patio adjoining the veranda, where the bike's kept under an awning. The rest of the compound is monsoon mud slivered with sky-reflecting water as if a giant mirror has been flung down and smashed. It'll be a big loss to Kalia when Kate's gone. She hasn't had the heart to tell him.

'I saw you,' she says. 'This morning at the train station.'

Kalia looks up at her out of his broad face the colour of Cherry Blossom dark tan shoe polish. Knobs of light wing his cheek-bones. His eyes are black, alert, with a slight Mongol slant. She remembers his shouting mouth revealing more teeth than she would have imagined. *Jai Hind! Janetge ya Marenge!* Before speaking he looks over his shoulder to check they're alone. Their shared reflex is caution. 'What will you do, miss?' he asks, quietly.

'Nothing,' she says. 'What would I do?'

Kalia looks down at the ground, blinks, revolves some conclusion he's already drawn. 'You could tell him,' he says. Him. Cyril.

'Why would I do that?'

Something's wrong, she knows, there's been a shift. She thinks back to the start of their friendship. On this same veranda one evening seven years ago she'd watched him quietly cleaning an earlier bike. Suddenly Uncle Cyril had appeared round the side of the bungalow, rushed up and kicked him in the back, and when he fell forward continued kicking him, saying, *What do you think I am – fucking stupid? You simple black bastard, I can* count, *you know* – throwing a handful of coins. *How many fucking times?* And she, Kate, unseen until that moment had said: 'Stop it!' startling Uncle Cyril, who for a split second cringed with a grimace that in spite of everything made her want to laugh. She nearly had laughed, he'd looked so idiotic. But he'd come up the steps and stood in front of her. It was the first time he'd been near her. She'd looked at her shoes in silence. *He steals.* Pause. *Didn't your mother ever tell you it's wrong to steal?* Cyril had stood with his fists on his hips, white shirt cuffs rolled back. The words *your mother* stung;

three days' inchoate feeling since her arrival at his house shaped
into resistance. *My mother* and *my father said it's wrong to steal*, she'd
said. Then raised her head to look at him. *And it's wrong to beat the
servants.* Cyril had looked away, made a strange movement of discomfort with his neck and jaw.

She kept imagining what it would feel like if he hit her, the
hand drawn back and then the swipe. That gold pinkie ring would
be a separate, additional pain. He was frowning, nostrils flared,
mouth corners down. One of the Hindu gods had this expression;
she couldn't remember which. She was sure he was going to hit
her. Between them it was as if a huge balloon was expanding; any
second it would burst, any second . . .

But instead he'd turned to Kalia with the look transformed
into one of amused disbelief. *See the bleddy cheek, eh?* As if the
kicking had never happened. *And I don't have enough with you
and that old bugger to look after already. Heh!* Cyril shook his head,
tutting. *I ask you. Honestly I ask you, eh?* He jogged down the three
steps. Didn't look back at her. *Go on hurry up and finish that. And
when Sumpath comes tell him there's two more for dinner. I can't hang
around here all day. Someone's got to earn the bleddy money in this
house.*

Since then Kalia has looked out for Kate, she for him. In torturous clandestine increments she's taught him rudimentary
reading and writing in English.

But there's been a shift. Today. Now.

'Why would I tell him?' she asks again.

Now *he* can't look at her. The rains have left sky-reflecting
puddles. It's a disturbing inversion, mirrored clouds moving across
gashes in the ground.

'Some of those people today,' Kalia says, 'they're against you.'

'Against me?'

'Against your people. Anglos.'

Kate is amazed. All the time she'd watched the demonstration
it had never occurred to her that anything could happen to her.

The only moment of fear had been the guard's hand on her arm and his voice in her ear. When she thinks of the scene now she sees it from above: the stream of wrangling bodies flowing round her, water round a stone.

'Why are they against Anglos?' she asks. It's a shock to her, to think that she, by virtue of belonging to a group, is caught up in . . . what? She doesn't understand. Outside the aura between herself and Uncle Cyril everything is a faint noise. Now, apparently, strangers are against her.

'Because you're like them,' Kalia says. 'The British.'

For a few moments they fall silent, Kalia applying the Brasso in soft whorls, Kate staring out across the water-logged compound. The dark bulk of cloud from the last downpour is separating into curdy masses. Low sun lights their edges with rose and gold, to Kate a bad-tempered beauty, two elements forced together. Because you're like the British. Suddenly she feels tired.

'Miss?' Kalia says.

She looks down at him.

'*I* am not against you,' he says.

At dusk (Cyril's gone up to the Institute for billiards but there's no knowing when he'll be back) Kate sits with her grandfather on the front veranda. The garden is a thirty-foot lawn surrounded by bougainvillea and plantains. Two banyans make humid tents of shade either side of the gateposts. The gravel path to the road glistens in the half-light.

'So?' she asks him. This is the umpteenth time she's tackled him about signing the Silvers wedding letter, her passport to freedom.

The old man smokes for a few moments in silence. Unequivocally old, now, Kate thinks. This last seven years he's made the transition, looks out at the world as if struggling to see through rain. Superficially he's the same, the bluster, the broad comedy, the rant; superficially the strength's still there. But she knows something's gone. Between them there's an understanding too painful to speak of, that the circle of his protection, such as it ever was, has shrunk. If you don't like the bleddy arrangement, Dad, Cyril had said, you know what you can do, don't you? Kate had been eavesdropping from the kitchen. Of late the old man doesn't look her in the eye. She understands: he knows, and can't bear that he knows. Can't bear that he's more bothered about himself, the roof over his head, fags, a whisky in the afternoon, a brown ale with dinner. Or rather he can bear it, is bearing it, is living daily with the reality of his own weakness. Between him and destitution there's only . . . there's only the arrangement, and If you don't like the bleddy arrangement, Dad . . . He'd had money once, apparently, but squandered it. All his life more money had come to replace what was spent. Then, suddenly, he was old and broke.

'I dunno what you expect me to do,' he says. While Kate's been staring out into the garden's gathering dark he's finished one cigarette and rolled another.

'Nothing, Grandpa,' she says. 'You don't have to do anything, just sign the letter and keep up the pretence that I'm at school. He won't know any different.' It's usual for her to stay in school during the short holidays. There are always a few dozen girls whose families live too far away or who won't have them at home unless they have to. The Leftbehinds, they call themselves, cold-comfortingly, through the long hours when the shadows revolve and the school's rooms echo. 'It'll be the same as always as far as he's concerned.' Money for the ticket will have to come from her grandfather, somehow. 'I've already written the letter,' she says. 'You just have to sign it. I'll be back in time for the start of term. *He* won't know anything. Please.'

The old man lights his roll-up from a matchbook. The flame-light in the cup of his knuckly hands illuminates his face, the big-pored nose and squinting eyes. He's had a haircut and shave this morning. The loose skin of his neck is flecked with missed silver bristles. The young boy of himself is visible in the shape of his head. He's been in India since he was seventeen. You could whore and drink and gamble and make money and still be a little raja. And when you wanted a wife, you could go and fetch one from the orphanage. He's outlived the wives, two of them. There won't be a third. He's surrendered to aloneness. That's what these sad hours on the veranda concede.

'You could ask Aunty Sellie to pay for my ticket,' Kate says.

The last of the light is going. The scent of next door's jasmine finds its way to the porch, strong for a few moments, then passes. Evenings here are rich with transient whiffs: goat, dogshit, orange blossom, coffee, someone's paprika'd roast lamb. Kate feels the mention of Sellie doing its work. The old man uncrosses his ankles, then crosses them again. She worries she's taken the wrong tack. He's guilty, yes, but you've got to know how and when to nudge. History's trickled out these seven years: he'd been against her mother's marriage; there was a fight. Her mother left Bhusawal. Since then the other daughter, Sellie, has been the favourite, has been given whatever he's had to give. Which these days is nothing but the burden of himself, his potential dependence if anything happens to Cyril.

He opens his mouth to say something, changes his mind. Takes another drag, exhales, clears his throat.

They sit for five, ten minutes. Kate keeps her mouth shut. There's a volatile emotional chemistry at work in him that mustn't be interfered with. It depresses her that she's beginning to understand the way people tick, that the way they tick is guilt and shame and desire and fear, that these are the elements of the heart's science. This knowledge trickles down from God in the dialogues. This is what people do with their freedom.

'Where is the ruddy letter, then?' the old man says at last.

It's after ten o'clock. Kate's in her room, packing. Her grandfather's still out on the front veranda with his whisky and his smokes. The holiday, the ordeal, is almost over. Tomorrow school.

A half-term to get through, then Lahore. Freedom. The city will show her a way. If the old man hasn't signed by tomorrow she'll forge the signature herself. She's never been to Lahore, though the name's familiar to her from childhood; her father's job (chief boiler inspector on the NWR) took him there occasionally. She imagines the city as an undecided entity on whose mercy she must throw herself. Just give me a chance, she's said to the cold God. Just one chance. That's not much to ask, is it?

She's had nothing in return. From Jesus and Mary, from the *old* cast of divine characters, yes, some nervy vague well-wishes – but from Him only the sustained icy stare.

'Come here! Come *here*, you fucking . . .' Uncle Cyril's voice in the compound. The sounds of feet *putch putch*ing in the mud. 'I give you a fucking roof over your head and this is how you repay me? Come here, you bleddy thieving *wretch*.'

Kate goes to the window and looks out. The veranda lamps show Kalia, with blood streaming from his head, down on one knee, one arm raised in defence. Uncle Cyril has a stick, a policeman's lathi, and is lashing out with a ferocity that makes keeping his balance difficult. Twice he slips and nearly topples, flails for a moment, grabs Kalia's sleeve, recovers. It would, with the slightest shift, look funny.

Hard to tell how long it lasts. Kate stands at the window watch-ing in silence, arms clasped round the book of Renaissance paintings. Kalia is thin, no match for ropily muscled Uncle Cyril. (What about your mother and father? she'd asked the servant years ago. Father not known, miss, he'd said. Mother is dead here ten years. Sahib lets me stay and work. You're an orphan, then, she'd said. Like me.) 'You bleddy thieving sonofabitch! How *dare* you?' When he's angry Cyril's face looks as if it's testing a dis-gusting smell, open nostrils and baggily downturned mouth. Again, with a slight shift this could be funny; comedy villains pull this face when they've been outwitted. You change how you look at something and it becomes something else.

Kalia gets to his feet and tears himself free. Uncle Cyril, grasping after him, slips in the mud and goes down on to his knees. Kalia, backpedalling, reaches the shed at the bottom of the compound. (Kate remembers the first time she looked in there: thin mattress, spartan table, one chair, old tins and jars – Tate & Lyle Golden Syrup, Bird's Custard Powder, Lyons Tea – filled with buttons, bottletops, screws, nails. Everything very neat and tidy. In more recent times other things have been added: old books she's salvaged from school; newspaper cuttings; a picture of Gandhi in a wooden frame he hides under the mattress.) Kalia moves with a purpose, suddenly; he ducks into the shed and emerges, upright, holding a heavily rusted machete (this is new; she's never seen this; he must have hidden it even from her) above his head. Uncle Cyril looks up, sees it, begins to say something – 'What? You raise your bleddy hand to—' but is cut off by the noise – not a scream but a kind of roared gargle – from Kalia's wide-open mouth. It's the loudest noise she's ever heard him make.

His open mouth and surprising teeth (the upper row slopes outward; it's why with his lips closed he always looks as if he's trying not to grin) remind her again of the demonstration, *all* the mouths shouting, the policemen's whacking out, the confusion of slipping bodies. Gandhi's in jail again, her grandfather had said not long ago, flinging down a *Times of India*. Good, Uncle Cyril said. This time they should *let* the bugger starve himself to death. Very little of it meant anything to Kate. The world was out there, people furiously angry. *Because you're like them, the British.* She thinks of the time in the bazaar, two Tommies with their English girls, arms linked. They'd made fun of her. Can you tell us, darling, where we can get the best *chutney* in town? She hadn't understood at first, had begun to say she didn't know because the servants did the shopping, but they'd interrupted – Your name's not *Mary* is it, by any chance? Then she got it: Chutney Mary. The girls' laughter tinkled from their dark-lipsticked mouths. As they were walking away one said to the other: You've got to watch these little cheechees, Emily. They'll steal a chap from right under your nose!

Kalia walks towards Uncle Cyril like an automaton, gargling, machete held aloft. She thinks, if he kills him now, if he kills him now brings it down on his head like that breaks it smashes his head then I won't have to I won't have to but they'll catch him and they'll know and they'll put him in jail or shoot him say he was trying to run. Uncle Cyril at first puts on a look of superior disgust, puffs his chest out, raises his chin as if he knows Kalia won't touch him – but at the last second flinches and ducks away, starts backing towards the house. Kalia follows him for four or five paces, then stops and falls silent. The two men look at each other, then Kalia looks away, as if he's lost interest in what was only a mildly amusing distraction.

'You dare?' Uncle Cyril asks quietly.

Kalia, with a kind of boredom or disgust, throws the machete blade-first at the ground, where it sticks in the mud for a moment then falls flat on to its side. He turns and, without saying anything, walks *putch putch putch* out of the compound.

Uncle Cyril stands bent for a few moments, hands gripping knees, breathing heavily, staring at the machete. Kate draws back from the window, so that if he turns he won't see her.

She knows her grandfather's in the house so there's a limit to her fear when, an hour or so later, Uncle Cyril comes to her room. She's sitting on the bed with the book of paintings open on her lap. Antonio and Piero del Pollaiuolo's *The Martyrdom of St Sebastian*, in which, despite being shot full of arrows by six archers at point-blank range, the saint looks merely bored. She gets to her feet as soon as her uncle enters the room.

'Finished packing, then?'

If you're on the bed you get up and away from it. You get to your feet. There are these minute adjustments you can make, for what little good they do.

'I'm on earlies tomorrow so I won't see you when you go,' Cyril says, yawning, massaging his left shoulder with his right hand. This is the demeanour, someone sleepily or with his mind elsewhere discharging a duty to which he's indifferent. 'So I'll wish you now.'

She says nothing, holds the book against her chest, arms crossed over it. He moves towards her, as always looking everywhere but at her. Her body sends its one fierce signal: no, no, no, no. She stands absolutely still. Her grandfather, not looking in, passes the open door with an empty tumbler in his hand, says, croakily, 'Kalia?' and disappears. He's only framed there for a moment, but she registers his craggy profile, waistcoat, braces dangling. A tall man starting to stoop, as if death is a low doorway to be got under.

'Well, have a good trip, then.'

When Cyril tries to kiss her she turns her face away, feels his lips and stubble on her cheek. He puts his hands on her hips, pulls her towards him. The hard book bumps between them. He leans again and she leans back, away, thinking in spite of the disgust that this is like the woman's melodramatic dip in the tango. It's wearying to be able to think this. He locks one arm round her waist and with the other tries to wrestle the book from her grip. She can feel him pressing against her. The crime your body commits against you is not letting you leave it. Confinement is absolute. Whether you like it or not the flesh continues to report sensations: hands on you; breath on your face; knot of hard heat there. It all happens as it always does, in silence, him smiling with what looks like indulgent humour, the grown-up benignly tolerating the child's little show of will. The book falls to the floor and he laughs, giddily, as if this is a lark to both of them. She closes her eyes, goes rigid. He never says anything when it gets to this. He can't speak, she knows, because language will take him out of the state in which it's possible for him to behave like this, will return him to the world and shame.

'Grandpa?' she says, not loudly, sensing movement again out-side her door.

'Aye?' her grandfather calls back. Uncle Cyril releases her – then suddenly draws his right hand across his chest in preparation for belting her. His face is dead except for the top teeth biting the bottom lip, as at the beginning of a violent F or V. The monkey eyes are lifeless.

She doesn't flinch. Closes her eyes and says, conversationally: 'What time do we need to leave tomorrow?'

Her grandfather coughs, approaches the doorway just as Cyril drops his hand and steps back. For a moment, silence, the old man sheepishly deducing. Kate bends and picks the book up, moves round her uncle, puts it in the open trunk, on top of her neatly folded clothes, starched white blouses and blue pinafores, white knee-socks snugly folded into themselves.

'Need to leave around ten,' the old man says. The room's still clogged with the moments before; his croaky voice abraids, beau-tifully as far as Kate's concerned. 'Don't worry, lass, I'm up at cracker dawn any road.'

Cyril looks out of the window. 'No point in calling for Kalia,' he says. 'I've given that little bastard his marching orders.'

Leaving the room he avoids touching the old man in the doorway.

'Here,' her grandfather whispers, producing the letter, sealed and addressed to the Silverses. 'I've signed it for you.'

Stairs, handrails, newels, benches, trestles, desks, kneelers, sills – Jesus and Mary Convent School has been Kate's introduction to things with a sad history of touch. The pathos of these objects is that they stay and you leave. Every year girls' palms and finger-tips and feet and knees, intimacy – then gone. You can feel sorry for a coat-hook, a doorknob, a bowl, a chair. When you sit on the stairs alone with your arms round your shins and your palms or calves on fire from the cane, the dark wood offers you its inarticulate sympathy, a moment you take, consume and forget but which it absorbs and will remember, uselessly, for ever. Some future girl will sit here and feel the same sympathy, years from now. You'll be a part of it, but she won't know and neither will you. That's the objects' sadness, that they connect the private moments of people who will always remain strangers.

Kate goes through the first half of term convinced every day something's going to go wrong. Nightly, when the other girls in the dorm are asleep, she checks that the little bundle of notes (it seems an increasingly paltry sum as the time for flight nears) is safe in its skirting-board cranny, that her locker's stash of tinned sardines and dates and raisins and corned beef and chocolate remains unmolested. These are strange hours, God in frigid vigilance over her. Just give me a chance. Silence. The star eyes unblinking. She reverts to the old prayers. Hail Mary, full of grace, the Lord is with thee. Blessed art thou among women, and blessed is the fruit of thy womb . . .

Eleanor Silvers can't stop yammering about the wedding. ('Silvers', the rumour is, has been strategically altered from the Goan da Silva. If true Eleanor ought by rights to be in the school's other division – perversely called 'English-speaking', to denote pupils who are neither European nor Anglo–Indian, but who none the less speak English. Since her fees are paid promptly, however, the nuns dismiss the rumour.) 'What are you *wearing*?' she asks Kate, the week before they're due to leave.

'My mother's dress. I've told you. White, with red poppies.'

'You should see my frock,' Eleanor says. 'Mummy made it. Lilac, with puff sleeves and a fitted bodice. And the gloves, my God. They're *too* perfect!'

Countless times Kate's on the verge of blabbing: I'm not coming back. One morning in Lahore you'll wake up and I'll be gone. But Eleanor can't be trusted. You tell her a secret and twenty-four hours later it's all over school. Kate imagines the family – these Silverses she's never met – coming to the shocking realization that she's missing. There's the bed cold, no sign; satchel, shoes, clothes, all gone. Eleanor's prim face with its almond eyes and pointy little chin quivering on the edge of tears. She'll think it's her fault. What kind of crazy child did you bring here? Your sister's wedding day, for God's sake. They'll call the police. A telegram will go to the school, and from school to Bhusawal . . .

Just let me do this, Kate thinks, pleads, demands. Just give me a chance. She's waiting for some sign of God's endorsement, a signal, a stroke of luck. But the school, the objects around her, buzz with His ambiguity.

Then, the day before she and Eleanor are due to leave, something happens.

From inside you.

In the toilets, bending to pull up her underpants after a pee, she feels a trickle down her thigh. Looks. Disbelieves.

Blood.

From inside you. Put *your hand there. You'll see.*

Obedient, incredulous, weak-kneed, she touches with her fingertips. Blood again. Knuckles seem to move inside her, the cramped fist of someone who's been asleep and is now awkwardly waking up. Another hot trickle, an intimate warm wet thread as when you feel a tear running down your cheek.

For what feels like a long time (the bell for afternoon lessons rings, to Kate a representative of the old friendly useless world, the world before this – her death, she thinks) she stands trembling in the cubicle, dabbing with her hanky, stopping herself crying.

Bizarrely, Sister Anne knows what she's trying to tell her. She takes Kate to the infirmary and shows her how to fold the cotton square between her legs like a nappy. 'This means you're a young lady now, Katherine, a young woman, do you understand?' Kate doesn't. Sister Anne lowers her voice. '"Unto the woman He said, I will greatly multiply thy sorrow and thy conception,"' she says. '"In sorrow thou shalt bring forth children." This is part of the sorrow, you see? Every month now this'll happen for a few days. It means that when you meet a man and get married you can have a baby. But every month now you'll get a little reminder of Eve's sin.' 'Do the boys get a reminder of Adam's sin?' Kate asks. 'The boys don't,' Sister Anne says in a tone of finality.

'Yes, but *why* does the blood come?' Eleanor Silvers wants to know, that night.

'It's so you can have a baby,' Kate says. This realization, that she's capable (technically, Sister Anne had stressed, big-eyed, index finger raised) of having a baby, has entered her confusedly, like a mild, fuddled demonic possession. She still has no idea how she can have a baby, how a baby gets inside you. It had been utterly incredible. For a few moments, listening, wrapped in the ridiculous cotton nappy, she'd thought Sister Anne had gone mad. But at the same time knew she hadn't, that the shape this garbled knowledge made was distantly familiar, her mother sometimes taking to her bed for a day or two, lying on her side curled up and her father very tender, saying, Poor girl, what can I get you?

'Let me in,' Eleanor says. She's a smart, mercurial, fidgety thing, sassy in the playground but prone to nightmares. One night a year ago she'd woken Kate and asked, tearfully, to get into her bed with her. Kate had been surprised and hadn't liked the idea of anyone else in her bed (the beds were small enough as it was); but she'd been so intrigued by the reduction of cocky bright Eleanor to snivelling pleading Eleanor (and, if she was honest, flattered that Eleanor had come to her) that she'd said all right, and Eleanor had climbed in and snuggled up against her. It's happened three or four times since. Kate doesn't mind. The only danger is both of them sleeping through until the nuns come with the bell for morning prayers. So far, by the grace of some inner clock, they've managed to wake up in time for Eleanor to scoot back to her own bed.

'I don't believe you,' Eleanor says.

'It's true.'

'I'm going to ask my mummy.'

'Don't!' Kate says. No queries that'll draw unnecessary adult Silvers attention. 'You mustn't. It's a private thing.'

Eleanor's quiet for a while, then says: 'I saw Lillian and Anthony kissing and he had his hand up her skirt.' Lillian is the bride-to-be, Anthony the fiancé. 'Lillian was wriggling like she had an itch.'

Kate says nothing. Closes her eyes. The cotton pad isn't comfortable; she can't imagine getting used to it. Sister Anne's given her a dozen, for which she'll have to make room in the already crammed satchel.

'It's what they do,' Eleanor says. 'Boys. Try'n touch you down there.'

Eleanor's brother comes down from Lahore to fetch them. He's a taciturn, bespectacled youth of twenty studying for a physics degree, keeps his nose in books the whole journey. From deep within her current state — rich but unfocused preoccupation — Kate is dimly aware that Eleanor feels cheated, is regretting having asked her to come. She, Eleanor, had been waiting for a mood of anarchic holiday. Instead she's got her boffin brother's indifference and Kate's self-absorption. 'I could have asked Vera, you know,' she says in a huff at Jaipur where, after several hundred miles, she's come close to the end of her patience. 'I thought we were going to have *fun*, for God's sake.' Kate, hauling herself up, determines to make an effort, for an hour or two plies her friend with questions about her family, but sinks back into herself. She doesn't know what's going on, only that something is confusedly coming into being in herself. Her mind returns to a handful of thoughts repeatedly: the blood's warm trickle; her uncle's hand drawn back to hit her; technically it means you can have a baby; you've got so tall, which turned out to be the last words.

She has four days with Eleanor before the wedding, largely spent mooching about, Kate drifting in and out of the here and now, Eleanor in and out of sulks. At night Kate lies awake, rehearsing the moment she knows must come. She sees herself sweeping an empty hotel room, washing dishes, bathing the children of strangers. Practical potentialities creep in and thrill her: the guests will be wealthy. She'll ask someone for domestic work. She'll do anything. She'll be free. It's a matter of days, hours. At night the city murmurs, surely a confirmation? Meanwhile Eleanor sleeps with her mouth open and her limbs thrown wide. There's talk of going to see *Casablanca* (the Metro gets Hollywood movies as they're released) but in the end it doesn't happen. Mostly the girls spend their time lying on their bellies in the garden moving their bare shins back and forth while leafing through Mrs Silvers's old *Photoplays* and *Screen Idols*. Eleanor's mother (by the number of Fonsecas and Devazes and da Souzas and Mesquitas who've descended on the home, there seems little doubt that the Silverses are indeed Goans, not that Kate cares) is a willowy good-looking woman with an elaborate chignon, whose pleasure in her elder daughter's advantageous match (the bridegroom's family owns property and a flour mill) translates into a general goodwill to everyone, flits around the place with a glassy smile that drives Eleanor mad. Mr Silvers, on the other hand, remains in a state of pessimistic anxiety, responds to every hiccup as if it's the catastrophe he's been expecting, the disastrous detail that will bring the whole of his daughter's remunerative future crashing to the ground.

'Anthony's not as handsome as Father Fonseca,' Eleanor says of her soon-to-be brother-in-law. 'Personally I don't know what Lillian sees in him.'

Because she's jealous, Kate knows. The older Silvers sister is a supple girl of twenty-two with her mother's good looks, slender hands and a thick fall of lustrous black hair.

'You can bet when *I* marry,' Eleanor says, 'it'll be abso*lute*ly for love.'

The morning of the wedding Kate wakes late, weak with

nerves. For a while she lies in bed, listening to the traffic and the household's bustle. Until now she's stopped herself noticing the city – even this suburban bit; some instinct has told her not to let the reality of it in until the moment she throws herself on it. But now the moment is almost here she feels the city itself (alerted by God, perhaps) putting out a strand of vague enquiry, as if it's noticed her presence, a new soul among its millions. Who are you? What are you doing here?

Eleanor tries on a dozen different pairs of earrings, clomps rapidly around the upstairs rooms from mirror to mirror in her high heels. They're slightly too big for her, Kate can tell. Mr Silvers keeps screaming at his wife to come and settle the bleddy cook, who despite specific instructions has failed to make any curry puffs. There's a terrible confusion when the gharis come, what feels like an hour of shuffling and reshuffling, of determining who travels with whom, of false starts and forgotten buttonholes, but eventually Kate is allocated a place with cousins from Sukkur, and in a moment (the same moment in which Ross and his friends are setting off for Mrs Naicker's and Ho Fun's) is on her way. Details of the unfamiliar streets are vivid whether she likes it or not: a red and white striped awning; a rickshaw having its buckled wheel changed; two fat ladies waving the procession on with white handkerchiefs; a tiny lone fruit stall crammed with oranges and limes.

The church ceremony goes by Kate in a dream. Again details flare and gleam: the bridegroom's extraordinarily delicate lifting of the veil; Mrs Silvers's hat of pink silk leaves; a brass candle stand when a cloud moves and releases its glow; Eleanor's sister on the arm of her new husband walking back down the aisle with her head bowed but then lifting it and giving a shy smile to Kate thought her but it was someone next to her.

Outside in the church's sprawling front garden where there's endless kissing and handshaking and embracing and kids running around in the sunshine glad only that all the shush, quiet, shush of the church is behind them, Kate in her mother's poppy print dress drifts at the perimeter. Throughout the service she's oscillated between nausea and tremulous excitement. You can bet when *I* marry . . . As an afterthought (slyly, it might have been) Eleanor had said: What about you? Will you marry for love?

The bride and her new husband stand facing each other, her hands in his, for a photograph. It's what you'll never have, Kate tells herself, unless . . .

The thought fizzles out. Your first period. My *what*? she'd asked Sister Anne. Your *menses*, dear. When a girl becomes a woman, don't you see? Very gradually over the last few days (it was happening all the long train journey up here, a gentle insistent transformation somewhere in her middle) the realization that this, her womanhood, her future, is the future she's never been able to quite believe in. Her satchel is packed. The thirty rupees are rolled and rubber-banded in the bottom of her purse. Tonight, in the small hours just before dawn, she'll creep from the Silverses' house and melt away into the city. She looks up at the sky. She'd forgotten it, the purer northern blue, the height of it. She remembers the Quetta winters of her childhood, the nights black and silver, the distant mountains gashed with snow. Her mother in thick socks and with the sleeves of her pink cardigan pulled down over her hands. The wall map in Mr Silvers's study says Quetta's only about 250 miles away. It's never occurred to her that she could go back there, seek out Edwin Hawes (poor Margot gone in the earthquake), ask for help. She remembers the fuss they used to make of her, the reservoir of untapped love their childlessness had left them with. She'd been aware of it, dimly, something she'd had no use for at the time – but when she thinks of it now the memory works like a talisman she never knew she had. Margot used to braid her hair, give her little trinkets to wear. They were kind.

Kate breathes deeply, lets the first filament of freedom settle on

her. Thinks, knowing it's a sentimental indulgence and a provo-
cation: I'm almost home.

'I suppose you think you're bleddy smart, don't you?'

At the voice she goes rigid. Fingers lock round her left arm.
They feel strangely cool. Cyril, standing close behind her, takes a
ceremonial-style step backwards, forces her to step back with him.
There's a line of trees behind them, a narrow avenue of cinnamons
separating the church grounds from a football pitch that's turned
to dust. Three more paces. This is impossible. Her mind begins to
plot the trajectories of explanation – then gives up. The how
doesn't matter. He's here. One way or another he's found out.
The first band of trees is between her and the wedding guests. He
wants them out of sight. She'll never be free of him. This is the
development God's been waiting for. Now that it's here Kate
understands it's been there in potentia for years. Perhaps ever
since she went to Bhusawal.

'You bleddy ungrateful little wretch,' Cyril says, yanking her
round to face him. 'I suppose you think you're the cat that gets the
bleddy cream with this little adventure.' His fingers have tightened
on her bare arm. There'll be bruises, dirty fingerprints. She pulls
against him. He hits her, once, backhanded across the face, the
pinkie ring leaves a scratch like the scar of a struck match. 'You've
got your bleddy granddad to thank. What do you think? What're
the odds? You'd have gotten away with it, madam, but he's sick.
Came to the bleddy school to fetch you, didn't I, like a Joe Soap?
Thenwhat? Oh, no, sir, not here. Up in bleddy La*hore*, if you
please.' He laughs as if genuinely tickled. He *is* pleased, she can
tell, the satisfaction of having at long last a rationale.

Three of the let loose children burst through the trees, one
with a length of pink ribbon clutched in his fist, the other two
chasing, laughing. For a moment his grip loosens. She tears herself away from him and runs, blindly, for what feels like miles, her
chest empty.

Dusty buildings and broad streets funnel into a warren of

narrower ways. There's a rickshaw stand, her purse clutched tight. The Old City, she tells the driver. It's the only destination she can think of. She and Eleanor were supposed to go there with her mother two days ago. In her panic she fishes out a dirty five-rupee note and tries to pay before they've even set off. No, no, miss, when we get there. Don't worry, I give you fair price.

Something is finished in her. The image of the bride and groom standing together for the photograph blooms, repeatedly, in her head.

I told you, God says – and in the moment of hearing this Kate accepts the thought that for a long time, possibly years, has been amorphously present in her head: that as long as Cyril is alive she'll never be free.

It's then, as a brilliantly sunlit silver-domed mosque looms up on her left, that she knows she's going to have to kill him.

CHAPTER NINE

lies

(London, 2004)

What's depressing about Janet Marsh is that she's a much less attractive Tara Kilcoyne. The resemblance (she has the same thin blonde hair and very white skin and an older, snoutier version of Tara's porcine sexiness, but she's carrying weight round her hips and thighs with a posture that says she's down to the last reserves of fighting it, pretty soon she's going to give in to being what the Americans would call a big-assed old broad) shows up my delusions: this is the Tara-type in my league, not Tara. I'm reminded of those people who are obsessed with celebrities to the point where they go out with someone who looks like them, that dismal glamour gap between the lookalike and the real thing.

'Look, as I said in the letter, my father's not up to it. He's eighty-three next month. I did ask him when we got your letter, but he's not interested. I can't believe you've come here, frankly.'

Frankly, neither can I. But I have. I sat on the District Line through Wimbledon all the way into town. Embankment. The walk up Charing Cross Road took me not just through London's after-work disgorgement but past the Limelight, Break for the Border, the George, the Astoria; none what they used to be but the ghosts of Scarlet and those mid-Eighties nights linger . . . Information Management Services turns out to be three slender tinted-window floors in the middle of a long tinted-window block on Rathbone Place. Halogened horseshoe reception desk in what looks like walnut staffed by a freckled woman in a toffee-coloured trouser suit body-guarded by a paunchy six-four black security guard with dark brown outward-pushing lips showing enough moist pink gum to make me think whether I like it or not of the close-ups in inter-racial porn. It's always the same reception flirtation double act, the black guy, the white woman, *that* whole thing.

No, I don't have an appointment, but could you tell her I'm the person who wrote to her about her father? A considerable pause, all this going from receptionist to PA to Janet Marsh and back again. The security guard makes a quick silent assessment – not for my threat potential but for my racial type – concludes (losing interest immediately the conclusion's made) that the dark blood's out of Asia or maybe South America, nothing African, no sexual competition; the women who go for black guys aren't interested in Pakis or Wops or Spics, and this is even before we bother with my being a short-arse he could beat up while smoking a spliff and drinking a cup of tea and languidly porking Freckles here. Eventually, a little sandy-headed nod and the phone returned to its cradle, Go up. First floor, someone'll come out for you.

'I know,' I say to Janet Marsh, once I'm admitted to the adytum of her fat-carpeted and low-lit office. 'I understand. It's just that your father's perspective would be invaluable: he was in India, mixed with Indians, wrote about them, and had his books pub-lished—'

'Book.'

'Had his *book* published in the UK at an incredibly interesting time, both in terms of what the changing boundaries were in the pulp fiction market but most significantly at a time when "race" and its representation was becoming a huge social and cultural issue.'

This feels the way I imagine it feels if you have to blurt out an ad hoc explanation to your wife of what you're doing in bed with her best friend: Well, you see, she's got this pain in her shoulder and there's this Balinese yoga technique that involves . . .

'I'm sorry,' I say. 'You must think I'm eccentric. Possibly mad. Believe it or not, people write PhD theses about these things and I'm one of those people. I realize I'm being a nuisance. He really wasn't interested?'

Janet Marsh is a businesswoman. The first thing was for her to decide whether I had power over her or she over me. She's done that. She has power over me. Money. Also control over what I want, her father. I could beat her up, true, but she's already decided I don't have what it takes for that; I'd always be too scared of the consequences. Therefore a layer of her physical formality drops away. I get the feeling there's something else – some big thing – on her mind. She sits back in her spaceshippish leather swivel chair, pinches the bridge of her nose, moves her fingertips out around the shallow orbitals, exhales. It's been, I infer, a *day*. Her make-up has the look of fine fracture, erosion. Under the short pinstripe jacket her black silk blouse buckles when she reclines, flashing a slab of burgundy-bra'd breast. Despite her desk, my only slightly less commanding chair, a coat-stand and the two oxblood leather couches at right angles in a corner behind me, the office still feels roomy. There's a wall-mounted (and muted) television to my right, showing CNN footage of George W. Bush at a press conference splashed by camera flash, speaking first with the inimitable expression fusing tickled smugness and intellectual vacancy, then, both hands gripping the edges of his lectern, animatedly delivering what might be news of the Second Coming. The feeling I always get when I see him (or for that matter any other person active in the political sphere) bubbles up:

this is your world and you're watching it go to shit . . . Yes, I know. But . . .

Janet Marsh squeezes her eyes closed for a second, gives a slight grimace, then opens them. 'How do you even know about my dad's book? It was *donkeys*' years ago.'

Something is definitely going on for her other than me and my visit. I've only been in the room five minutes but it's long enough to know there's been some seismic shift (today?) in comparison to which I'm a detail, tolerable only in its aftermath. Any other day I'd have been turned away via telephonic proxy at reception. I wonder if she's just started an affair, or won the lottery, or knocked someone down in her car, or been told the lump's benign, or had some sort of Blakean vision under one of London's streetlamps.

'I came across a copy in a second-hand bookshop in Wimbledon,' I tell her. 'Just blind luck, really, unless you believe in there being a Divine Plan.'

I meet her eyes. She's looking at me but still, manifestly, suffering or relishing the effects of that earlier event. Whether she's conscious of it or not, these effects have drawn her mouth into a slight smile. Oi, I want to say. Look at me *properly*. I'm sitting here lying to you. I have a scheme. My father wants *revenge*. Pay attention for Christ's sake.

'I'm sorry,' she says, coming back into current time and space with a visible effort. 'I really don't think my dad wants to talk to anyone. He's got his little routine and he doesn't like it disturbed. I don't' – she frowns with pleasant incomprehension rather than suspicion, some of the faculties switching back on – 'I don't really see what you'd expect to get from talking to him, anyway. The whole thing sounds a bit . . .' She doesn't finish, offers instead the crumpled mercantile smile of pity for the harmless, unremunerative (but, if she thinks about it too long, annoying) world of academia. The whole thing sounds a bit small and pointless, she means. I don't blame her. What was I thinking? I should have just tailed her. I should have gone in for surveillance, which is what

I'm going to have to do now in any case; a joyless prospect, first because now she knows what I look like, which will make shadowing her tricky, and second because reality's narowed my scope for whatever fantasy I might have projected on to her: she's no longer a blank canvas.

'Do you mind my asking,' I say, 'how good your dad's memory is? I mean, hypothetically, would I be able to have a conversation with him about his past? About the book, I mean?'

She'd leaned forward, elbows on desk, hands (which without the vampiric nails would be mannish) toying with a corpulent fountain pen to give me the previous brush-off; now she sits back again and relaxes. A soft double chin. 'His memory's all right,' she says. 'Ish. I mean, lousy for present-day things, short-term, but, yeah, you could have a conversation. It's not that, it's just he doesn't like his routine interfered with. It'd be a bother to him, you know? Sorry.'

'I understand,' I say, raising my hands. 'No problem. Just thought I'd try, you know. It would have been . . . Well, never mind. I'm sorry to have—'

There's a knock at the door.

'Yes?' Janet Marsh says.

The door opens and a sharp-faced girl in her twenties with short and complicatedly cut black and gold hair pops her head round it. 'Oh, sorry,' she says to Janet. 'All right if I shove off?'

'Yes yes you've got your thing tonight,' Janet says, getting up. 'I forgot.'

'See you Monday,' the girl says, and without looking at me withdraws her head and closes the door.

'I'll tell you what,' Janet Marsh says, as I, taking the hint, get to my feet. 'I'll ask him again. If the answer's still no, then that's your lot. Okay?'

That she walks me out of the office and that we board the lift together is further evidence of something else on her mind. You don't share space with a stranger unless you have to. My ego angles for the flattering reading, that she, Janet, is attracted to me. She is, after all, sufficiently not good-looking, sufficiently not Tara. But that isn't it. She's pleasantly throbbing from something big having been lately settled. Her limbs (I imagine her bare white arms and thighs possessed of Botticellian asymmetry and heft) have shucked their tensile apparatus; I can't help thinking of a horse walking free of its harness, the giant, sad liberty. She's almost, but not quite, too tired to enjoy it.

'It's really just a perpetually updated database,' she says, when I ask her what IMS does. 'We match the top advertisers with the top five hundred UK companies. The database means any brand manager can pinpoint any advertising executive – and vice versa, obviously – at the touch of a button. Clients are subscribers. You pay so much a year, you get twenty-four/seven online access to the information you need. The object was to make a tool the industries couldn't afford not to have.'

'It'll probably come as no surprise to you that I have absolutely no idea what any of that means.' Since I'm playing the academic I try to sound the part.

She's not too far gone to smile, though with obvious tokenness. The whites of her eyes are pinkish. Suddenly my own eyes feel exhausted. 'You see a TV commercial,' she says, 'and you want the person or team who designed it for your new product. The database will tell you who they are, where they are, and how much it's likely to cost. Or you're an ad company. The database means you'll be among the first to know if Mars is planning a new chocolate bar, which means you'll be among the first to pitch a campaign. Yes?'

'Incredible. Who thinks of these things?'

'Me and my ex-husband.'

'Looks like you're doing well.'

Her response is a lifted chin and a wobbly smile in the manner of Goldie Hawn.

(I remember Scarlet years ago wondering aloud why writers

still bothered describing a character's physical appearance. There are only so many types of face, she said, and we've seen them all on screen. Why don't they just say, She was a bit like a young Sharon Stone, but with dark hair? Or he was like Larry Hagman with a beard? She insisted that everyone could be seen, if they had to, in terms of looking like someone famous. In the pub she'd go through every person; she wasn't satisfied until she'd wrung resemblance to someone famous from each of them. It morphed, naturally, into the game we came to call Celebrities. 'Rutger Hauer's over by the bar,' she'd say quietly, interrupting me. I'd have to turn and look. The object was to find someone who looked like a famous person only if you applied the widest and most absurd latitude. Thus 'Rutger Hauer' would be a rheumy octogenarian with a rinsed quiff, dentures and a cravat, but also with, if you really reached, a look of Rutger Hauer.)

A wobbly smile. To indicate what? Irony? Understatement? Either way this smile is the first that brings her — that is, *her*, Janet, the woman rather than the professional — into play. It's the first acknowledgement of me — that is, *me*, Owen, the man rather than the irritating chore — she's offered. It's such a shift — the guaranteed aphrodisiacal clout of moving from the formal to the intimate — that I get a little twinge of lust. All her heavy-bodied appeal suddenly intrudes. The long day's left horizontal creases in her pin-stripe skirt just below the abdominal tyre. Her armpits will have the rousing mix of deodorant and sweat, the nyloned zones their own foxy heat, all her body's responses to the day's provocations, the spent chemicals, a lovely text written in the hours since her shower this morning.

'Oh, we've done okay,' she says. 'It was timing, really. It's always timing.'

On the other hand, our briefly meeting and hurriedly looking away eyes concede, she did say 'ex'. She didn't need to say that. In the glance she seems hyperconscious of our erotic potential. It's not me. It's her mood, the post-ravished state she's been left in by whatever it was. I know it's not me. She knows, too. We know a lot in this lift, which has one mirrored back wall and three others of something which looks like black onyx but which I assume isn't. Like the rest of the corporate world it smells of non-smoking: Pledge, floor wax, Windolene. I imagine a hidden camera sensitive not to infrared but to unsaid things registering all ours like a cat's cradle of lasers stretched between us. Just as the lift comes to a stop on the ground floor Janet Marsh and I glance at each other in the mirror a second time. Another wobbly smile and the watery eyes awake. The space is so confined it's as if we've just flashed our parts at each other. I'm convinced that if I ask her what, exactly, I'm doing here she'll have forgotten. The doors open. I do the after-you gesture and she steps out into the gleaming atrium. Freckles has gone home. The black security guard stands alone with his back to us looking out of the tinted automatic doors like someone longing for his lost home on another planet. He turns, smiles gummily, lazily at thick-calved Janet *tuck-tucking* towards him on her high heels. He points a gizmo at the keypad and does a satirical doorman bow as we pass. 'Goodnight, Mrs Marsh.'

'Goodnight, Tony.'

I nod an acknowledgement to him but get only a raised eyebrow in return. You porking her? Jesus Christ. Little beige fucker like you? World's gone mad.

Two strange things happen out in Rathbone Place. The first is that Janet Marsh and I stand for a few moments, smiling and saying yes thanks okay fine and phatically not quite saying good-bye, though there's a handshake and me backing and nodding like a lobotomized dog and her standing in the black overcoat with the soft pale-blue scarf loosely looped and one ungloved hand (the size of which surprised me when we shook, its broad, plump, warm apricot-handcreamed palm I imagined manfully masturbating me) holding her tan leather satchel and looking, now that the cold air has tightened her, statuesque rather than baggy. The second is that

I end up so close to the kerb that the wing mirror of a slowly passing lorry cracks the back of my head.

There's a split second of atomic red-black detonation, time enough to register the sound of the blow – a deafening and censorious *bok* – then I'm out.

When I come to I find myself sprawled on the freezing pavement with Janet down on her haunches trying to roll me from my front on to my side so she can get a look at my face.

'Oh, my God,' she says. 'Are you all right?'

It's a strange feeling to be suddenly whipped out of time then rushed back in. I'm very aware, as I take my first inhalations, of the sensuous secrets of the pavement, which it turns out have remained faithful these years, the glittering pixels and whiff of stone and old gum delivering without rebuke all the wealth of my childhood they've held in trust. A beautiful peaceful salving thing, lying on the pavement. No wonder drunks do it so much. And it's free.

'Look at me. Are you all right?'

I blink, open my mouth, experience a curious inner delay and a second wallop of that red-blackness precursory to oblivion. I resist, hear myself say, 'Jesus Christ,' from a distance away, but there's distraction in the form of Janet's complex perfume and from this angle large nostrils and that doughy double chin. I lift my head and my face bumps the soft weight of her breasts. She's been looking into the lorry's slipstream at the shrinking number plate I know intuitively she's missed. I hear the driver downshift, slow, round the corner, pull away. Compensation (against which concept even this state of near unconsciousness isn't proof) offers a few sparks, then fizzles like a dud.

She ignores the breast bump, helps me up on to my left elbow – then remembers (as do I, with the first rush of nausea) that maybe I shouldn't try to get up too quickly.

'Actually, keep still a minute,' she says. 'Let me look at your head. Christ, I can't believe that just happened.'

Since being able to see is makes me feel sick I close my eyes, but am immediately yanked into a waltz that make me feel sicker. I open them again. The street's like a bit of looped footage: it lurches from right to left, flickers, jumps back. I know the thing to do is keep watching; it'll slow and, like the drunk's spinning room, eventually stop. But tracking it makes my eyes feel like they might vomit all on their own.

'Anything?' I ask. Her big black nyloned knees tick as she adjusts position to get a better look at my head.

'Well, you're not bleeding,' she says. 'But there's a lump already. I'm going to call an ambulance.'

'No, no, Christ. I'm all right. I don't need an ambulance.'

'Look, you can get an aneurysm from a bang on the head like that.'

'I'm fine. Just give me a sec.'

'You'll be concussed. Let me call an ambulance. Are you going to throw up?'

'I might. Look, please don't call an ambulance.' I don't know why I'm so resistant, since I feel I might, actually, need one. Some televisually conditioned reflex, presumably. Whenever someone in a drama suggests calling an ambulance the injured person always says no, no, I'm fine.

She's got her mobile out and her thumb poised for 999 (I wonder if she's ever had to dial it before) but I lift my hand and place my fingers on her gloveless wrist. 'Seriously,' I say, 'I don't need an ambulance. Honestly. You'll be depriving someone who does. Put the phone away.'

We look at each other. It's exciting to both of us that something's happened. Her sore eyes are wide and her lips are parted. I imagine kissing her will taste of stale humanity, though it's nice to think of the chill evening just now passing through her lips and nostrils. Behind her head the buildings of Rathbone Place are half attending to us, half given over to the deepening cold and darkening sky.

★

'I've got a confession to make,' she says, when I return to the table with drinks, Laphroaig for me and a white wine spritzer for her. I know the way she's seeing this: her first act of experimental indulgence in the world after the liberating trauma, whatever it was. She's pretty sure that she can have me, that enough of the goods are intact, that like her I've been turned on by the accident, or else why bother suggesting the drink?

Her car, an Audi, was in a car park just off Tottenham Court Road. The compromise after I queasily got to my feet was that she would drive me home, via hospital if I showed en route signs of being about to die. Via, as it turns out, Neon Hallelujah, since when we pulled up at the lights opposite it and I said let's go and have a drink she said okay, with a smile compressed to acknowledge the inevitability of the last hour's drift – okay, yes, it's *this* – and pulled over. The first intimation had been when I'd said well only if it's on your way (knowing it couldn't be) and she'd said well it isn't but I think I should and I didn't object further and we let the truncation and silence stand for a while before I said where *do* you live, and she said, not surprisingly, west. Holland Park. Handy for my dad; he's in Shepherd's Bush. Everything after that – not that there was much; she drove confidently, fast, largely without speaking – had carried Eros' imprimatur. The glaring confirmation was that beyond his postcode we didn't discuss her father, *Raj Rogue*, the proposed interview. The mutually intuited danger was that, if we did, something (the truth, for example) might emerge which would compromise her ability to have sex with me, now, with dreamy casualness, courtesy of the long day's surreal momentum, its surprising amoral necessities.

We sat in the Audi in what might have looked to an observer like a state of mild trance, me, driver of Maude's cast-off '92 Fiesta, unused to top-of-the-line car interiors, thinking among other things that now they looked like the cockpit of the Millennium Falcon, and how quickly that had happened, but then no, not quickly, because *Star Wars* was almost thirty years ago, her with her slightly bulbous wet and pink-prone eyes drinking the road, smiling very slightly as the reality of whatever freedom she'd inherited today shaped its current around her, said yes, there's all sorts you can do now, screw strangers, just relax into it. This is the brave new world.

I sit down, hand her her drink, take a sip of mine and wait for the single malt flower between the lungs which opening says *shshsh*, be calm, all is well. There it is, testifying once again to the reliability of alcohol. I imagine it like a Buddhist lotus, a gorgeous manifestation of inner peace smack in the middle of the heart chakra. Neon Hallelujah's dark and quiet around us. It's still early. Rowena's lighting the table candles. The execrable Dido warbles as with deformed oestrogen from the speakers. Janet's been to the loo while I ordered, touched up her make-up, Optrexed her eyes by the revived look.

'I've got a confession to make.' She's smiling again, or rather, with head down and fringe hanging, making a show of not being able to keep a straight face.

'So have I,' I say. 'But you first.'

'I sold the company.'

'What do you mean?'

'I mean today. Signed on the dotted line. Another company, an American company, bought IMS. They'll make the whole thing international.'

No further explanation needed. That crack from the wing mirror was the icing on the cake, the event that plucked one of the myriad potentialities from the ether and handed it to her as an actual. Go to bed with him if you want to.

'Which means .`. . you've made a lot of money?'

'Well, yeah. Some. The main thing is I'm out. I don't have to think about it any more, thank God.'

This is more than a warning for me not to set any store by what might follow; it's also a reassurance that she's not, as I might have been wondering, mad.

I raise my tumbler. 'In that case congratulations.'

She does smile, properly this time, with a little access of genuine pleasure when we clink. Her left upper canine is grey. The promise, as ever, is finite, but there's no doubt I want her. Her look suggests a repertoire of skills (acquired with the sad diligence of women who know the way the world goes, who'd rather have such skills and not need them than need such skills and not have them) and beyond the repertoire an uneroded part of her sexual self she's been consciously or unconsciously saving in the hope that one day she'll have the time and space (not angry, not depressed, not bored, not stressed, not exhausted) to use it. If we go to bed together she'll be more than sufficiently self-involved for me to enjoy her as an object.

'What's your confession?' she says.

Dad, listen to this. You'll love it. I'm fucking Skinner's daughter.

'I work here,' I tell her.

Vince, God bless his homosexual soul, is already out when I call him before leaving Neon Hallelujah, and won't be back until the small hours unless he gets lucky (or unlucky, as we've started saying) in which case not until tomorrow. 'There's double *Friends* and double *Sex in the City*,' he reminds me, 'so don't forget to set the video. Who is she, by the way?' 'A rich English businesswoman, but it's a long story.'

I trip, with clatter, skid and comedy flail, over the bootscrape on the way into the flat, which makes her laugh. (The second drink was a scotch and she drank it pretty fast, still a dash of Dutch courage required. Don't you have plans for this evening? I'd asked her, eye to eye. She shook her head: the plans were dismissible. After the second drink she said, I'm off to the loo and then I'll drive you home. She said it with almost innocent briskness. My compressed call to Vince in the five minutes she was gone. When she came out and our eyes met across the room she raised her heavy chin and looked sidelong then back at me and that was the signal that yes, the plans had gone.) 'Are you always this clumsy?' she asks in the hall, after I've closed the door behind her.

'Only when I'm not one bit nervous.'

The door's closing has given us sudden shocking still privacy after the warm bar and the cold street and the flow of traffic around the car. It's as if we're in the lift again. Now that it's come to it having sex with her (going into my room with her, undressing, seeing all the secrets of her broad body spoiled in a twinkling), if having sex with her is what this is, now that it's come to this it seems ugly and absurd; if I'm not careful, hilarious. But that's the way it always is if I let my mind go. She hasn't done quite *this* before but she's had sex with people she's not been sure about, encounters in the raw space she's had to inhabit around the berg of the failed marriage. I try it, mentally, as an aphrodisiac, Mrs Janet Marsh. Kept the name but not the ring. A ring would have helped, seeing it on her finger when her hand grasped my cock or (with me guiding her wrist) fluttered at the lips of her cunt, the little gold band saying broken promises, failure, death. (This is a recent reversal in my life. It used to be sex made me think of death. Now death makes me think of sex. With Scarlet, but since she's gone . . .)

It's only a few seconds since my line about not being nervous but the silence has fattened between us. Neither of us is up to protracted flirtation. The obvious immediate future, in which I take her coat and laptop and she follows me into the kitchen and I open a bottle of the for-special-occasions Châteauneuf-du-Pape and we clink and drink and have to keep thinking of things to say which will somehow enhance the idea that it's going to be a good and natural and sensually life-affirming thing for us to go to bed together, this obvious immediate future is in the silence with us like a lump of dangerous energy. The hall's bits and pieces — coat-stand, fake Persian runner, occasional table with topaz-shaded lamp, Maude's startled self-portrait in oils from art college days – are vivified and attentive. This isn't what they're used to. It gives me a flicker of pride that I've surprised them.

Janet opens her mouth to say something, thinks better of it, risks one final look at me; if I can't make it fly from this it won't fly at all. There's enough of her unspontaneous self available to haul her off, more than enough memories of men, the countless ways they disappoint. Seeing all this I move towards her and, since she doesn't flinch, lower my head to kiss her. There's a split second before she lifts her mouth, cooperatively, then we are, with uncertain pressure and what feels like flaccid lips, kissing, in the flavours of whisky and nicotine and caffeine, the taste, I tell myself, of excitement trying to struggle up through fatigue. Her head when I open my eyes looks huge, great scrolls of mascara'd lash and powdery blue eyelid, tiny white hairs, thread veins, around all the pale blonde corona like a signal of warrantless optimism. Her mouth's bigger than mine, with a masculine tongue that moves uncertainly, sometimes seeming to back up. We'll have to go fast from here if the moment isn't to start leaking spontaneity, but it's apparent to both of us that a filmic hump right here up against the cold wall, trousers dropped, pinstripe skirt hoiked, isn't an option. We don't have the momentum of passion and her body's already told mine it's too heavy for that sort of thing or that I'm not heavy enough. I slide my hands inside her coat and jacket, feel through the silk blouse her big rib-cage and strong back. The sexual clinician in me says stocky, keep the high heels on to lengthen those legs, but knows it won't happen, they'll have to come off to release the nylons, which I doubt are stockings, never mind never mind just get on with it.

The terrible question of what to say when the kiss comes to its conclusion starts bothering us while the kiss is still going on, makes me think whether I like it or not of that poor bastard who died of a heart attack applauding Stalin because no one once the applauding started wanted to be the first to stop. None the less we separate an inch or two, kiss lengthily again, her tongue livelier now, letting me know that assertiveness is one way she can go, if need be. We do the little after-kisses, as if plucking crumbs from each other's lips, the friendliness or suggested familiarity of which jars for both of us. Younger versions of ourselves would be tempted to let the first notes of self-congratulation in: *When did you first realize? I had a feeling about you. You must have known.* But we're not young any more, make no assumptions. This is just something that's going on at the moment and could in the next moment or the next or the next be knocked into inertia by any one of a thousand little miscues. Best not to say anything. I nearly say that out loud: best not to say anything.

'Where's your bedroom?' she says.

'I'll show you.'

'I need another drink.'

'There's wine or whisky.'

'Whisky.'

'I've got grass if you prefer.'

'Grass?' Then she understands. 'Oh. No, I don't have that. It gives me palpitations.'

She moves away from me and goes to the bedroom door. I thank God for the tidiness gene I've inherited from my mother. Bed's made, laundry's basketed, CDs are cased and shelved, ashtrays empty, porn stashed in the bottom drawer of the dresser, though Janet's past surprise at that sort of thing. *Lesbian Ass Suckers 6.* I imagine her tired shrug. She's one of the women it's old hat to, the way men are. She knows sex with them is always going to be a negotiation with all that rubbish.

I watch her push the bedroom door open and peer inside.

'It's okay,' I say, passing her on the way to the kitchen. 'It's safe to go in.'

In the kitchen I make two quick Jameson's on the rocks, burra pegs, as Pasha would say (Skinner sits shrivelled somewhere in a winged chair waiting for me, for us, but I don't want to think about it now; enough of Janet has got through to me to make me feel guilty about the *Raj Rogue* subterfuge), and turn the central heating up. She's still at the bedroom door looking in when I return, still with her coat on. Her laptop case stands in the middle of the hall. I hand her the tumbler, and here we are clinking and drinking after all. I squeeze past her, go into the bedroom, turn the bedside lamp on.

'Not stopping?' I ask.

She smiles, puts her drink down on the dresser, slips the coat and jacket from her shoulders. I move close to her, put my hands on the soft curve of her waist. I'm wondering if she's going to want to do anything, go to the bathroom, put a diaphragm in, lay down some rules, I don't take it up the arse, you can't come in my mouth. I remember the idealistic days when it was impossible to keep a hard-on through the dismal palaver with the condom. She lifts her mouth again and we kiss. Our breath can't be great but alcohol and that bowl of Neon Hallelujah's marinated olives have left us on level terms. The curve of her waist feels good and female between my hands, gives me the first real twinge since the lift. It's going to work, what she's got, the heavy whiteness, all the salient womanly bits just past their best, a comma of Andrex left behind in the anus's crinkle saying shit, human, unethereal. That's the tack to take, that and the self-made money, the commercial boredom I'll imagine having detected like a tired odour in her armpits, navel, crotch. Oh yes.

'No one's going to walk in, are they?' she says.

'No.'

The radiator clanks, twice. Heat's entering the room like a supernatural manifestation. Awkwardly, since I still have my hands on her waist, she twists to retrieve her drink from the dresser, downs it in one, shudders as it makes its fiery way to her guts.

'Okay then,' she says, and kisses me again.

Skinner's daughter. The soap-operatic beauty of this is like a heaped platter of vulgar food from which I could, if I wanted to, gorge until I was sick. I don't want to think about it. There are other things to think about. The dilemma at our age is whether to attempt the minefield of mutual undressing. She surprises me: when I sit on the edge of the bed and pull my shoes off she straddles my lap. Her weight's exciting, suggests (I don't know if she intends it, likes it, or has been forced by physical type into recognizing it as her strong suit) that submissiveness from me might be the way to go. The natural place for my hands is her bum, so they go there, and after a succession of more aggressive kisses push the pinstripe skirt up to reveal, as suspected, tights rather than stockings. She reaches down and pulls my sweater and T-shirt with a crackle of static off over my head. The exposure of my nipples (there's the awful second of darkness just before sweater and T-shirt clear my head) makes me think of the comedic gap between Brad Pitt's chest in *Meet Joe Black* and mine, here, now. One of Janet's shoes falls from her foot to the floor with a clomp. I reach up for her breasts, risk the blouse buttons, by the grace of God get all four undone without feeling time too loudly passing. A slight brief frown of excitement wrinkles her powdered brow.

As if with telepathic agreement to quit while we're ahead, we roll, kiss and separate to remove more clothes, socks and jeans in my case, blouse, bra and tights in hers. We do it quickly because to do it slowly will remind us that we're complete strangers. Under the duvet (which will be too hot in a minute) we lie on our sides facing each other – which we're not ready for and so kiss again with ungenuine urgency, teeth bumping.

I think, as Janet Marsh reaches down and pulls my underpants off, of writing a novel narrated by a double bed; that's the sort of thing you've got to do these days, Nick Gough told me. Rain rattles on the window pane, says yes it's bleak to scrape through the world alone, we move forward into darkness and darkness closes behind us. I think of Vince out there in the hollow of Friday night, imagine him laughing in a twinkling bar, feel such a surge of affection for him I nearly lose my erection.

While I kiss down the length of Janet Marsh's torso Scarlet's retribution theory flutters in and out of my head: colonial bas-tardry takes erotic revenge, fucks England, Great White Male reinvented for heterosexual accommodation as Great White Bitch. Janet certainly is white, with veins showing in the loose-knit belly and breasts. It occurs to me that my dad will disapprove. Cheh, that bugger's flesh and *blood*? The rain is a sad intelligence against the house. Janet Marsh is sad, too, I decide, underneath the new adventurous madness to which her wealth has entitled her. As I pull the duvet down and she bends one knee (the legs make a tri-angle, the left straight, the right with the knee as apex) I think: You can't hide sadness. You can't hide sadness and you can't hide fear of death. Her current posture reminds me of those Victorian etchings, *Britannia and Her Empire*. We're missing, one at her blonde head, the other at her formidable feet, the two smiling female representatives of India and Africa, brown bodies draped with fruit, silks, jewels, ivory.

These and other thoughts twitter. It takes a silent while to get the functional measure of each other. What we do (reciprocally) orally we do with learned patience and calculating hesitations. I haven't gone this carefully or slowly since Scarlet. It becomes, in my mind, a sort of ethical project, to get Janet Marsh turned on. In the elusive way of these things it's the breath from her saying, quietly, 'That's it,' close to my glans that at a stroke turns *me* on, which in spite of everything I'm not expecting.

'Have you got something?'

Unsixty-nined our perspiring faces meet and surprise each other. She means a condom. With someone else I might make a joke – you mean, like the clap? – but not with her. We're not ready for jokes. The condoms are in the bedside drawer. I've never been one for having a prophylactic put on me by a woman. The idea that something so manifestly unerotic can be made part of foreplay is well-meaning Family Planning clinic idiocy. But she takes the foil packet, slides down, administers a languorous kiss and deftly rubbers me. I now know that after fucking her I'm going to want to fuck her again, in a different position. In all the different positions. Which will mean more time together. Which will mean hoping she doesn't leave straight away. Which will mean disappointment if she does.

She's heavy and soft-hipped underneath me. The large breasts have a look of fatigue. She's away to one side watching but occasionally returns to within herself, looks out at me with what seems genuine unanalytical imprisonment in the moment. God knows whether it's doing anything for her down there. Her getting-pleasure face – slight frown, flared nostrils – is like a little girl's you've-offended-me face, but I've seen the expression on other women's faces before, that hurt look as if the pleasure's an affront or a perplexing betrayal. It's another while before we are, actually, fucking. But eventually, if she's to be believed, we get into a rhythm.

Not that she's going to come like this, I can tell. (When you've seen as many lasses as I have nowhere near comin', I've told Vince, in the northern stand-up voice we use for such things, you get to recognize the luke.) 'Do you want to be on top?' I ask, depressed by the sound of my voice. Her nod is revealingly urgent. We manoeuvre carefully so I don't slip out. Now that she can use her hands on herself she releases the remaining inhibitions, incrementally, until after a few minutes I might as well be a waxwork. Her chin goes up, shows me otherwise private horizontal creases in the soft white meat of her throat, and she does, with a modest quartet of shudders, come. Followed sixty seconds later, after a heavy roll back into our original position, by me.

After several minutes she says: 'Well.'

I've rolled off her on to my back, arms out, muscles unstrung, post delicious crucifixion. The thing, both of us know, would be for her to turn towards me, rest one hand on my chest and her head on my shoulder or in the crook of my arm the way couples in films do. But it would connote a tenderness we're not going anywhere near. I'm divided between the reflex to get her up, dressed, out of here so I can sit in peace with a drink and a fag and think about it, and the novelty of having someone – anyone – to share a night with.

'Thank you,' I say.

She laughs, once, with contented dog-tiredness. 'You're welcome. And thank *you*.'

'You're losing your voice.'

'I've been talking all day. All year it feels like.'

'Do you want something for it? We've probably got something.'

She swallows. 'Don't bother. You like it at first, anyway, sounding not yourself.'

These are the first notes in an improvisation, seeing where it'll go. The rain's hurried static says stay indoors, leave outside to the night's cold, rough gods. I think again of Vince and all the other poor bastards still with Friday's black hollows and small hours to deal with. If we were twenty years younger I'd ask her what she was thinking and she'd say you want me gone, which would either start something or stop it starting. I can, however, feel her thinking that I want her to go. I can feel her lazily in her new freedom thinking gently, Oh, well, fuck him, just give me a few minutes.

'I'm starving,' I say. 'You must be, too.'

She smiles, closes her eyes. This not getting up and going is like ignoring the clock in the morning, the moments of denial melting on contact like snowflakes you've put out your hand to catch. Then I remember she's done with all that for a while, having to get up and go somewhere. I wonder how much the Americans paid for her company.

'I'm starving and exhausted,' she says.

'In which case food and rest,' I say, balking at saying food and sleep, though the thought of us passing the night in my bed excites me, sharing the tossed journey through dreams. Surely after everything that's happened there'll be dreams? 'What would you like?' I ask.

'Tea and toast.'

'Well, that's available.'

'You don't have to.'

'It's on its way.'

'What do I have to do?'

'Nothing. Lie there and don't get dressed.'

She swallows again, enjoying the soreness. Thinks about it. 'Okay,' she says.

'Promise you won't put your clothes on.'

'I promise I won't put my clothes on.'

After the tea and toast we have sex again. I come before her and have to get her off first with my hand, then with my mouth. She can have three or four or five one after the other, it transpires. 'This is why you didn't want me to put my clothes on, I now see,' she says, which makes me like her. The tiredness and having arrived late at her freedom make her sound wise. I get up again and make, since I can, farfalle with smoked salmon, lemon, cream and fresh dill. There's a bottle of Jacob's Creek chardonnay in the fridge that's been there for God knows how long, since Vince and I only ever drink red, but now it's just the thing. We eat in bed.

'I don't do this very often,' she says.

'Go to bed with strangers?'

'Eat in bed. With or without strangers. This is delicious, by the way.'

After this second meal we make each other come again, with a meandering self-involved slowness that borders on the meditative. No more, our bodies agree. We've tasted the sweet fruits that grow in that narrow margin between satiation and disgust. Besides, my cock's starting to smart.

'I'm taking it for granted that you're not planning on going anywhere,' I say. My head rests just below her navel. Her pubic thatch is thin, almost a mohican, damp-darkened but in any case not quite the blonde of her head. The marshy odour of our excess wafts up from her flattish cunt, a hint of brine, tinned pears, wet peat, just the right side of unpleasant.

'Eh?'

'I mean, I'd like it if – assuming you don't have to be anywhere else – you stayed here tonight.'

'Oh,' she says. 'Well, I suppose I could. I can't drive, anyway.'

All the drinks, of course. That must have registered. 'Thank God it's Saturday tomorrow,' I say.

'Every day's going to be Saturday for me for a while.'

'What will you do?'

'I don't know. Not get up till noon. Have long baths. Go on holidays. Lose some weight.'

I'm not keen on this line. My own fault, bringing up the Future in the shape of tomorrow. It pulls the shadow of our context over us, how we met, my letter, her father. My father. The fucking *Cheechee Papers*.

'What's your thing about, really?' she asks. She means, since her radar's live, too, the mythical PhD thesis.

'Do you really want to know? It's pretty boring.'

'Go on, I'll stop you when I'm bored.'

'It's about . . . the way popular culture – in this case, pulp fiction – presents the foreign or the exotic as a frame within which moral behaviour excusably changes.'

'Okay, I'm bored.'

'Thank God for that.'

'I don't have brain,' she croaks. 'Not that kind.'

'No, you have the kind that enables you to retire by the time you're however old you are.'

'I'm forty-two and it's easiest if you just say nothing because if you're lying I'll know and if you're not I won't believe you.'

I think about that for a while, unpack it, then say: 'Okay.' It didn't pass me by that she chose the Winnie-the-Pooh idiom of 'having brain'. A little invitation to intimacy which made me, since I can't help myself with such things, suddenly think we might be able to have a relationship. Then immediately think, No, we couldn't. I wouldn't be enough for her. And the baggy body would get me down in about two weeks.

'And you work at that bar?'

'Yes.'

'Wouldn't it be easier just to teach?'

'Actually, I like working there. I like the staff. Obviously they come and go, but there are periods when it feels like a little family.' I'm not helping myself with any of this. Winnie-the-Pooh notwithstanding, Janet Marsh will, I suspect, tolerate only so much namby-pambyism. In the end she wants a man who can change a tyre and punch some other fucker's lights out. I don't blame her. If I was a woman I'd want one like that myself. All this cooking and having brain is going to be of limited use here. There was a time back in the Eighties when you got into the pants of educated girls by being sardonically unmasculine but those days are gone, and in any case Janet doesn't have that kind of education. I nearly blurt out that I write porn as Millicent Nash for Sheer Pleasure, but that's more namby-pambyish than cooking. Besides which, my Sheer Pleasure career is over. There was a message on the phone from Louisa Wexford: 'I can't believe you're choosing to let it be like this, Owen, but I'm afraid if you look at paragraph 7.2 in the contract . . .' I keep asking myself why I stopped halfway through *Bound to Please* (the last, truncated utterance of which was, appositely enough, 'Jacqui felt her anus yawning') but I'm not coming up with much. Boredom, I tell myself (and note for the first time in my life that boredom is an anagram of bedroom), though I know there's more to it than that.

'D'you think he's wearing his wire again?' Janet Marsh rasps. Her wrecked larynx is making me feel fond of her, but also, if I follow the fondness, aware that there would come a time in the not-too-distant future when it wouldn't have that effect, would be an annoyance; time lets the air out whether we like it or not. For the past couple of hours we've been lying side by side alternating between twitchy sleep and surreal wakefulness. She said she liked to fall asleep to the telly so I put the portable on. BBC News Twenty-four. The clip is of George W. Bush 'debating' with John Kerry. This is the second of the three scheduled encounters between incumbent and challenger. After the first, more than a week ago, there was a big fuss because it appeared in photographs from a certain angle that the president was wearing a wire, presumably as a conduit for instructions on what to say. Instructions from Satan, Vince said.

'Frightening to watch, isn't it?' I ask.

'Do you follow it all? This stuff?'

'No. This guy though . . .'

'We all thought there was weapons there, Robin,' the president says, in response to an audience question. 'My opponent thought there was weapons there. That's why he called him a grave threat. I wasn't happy when I found out there wasn't weapons, and we've got an intelligence group together to figure out why.'

'*Wasn't* weapons?' Janet Marsh says.

'Don't get me started.' My hand rests on her belly. Unbra'd, her breasts roll away from each other as if each is in a huff; they're broad rather than pendulous and even when she's upright spread rather than droop.

'It's one thirty,' the newsreader says. 'The top stories tonight. Unconfirmed reports on Abu Dhabi television say that Ken Bigley, the Briton taken hostage twenty-two days ago, was killed on Thursday after a failed escape attempt. The second of the US presidential election debates took place tonight . . .'

'That poor chap,' she says.

'Yeah, it's a mess out there.' I use the remote to turn the volume down to a murmur. The in and out of sleep has sobered both of us up. I'm considering a trip to the kitchen where, for no good reason, the fruit bowl has become the place Vince and I keep our weed. It gives her palpitations, fine, but she won't mind if I go

ahead. On the other hand, I don't want to spoil what we've got.
It's precariously good to lie here and stroke her thighs, midriff,
flanks. If we were out in public as a couple I'd wish she was slim-
mer and better-looking – wish she were Tara Kilcoyne, in fact –
but here in private I'm filthy rich. Every time I think along those
lines I become aware of another thought running underneath it
like a culvert, that everyone and everything, Janet and these
moments included, is just me killing time until Scarlet comes
back into my life.

'I don't know how they do it,' she says. The footage now is of
a small anti-war demonstration somewhere that doesn't look like
London. People with faces pink from the cold, the wind lifting
their hair. Lots of them smiling. 'Get out there with banners and
shouting and whatnot.' Her voice is getting worse with every
utterance. The thought of entering her again, the big body with
its hot cunt and tired throat, futilely tugs a thread of blood in my
cock. She was so strong and undulant when I got on top of her
that I kept thinking that never before had I really been given, as
the slang has it, a *ride*.

'They care, I suppose.'

She rolls over on to her side facing away from me, but still
touching. Spoons is on offer but for the moment I stay where I
am with my hand on her right buttock. 'That's what I mean,' she
says, yawning. 'I don't know how they manage to care. I couldn't
give a fuck, really.'

'It's difficult,' I say. 'We're all lazy.'

'I'm not lazy,' she says. 'Just selfish.'

I don't like any of this but at the same time it feels inevitable. I
imagine a snapshot taken looking down at the two of us lying
here, our telly-lit bodies with their bones and blood and nerves
and consciousness. Then imagine the shot magnified times ten.
Then times ten again, and so on, the way I've seen them go from
atom to cosmos. Sooner or later you see the city, the country, the
continent, the planet. A leaflet handed to me on Charing Cross

Road a while back said: 'It's your world. What are you letting them do to it?'

'I see all this stuff and I keep thinking I should be bothered about it,' she says. 'But I'm not. All I've had in my head for the last year is this bloody deal, the company.'

'We've all got our excuses,' I say, thinking not just of Scarlet and the day at St Thomas's but of an Amnesty International insert in Vince's *Guardian* a while back which fell out of the paper when I picked it up (as it was no doubt intended to) and said, in big black letters on its front: 'WHAT'S YOUR EXCUSE?'

We return to silence but I know she's still awake. I'm beginning to wonder what the morning is going to be like. We'll fuck again, I daresay, which will be a mistake because we'll both look a lot worse than we do now, which won't matter for the sex but will matter immediately afterwards, my burgeoning pot belly and putative bubs, her thick ankles and that suggestion of flab on her upper arms. The general cosmetic of night will have been rubbed off. The weight of all our lives' failures and approximations will be upon us. Will we sit at the dining table over a pot of tea? Will we have to deal with Vince, who'll be elaborately hung over, slippered and dressing-gowned, grumpily full of his night's escapades or hurt in his heart by his night's emptiness? Hard to imagine she'll want to stick around. The more I think about it the more I imagine she'll want to be up and gone. I picture her at home (a large, high-ceilinged flat), moving slowly, drawing and with much sorrow for herself gingerly stepping into a deep, hot bath. The first adventure in her new freedom will have depressed her, if she's honest. And all she has to look forward to is more of it.

'Do you believe in God?' I ask her. The rain's erratic now, by turns stirring itself and fading. The wet night's into its tough hours for the West End's lonely, the lights shimmering in the gutter streams. I wonder where Scarlet is. What she's doing. If she's with someone.

'No,' Janet says. 'Not really.'

'If you don't believe in God you've got to come up with some other reason for doing the right thing. People, maybe.'

She doesn't answer straight away, but eventually says, in a threadbare, sleepy voice: 'Yeah.'

'I try to think of whether my parents would think something was honourable,' I say.

Again there's a long pause before the fading 'Yeah.' Then after a while, barely audibly: 'I'm going.'

I turn the television off and slot in behind her. The darkness is balm on our eyelids.

I'm not prepared for it when it comes. I never am.

'What is it?' she says, unable to disguise the fear in her wrecked voice. 'What's the matter?'

A gap in the curtains reveals a sliver of magic-hour light; the night's first concession to the idea of dawn, enough to show the wet of her eyes and the mirror's glimmer; the rest of the room's bits and pieces are lumps of shadow. It takes me a moment to remember who she is, how she got here, what we did.

'Sorry,' I say. 'This is embarrassing.'

I've woken myself with a terrible falsetto inhalation. If I give in to what's going on in my chest I'll sit there and sob. Her wide-awake force field crackles with the checked reflex to get the fuck away from me. A woman goes to bed with a man she's never met before, she goes to bed with his potential psychopathy, never mind tolerable sex and Winnie-the-Pooh.

'It's all right,' I tell her. 'I have nightmares. It's nothing.'

Hardly. She can see, or rather feel, the state I'm in.

'It's really okay,' I say. 'Honestly. I'm sorry.'

A pause. Her inner deliberation might as well be audible. Get up, get dressed, get out. Don't panic. Think. Stay. He's not crazy. Her hand comes up through the dark behind me and its touch between my shoulder blades gives a glimpse of how unsatisfactory it would be if we had a relationship, the precise degree to which it wouldn't be enough.

'Christ,' she says. 'What were you dreaming?'

I don't know what to tell her. It's not the dreams but the feeling they leave in the moments after I've woken myself up. The future's promise of loneliness. The overwhelming dull certainty of my death. The melodramatic absurdity of getting worked up about it, a man of my age and education.

'It won't sound like much,' I say.

Actually, there is comforting heat coming from her hand. Tears, whether I like it or not, are trickling down my cheeks, all my childhood still there, as confirmed earlier by the Rathbone Place pavement. That's one of the things that hurt, how much I remember, and that all that will, when I die, be lost.

'Come on,' she says. 'Lie down. You're all right.'

I could turn on my side and press my face into her breasts. They're available. But the mother-and-childness of it puts me off. I wonder (inconclusive stretch marks) if she and the ex have kids. Somehow I don't think so. There's been that slight inquisitive lift to her chin the whole time, the world-curiosity motherhood generally kills. Also, in the movement of her hips when we were fucking the ambivalent admission that this was still what defined her cunt, that there was something anachronistic about its not having gone on to the higher calling.

'I see things speeded up,' I tell her. 'Different things ageing really fast. Just now I was dreaming that I was walking towards two trees in a field. Green grass and blue sky and these two big trees. Then, suddenly, they started . . . It was as if I was watching them going through all their seasons one after another incredibly fast, leaves falling off and growing again, over and over. I saw them get old, ancient, wither, then die, all within a matter of seconds. Doesn't sound like much, I know.'

She remains silent, very lightly stroking my wrist, where my pulse is throbbing.

'Sometimes it's animals,' I say. 'A family of dogs, all their flesh dropping off them and their skeletons crumbling. It's the knowing it's coming, in the dream, you know? Like I recognize it's going to be one of those dreams and I can't stop it.'

'What sort of trees were they?'

'I don't know. Big, leafy. Why?'

'I've got a dream dictionary at home.'

'I don't think the type of tree matters. Sometimes, like I say, it's dogs or fish or foxes. It's the speeding up that's the thing.'

We lie in silence side by side. The house's ether tells me Vince hasn't returned. I hope he's had sex with someone, that he's safe, that it hasn't left him feeling more alone. He fell out with his mother and father years ago and his brother, to whom in any case he was never close, emigrated to Australia a long time back. It occurs to me that apart from Vince I don't have any friends. Melissa and Maude are out there like energy centres on which I can, no matter how distantly, draw. Even Carl and I have, this last decade or so, found a groove. (It began when we realized we were both readers; books licensed us to concede kinship in spite of having nothing else in common. Now it's a joke between the girls that Carl and I stick up for each other against their criticism, that at this preposterously late stage in the game we've decided we're brothers.) My mum and dad. I think of my family and then of Vince, effectively without one. And all of London and all of life to roll around alone in.

When, after perhaps ten minutes, Janet Marsh moves her hand slowly from my wrist across my hip and down – gentle insinuation then bald statement – to my cock I know it's because we don't have the resources for anything else. We're existing now in that state of knowing there's no future in this but putting the knowledge to one side to get through the present. There have been moments, the shared food, the more or less successful screwing, but they seem paltry now with the encroaching light and the faint sound of the first train. All that we don't know about each

other and all that doesn't fit forces us back into sex, since the alter-
natives are lying here acknowledging it or getting up and dealing
with whether she's still too drunk to drive home. (I've felt her
turning this over, these ten minutes, the business of getting home.
If she takes a cab she'll have to come back later to pick up her car.)
We turn towards each other, kiss, achingly and stalely start up
again, though, not being the man I used to be, I'm wondering
what dirty twist she can add this time to get me going.

CHAPTER TEN

❧

The Deal with God

(Bhusawal, 1945)

It did occur to Kate, cycling to her aunt's one Monday morning three days before her eighteenth birthday, that she'd gone mad. If she stopped, made the shift to one side of herself and looked disinterestedly at her life, a version of her voice said, quite calmly: You're living in a state of madness, a meandering fever, a dream. And she, quite calmly, replied: Yes, I know. Three years, after all, had passed since Lahore; and Cyril still lived. Not because her resolve had failed but because having decided to kill him she found she'd given herself, perversely, an increased tolerance of her own suffering. It was as if knowing she had this potential allowed her to take her own time realizing it. Murders, apparently, had their peculiar gestations. At some point – she couldn't say when, exactly – the date of her eighteenth birthday had hardened into significance. You've got until then, she'd told God, in the no-nonsense idiom their communiqués demanded. After that, I'm doing it myself. She hadn't been able to shake the feeling she was being tested, offered some sort of deal. Sometimes now in the loveless face of God (there were star-strewn nights she spent hours staring into the heavens as if in direct confrontation) she believed she saw a smile. No benevolence; just the faintest suggestion of amusement at her own writhing freedom. You *can* kill him, yes . . .

But?

She didn't know. Only that she was the subject of divine experiment. This, she incrementally understood and accepted, was what God did, was why He'd given us the freedom to choose in the first place: not out of love; out of curiosity.

Fine. You've got until I'm eighteen. Then I'm doing it myself.

Since having been taken out of school after her grandfather's stroke Kate had been forced into domestic slavery at her aunt's, though she still lived at Cyril's. Sellie, small in her upper body but going heavy in the hips, had a tiny-boned moist face and a thick mop of centre-parted hair. Some resemblance to Kate's mother around the eyes, but very slight. The milky-coffee colouring was the same but the face had a hint of Cyril's monkeyishness about the mouth. Kate imagined her in a tree, nibbling a pomegranate held in her small dexterous hands.

'The dhobi's been,' Sellie said, putting her head round the bathroom door where Kate was flannel-washing Dalma and Lucy while Robbie, naked but for chuddies, hung by his hands from the corner of the water tank. The floor was stone-flagged and the walls were brick painted buttermilk yellow. One window with blind slats missing admitted stripes of light into and out of which two bluebottles chased each other. Hot water steamed from the washbasin. Dalma, who was a skinny little thing with a huge nest of tangled black hair, was still half asleep in her nightdress.

'The clothes are on the chest in the hall so you'll put them away when you get back, okay?'

'Okay, Aunty,' Kate said. All this could go on. The world didn't stop just because murder was maturing in your blood. She let the thoughts – specifically the word *murder* – have their play to see if they detonated anything from God. Nothing. Only the steadily increasing weight of His presence. Kate held aloof; their terms were understood. He had three days to stop her, or to make the killing of Cyril unnecessary. There was no need for further dialogue.

'Hi-ho, *Sil*ver,' Robbie said.

'He's going to tip that over,' Kate said.

'Robbie get *down* from there,' Sellie said.

He ignored them. 'Hi-ho, *Sil*ver,' he said. 'Away!'

'What to do with this child?' Sellie said vaguely, and withdrew.

Kate dried Dalma and handed a separate towel to Lucy, who could dry herself. 'Go on, Robbie,' Kate said. 'Clean your teeth quick or we're going to be late.'

Robbie propelled himself backwards from the tank, landed on his heels, then stuck his palms in his armpits with a grimace of pain.

'I told you you'd hurt yourself,' Kate said. 'It's all rusty on the edge, you silly boy.' He was, Kate thought, a bit mad. He kept up bizarre monologues, got fixated on things, laughed if he hurt himself doing something stupid.

'I *am* a silly boy,' he said, pulling a face of shuddering agony. 'I am an *ab*solute silly boy, dear God.'

'Hurry up and wash,' Kate told him. 'Go on while I get these two dressed.'

'I hope it's kippers for beakfast,' Robbie said, stretching the elastic of his chuddies and looking forlornly at his genitals. 'Please, St Francis, make it kippers.'

'There aren't any kippers, stupid,' Kate said. 'There'll be porridge and toast and tea – *if* you get a move on.'

'It's the end of the Empire!' Robbie said, this being one of his father's habitual utterances. 'God save the King!'

The day went as usual. She took Robbie and Dalma to school on her bike, Robbie on the back, Dalma on the handlebars, then rode back to find that Sellie's half an hour of looking after Lucy had exhausted her. 'Kit, you'll have to take her for a while, honestly I slept so badly last night.' Thereafter all chores performed with Lucy on her hip or clinging to her leg or screaming or breaking something or choking on something she'd swallowed. '*Please* keep her quiet, Kit, for *heaven*'s sake. It's Uncle Will's lie-in today and he's not feeling too good, either.' (Sellie's husband, Will Lomax, was an Anglo fair-skinned enough to be taken for an Englishman, albeit of the pinkish boiled variety, with a bald, freckled head, bulldog jowls and a coin-slot mouth. He was one of those men, Kate thought, who enjoyed pretending to be irascible, barking at people, bellowing that there wasn't enough oil in the curry, standing with hands on hips and slot-mouth open in amazement at your effrontery that in reality he not only didn't mind but loved. He played this character full-time, enjoyed it, very occasionally stunned you by dropping out of it and saying something from his true self, quietly. If he thought about it at all, Kate knew, he was on her side: the hell of Cyril, the exploitation by Sellie, but he wasn't a man to dwell on things that required his ethical action. He was more likely to lift his burra peg up to the evening sunlight as if inspecting the scotch for foreign bodies and say, 'My God what a world,' before closing his eyes and taking a soothing sip.)

Kate put the clean laundry away, washed the household's yesterday socks and hung them out, polished the family's shoes, refilled the water chattis when the taps came on, kept Lucy amused. She went home for lunch with her grandfather, then returned to Sellie's for the afternoon's babysitting. She picked Robbie and Dalma up at four, rode home with them, oversaw their tea, then took all three children out on foot to the Railway Institute, where before the evening's adult socializing began youngsters gathered at the compound's swings, roundabout, climbing frame and slide. (The other children were there in the care of servants. Kate had heard one of the boys ask Robbie,

'How come your ayah doesn't wear a sari?') Then, with the sun lighting soft columns of evening gnats, back to Sellie's to bath the children and get them ready for bed, at which point Sellie materialized to comb her offspring's hair and coddle them for ten minutes before they went to sleep.

'I'm off, Aunty,' Kate said, hurrying to her bike.

'Don't be late tomorrow,' Sellie called. It was what she always said.

All this goes on. Murder. All this can go on. The world doesn't stop but turns up its dial, gets more itself. She had maybe an hour before the lamps were lit. Cyril's curfew. The place was off the south side of the bazaar. She pedalled hard past a bullock cart, the animals' pale golden haunches gleaming, the chorus of flies busy at their beshitted rears. The bike seemed twice its normal weight. Her calves and thighs burned. The market deserted depressed her, flecks of food and the bony dogs nosing. There'd been a downpour while she bathed the kids at Sellie's, what felt like the monsoon's last utterance, that shift up there, something leaving the sky.

The ground inclined and she stood up on the pedals. An Anglo woman carrying a wicker basket over her arm hurriedly crossed in front of her, gave her a glance from under the brim of her sun hat. Kate felt the stare on her back as she passed. As far as the town was concerned, she knew, the worst had all happened; it was all already as bad as it could be. That's Cyril Starkey's niece. Poor wretch. She'd caught the lowering of voices, seen the looks: pity; curiosity; disgust; satisfaction. Satisfaction that it was someone else, as if it validated them. The irony was it hadn't *all* happened. It could, she knew, be worse. There were long periods, sometimes months long, when Cyril left her alone. She wondered if he was governed by an astrological cycle. At first it had surprised her every time he drew back from doing what he could, with force, have done. It had surprised her until she understood how much he lived in fear. Fear was at the centre of him. If he raped her he'd have to find in himself the resources to justify it. If he couldn't, there would be no escape from his own self-disgust. Finding the justification would be one kind of madness. Failing to find it would be another. It was what her eyes confirmed for him when he could bear to meet them: This is what you are. She meant, at the eye of the storm of meanings, a coward. Therefore he beat her. The beating was the crescendo, the surrogate consummation. After the violence, new rules and proscriptions, their only purpose that they guaranteed her infringement. I'm still the roof over your head and I'm still entitled to a bit of bleddy respect. The mandatory kiss goodnight, this was. Facilitating all the vulgar touches. His hands leaving invisible filthy prints. Which over the weeks would build. Desire against fear. Fear won, but the margin of victory got smaller, smaller, smaller. She could see it. He was working himself up. Once or twice her grandfather had got between them. The furious raised male voices, but always in the end the old man beaten back, skulking, hot and rosy with his own dependence (for all his favouritism Sellie had made it clear she wouldn't take him), ready for the raging retreat into drink. Now he hid behind his own feebleness. *When he's dead*: every look of Cyril's said it; all three of them thought it. It was in the bungalow with them like a fourth person.

She used to play a scene out in her head. A policeman, Cyril's friend and billiards accomplice Sergeant Rhubotham, small-eyed and with a high forehead from which the hair went back in a dozen glossy ripples, saying, Now, Miss Lyle I realize this is difficult but I must ask you: Did your uncle . . . Are you saying your uncle *raped* you?

No, but he was going to.

How do you know? Are you seriously asking me to accept that your—

Accept what you like. I don't care. Do whatever it is you're going to do and get it over with.

Superficially the dialogue within herself was conducted as if the question was what she'd do immediately afterwards, how she would, as the phrase was, get away with murder. The fantasy of simple admission to Sergeant Rhubotham had some time ago been replaced by the business of concocting alibis, stories of thieves in the night, jumping a train, going in disguise, making her way back to Quetta where Edwin Hawes, who'd been working the Mail to Hyderabad when the earthquake struck, still lived in the city they were rebuilding. Whereas in the earlier phase the mere fact of Cyril's death was her reward (she'd own up to Rhubotham, yes, but in the last days of her life enjoy sensuous cleanliness, the freedom to relish the world's bits of beauty, even the play of sunlight on the bare brick of a prison wall), now she planned to survive, to navigate beyond the crime, to find a way into the future, whatever the world (or God) might do to her by way of retribution. This, superficially, was the inner dialogue. The other dialogue, the real dialogue – about how she would (how she *could*, practically) do it – wasn't a dialogue at all, but a murmur of forces never allowed to come to the surface, to thought, to language. She'd given no thought to the machete since the day of Kalia's dismissal, but one evening, months later, when she was chasing pariah dogs from the compound she'd come across it in the long grass near the fence, lobbed there, presumably, by Cyril. She'd picked it up and brought it like a sleepwalker into her room. Wrapped it in a rag and hidden it under her wardrobe. She hadn't thought anything, simply done it. The forces moved her and she was content to let them. The less she had to think about it the better.

What she did have to think about was Kalia. Doing something, now, miss, he'd told her. This is my country. Poor people don't realize how many of them there are. They are like the body, you know, but without head and brain what good? Disowned by Cyril, he'd jumped a goods train to Bombay. A year ago he'd got a message to her through the butcher that he was back in Bhusawal, secretly, since Cyril had reported the 'assault' to

Rhubotham. Since then he'd come and gone a few times, stealth-ily. I will help you, miss. You can count on me. He still found it difficult to meet her eyes, but less so than formerly. Something had hatched in him but remained deformed, a profane inclination beyond the accepted boundaries. Somewhere in Kate's meander-ing fever was the phrase *He loves you* and the adjunct *like that*. He wouldn't think of it in that way, wouldn't think of it at all, would experience it only as a piercing need to be of use to her.

She turned left into a cramped street of poor houses and huts. Here the maze began. Washing hung like dismal bunting, a stink of shit and stagnant water, cut through here and there by spicy cooking whiffs and strands of woodsmoke. She'd been here before but had to run the directions through her head. Miss, there is one pale blue house on a corner and a place with a striped thisthing opposite. Awning, he'd meant. If you get lost ask for the house of Jagrilal the tailor. He dropped into English erratically. In the old days he'd been reluctant, said it was disrespectful of him to talk to her in her language, which wasn't his. But how can I teach you if you won't repeat? Eventually, he'd made himself do it, in an agony of embarrassment, not meeting her eyes.

Another left, three small huts with rotting roofs. Turn right. There was the awning, and the pale blue house opposite. Kalia was peeping out from behind the door's curtain.

'All right, miss?'

She nodded.

'Best to bring your bike inside.'

The curtain opened on to a small, low-ceilinged room with a big bed in one corner and an open cooking fire in the other. A dark infant with a head of wild black curls lay asleep with its mouth open on the bed. A girl of four or five lay on her belly next to it, moving her shins back and forth and singing quietly to a filthy homemade cloth doll. An old woman in a shapeless shift squatted on her haunches watching a pan on the fire, while a sari'd woman in perhaps her late twenties sat in the back doorway, orangely lit by the dust-filtered sunlight, grinding spices on a curry stone. It had astonished Kate that Kalia had friends, an existence beyond Cyril's.

'Miss, Thursday night, after midnight, I will be there. When you come we'll go by the back way to the river and my friends will take us.'

'Yes,' Kate said. Given no more than cursory glances from the house's inhabitants, she'd been led by Kalia into a small side room, the curtained door of which opened on to an acre of shantied scrub. 'But why would they do that? Your friends – for me, I mean?'

'They are coming for me. We're going to do something, some work in Nagpur. In Nagpur there is a place you can stay safely . . .' he hesitated. 'For some time, anyway. I've arranged it. I do good work, you see, so have some pull. I never forget you.' They'd been speaking Hindi but the last two sentences he uttered in English.

Something went into the skillet next door with a sizzle. Onions. Her eyes prickled. She hadn't liked the way he'd said that, *pull*, the hint of puffing up. She'd never asked what work, but thought now she knew. She remembered a burned-out military vehicle in the street near Eleanor's in Lahore. Other overheard snippets and glimpsed headlines, her uncle arguing with Mr Knight next door, They're saying anarchists, anarchists, but if you ask me Congress is *paying* these bastards. It's all bleddy mochis and sweepers, who else?

'Miss, you should let me do it,' Kalia said.

'No. It's not for you.'

'But—'

'It's between me and God.'

Sister Anne used to say: He tests most severely those He loves most. He knows you. He'll never give you more than you can bear.

'If I don't come,' she told Kalia, 'it means I've changed my mind, okay?'

'But what if something's happened?'

'Like what?'

'Something happened to you, miss.'

'It won't have. If I'm not there it'll just mean I've changed my mind.'

'Are you waiting, miss, for your God to help you?'

She looked past him to where a slight breeze lifted the door's curtain. The light was fading. 'I've got to go,' she said. 'They'll be lighting the lamps soon.'

Tuesday went slowly. No rain, and a conviction from sky to earth that there would be no more. The town's collective mind understood, stopped expecting it, went about its business having made, elusively, as if some spell had been cast during the night, the seasonal shift. Her grandfather ate very little at dinner, hobbled off to the veranda straight afterwards. His heart wasn't in anything, these days. The stroke had left him with a paralysed left arm and a weak left leg, also a droop to the left side of his mouth that slurred his speech. He walked with a stick, needed help with buttons, shoelaces, braces, neckties. His food had to be cut up for him. He'd been diagnosed with angina and, off-stage, to Cyril and Sellie by Doctor Bannergee, as showng the first signs of Parkinson's disease. All that was not of the body was going bad, too, the mind, the soul, the conscience. He drank more, stewed, muttered, was sometimes found weeping, in the end for himself, Kate knew, though there were half a dozen litanies, mainly I can't believe after all these years, after all we've *done* that we're just going to pull out like leaving a bloody camp. 'We' were the British. It separated him from her further. He never talked to her about the earthquake, their miraculous survival, ruddy *destiny*. All they'd shared in the past now gathered and turned as if with a spotlight on the one thing they shared in the present. Cyril. Him. Her.

'What are you looking at?' Cyril said.

'Nothing.'

'Nothing. Don't try'n get smart with me.'

She didn't respond, began collecting the plates. In the kitchen he came behind her and put his left hand in a tight grip round the back of her neck, pressed himself against her. The cuts from the belt beating hurt. She closed her eyes, forced him to feel her inertia, the deadness past even revulsion.

Nothing. Him silently raging. Time stopped when this happened, asserted the impossibility of anything else happening, ever.

Then, in a complete inversion of reality he kissed the back of her head, as with brisk affection, and pushed himself with a final neck-squeeze away from her. 'Right,' he said, slapping his hands together and rubbing them as with eagerness for a challenge. 'Time to go and skin those poor buggers.' Billiards. Tuesday night, the Railway Institute. He'd be back late. Three times recently she'd woken in the night and found him standing in her room. Hadn't known whether he knew she was awake. The light was always behind him, left him in silhouette. She'd frozen, closed her eyes, heard the breathing, some compressed movement. Eventually his steps moving away, the door closing.

She stood still, holding and leaning on the stack of plates, letting her body return by degrees. She washed up, filled the goglets for the night, put the crockery and cutlery away, and went to her room. The waiting was almost over. Now only the murmuring forces lulled her, a rushing stream to the sound of which she was falling asleep. God's dark-starred face flirted, incessantly. She kept feeling it above her head, kept looking up, catching every time the last shimmer of its dissolution. It was hard to think. Thinking required separation from your experience. But her experience had lost the barriers that made it hers; it bled out, fused and mingled with everything around her. Resisting – several times she tried to haul herself out of the dream – depleted and soon exhausted her. She tried getting thoughts started: *If he . . . I don't . . . mercy means even the Devil . . .* but each one frayed into nothingness. She felt immensely heavy in her limbs. The weight was God's moment by moment increasing interest in her, in what she was going to do.

She got down on her knees to drag the wrapped machete out from under her wardrobe, but found she couldn't, couldn't look at it even, and instead lowered herself and lay on her side on the floor. The stone was cold through her nightdress, a brutal bliss, the way an angel might . . . But again the thought frayed.

Eventually the cold hurt. She got up, turned out the lamp and got into bed. For a while she lay in the dark with her eyes open. Heavy enough, she thought, to crash through the bed, the floor, the ground. She'd go through and watch walls of raw earth racing upwards past her. Hell? Some core of heat miles below her, the faintest edge of which she was already beginning to feel. Well, if she was going to Hell she'd go.

She fell asleep and dreamed. She was on a train and it was night. Not a passenger carriage but the guard's brake van, no sign of the guard. The door was wide open to the rolling night. A sky of stars stretched down to a line of distant hills. Between the hills and the train a vast empty plain. Suddenly she felt a pain in her side, then lower, in her womb. She lifted her dress to look and there, sprouting from her thigh in a little gobbet of blood, was a small unopened green bud. She pulled it and it came away with a twinge, as if some tiny root had been plucked. She cupped her hands over it, feeling panic starting to rise. As soon as she closed her hands over it it started to get heavier. The dream shifted. She was in the passenger compartments, searching for her mother and father. People kept telling her they'd just seen them, there, but when she looked where they were pointing, no one. Then suddenly there *was* her mother, coming towards her, squeezing past people, smiling. She said, Oh, God, Mummy look what I've done, but her mother just smiled and said, What? what's wrong? it's beautiful. She looked down to where it felt like her hands were still cupped around the little bud only to find that they weren't, and that instead she was holding, uncomfortably, as if it was a sodden cat, a naked, heavy, calm-faced baby.

The dream hung over, added its weight to the leaden unreality into which she woke. At Jesus and Mary once they'd sat her in a chair and blindfolded her. Eleanor, Vera, half a dozen others. Told her that first they were going to make her very heavy, then very light, so light in fact that she would float up to the ceiling. One by one they'd put their hands on her head, increasing the pressure until it was almost beyond bearing, then one by one had removed them. The sensation of lightness had been unnatural. It was if the top of her head was pulling her upwards. Her chair had wobbled, left the ground, she'd felt herself rising. Her head had bumped the ceiling. Afterwards they'd shown her how it was done. The chair was lifted an inch off the ground by four girls. The 'ceiling' was a big dictionary brought down to touch her head.

This, cycling to Sellie's, was that heaviness, God in tiny increments adding the weight of His interest like their one-by-one hands. She wondered how long she'd be able to keep moving under it.

'Oh *God*, Kit, thank heavens!' Sellie said, rushing up the front path. Her thin face was shiny with sweat. 'Quick! Quick, go and get a ghari!'

'What's wrong, Aunty?'

'Robbie's fallen and I think he's broken his arm. Go *on*, child, for God's sake. Hurry!'

It took a while. The nearest ghari stand was a mile and a half away at the market. Robbie getting into it was a miserable sight. He'd screamed at first, Sellie said, then gone very quiet, holding the broken arm. It was as if he and accident had throughout his life been playing a violent thrilling game and accident had suddenly changed the rules. Kate felt sorry for him.

'What were you doing up on the roof, silly?' she asked him. He sat next to her, violated. Sellie had stayed back: No no, Kit, you

go. I can't stand the smell of a hospital, honestly I'll be sick. He
wants you to go, anyway, don't you Robbie? Robbie had nodded,
sadly, and it had occurred to Kate for the first time that the boy
loved her.

'Looking for those things,' he said.

'What things?'

'Those *green* things.'

She didn't push it. Robbie lived in his own world.

This was better, the morning air a gentle ravishment of her bare
arms, shins, throat, face. The day was making the first of its shifts
of light, from the dusky peach (which tinted beggars still rolled in
their rags like giant bidis, a dog sleepily nosing a drain, someone's
bearer leaning against a porch post, smoking) to bleaching white.
Doors were opening, breakfast smells drifting out. A doodh-
wallah led two milk buffalo with bony hocks and *tunk-tunking*
bells door to door. Kate, in the pink cardie and the sundress of
tiny pale-yellow check she'd made herself, leaned back in her seat
with her arm round Robbie's shoulder. The weight was still on
her, God's hands pressing down on her head. You're getting heavier, Eleanor and Vera had said, mimicking hypnotists, heavier,
*heav*ier . . . but this was better. And God was a hiss underneath
every other sound, and God was an eye that watched her through
every detail of the burgeoning morning. Tomorrow, she would be
eighteen years old.

While Kate was preparing herself for murder, Ross was preparing
himself for bribery and corruption at the doctor's office.

'Monroe sahib?' the doctor's peon said. Ross, next in the waiting room's small crowd, got to his feet. Don't forget the peon,
Eugene had warned him. The peon is important. Few pice or a
cup of char. Don't forget.

'Monroe sahib?' the peon repeated.

Ross coughed, looked down, slipped him two coins and
entered the doctor's office.

Dr Narayan, whose plump moustache and long eyelashes would have made him handsome if not for the womanly curvature of his face (which combination made him instead a sort of erotic curio, disturbing to both men and women), sat stethoscoped in a short-sleeved white shirt and khaki trousers behind his desk, writing in what looked suspiciously like an accounts ledger. The office smelled of camphor and disinfectant. One wall displayed a large year planner with as far as Ross could see nothing planned; next to it a life-sized illustration of a human male, the left half of the body stripped to reveal circulatory system and vital organs, the right half to show musculature. Light from the one window backing the desk glistened on the doctor's oiled and side-parted hair. In spite of Eugene's reassurances Ross was nervous. The peon gestured to the chair. He sat. The doctor continued writing for a few moments (as doctors must, to show your negligibility in comparison to other cases, to remind you their time is precious nectar of which you're fortunate to be getting a drop) then looked up with a smile. 'Well then, Mr Monroe, what seems to be the trouble?'

By the time of his demobbed homecoming Ross knew he was going to the Olympics. He'd fought and beaten all the bantamweights in the IAF and half their RAF contemporaries. A *Times of India* journalist told him to stop wasting his time fighting Tommies. 'If you want to go to the Olympics,' he told Ross, 'fight for India. You've already beaten the competition. You want to box for Britain, you'll have to get bloody papers and citizenship and certified proof of your great-great-granddad's lilywhite prick. Plus you might get a kicking from some Tommy between now and 'forty-eight. Box for India. It's your ticket out of here, I'm telling you. And then you tell the promoters there that you want to stay and go pro, they'll sign you up like a shot.' Ross had listened. The trials were two years away. In the meantime all he had to do was keep his hand in and stay alive, which meant a job. Which in Bhusawal meant the railway. He'd moved back into the family house in Bazaar Road and his father had got him started as a goods fireman.

Keeping his hand in and keeping a job were, it turned out, one and the same; within three days of his starting on the goods locos both football and boxing managers had sought him out. Word of his talent had been spread not only by the sporting press but closer to home by Eugene and Ross's older brother Hector (now a passenger guard working the BB&CIR line out of Bombay), who until transferring had captained the GIPR football squad for the last three years. (Bombay's Hector-gravity was a married woman, Mrs Bernice Gallagher, with whom he was having a self-destructive affair. She was a slender, light-skinned, highly strung Bhusawal girl Hector had gone with, chastely, on and off, but who during one of the offs had suddenly married an English hotel owner she'd met on a day trip to the Ajanta caves. The Englishman had whisked her off to be queen of the Albion in the city. When I was friendly with her before, Hector had confessed to Ross one night, drunk, it was all shut-up-shop down there, you know? A kiss and a cuddle but nothing . . . And now? Hector had shaken his head. Jesus Christ. You don't know how it is, brother. It's the same for her too. Then his face changed. He made the finger and thumb rubbing gesture meaning money. But she wants the bleddy royal life, doesn't she, eh? Three bags full, memsahib. Oh *Christ*, you don't know what this is doing to me. Ross did know, or at any rate had never seen his brother looking worse or drinking more.)

Football was under the eye of Reggie Hodge, foreman of the engineering workshops in Parel, boxing of Clem McCreedy, or 'Old Clem', a retired assistant yard foreman and former Inter-Railway Lightweight Champion. 'Now look here, Monroe,' Old Clem said, wagging his finger. 'We've heard great things about you so I expect you to bleddy deliver.' He was a small, round-shouldered man with a brown, mottled cannon ball of a head set off by a snowy moustache. He had no eyebrows at all; punched off, he said, over twenty years in the ring. 'And I don't want to hear any cribbing from you about any*thing*, because you're going to be living the life of bleddy Riley, okay?'

The only problem, as far as Ross could see, was the railway's attitude to training, namely, that they didn't bother doing any. He was used to the air force's no-nonsense regimen: up at 6.00 a.m. for a fourteen-mile run punctuated on the half-hour with push-ups, squat-thrusts and sit-ups. Back to base for breakfast, followed by two hours of co-ordination exercises in the gym. Lunch, then a long rest through the afternoon (tournament boxers had been excused all duties during training: yes there was a war on, yes there were parts to be inventoried, yes there was fuel to be kept flowing, but primarily, *primarily*, there were fights and football matches to be won) until the evening session at 4.00 p.m.: three rounds of sparring, three rounds of skipping, three rounds of shadow-boxing and three rounds on the heavy bag. Then you were done for the day, limbs humming with the peace of exhaustion, masculinity reverberating like a well-struck bell. The evening's first drink was a sensuous seduction. But without someone to bark you into shape, Ross knew, you were on your own. Was he up to maintaining, as Rockballs would have put it, his focus?

'And you're double lucky,' Eugene told him. 'You'll be picked for boxing *and* football.' Eugene (innocently enhancing the appositeness of his Quickprick and Sprintfinish nicknames) was a speedy right winger, and had been playing for the GIPR First Eleven since he arrived in Bhusawal three years ago. The night of the *common brass* diagnosis he'd gorged himself at Mrs Naicker's, got a dose of clap and, in a panic (he'd joined up under age to escape a violent father and was irrationally terrified that in getting himself treated the truth about his age would come out), decided to desert. Ross, when he'd seen there was no talking Eugene out of it, had agreed to help get him over the barracks wall after dark – but only on condition that Eugene went straight to Bhusawal and presented himself to Agnes for treatment. *Sister*, Ross's note said, *This is a good fellow and a close friend who's got himself into difficulty. Please do what you can for him.* Agnes had got Eugene treated, but not before giving him the roasting of his life. Eugene had survived, however, and become a friend of the Monroe family. Ross's father got him fake medical discharge papers (more bribery and corruption) and a job on the GIPR. By the time Ross came home in the summer of '45, Eugene was a goods driver and Bhusawal was home. (But his Troubles with Women had continued. The great tribulation was an affair with the allegedly 'professional' Cynthia Merritt. If she took money from other buggers, I can tell you she didn't take any bleddy money from *me*, he'd told Ross. Ross was inclined to believe him. If he had paid for it Eugene wasn't the fellow to deny it. Cynthia, whom Ross remembered as a small but long-legged woman with a wheaty complexion, extraordinarily large dark eyes and a quiet sexual confidence that surprised and drew you, had, after a row with Eugene, packed up and gone back to her mother's in Jalgaon a year ago. Eugene, uncharacteristically reluctant to make a yarn of it, left Ross to read between minimal lines. Cynthia had loved Eugene. At first Ross thought Eugene hadn't loved her. Then the more depressing reading: Eugene loved her but couldn't, thanks to masculine hypocrisy, get past her reputation. The affair had sewn a thread of self-loathing in him, and to punish himself he'd started courting the large-breasted but perennially furious Mitzi Donnegan. A year had passed. Eugene and Mitzi were getting married.)

'Well, Doctor, I'm not feeling too good, you know?' Ross said. The wedding was on Saturday and Eugene was demanding two days and nights debauchery to say farewell to his bachelorhood for ever. Ross, his best man, was required. Which meant getting Thursday and Friday off.

'Yes?' Doctor Narayan said.

'I had vomiting and diarrhoea last night, and I feel a bit shaky today.' Don't be too specific, Eugene had said. Keep it general. That's the understanding. Generality.

Dr Narayan raised his eyebrows but simultaneously lowered his heavy upper eyelids. It looked like a sexual display of the showgirl eyelashes. Alternatively a sign of medical cogitation. 'I see,' he said.

'It's hard to say, specifically,' Ross said.

'Just feeling a bit weak in the guts, generally, yes?'

'Yes, generally.'

'Stand up, please. I'll have a listen to your chest.'

The doctor rose and motioned for Ross to step to one end of the desk. Set in the end of the desk (for a bizarre moment Ross found himself wondering whether such a thing was customized or made like that) was a small drawer, which while listening to Ross's chest the doctor smoothly opened with his left hand. The hand had the same womanly plumpness as the face.

The peon coughed, and, when Ross looked at him, indicated with a slight nod. Ross dropped two rupees into the open drawer.

'I think a couple of days rest should see you right,' Dr Narayan said sleepily, removing the stethoscope from his ears and returning to his chair. 'Get plenty of fluids and keep your room well ventilated. Please, have a seat while I write you a note.'

Ross relaxed. This was India, money warmly slipped from hand to hand, an impersonal friendship or subscription to a universal religion embracing everyone from princes to peons. Lousy way for a place to run – collapses and breakdowns inevitable – but he wasn't going to worry. Two years' cushy living, Inter-Railway champion, Olympic trials, London, promoter, sign up, you're off. Retire at thirty-five and have all the sweet pussy you want. Don't repeat that.

Which brought up – increasingly there was no getting away from it – sex. Women. His virginity. He was the only one not having woman trouble because he was the only one not having women. He'd lied to Eugene, elaborated two stories, one of a nurse in Secunderabad during the six months' flight mechanic's training after basic at Walton, the other of a stenographer in Allahabad (where he'd been subsequently posted) at a New Year's office party he and a friend had in uniform gatecrashed. In reality there had been with both these (Anglo) girls what Eugene would describe (with up-and-down eyebrows and chimp grin) as slap-and-tickle. With the stenographer, hurriedly, using hands only, a denouement. A denouement for Ross, at least. She'd said, No, no, pack it in, when he tried to reciprocate. I'm too drunk to feel anything, anyway. It had astonished him that she'd said this, that she knew herself well enough to be able to judge, that she had experience to draw on. It had made her so dirtily alluring he'd persisted, until her gin-flavoured laughter had dried up and she'd said, Look for Christ's sake it's not going to work. Come on, let's get a drink. She'd agreed to meet him the next day but never turned up. He was so convinced something must have happened to her he went back the following evening to the office building and watched from a newsstand opposite. Out she came at five o'cock, laughing with a female colleague, the two of them with linked arms hurrying off before he could think of what to say.

This had relaxed him, too, that there were such women in the world, but at the same time depressed him because he knew he wanted something more, something fierce and private, a contract against loneliness, against, if he thought about it, death. He wanted, he supposed – the word was a shock to him when he arrived at it – love. The way the stenographer had been was exciting in flared-up moments but underneath the sensual pleasure there had been a cold horror of mutual privacy, as if no matter how hard they looked at each other (and most of the time they hadn't been able to; she'd put her head back in what even then had seemed to him a pretence of enjoyment, so much so that when he thought of it now he imagined her looking at a clock over his shoulder) they would remain separate and unknown. There was only the superficial allegiance, the bodies. If he'd died the next day he'd still be dying sexually alone, having made no real connection with a woman. It made him think of the fights. There were moments in the ring when you and the other man enjoyed a profound mutual visibility and understanding. You made a connection so powerful that neither of you would go to his grave having never seen into and been seen into by another human being. Like that, but with a woman, the other combat that was really an allegiance. That was what he wanted.

'You don't understand,' Hector had said to him, again liquored up (he'd lost weight, Ross noticed; there was a boyish poignancy about his neck and ears and wrists), 'at that moment . . . At that moment . . .' Hector had closed his eyes and made a face of something like disgust, as if withstanding torture which beyond the pain filled him with ethical loathing for the torturer . . . 'I'd sacrifice everything, *everything*. When we're together like that and she looks at me . . .' He'd checked again, a few degrees shy of the drunkenness that burned the last boundaries; checked, shook his head, looked away. He hadn't needed to finish. Ross had heard it before: *when she looks at me like that, in that moment, I'd sacrifice anyone or anything to keep her. Nothing else matters.* Whenever this realization had come to Hector it left him in denuded shock, shown him an entirely new version not just of himself but of the world. This was the having false gods before God, why God had bothered making it a commandment in the first place. They'd all grown up imagining the Golden Calf, but it was this, discovering that the price of your soul was the freedom to fuck this woman, to keep fucking her, for ever. Aside from the shock of seeing his brother so much reduced, it showed Ross Bernice in a new light. He'd remembered her as a twitchy girl with a slightly annoyed horsy face and a piercing nasal voice. Now he had no choice but to visualize her under his brother (or was it himself?), equine nostrils flared, legs welcomingly spread, conjuring a look that made you willing to sacrifice everything, *everything* . . . The affair was a terrible silent fracture in the Bazaar Road household, his father,

Ross suspected, jealous of the intensity, his mother jealous simply of Bernice, who had, in the apocalyptic idiom, taken and murdered her son's soul. It was anathema to her that her sons must leave home and find women at all, tolerable only if they found women they could learn to despise; then they would seek and receive her allegiance in the despising. (It had been a bad year for his mother, Ross knew. Hector's desertion; trouble with her hip; Rose marrying a goodfornothing; Agnes turning down the visiting eye specialist from Jabalpur. All this on top of his cock-and-bull story about the 'robbery' – Mumma there were three of these buggers and I don't know where this first chap was hiding but when I woke up they'd taken my watch and money as well – of Raymond Varney's bloodstone ring, which she hadn't quite, he thought, believed . . .)

Mulling over all this, with his bought and paid-for sick note in his pocket, he stepped out into the hospital corridor not looking where he was going. Something bumped into his legs. He looked down to see a small boy with his arm in a sling turning and looking up at him. The boy hadn't been looking where he was going, either.

'Hups,' Ross said. 'Are you all right?'

'Are you all right?' the nurse asked Kate, reaching out to steady her.

'I'm fine,' she said. 'Just a bit dizzy. No breakfast.'

'Sit down here for a minute. Doctor, you should have a look at this young lady, I think.'

The doctor, third in rank after Bannergee and Narayan, was a young Muslim with a gentle voice and a soft beard that fringed his face from ear to ear. Would be better with the moustache, Kate thought, but lots of the Muslim men went for the beard only. Made them look like flowers, the face the heart and the beard where the petals would be. She'd forgotten his name already. 'Oh no, I'm all right,' she said, being guided down on to the wooden chair next to the trolley on which Robbie, arm plastered, was perched, having his sling fastened. 'Just a bit tired.' Have a look meant examination. She didn't want that. And in any case the problem was the weight pressing down on her head. It was absurd, but since she'd remembered the game at Jesus and Mary, Eleanor and the girls with their levitation trick laying their hands on her skull and recognized the feeling, the gradually increasing weight of God's watching her, she'd been unable to think about or feel anything else.

'Let's have a look,' Dr Azad said, getting down on his haunches and peering into her face. The nurse, a Tamil in her early twenties with a tiny pointed face and the large black eyes of a doe, lifted Kate's wrist to take her pulse.

'She doesn't look right to me,' Robbie said. The business of plastering his arm had brought him back out of misery. Now he sat swinging his legs, intrigued and impressed by this new sling-wearing version of himself. Can I have an eyepatch? he'd asked. The nurse and doctor had laughed.

'Don't pay any attention to him,' Kate said. 'He's mad.'

'Not necessarily,' Dr Azad said, shining a pen torch into her left then right eye. 'You look a little anaemic to me. Are you eating regularly?'

'Yes.'

'She doesn't eat enough to keep a bird alive, my daddy says,' Robbie said.

'Robbie. Shush.'

They found nothing wrong, naturally. Heartbeat, pulse, temperature, all normal. No chest pain, no abdominal pain. Admittedly she underplayed the headache, but what was she going to say? God was pressing on her because he was waiting to see if she committed murder? Dr Azad had other patients to attend to. Robbie would have to come back for a check-up in a week. The nurse told her where the canteen was and recommended a cup of tea and some toast before making the journey back. All this can go on, Kate repeated to herself. All this can go on.

'Come on, mister,' she said, taking Robbie's free hand in hers. 'Let's get you home. I suppose you'll want the day off school for this?'

'I want pancakes,' Robbie said.

Suddenly the pressure on her head started to ease. The sensation was so strange it stopped her in her tracks. The hands were lifting, like birds taking off. She took three more steps. Three more hands. Robbie ran on ahead. You're getting lighter, now, Eleanor and Vera had said, in quavering voices, lighter . . . lighter . . . *so* much lighter . . .

She was tempted to laugh, but it was unnerving, too, the feeling of lift. Carry on walking and eventually your feet will leave the ground. The thought for the first time that there might, actually, be something medically wrong with her

'Come *on*,' Robbie said. 'You're so *slow*.'

Something's happening, she wanted to say to someone, anyone. Something's happening to me. Couldn't be more than two hands keeping her earthbound. The lightness tingled in her shoulders, knees, ankles, toes. Very vividly she saw herself lifting off, feet dangling, one shoe dropping off, the half-dozen people milling about looking up, mouths open, astonished. God's interest settled on you gradually but abandoned you with shocking suddenness. That was the thought that at last unravelled: God, with a final glimmer of the wry smile, was turning His attention elsewhere. We'll play again, Katherine, but for now . . .

'Kitty,' Robbie said, looking back at her, 'can I have an ice—'

'Hups,' the young man said, looking down at Robbie. 'Are you all right?'

Kate watched Robbie nod. Then the young man looked up at her.

She thought, afterwards: He must have assumed he was making good ground because I kept smiling and laughing. Either that or he must have thought I was simple. The truth was she couldn't help it; the release from the weight's pressure, the extraordinary sensation of lightness, of being on the verge of flight. She would have been giddy with anyone. (Robbie said, Why are we *walking*, for God's sake? but didn't argue when she said, Because I want to. He ran on ahead, examining things along the road or having bizarre, truncated engagements with total strangers, content now to accept the broken arm and sling as a novelty rather than a betrayal.)

Why don't you come to a dance with me next week? And without thinking she'd said, All right. I can't believe, he'd kept saying, I can't believe it's *you*. She was a *you* to someone. You had a scratch on your face. How did you get that? I don't remember, she said. And you were wearing a white dress with poppies on it. It was my mother's. And you bought pistachios in the market. Did I? And you looked like you might be being followed. And you, and you, and you.

It was a strange shift, as if the world had put out its hand and for the first time since her mother's death she'd taken it, wondering why now, why never before? Simultaneously understanding that your life had its own secret appointments. The feeling of lightness got in the way of what she thought of this young man to whom she was a *you*, almost. But not completely. Almost but not completely got in the way of the other thing, too, the accrual of loathed touches, the contagion. Already – him saying he always looked for her in Lahore after that (was that possible?) – she was thinking: sooner or later someone'll tell him, Cyril Starkey's niece, poor bitch, you didn't know? Oh, everyone knows . . . Already she was getting an inkling of the courage (or indifference) she'd need to give him the facts and nothing else. She imagined herself saying it. I'm telling you now because if you don't hear it from me you'll hear it from someone else. How would he react? She surprised herself, leaping ahead with the certainty that there would be a future. He had a good bony face, she thought, life in the deep-set eyes, a look of appetite for the world, something out there. There might be swagger later, when he remembered himself, but for now he was genuinely in the moment. Monroe the surname. She'd heard it; father a driver, brother a passenger guard so Cyril probably knew them, must be where she'd heard it. I cannot be*lieve* it's you, he kept repeating. He must have thought he'd never met a girl so easy to make smile. It's destiny, he'd said, and laughed. There's no other explanation. So you'll come to the Limpus with me next week? Or you know, there's my friend's wedding on Saturday. I'm best man. D'you want to come along? Shall I call for you? She thought, afterwards: He must have felt like the cat's whiskers, asking and me saying yes straight away. He must have thought I was crazy.

She thought all this afterwards, when there was time.

'What's happened?'

At the bungalow Mr and Mrs Knight, the neighbours, stood in their front garden, heads inclined as if listening for something. Two full-faced sloe-eyed servants' children with a hoop and stick also stood frozen in the street. It was almost three in the afternoon. The heat was a soft sustaining presence against her arms and legs. (She'd kept her cardie over her shoulders on the walk back from the hospital – two bruises there was no need for him to see – but taken it off once he'd left her, a hundred yards from her aunt's at her request.) Sellie, in an idiotic panic, had kept Dalma home from school. Kate had dropped Robbie off and hurried back, wondering if her granddad had managed to feed himself, since he wouldn't suffer anyone's help but hers. She'd ridden home feeling the first (disappointing) suggestion that her natural gravity, neither the weight of God's cold interest nor the giddying lightness of His abandonment, was returning. Details had been here and there vivified as she rode: a red door; two golden dogs lying in the sun; a spices stall with heaped earth-tones powders. Now, as she got down off her bike with sweat cooling in the nape of her neck, this. Dense, static energy emanated from the bungalow.

'A shot,' Mr Knight whispered. 'Shouting, and something like a shot.'

She went cautiously. The tattis were up in the windows, though they needed damping again. In the living room Cyril lay on the floor with his head on a cushion. Sergeant Rhubotham knelt next to him. Cyril's shirtsleeve had been raggedly cut off. Rhubotham was using both hands to put pressure on her uncle's shoulder. Two or three trickles of blood crept out from under his palm. The room was slightly upset, rattan coffee table knocked over, the painting of the tiger in the river askew, mantelpiece ornaments scattered. Near Rhubotham's foot, a short, wooden-handled dagger, shiny with blood.

'What happened?' Kate said.

Rhubotham got a fright at the sound of her voice, twitched, turned. Cyril's head lolled towards her with a groan.

'Miss,' Rhubotham said. 'First-aid kit. Have you got one?'

'What is it? What's—'

'*Now*, please. Or a clean hanky or something.'

Kate ran to the kitchen, came back with the tin.

'Bandage and pad,' Rhubotham said. 'Quickly, please.'

'There's no pad.'

'Just give me the tin.'

'Oh, God,' Cyril said, grimacing. 'Fuck.'

Rhubotham worked fast but not deftly. His hands, Kate observed, were shaking.

'I can't believe it,' Cyril said. 'Never in a million years would you think a bleddy—'

'Don't talk,' Rhubotham said. Then to Kate: 'Does anyone here have a telephone?'

'I don't think so,' she said.

'You'll have to go up to the Institute. That's nearest.' He hesitated. 'Wait here a moment,' he said.

She didn't wait but followed him through the back of the house. A cricket sprang away as she stepped out on to the veranda.

Afternoon light seared the compound. Kalia lay face down on the ground. A small puddle of blood had formed at his side. A few feet to the left a revolver shone in the sun.

'Sheer chance I came in when I did,' Rhubotham said, quietly. 'Happens like that sometimes. He wasn't planning to use the gun, I suppose, for the noise.' His voice quivered. He stepped a few paces away, bent double, vomited. Kate looked down at Kalia's face, the wide, tough cheekbones, the too-many teeth that his lips always struggled to cover. His mouth was open, the tip of his tongue visible, as if tasting the dust. His half-closed eyelids showed two crescents of white. Are you waiting for your God to help you, miss?

'I'll have to stay here,' Rhubotham said. 'Crime scene. You go up to the Institute, tell them I sent you and you're to use the telephone to call—'

'Get someone else to go,' Kate said.

It threw up a sheet of silence between them. She ought to be feeling something, she knew. She felt nothing. She thought of reaching down and closing Kalia's mouth, started the move towards doing it, but stalled, straightened. Rhubotham came nearer, smelling of sick. When he stood alongside her it was as if Kalia was their sleeping child, forcing a shared intimacy on them. Rhubotham, sensing it, spun on his heel and hurried back indoors. Kate stood for a few moments. Dogfighting flies scribbled in the space around the body. Her natural weight had re-established itself but the last veil of her childhood had gone. She turned and went back into the house.

Rhubotham was out from, issuing instructions to Mr Knight. Cyril lay as he had been left, bandaged, head on cushion. He was shivering, face yellowish pale and wet. Standing over him, she realized he hadn't acknowledged her presence since she'd come in. Even now, with her shadow crossing his chest, he couldn't look at her. Rhubotham came back inside. Opened his mouth to speak, but something about the girl standing over her uncle like that stopped him. It was Kate who spoke.

'You will never lay another finger on me,' she said. 'If you do, I'll kill you myself.'

Cyril said nothing, but wetly shivered. Rhubotham, who had found his cap, put it on, slowly, as if with new reverence for the smallest acts. He moved aside to let Kate pass. She went through the door and out into the street, where a murmuring crowd had gathered at the gate. The murmurs ceased when she appeared. In silence and the day's bleaching light Kate took her bike, wheeled it past them, mounted, and rode slowly away down the hill.

CHAPTER ELEVEN

witnesses

(Bolton, 2004 & 1971–1972)

In the small hours, woken by another things–speeded–up dream that left me with sweat cooling in the digital clock's salving green light, I get up and prowl.

I'm back in Bolton, a week after my night with Janet Marsh. Today was my mum's seventy-seventh birthday, and Melissa, Maude and I have made the Herculean effort and convened (at Maude's) to celebrate. Carl makes only one trip a year from Arizona, a product less of economy than of the stingy American holiday allowance, and he's already been this summer for the parental wedding anniversary. (Our claim, mine, Maude's and Melissa's, has always been that Carl is our mother's favourite. Of late I've revised. He's not the favourite, I told the girls. It's just that he's not demonstrative. Mum needs a lot of affection. Hugs, kisses, all that. He withholds. Not like us, Melissa said. We're cheap. We're like affection *whores*. This is true. Actually, I told them, I don't think it's a bad thing. This pining for Carl keeps her involved, leaves her motherhood unfinished. She's better than she'd be without it.) Spouses, partners, grandchildren, great-grandchildren, none of them is here. As they get older Mater and Pater want the whittled-down family. The grandchildren were fascinating when they first came along, introduced my parents to another version of love, but they've grown up and become remote. There are too many of them. They're out there with the internet and video phones, having kids of their own and changing towns and countries every ten minutes. When they're all present it takes the old man for ever just to address someone, all the false starts, Ben I mean Mike I mean Carl Rick Owen – bleddy *hell*. He only wants a refill. I've told him to just sit there and hold his glass up and keep bellowing Whisky until someone supplies it.

The frail nobility of houses at night: the little islands of LCD light; the timid sentience of coat-stands; the well-earned relaxing *tonk* of a cooling radiator. Garp, I recall, got a kick out of watching his kids sleep. I've got a similar penchant, not for kids, since there aren't any, but for my family. The role comes naturally, insomniac or dream-spooked guardian in the dead nocturnal spaces; it gives me a profound feeling of sadness and well-being, as if my vigilance hangs above them like an imperfectly protective veil. There they lie, lumps of darkness in the room's dark. I exhale, quietly, feeling the last vestiges of the nightmare evaporate. These are the moments, alone, keeping watch, when my muscles and bones ease into their right alignments. I know what Vince would say: And you don't think this is a sign there's something wrong with you? You're like a sort of perverted addict, he told me, the last time we had the routine conversation, a grown man addicted to his family. It's really awful. What about *your* life, for fuck's sake? I couldn't answer him. I wanted to. I wanted to say: They had gold bars and bloodstones and machetes and murder plans and God and India and Destiny. I've got a teaching job and a broken heart. What fucking life?

It's been a good day. The perennial Monroe offspring project to get Mater tipsy (getting her drunk, or as she would say *blotto*, is out of the question) today met with success; she sank three – yes, three – Harvey's Bristol Creams and entered the state of mild word-muddling inebriation from which we, the degenerates, derive disproportionately devilish pleasure. Cheeks flushed, eyes moist, she said: I feel a bit giddy. That's the point, Ma. That's what it's *for*. Oh, no, I don't like it – trying to blink herself sober, giggling, hiccupping, for God's sake. She had to go to bed early, but came downstairs a couple of hours later, ostensibly to get a drink of water, really because the gathered family is irresistible for her. She has a way of doing this, gravitating in her nightie back to the bit of the household still awake and poking her head round the door, frowning and rubbing her arms and somehow conceding that this is where the fun is still going on and that she's a sucker for it. She'll stand in the doorway for an hour, or perch on the arm of a chair, knees together, keeping up the appearance of being just about to go back to bed. 'What are y'all watching?' she asked. We were watching Channel Five's *Cosmetic Surgery Live*, of which Pasha, Melissa and Maude are appalled fans. The programme included a feature on anal bleaching. (It's quite something even to someone of my generation that you can be watching a terrestrial commercial channel at eleven-thirty at night and hear: 'Coming up after the break: anal bleaching', along with a teaser shot of a young, attractive Latina down on all fours with her dark Levis and white knickers round her ankles.) And sure enough, after the break here was the young Latina, having her anus, well, bleached. 'I juss like to feel, ju know, that everything's nice an neat back there.' She was being interviewed *in situ*. 'A lada dorker-skinned ladies now are lightening up in the anal area.' This was the bleach-pasting 'doctor', American, naturally, female, mid-forties, humourless, piping up adenoidally from behind her client's upraised arse. It wasn't that it wasn't funny to her (any profession soon bleeds its funny stuff of funniness); it was that it had never been funny to her. Pasha was sitting forward in his chair, glasses on forehead, squinting as if in poor light, trying to get his head round the concept. Melissa and Maude were delightedly agog (that's the way for unpoliticized women; yet it goes in, adds to the weight of depression, the dully intuited mass of torture men coerce them into inflicting on themselves). 'Look at this, Ma,' Maude said. 'It's women who have their *anuses* bleached.' My mum stood there holding her elbows and trying to unpack what she'd heard, then said, after a crinkle-faced moment, 'Dear *God*,' which sent us into hysterics. And if that wasn't enough, she asked in genuine puzzlement: 'Who's going to be looking back there?'

On Maude's shag-piled landing I stand and smile, thinking of this. My mum's sexual naivety and that shy nightied way she has of coming back to where the kids are still up will, when they're gone, leave a terrible gap in my world, a unique loss.

Barefoot I creep into my parents' room. A palpable aura of body heat cocoons them. Pater sleeps (marking time in sonorous snores) as he's always slept in England, with the sheet wrapped bedouin-style round his head against Night Chills, to which he refers in an undertone, as if they're malevolent spirits who might be listening. My mother sleeps on her side facing away from him, knees tucked up, a slight frown on her shut face. Her last set of dentures has given her a very slight underbite none of us is happy about. She's not happy about it herself, but we've all stupidly nagged her about it as if it's her fault, as if she's betrayed us by sud-denly changing her face in her late seventies. 'Anyway,' she told us this morning, 'I've made an appointment to have these teeth replaced, you'll all be glad to know.' It made us realize how lousily we'd handled it. We're such bullies, in our mild angry loving ways.

It hurts my heart to see Mater and Pater like this deep in their dreams (dead to the world, as the pitiless idiom goes), especially her; the fragilely held balance of her seventy-seven years forces me to remember the gaps between her children's world and hers, all the ways modernity (us, the kids, with our deranged lovers and boozing and disappointment and gadgets and boredom and ambivalence and secrets) has left her behind. I try to imagine her – as *The Cheechee Papers* insists I must – as the orphaned child, the near-destroyed adolescent, the dreamily (I'm tempted to say somnambulistically) plotting murderess. Hard to believe it's the same person. More than half a century ago those hands (phthisic now, the skin worn to transluscence by the years of feeding us, clothing us, picking up after us, First Aiding and caressing us) that lie as if in unconscious prayer together by her cheek, lifted the machete abandoned by Kalia and felt the heft of its promise, the implicit potential, the one great liberating trajectory it offered. What was the plan if not to smash Cyril's head in with it? But would you really have done it, Ma? I've asked her God knows how many times. She shrugs, then thinks, then says, Yes. Definitely. He disgusted me. I would have killed him. It's lucky I met your father when I did. Is this the same woman, girl, child? Can the identity really have survived? This is the question like the buckled heat of a furnace *The Cheechee Papers* forces me to face. Again I remember the look of her, delightedly frowning, arms wrapped round herself, rejoining us in the living room earlier. The little self-allowed indulgence: 'What are y'all watching?' How can it be the same person? But the facts insist. Katherine Lyle, now Katherine Monroe. Dearie. Ma. Mater. Mum. You write what you want, Sweetheart. None of that can touch me now.

Melissa and Maude sleep with their doors wide open, Maudy, who's inherited Pasha's intolerance of the cold, with the duvet pulled right up under her chin, her long dark hair spread coronally on the pilow; Melissa (years with Ted on the icily draughted farm) with the duvet half off, one arm bent up as if she's just been relieved of a badminton racket. Whether I like it or not it's a pleasure to see them without their men. (Ted's never in any hurry to join these gatherings, from which we can't help making him feel excluded; neither is Maude's man, Greg. We're insufferable together, we know, *liking* each other; it's best if we're left to get on with it.) I have to remind myself that my sisters are women now, Melissa a grandmother, for Christ's sake. Maude's daughter, Elspeth, has just moved in with her boyfriend. They used to be the Girls. Their bodies have filled out certain schedules: grown breasts, assimilated the monthly bleed, fucked and been impregnated by men, carried and given birth and milk to children, worked, walked, ached, suffered divorce, drunkenness, 'flu and fad diets, soaked up sun and poisons, begun to slacken, to wrap and put away certain small treasures. Love's been. Left. Sent its less fierce relatives along later. Life's tiringly manageable. Matters of the heart that might have killed them haven't; now there are only the matters of the body to worry about. Their offspring still draw them into the future, but without the blind ferocity there once was. They're starting to see that the main shape of their lives, the bulk of the relevant information, is already in. Only the death of one of their children could really open the book again, and even that (though I know they'd never admit it), since the kids are adults now and God more or less dead, wouldn't start the apocalypse it once would have. By the Nietzschean law they've survived too much to be destroyed. They're starting to see, without, most days, minding, that they've only got one mystery (the big firework saved till last) left.

The stair carpet receives my tiptoed descent with, I decide, a sort of terrified collusion, recognizes me, the small-hours prowler, the family voyeur, the communer with the mute souls of domestic appliances. I pause in the hall, abristle with selfhood, privacy, certainty of my own eventual death. I tell myself there are all sorts of things I might do: make a cup of tea; play a game or two of patience; start Maude's abandoned copy of *The Sea, The Sea*; step out into the moist, conifered back garden for a sensuous shiver; but I and the tense hall know that's all smoke.

From my rucksack by the telephone table (there's a nonworking grandfather clock here that makes me think of *Tom's Midnight Garden*) I unpack the envelope files I've brought with me.

All three of them. I'd intended to bring only *The Cheechee Papers* and Skinner, but found after I'd packed them that leaving the Scarlet file behind felt wrong. I've started working – the writing, The Book – on the computer at home (which when I open the desktop still confronts me with a folder marked 'Sheer Pleasure/ Millicent Nash') but the attachment to the physical files now is superstitious. Besides, a great deal of what's in them is without backup or copies. What if there was a fire in the flat? Scarlet's photos. I tell myself, settling on Maude's lounge floor, that I must make duplicates of everything.

I sift, unproductively, circularly, through *The Cheechee Papers*. 'The gods and goddesses of romance make their inaugural demands,' one sheet begins, but the sentence isn't finished. The material, I tell myself for the thousandth time, is difficult. Progress is bound to be slow. I'm cursed with memory: I remember every-thing. That's the problem.

No point in opening the Skinner. Tomorrow morning, if I can get him alone, I'll tell Pasha I've found him.

The cat-flap squeaks and thinly slaps and Maude's cat, Fergus, comes in with a tinkle, smelling of damp lawns, the night. I would like him to curl up in my lap, but he doesn't. Instead sniffs me, goes once abstractedly round the room's perimeter, then stops, comes alert, listens. In a moment, he's gone, *tink tink tink tink*. That's the appeal of animals, why we can watch them for hours: they can't choose, it's all call and response. They have fear, but not anxiety.

I switch the television on, mute it and channel surf until I find late-night boxing, *Great Fights of the '70s*, Ali vs Frazier in Manila, which, at the retirement flat on the other side of town, the Mater and Pater VCR will be whirring into life to record. I remember the fight. The big contests were festival events in the Brewer Street household, like Easter or Christmas, brought the distant glitter of America into our living room. (I always knew Pasha's analysis of Ali's superior boxing was incontrovertible, but secretly

I was with my mum in the Frazier camp, took Ali's bullying big-headedness at face value. Frazier looked like a nice guy, but with his style, that monotonous, loose, forward-stepping chug – like a drunk trying to lean on a bar that kept moving away from him – and all but folded arms as defence, you knew Ali'd get him sooner or later.) What always frustrated me as a child was that you could never get a clear view of the half-naked girls who came on to parade the round number-cards in the intervals. Maddeningly, the camera stayed on the gasping boxers getting sponged and barked at; every round you thought someone would get wise and shift the shot a few degrees left or right, so that instead of a torturous glimpse – one long leg, a nude armpit, a sliver of spangle-pants'd buttock – you'd get the whole glorious sight. But they never did. Further maddeningly, you sometimes got a pulled-back shot of the ring just as the girl was clambering awkwardly out. There was, it seemed, a minder whose job it was to part the ropes and give her a hand down. It infuriated me that these men never seemed particularly interested in the girls, did their rope-parting all the time looking past them, at the slumped fighters in their corners. These girls struggling to negotiate the ropes and the step down in their high heels hurt my childhood heart with their suddenly revealed humanness; I loved them, wanted to marry them. How could the minders be so oblivious? Even the crowd's between-rounds wolf-whistles sounded token, bored, impatient for the action to begin again. It was American boredom, a col-lective satiation that added in spite of myself another layer of sinister glamour to who my mum and dad called the Yanks. You could see that for the crowd there was a fine line between being bored by the girls and hating them. (When we grow up, I said to Scarlet, countless times, we'll go to America.) It's different nowa-days. The broadcasters have wised up. Now you do get the camera shift between rounds; the blonde with the porn body and *Sunday Sport* crop-top and high heels and deadened smile. The world changes, the old order passes away. And that's just my meagre

quartet of decades. At St Aloysius Pasha read science fiction tales
about people going in rockets to the moon. Science fiction.

The papers in the Scarlet file are held together with a bulldog
clip. It's with a familiar feeling of shirking my duty that I prise it
open and slide them out.

She came to live with us at the Brewer Street house (when she and
I were going on six years old) because her mother, Dinah, was mad.

'Aren't you going to give Owen a kiss?' Dinah said to Scarlet, as
if to prove the issue. Scarlet stood holding on to a leg of our dining
table. At the mention of a kiss she twisted herself round it in embarrassment disguised as abstraction. (I see it now as a foreshadow of
the move that would come later round a pole in stilettos and her
underwear. Can we trust the way a grown man remembers the
behaviour of a little girl? When the grown man is me and the little
girl Scarlet, yes. I remember everything.) 'Come on, silly,' Dinah
said. 'Don't be shy.'

There was no kiss. Throughout dinner my mum and dad
exchanged looks. I'd seen enough welcomes to register the qual-
ification in this one. Dinah, who had a moist, pretty, antelopish
face (and I'd noticed bruises on her shins like fingerprints), ate
very little. Scarlet consumed only half a frankfurter and three or
four chips. When she ate she curled her lips away from her tiny
teeth and bit, nicely. 'Aren't you *pretty*,' Melissa had said to her.
Scarlet had lifted her chin and looked sidelong.

'They came with me, you know,' Dinah said. I'd been lost in
Scarlet's big-eyed face and emerged not quite at the utterance
but at the lump of silence it deposited like a stone in the middle
of the table. My mum and dad glanced at each other then both
opened their mouths to say something before anyone could ask
but they weren't quick enough and Maude said, 'Who came with
you, Aunty?'

'Who do you think as if you don't know. They don't realize I
can see them, plain as day. But I can.'

'You know Dalma's getting married?' my dad said.

Another silence. Then my mum said (Maude trying to work out whether she'd misheard): 'Yes, to a doctor. She went into hospital for her tonsils and this young chap fell for her.'

Dinah laughed, not in response to this news but as if someone else had just whispered something to her while it was being delivered.

''Course, Sellie thinks she's the cat's whiskers now,' my dad said. 'Daughter marrying a doctor and all.'

Maude was looking around the table for confirmation she wasn't suffering some sort of delusion.

'Maude, can you help me clear, please?'

Dinah said: 'You think I don't know y'all are all in on it anyway, waiting so you can phone them.'

'Maude,' my mum said, 'take Aunty's plate. Come on.'

I saw all this, didn't understand, observed looks passing between my sisters and brother and mum and dad, Dinah's attention apparently engaged by something on the carpet. Scarlet tugged Dinah's sleeve, repeatedly, until, as if after hauling her mind against the elsewhere gravity, Dinah turned and looked at her, and Scarlet cupped her hand and whispered something behind it, which turned out to be that she wanted the toilet, and wouldn't be shown where it was by anyone but her mother.

'She's bad again,' my dad said.

'I thought she was all right?' my mum said.

'What the bleddy hell to do now?'

'What's wrong with her?' Maude said.

'She's not well, Baby. You were too young to remember last time.'

'I remember,' Melissa said. 'She told me there were people after her.'

The toilet flushed. 'Owen, not a word, okay? You don't repeat – got it?'

It had happened too fast for me to be *able* to repeat, but I nodded.

After dinner Melissa went out with her long-haired boyfriend,

Mick – English (or at any rate white), bony of face, thin-legged, leather-jacketed, a wearer of psychedelic shirts and an earring. 'That bleddy *gandu* bugger' was how my dad referred to him, though for me the house's ether quivered whenever he came in. Melissa was going on twenty-one, glitterily green-eyed, full-lipped, supple. (I see photos of her from then and think, Christ what a package; those guys, did they *realize*? Did they have a *clue*?) Maude, fourteen, who despite having the look and pent sex of a moody young squaw was as yet steering clear of boys, long-sufferingly sat down to her homework at the dining table. Carl – the Quiet One – went up to his room to read. The year before I'd given him the mumps and he'd missed his A level exams. He'd never been wild about me; now, after a year of part-time jobs he hadn't planned on, dialogue between us was non-existent. I was commanded to play with Scarlet, so tipped my tub of Lego out on to the rug; the familiar abrupt plastic avalanche, the sound of limitless constructive possibility. Scarlet, kneeling with straight back and hands on her thighs, watched. Outside the colours of dusk softly endorsed my creeping excitement. Above the back wall a streetlamp was visible in its first blood-orange phase. Brewer Street had such a wealth of greys that these first moments of the streetlamps were tropically glamorous, as if giant fireflies had arrived.

'My mummy's boyfriend wore a wig,' Scarlet said. Our hands among the red, white and blue Lego bricks had revealed that we were exactly the same colour. 'I saw it on a plastic head when I went into their room.'

A conceptual traffic jam. A mummy with a boyfriend. A boyfriend with a wig. Mummy, boyfriend and wig all sharing a room. 'When we left she called him a fucking bastard.' I looked up to check we weren't being overheard. I'd never heard someone who wasn't white say 'fucking'. Maude had sneaked the telly's volume up a couple of degrees at David Cassidy's appearance on screen. (David Cassidy had the American inhuman sparkliness you couldn't see and not crave. A threadbare family joke was that when my Uncle Ronnie asked me what I wanted to be when I grew up I said American. Maude was in love. There was a *Jackie* in her room – which was also my room and Melissa's room – permanently open at a page that said: 'ONE HUNDRED REASONS WHY DAVID LOVES *YOU!*') Neither she nor the adults had heard us.

'But they *shot* those children,' Dinah was saying. 'And they weren't part of the demonstration even.'

'Oh, the Americans won't stand any bleddy nonsense,' my dad said, with a sort of relish. 'It's a mess. Now they've started with Cambodia, too.'

'But those children weren't even *dem*onstrating. That's what it's like. They don't need a reason. They're everywhere.'

Shot. Demonstrating. I didn't know what demonstrating was but I remembered a television image: A student (I couldn't tell whether a boy or a girl) lay face down as if deliciously asleep on an asphalt road next to a lawn of scraggy trees. Even this minimal topography established it as America, something about the pale curb, sandy grass, chain link fence, even a passing dog was unmistakably American. Also the grain or snowy sparkle of the footage. Next to the body a girl was down on one knee with arms out (like Al Jolson, I'd thought), screaming. Other students with long hair and torn jeans, one in a suede jacket with tasselled sleeves like Buffalo Bill, stood around, some looking at the corpse, others looking elsewhere, still others looking as if they weren't aware that anything unusual had happened. Then a young bearded and bushy-haired man being interviewed, looking like he was trying to be angrier than he was. There was something artificial when he swore and it was bleeped out: 'This is the National f★★★in' Guard and they f★★★in' murder four innocent people, man.' His worked-up face and slightly bouncing bush of hair had been followed by images of American soldiers walking across a long-grassed plain with a bank of smoking jungle behind them. All of them had their trousers tucked into their boots and the chin straps of their helmets dangling. The uniforms had lots of pockets and the soldiers walked with confident exhaustion, carrying their guns casually. One of them stopped to light a blinding white cigarette. Another grinned at the camera and said, 'That's all, folks,' which was what came up at the end of *Bugs Bunny* cartoons. They were like strange angels to me.

'How can your mummy have a boyfriend?'

'Because she can.'

'What about your daddy?'

'My daddy's gone away.'

'Where's he gone?'

'Just away. Before I remember.'

Without any good reason I imagined he'd gone to America. There were bone-white car-chase roads that crossed prairies and deserts. Also the jazzy neon-lit spaces between dark skyscrapers. There was always a scene in films when a detective went into a bar with a photo of a missing girl and the bar had a stripper with tasselled nipples or spangled knickers toplessly wiggling and showing her bum while moustached men in sunglasses or fat men with cigars smoked and stared and often didn't even seem to be sitting with their faces to the stage. It always disturbed me that some of them didn't bother to look. That was something about adults, how they were. It was as if the telly knew something dead or bleak and it was slyly showing you, enjoying making you feel uncomfortable. Scarlet's dad knew now, too.

The guests were offered beds (Carl's or Maude's or Melissa's or mine) but insisted the couch was good enough. I, thrilled by the house's disturbed routine, demanded in on the adventure and was allowed to sleep with them in the front room downstairs.

'He called her a nigger bitch,' Scarlet said, returning to the subject of the wigged boyfriend. She and I lay side by side with the covers half off, shoulders touching, her foot occasionally kicking mine. Dinah was asleep. There was a streetlamp outside the bay window. The curtains filtered just enough of its light to orange the darkness, show Scarlet's teeth, fingernails, the liquid black of her eyes. At some point it had been agreed by our bodies that we could fidgetingly hold hands or drape our arms over each other. My hand found the rubbery whorl of her navel where the T-shirt had ridden up. This was meant to happen. In fact, surely it had happened before? Somehow in the interim we'd forgotten each other, but now here we were, remembering.

'A nigger's a Jamaican,' I said. Taxonomy courtesy of Brewer Street. Niggers, nig-nogs, darkies, coons, blackies and chocolate drops were one thing, Pakis and wogs were another. Muhammad Ali, for example, was a coon, whereas Mrs Gandhi was a Paki. I put my leg over hers. She pulled it out from under and put it on mine. We giggled. Did it again.

'Shshsh,' I said. 'That's my sister. And Mick.'

Footsteps outside the bay window. Two lumps of darkness in the minimal light.

'Let's see,' Scarlet said.

It was a job to get to the curtains without a sound. A further ordeal to lift the hem without Melissa and Mick noticing.

'They're kissing,' Scarlet said.

Yes, they were, aggressively, the way lion cubs bashed their muzzles together. Their heads kept changing angles, as if they couldn't find the right one. It was awful the way they kept their eyes open and the way the dark windows and doors opposite dumbly watched, as if they couldn't believe what the world had come to.

'Look at his hand,' Scarlet said.

Melissa had her patchwork suede (fake suede, she's told me since) jacket on, with underneath a ribbed short-sleeved crimplene top. Mick had pushed this up and with his left hand was gently squeezing her lacily bra'd breast. His thumb did some jiggery-pokery and there suddenly with a turgid pop was Melissa's nipple. To my utter astonishment, he bent his head and kissed it, put it in his mouth, appeared to suck. Melissa drew a sharp breath in as if she'd touched something icy, turned her head away with her chin lifted, closed her eyes, swallowed, visibly. It was a terrible pain to me to see her do this.

'They're doing the things,' Scarlet said.

'What things?'

'Like in the pictures.'

Like the strippers in the American bars the detectives went in, I assumed she meant. I bet they don't go anywhere *near* the pictures, my dad had said. What are you seeing? my mum had asked. *Butch Cassidy and the Sundance Kid*. I'd thought Butch Cassidy must be the brother of David.

Mick's hand abandoned Melissa's breast and with the tautly splayed fingers of a male go-go dancer travelled down her ribs and the dip of her waist, waistband, skirt. At the hem it paused, then snuck under. While he kissed her neck Melissa's head tipped back and her eyes seemed to be trying to think of an elusive specific thing. There was something mechanical about the movement of Mick's hand under her skirt, like a wind-up toy that must sooner or later run down. Melissa let it go on for a minute, then grabbed his wrist and forced his hand away. Then the kissing again, such violent snout-clashes I feared for my sister's teeth, and gradually the hand under the skirt, mechanical movement, allowed for a bit, forced away. Repeated countless times.

Eventually, after several false endings, Melissa disentangled herself, prised Mick away (he made a little boyish performance of clinging and pouting which I could tell from her face Melissa was embarrassed by) and came with stealthy turn of key and latch-held close of front door inside. Mick walked back to his Vauxhall Viva, got in, started up with a blast of the Who going 'Why don'tcha all f-f-f-fade away', then drove off. The front room door was ajar. Melissa put her back-combed head round it. Saw what we wanted her to see: Dinah genuinely asleep on the couch, Scarlet and me with flung limbs ostensibly asleep on the floor. We lay still with our eyes closed until Melissa had crept upstairs and the house resettled.

'They were doing the things,' Scarlet whispered.

I didn't know what to say. Scarlet's head seemed a small, hard, big-eyed thing with all her soft dark hair spread out on the pillow. Her mouth was a blob of blackness.

'Let's play doing them.'

Another hard-boiled egg lodged in my gullet. One of Dinah's long bare arms was just visible outside the sleeping bag. At dinner her big-knuckled fingers had been greasy from the parathas. When Melissa and Mick adjusted their face angles you saw their glistening tongues. The gullet egg went down in an ecstatic swallow, was within moments identically replaced; there was another one somewhere else, I wasn't sure where, in my belly or up my bum. Scarlet rolled over on to her back and took hold of my hand.

'Okay,' I hissed.

There was a lot of lying on top of each other with mouths pressed together, mutually exchanging hot nostril breath. I liked the weight of her on me, the hard of her ribs and soft of her belly. There were repeated stabs (cranium, shoulder blades) of God watching, Jesus, too, who from the landing's Sacred Heart swivelled his blue eyes down and left, seeing – through staircase, wall, ceiling – us, doing the things in the pictures. Dinah in her sleep rolled over on to her side facing away from us, gave us another layer of privacy. We touched tongues, poked them between each other's lips, held them there. Every move had its intuited duration, as if we were working through a specified performance. It was difficult to keep hold of the feeling, which was a good feeling, because it was so good you kept slipping to one side of it to see how good it was. Once or twice God threatened through Dinah's tossing and turning – I'm *warning* you – but we stopped, the threat subsided, we started again. Hard to say how long it went on. Eventually, we fell asleep.

The following morning, Dinah was gone.

★

It couldn't, as I believe I'm old enough now to say, happen today. Dinah would be sectioned, Social Services would step in, Scarlet would go into care. The creaking penniless unthanked system would do what it does and love wouldn't have a chance. But thirty-two years ago administration meant people writing things down on pieces of paper and sending them to other people in an envelope. Crazies were evaluated with beard-stroking puzzlement. And how does *that* feel? Like my head's full of wet sand. I see. It might be time to give *these* a try. Dinah went in and out of Bolton Royal's psychiatric unit, lived sometimes with us, sometimes with mysterious 'friends', sometimes disappeared altogether. There were dodgy men, always. When she reappeared there were long talks with my parents, eavesdropped on by Scarlet and me, hiding behind the living-room door.

'You've got to think of your daughter,' my dad said.

'I know.'

'There's only so much chopping and changing a child can take.'

'I know.'

'Then?'

Silence but for the gas fire's exhalation, the particular absence of speech that meant Dinah sitting with head bowed and knees together, hair hanging forward, tears *pit-pit*ting on to her skirt. Sometimes Scarlet would leave me, run in, climb into her mother's lap, cling. Other times she'd turn and creep away to bed and lie with her eyes open staring at the ceiling. Most of the time (increasingly, the longer Dinah kept up the now-you-see-me-now-you-don't routine) she stayed sitting by my side, listening, saying nothing.

She came with me to school. The expectation no doubt is that we were horribly racially abused. (That was another of Nick Gough's options: playground fable. All his options, now that I think of it, are a long way from what I've got, from the bloody *Cheechee Papers*.) At St Thomas's we were either too visible (pah*kie*, pah*kie*, pah*kie* . . .) or, when it came to being picked for a team or included in a game, not visible enough. There must have been a handful of non-white Roman Catholics in Bolton, but none of them was at my primary school. We were abused, of course, but there were two of us and that made all the difference. Certainly I got beaten up, but usually because I'd hit out at someone who'd insulted me or Scarlet. I was very good at losing my temper, not very good at fighting. (Where are your father's genes when you need them? I could have inherited boxing skills. What did I get? Sticking-out ears, or as Pasha would say, yurs.)

'Speak Paki language,' I was commanded one sleety morning, having been cornered by a group of boys led by Ant Hargreaves. 'Go on, say sommat in Paki.' I could count up to ten in Hindi (Melissa had taught me) but I wasn't going to. *Aap kya khana mangtha?* I might have said: *What's for dinner?* Pasha liked to ask it in musical Hindi, a joke that the days of having servants were so long over and my mother – Kate Monroe! – was in the kitchen. 'Get fucked,' I told Ant and his fellows, and kicked out at the nearest one. They sat me down in a puddle then spread the story that I'd wet my pants.

Teachers, too, had the choice between bringing us into the existential limelight – 'And what do *you* have for Sunday lunch at home, Owen and Scarlet?' (simian hysteria when I answered, 'Chicken curry and rice, miss') – or reminding us that we weren't really there. 'If you've brought back a letter signed by your mummy or daddy about a musical instrument, please leave it on my desk before you go out,' Miss Livsey said. Scarlet and I looked at each other. What letter? There was for both of us a constant nervousness about having missed something, some way things worked. And there on Miss Livsey's desk at the end of the lesson were a dozen or more letters. What should we do? I asked Scarlet. Should we say anything? No, Scarlet said, we shouldn't. We might get into trouble. Over the next few weeks some kids started bringing to school as well as their gym bags or satchels cases carrying musical instruments. They, by occult English

metamorphosis, had become the Orchestra People. I was King
Herod in the nativity play. Scarlet was the lousy innkeeper's wife.
It ought to have all felt desolate and terrible, but there were, I
repeat, two of us. At a parents' evening my mum and dad were
told Scarlet and I had trouble mixing. 'They'll mix when there's
someone worth mixing with,' my mum said, and that was that.

We found our way into the burned-out house towards the end of
the summer term. A miracle its gravity hadn't drawn anyone
else. At one edge St Thomas's playing field was bordered by a
two-foot-high bank and a line of railings with a thicket of trees
beyond. Between the back of the bank and the railings was a
narrow gully you could crawl along unseen. If you followed it far
enough it brought you to where the railings ended and, at right-
angles to it, the hedges of the houses that backed on to the field
began. The burned-out house was the first in the row of four. A
hole barely big enough to squeeze through, but when you did,
there you were in the darkly enclosed space, fenced on either
side, with the great mystery of the fire-eaten house in front of
you.

In the kitchen I kissed Scarlet and put my hands on her hips.
These warmer days we'd made this our place. The feel of her was
the same bloodwarm miracle every time as if for the first time.
The hard of the hip was so you understood the soft of the waist;
ditto knee and thigh, rib and belly, jaw and throat: hard–soft.
School dessert had been chocolate sponge and chocolate custard.
Our mouths were sour from it, milk powder in the custard that
outlasted the cocoa, lingered on the tongue. She stuck hers out for
me to suck, hummed a tune while I did it. The pleasure of holding her and sucking her tongue was so intense that every moment
I thought something must happen to stop it.

She disengaged, stepped back, leaving me open-mouthed leaning out into nothing. Light from where a window-board had
slipped came in and gave one half of her hair a nimbus. The St

Thomas's girls' uniform was a pale-blue cotton dress, white knee-socks and an olive-green jumper or cardie. Scarlet had the cardie, two buttons missing.

'Let's do the you know,' I said. I didn't like the way she'd been recently, the suggestion of boredom or irritation. Her attention was moving past me. She'd noticed the bright edge of Elsewhere, I thought, exactly as Melissa had in the months before she'd left, as Maude was beginning to, of late. A female tropism, I decided. Moments like just now, her stepping back, suddenly reclaiming her tongue, gave me a glimpse of how desolate the world would be without her. The alienness of brick walls and cars and other people's faces and twirling umbrellas and teachers would surge back into awful unmediated existence, demanding I made something of them; impossible without her.

'Scarlet?'

She put her hands on her hips and her head on one side, as if I were a perplexing but only mildly interesting painting.

'Come on. Take your knickers off.'

She stared, slowly righted her head. She did this not-speaking-to-me routine from time to time, or carried on as if I wasn't there at all. It brought all the violence I could do to her (if not for the great wall of love and worship in the way) to the surface.

'Upstairs,' she said.

The staircase of the burned-out house was intact but what was left of the upper floor was precarious. The fire had eaten from the front of the building towards the back at a tilt. One bedroom had no floor, another's was undamaged, but the one Scarlet preferred had half its floor missing, the remains a jagged crescent. You had to edge round the drop, looking down past the blackened stumps of the joists into the scorched living room below. From its glass-less window (two or three planks cursorily nailed up) you got a view of playing field and playground, saw the whole St Thomas's population in its constituent clusters: girls skipping; loners mooching; boys chasing soccer balls. It was small and sad seen in its entirety, bits of life you knew felt huge and urgent if you were down there in them. Perhaps it was how God saw the world.

'And I don't know why you're calling me Scarlet,' she said, as we went up, vertiginous me clinging to the wall. 'My name's Sabrina.'

Another thing she'd started lately. Sabrina, Megan, Chrissie, Natalie. It gave me a dirty feeling using these aliases, but she wouldn't answer me if I didn't. She'd let me get used to calling her by one false name then switch to another. It made me think of Dinah. They came with me, you know.

'Can I kiss you there?'

I knelt and she lifted her dress, the cool cotton tent over the soft warm middle of her. I was aware of the floor's edge at my back, the drop like a cold open mouth. The house smelled of wet dust and charcoal. Scarlet's green-cardied shoulder blazed when she leaned into one of the window's slats of light. It used to be that she fiddled with me, too, stretched, twanged, squeezed and put in her hot soft wet still mouth my twitching prick, but recent weeks had reduced us. For me these games never stopped prom-ising something – but what, I didn't know – beyond themselves. For her it was as if they'd failed to deliver.

At the burned edge of the drop I stood releasing at Scarlet's instruction an arc of piss into the room below. Sunlight passed cheerily through the hot stream.

'There,' she said, pointing to a patch of exposed brick. I shifted aim. Hit. She laughed.

'There, where that writing is.'

Another hip-swing. Another hit. The graffiti of evening van-dals.

'I'm running out,' I said. 'Hurry up and—'

'Shshsh! What's that?'

My piss stopped. 'What?'

'Shshsh!'

Voices in the garden. I tucked away and zipped up, pronto.
Scarlet with black eyes wide put her index finger over her lips.
Quiet. Together on tiptoe we returned to the window and peeped
between the boards.

Gary and Wally. Gary Dempster, 'Cockertskoo' (*tr.* 'Cock of
the School', i.e., the boy no one could beat in a fight) and Robbie
Walsh, a.k.a. Wally, Little Wol, Rolly, and, by recent poetic fiat of
Gary Dempster, Wally Da-Da. Wally was unnaturally small with a
pudding bowl haircut that made his head look like a mushroom.
He was catarrhal and red-faced with rheumy blue eyes and pre-
maturely detonated capilliaries in his cheeks. (Walsh, Mrs
Shepherd had once famously said, you're like an offensive alcoholic dwarf. Do something about yourself, can't you?) Gary
Dempster, Cockertskoo, skinny, big-boned, with a mop of dark
hair, sad grey eyes and a full-lipped feminine mouth, won all his
fights because he had rage. If there was a brick he'd grab it and
smash your head with it. He'd come to St Thomas's two years ago
from Burnside Children's Home. We got these terrifying children
now and then who smelled of stale piss and wrote like Infants and
if pushed screamed obscenities at the teachers. Gary had been suspended, let back in, suspended, let back in. In Miss Livsey's class
he'd thrown a chair through a window, and he'd called Mr
Entwistle a bald cunt to his face. He'd had what looked like an
epileptic fit in the corridor, which had brought teachers running,
with versions of their faces we'd never seen before; they were
people, we discovered, with an access of horror. This was Gary's
last year and the word 'borstal' kept being said to him. Once, I'd
come out of a toilet cubicle and found him standing alone in
silence staring at the tiled floor, hands uncharacteristically out of
his pockets. My scalp shrank as I walked past him – the swipe, the
lash out – but he didn't even look at me, just carried on staring at
the floor.

Certain things disgusted him. Wally was one of them.
Therefore he went through phases of forcing his company on

Wally, making him go around with him, getting him into trouble. Over the last week or two he had made Wally his 'leader', the Great Wally Da-Da, whose job it was to pick boys for Gary to beat up. Wally, in visible misery, had no choice but to play along.

'I don't reck we're sposed be in here,' Wally said. Gary, inspecting the gap in the boarded-up door directly below us, ignored him. 'Oi, Gary, don't you reck we shouldn't be in here?'

'Shut it,' Gary said. 'Get over here.'

Wally stood in the middle of the overgrown back lawn with his mouth open and his arms held slightly away from his body. 'Let's go back,' he said. 'We can go back and—'

Gary turned, walked over to Wally, quickly.

'Don't Gary don't please, please—' Wally cringed, arms crossed and wrapped tight round his face. Gary calmly grabbed a fistful of Wally's hair and yanked. Wally screeched and dropped to his knees.

'Fuckin shuddup,' Gary said.

We heard them coming in, got down on our bellies. They were in the kitchen, Gary poking around. It was depressing seeing the two of them together, Gary moving about, occasionally turning and making strange faces at Wally, Wally exaggeratedly snorting and snickering. Gary kept up a quiet soliloquy, or series of soliloquies, since he changed voices repeatedly. Scarlet and I lay on our bellies at the edge of the drop.

'Hygiene inspection,' Gary said. This was him impersonating a grown-up. 'By your bed, now, laddie.'

'Gary, don't.'

'Come on, now, laddie-boy, no nonsense else I'll 'aff teck measures.'

'Gary, I don't *wan't*.'

'Right. I'm teckin . . .'

They came into view below us. My shoulders tightened. Wally was crying, silently, with his face screwed up. Gary was behind him, not looking at him. A weight came up off them and pressed on my head. There were those minutes before a thunderstorm, the space between you and the sky filling with invisible tons.

'Stop fuckin . . .' Gary said. Then, as if to an invisible colleague, in a nasal, W. C. Fieldsish voice: 'The boy's a grizzler. The boy's a grizzler.' Wally's hands covered his face. Scarlet's body pressed against mine. I wanted to move back but any sound might draw their attention. Hygiene inspection was when Nitty Nora the Bug Explorer, a mountainous blue-eyeshadowed nurse with an odour of flour and antiseptic, pulled you close and rummaged your scalp for nits. A surprisingly delicious experience, your vestigial ape reduced to boneless ecstasy. You went away half devoted to the woman.

I daren't turn my head to look at Scarlet in case it made a noise. All either Gary or Wally had to do was look up. Gary had gone over to a corner and taken a piece of folded-up newspaper out of his pocket. He looked at it for a few moments, breathing heavily through his nose. It was the same emptied look I'd seen that day in the toilets, as if he was staring into nothingness with nothing inside him. He folded the piece of newspaper back up and put it carefully into his pocket. 'Hygiene inspection,' he repeated, not looking at Wally, wrinkling his nose as at the detection of a bad smell. 'By your bed, laddie. Let's be 'avin you, now, chop-chop.'

He approached Wally. Wally's head shuddered; he was jamming his jaws together. Gary observed this for a moment, then grabbed Wally by the hair and pulled his face close to his own. They remained in this Eskimo greeting for a few seconds, Wally with head shuddering, Gary with nose wrinkled and eyebrows raised. There was a curious little shuffle, both of them moving together, then I saw that Gary was trying to pull Wally's pants down. Wally, with pained face, making a pointless fight of it, grabbed Gary's wrists. Gary giggled, flicked Wally's hands away, slapped him, lightly, across the face, then with brisk disgust in three awkward yanks forced Wally's shorts and underpants down.

'Ands on yer ed!' Gary barked. 'And stop that snivellin, now, laddie boy, if you don't mind.'

Wally, trembling, raised his hands and put them on his head. The gesture lifted his sweater and shirttail higher, revealed the elastic-marked waist and pale pelvis. Gary stood with his fists on his hips for a few moments. Turned and took a few steps away. Then turned back. He took the piece of newspaper and a pencil from his pocket, unfolded the newspaper, hurried round to face Wally, held it out to him. 'Hold that, laddie,' he said. Wally was quiet, shivering, but I had the sense he'd gone into himself. '*Hold* it, I said,' Gary said. 'Never seen one of them before have you, laddie, eh?' Wally with shaking hands took the newspaper clipping. We couldn't see what was on it. Gary seemed to be fighting persistent boredom. He circled Wally, but veered away, went to the window or kicked about in the rubble. Eventually with a sigh he approached Wally and began poking his buttocks with the rubber end of the pencil. Every time he did, Wally, hobbled by his dropped trousers, flinched and shuffled forward. 'Move again, laddie, would you?' Gary said, poking repeatedly. Wally was in a very thin voice mumbling to himself. Eventually he was up against the wall. Gary leaned back and with a dentist's weary concentration carefully aimed and pushed the pencil between Wally's buttocks while Wally in his own honking voice said loudly but not shouting, 'Ow, ow ow,' as if counting.

After a moment Gary, breathing heavily through his nostrils, pulled the pencil out and tossed it away. Without being told to Wally dropped the newspaper and pulled up his pants.

Just as he did this two things happened. The floorboard underneath me gave a loud tick that made both boys look up, and an adult female voice suddenly musically bellowed, 'What on *earth* are you boys doing in here? Get out this *minute*.' This was followed by terrible snapping sounds, the plywood boards being with grown-up strength ripped from the door. Slats of light shot in and picked out hurrying dust. Scarlet pushed herself away from the edge, stood up and backed to the window. Not a woman but a man came, with heavy crunches of litter and clattering of debris, into the room below. I'd never seen him before. I caught a glimpse of short grey hair and a reddish T-shirt before I backed from the edge and got to my feet. As in *Scooby Doo* I tiptoed in reverse. 'Right, you boys,' I heard the man say. 'Out, *now*. This place is a deathtrap for God's sake.' Then my foot went through the floor.

We were an odd foursome in front of Mr Tyrell, the headmaster: Gary, Wally, Scarlet and me. The office was set below the level of the playground, like a bunker. The window's dark view was of half a dozen concrete steps going up into the yard. Tyrell behind an MFI desk in a squeaking swivel chair with what little light came in glinting on his spectacles, speaking to us very solemnly and slowly about his disappointment in us. I wondered how he stood it in here, that pea-green carpet and the moody wood panelling. Other than the desk and chair only two gunmetal filing cabinets and a few framed school team photographs. Our parents would have to be informed, he said – then when the silent charges detonated visibly realized that Gary didn't have any and Scarlet's were absent. Gary snorted quietly, and put his hands in his pockets. Mr Tyrell sighed, sat back in his chair, then as if he'd forgotten until this moment to lose his temper with us leaned forward again and in a very loud voice said if he ever, if he *ever*, had reason to believe we were anywhere near that house again we would face *extremely* serious consequences, did we understand? He said did we under*stand*? Wally, shirt still untucked, cried without a sound through the entire interview. Now get out of my sight, all of you.

'Look,' Scarlet said to me when we got home. We were in our bedroom, alone. Downstairs we'd left Maude doing her homework at the dining table, my dad with his glasses pushed up on to his forehead watching the ITV news and my mum in the kitchen getting tea ready. Beef and potato and pepper stew, the hot sour of tamarind that like a pair of pincers squeezed your salivary glands. We were both starving after the day's ordeal. 'Look at this.' She took out of her pocket the much-folded piece of newspaper Gary had made Wally look at. 'I picked it up,' she said. 'No one saw.'

It was without doubt the strangest image I'd ever seen.

Five Vietnamese children a few yards apart from each other came down a wet tarmac road towards the camera, loosely shepherded by three helmeted soldiers in the background. Nearest to us, in the left foreground of the shot a boy in a white short-sleeved shirt and dark shorts was doing something extraordinary with his face. It was only crying, this extraordinary thing, but the camera had caught him in such a way that his open mouth looked cartoonishly too big for his face, a rubbery black cavity like Linus's when he bawled. Back down the road a little girl held a smaller boy's hand as they hurried towards us. Slightly further back, with her head turned as if to check that the soldiers were still behind them another little girl (she looked about five) was running. The soldiers didn't look as if they were in a hurry. The side of the road showed rough grass and a hint of puddles. The horizon was a blur of what might have been smoke.

'Look at her,' Scarlet said.

The fifth child was exactly in the middle of the shot, a girl who might have been seven or eight years old. She was completely naked, holding her arms away from herself, wrists limp. The logic of the scene said she was moving towards us but she looked posed with a static grace. As with the boy in the foreground the camera had frozen her mid-scream, and like his mouth hers appeared unnaturally large. You couldn't believe she was naked, but she was: diaphragm and ribs, navel, thin shadowy mons. Naked in the centre of a wet tarmac road in what looked like the middle of nowhere.

'There's something wrong with her,' Scarlet said. 'Look at her arm.'

'Is it burned?'

We fell silent, the picture was so strange. I was thinking of the way Gary had taken it out, then put it away, then taken it out again and made Wally look at it. Never seen one of them before, have you, laddie? The girl's thing, he meant.

'What shall we do with it?' I asked Scarlet.

'I'm keeping it,' she said. 'It's mine now.'

Two days before the summer holidays I stood alone with the headmaster in his office. Wally had been absent from school since the incident. His parents had been in to see Tyrell. Rumour was filling the school like a gas leak. Something Serious.

'Are you sure you're telling me exactly what happened?'

'Yes, sir.'

'I don't want you to be frightened. I want you just to be sure you're telling the truth. Are you?'

'Yes sir.' A heavy smell of mown grass came in through the office's long upper window. Scarlet had said: They won't believe us, anyway.

'All right, you can go. Send Scarlet Reynolds in, please.'

I closed the door behind me to get a moment. She was leaning against the wall opposite with her hands in her skirt pockets and her chin down on her chest. She looked up at me, brought herself back from wherever she'd been.

'Did you tell him? Like we said?'

I nodded. 'He wants you to go in.'

She pressed her face against mine, nose to nose, as if to evoke Gary and Wally's version of the gesture from the week before. I got the hairwashed smell of her, and when she pulled away saw the faint freckles sprinkled under her eyes.

All the way to Miss Livsey's I kept thinking of how Scarlet had said: They won't believe us anyway. They won't believe *us*, she'd meant. Herod and the lousy innkeeper's wife. Chicken curry and rice on Sundays.

★

Two weeks later, Dinah, with a silent, damp-looking cold-eyed man I'd never seen before, came and took Scarlet away.

There's a Post-it I'd forgotten about stuck at the bottom of this page. It says: Parallels: Kate orphan loses everything creates family. Scarlet orphan loses everything rejects family.

I sit back in Maude's armchair and pick up the TV remote. *Great Fights of the '70s* finished a while back. Since then, in and out of reading, I've been flicking (still with no volume) between Iraq coverage on BBC News 24 and *Supergirl* on Channel Five. The actress playing Supergirl (yes, as in the girl version of Superman) is so Americanly blonde and youthful and healthy and pretty and angelic it's been hurting my heart to watch her. It's a sweet pain to me, the supernatural freshness of young American actresses. I can forgive America anything for these girls it produces.

Deciding enough's enough I hit the Off button and the picture disappears with a thump–tick–crackle.

'You're still awake?'

Pasha's voice startles me. I hadn't heard him come down. He's groggy and pinch-eyed, but sees me jump and quietly laughs. He stands in the doorway in his ivory cotton pyjamas (the man from Del Monte pyjamas, my mum calls them) and bedsocks, hair sticking up, one hand gently rubbing his belly. He'll have got up for a pee and seen the line of light from the lounge door. 'What're you doing?'

'Just going through some stuff.'

'It's nearly four o'clock.'

'I know.'

He rubs his hand over his face, half waking it. He's not a night prowler but he's seen the files there on the floor. 'I'm going to have an Eno's,' he says. 'You want one?'

'No, I'm all right, Dad.'

'Bleddy stomach's griping.'

He turns and goes to the kitchen. Eno's anti-acid powder is the panacea. Heartburn, indigestion, constipation, pimples on the tongue, trapped wind. As a child the ritual fascinated me, the soft white powder, the panicky effervescence, Pasha hurrying the glass to his lips before the whole lot frothed over the brim. He used to save me a mouthful. It tastes like fizzy salt, Dad. Don't give him that rubbish, my mum would say. The great magic was its conferral on me of the ability to produce burps of adult magnitude, which in spite of herself made my mum laugh.

When he's had his drink (he burps, *baaaarouwp*, as if in solemn praise of a primitive god) he comes back to the lounge doorway. There are these moments when he looks not his age, but shockingly older than my mental image of him. The belly remains redoubtable, the dark hands elegant and cunning, but the skeleton in places – knees, clavicles, elbows – is beginning to assert itself, to speak of essential structure.

'You're not going to bed or what?' he asks.

Outside it's still dark, but there's been in the last minutes a perceptible weakening of the night's concentration, as if it's raised its head from hours of study. 'I will,' I say. 'I got sidetracked with all this.'

He comes in, burps again, goes to the bay window, lifts the curtain and looks out. It's still surprising to him and my mother that the kids have houses like this, big rooms, gardens. Melissa and Ted have a swimming pool. Mater and Pater have swum in it, but still more or less refuse to believe in its existence.

'I wanted to ask you something,' I say.

'She's forgotten the bleddy crook lock again.'

'Dad?'

'Eh?'

'How come in India you weren't really aware of what was going on?'

'What do you mean?'

'I mean politically. You must have known things were going to get lousy for the Anglos once the British left.'

He yawns, gigantically. 'Yeah, we knew, but what were we going to do? Handful of people in millions. The ones who could get out got out, that's all.'

'Didn't you feel there was anything you could do? Get involved, I mean. Organize?'

He shakes his head. 'It didn't occur to us. Well it didn't occur to me. Hector got obsessed with politics for a while after '47, but I could never be bothered.'

'But I mean the whole shape of the *world* was changing. Didn't you . . . ?'

'We didn't think about it, much. Don't forget I was boxing. That was always going to get us out.'

Which draws down silence.

'What you've got to understand, my son, is that I wanted to be in the *ring*. It always felt to me like . . .' He purses his lips and shakes his head. 'All the bleddy this and that, politics, news, work, money, the British, the Indians . . . In the ring all that meant nothing. It was like a kind of *purity*. There's the man and you've got to knock the bugger out, you see?'

'Nothing else mattered,' I say.

'Nothing else mattered. You haven't been in the ring, so you don't know. Everything else . . . There's nothing comes close to it for the purity of the thing. I haven't got the words.'

Like sex, I want to say, thinking of Scarlet. I've been in *that* ring, Dad. 'Like being in love,' I opt for.

He's not stupid, he knows what I mean. He laughs, makes a slight dismissive gesture that somehow leads both of us to look at the contents of the files scattered on Maude's taupe carpet.

'How's it going?' he says.

'Slow. A lot of other stuff keeps creeping in.'

He doesn't mean the Book, *The Cheechee Papers*. He means Skinner. The Gas Board bugger didn't remember him, I'd lied. It's another dead end. All day I've been rehearsing the words: Dad. Listen. I've got something to tell you. I've found him. I'm waiting for the daughter to call.

But something gives me pause. The briefest loosening of his face. He's not thinking about Skinner. He's suddenly arrested by the oddness and the hour, standing in his pyjamas not even in his own flat. He's an old man and he doesn't like his routines disturbed. There is the perennial swarm of worries — about money, about Maude's crook lock, about getting mugged, about how Carl's running three cars and putting two kids through college, about me and my neither here nor there wifeless life, about what'll happen to Mum if he dies first, about what'll happen to him if she dies first, about the pensions crisis, about Elspeth's moving in with her boyfriend, about the NHS waiting lists, about terrorists, about his prostate, his kidneys, his bowels, his feet and his teeth — there's this swarm of worries and ever-increasing feeling of his diminished say in the world, his grip in subtle increments loosening. Sometimes his face, as now, relaxes for a second and I know he's seeing it clearly, that the bulk of his strength has gone. Unopenable pickle jars are passed to me, these days. The first time it was thrilling; since then a negligible acute sadness. When I see him seeing it like this, a feeling of febrile insubstantiality takes me, a manageable panic.

'Is that Scarlet's picture there?' he says.

'Yeah.'

'Show, let's have a look.'

He studies the Elvisish headshot. 'I don't remember her having her hair short like that.'

'It was at the end. Just before we broke up.'

'You never hear from her?'

'No. I think she went to America.'

'Acha?'

'Well, it's just a feeling. I don't know. She could be anywhere.'

I know he knows the score; my mum will have enlightened him: Scarlet Broke Owen's Heart.

'We all thought you two were meant for each other,' he says, dropping (carefully; he's not insensitive to these things) the photograph back on to the papers on the floor. 'I mean, when you met her at university after all those years.'

'Yeah.'

'Destined to be together, I told your mother.'

'There's no such thing as destiny, Dad.'

'Well,' he says. Pauses. Belches softly, *bouwp*. 'There used to be.'

Familial ESP is keeping him hanging around. He doesn't know what's in the air but something is. He goes to the doorway, hovers. I could tell him, now. The cat-flap goes again and Fergus appears, slinks with abstracted sensuality between the old man's ankles. Pasha's fond of this cat, to his own surprise, is quietly flattered when Fergus appears to recognize him or chooses his lap to curl up in. Old age is sparing with its gifts but this is one of them: there's room and time to take in the personalities of little creatures, find these late, small, uncomplicated relationships.

I know what's holding me back. I imagine discussing it as if it's a novel with my Friday three o'clockers. Daniel's weary analytical acumen, half of them not paying attention, heads full of mobile phone numbers and contraception, hip-hop lyrics, diets, the gaggle of celebrities having a permanent soiree in their brains. Not to be*labour* the point, Daniel would say, not to *state the obvious*, but the reason he holds back from telling his old man is because maybe, just *may*be, this lifelong quest for Skinner is what's keeping the old boy, you know, engaged. Actually *find* the fucker, deliver him, you know, then what's his dad got to—

Well I think *live for* is a bit strong, Daniel, but yes, that's more or less it.

'I'm going to clear all this up and go to bed,' I say.

CHAPTER TWELVE

꧁꧂

The Tryst with Destiny

(*The Cheechee Papers*: Bhusawal and Bombay 1946–52)

That first Inter-Railways season, March to September 1946, introduced Ross to the absurdly privileged life of the sports star. For
their six-month sojourn in Bombay the teams were housed in stationary first-class carriages in the Victoria Terminus sidings,
commodiousness and luxury Ross had never known. Plush berths,
tin baths, self-contained toilet and shower closets, cooks, bearers.
'I told you,' Eugene said, laughing, uncorking a bottle of Three
Barrels rum. 'This is the bleddy *life*, men, what?' The bleddy *life*
was, on the whole, getting paid for lounging around drinking and
smoking (plus in Eugene's case womanizing) and being waited on,
with the odd bout and game of football thrown in as if to remind
them apologetically what they were there for. Many of the Anglo-
Indian fighters and players brought their wives, families and
servants with them. Not Eugene. He'd been married to Mitzi for
six months, long enough for the novelty of fidelity to be wearing
thin. She'd disappointed him between the sheets. Years of knock-
ing-shop gymnastics – and more recently the affair with Cynthia

Merritt — had left Eugene with a broad sexual palette. Mitzi was
not only not interested, she was morally stung. 'You're hopeless,'
Ross told him. 'I don't know why you bothered getting married
in the first place.' Marriage was much on his mind.

Kate had said nothing of dreams and weights lifting off her head
and machetes and God. She did say, after their first dance a week
following Kalia's death, when Ross put his arm round her on the
walk home under a dust of stars: 'I'll tell you this once. Once must
be enough. I know what the talk is. I know they say I'm his mis-
tress. I'm not and never have been, nor ever will be as long as I
live. If that's enough for you, we never have to speak of it again.'
She hadn't rehearsed it that way but when she opened her mouth
found that was all there was. Six sentences like a line of stones.
He'd said (after a pause in which she was thinking how strange it
was to have someone's arm around your waist, how all her life
since the death of her parents there had been nowhere for physical affection to go, how if the door into love and family opened
the terrible force of her affection would come rushing out, that
she knew now she would love her children with ferocity, beyond
any kind of control): 'It's enough for me.' And she'd said: 'Good.
I'm glad.'

'So that's you, is it?' Cyril said to her one night a month later,
when Ross had walked her all the way to the gate. Since the stabbing her uncle had barely spoken to her. Death had come close,
shown him what he would have to take with him. It had left him
shrivelled round his core of tawdry rottenness. He never said, You
put him up to it, planned it. That would be to admit the magnitude of her hatred, which threw him back on the question of his
hatefulness. No. Intolerable. Instead his face had taken on a new
look, curl-lipped and wet-eyed, between disgust and imprecation,
as if in this courtship with another man she was betraying him.
Sometimes just the sight of the back of his head made her feel
physically sick. Contempt kept her from vomiting. If he had
touched her then, she would have killed him out of sheer disgusted

reflex. But he didn't touch her. Instead started these small-mouthed non-questions. 'So that's you, is it?' She ignored him.

In February her grandfather had another stroke. He survived, wheelchair-bound, with further diminished powers of speech. Kate, still the unpaid labour force at Sellie's, had her hands full. At Sellie's the talk was of leaving for England. 'This place is going to go to shit,' Will said quietly, on the veranda, holding his evening wet up to the sun as if proposing a toast to the idea. 'Only one place for us now and that's home. This time next year we'll be gone, Kitty.' This was the current that wrecked her nerves. Cyril was afraid of emigrating to England (where he'd be no one), and carped endlessly about Sellie's selfishness in leaving him with the burden of the old man.

Ross, meanwhile, had to wait for victories in the ring and on the pitch, the leverage they'd provide. He knew he wanted to marry her (she had it, the instinct for fierce allegiance, the hunger for making a knot of shared life against the gale; there was a bot-tlenecked power in the girl which he in his moments of naked intuition was afraid of, and on top of all that the great Godswirl of destiny [the stars that first walk home had seemed to allude to] that had connected them) but not on a fireman's wages. Look, just be patient, for Christ's sake, Eugene had told him. Win the boxing in April. Win the football with us in September. Get up to goods guard at least. She's not going to want to marry a bleddy pauper, is she?

And so the courtship crept on through 1946, both of them waiting, her for him to ask, him for a life worth asking her to share. He dropped what hints he could, back in Bhusawal between bouts or matches. 'Listen,' he told her, during a slow dance at the end of an evening at the Institute (she was exhausted from the day with Sellie's kids and her grandfather), 'when the season's over I'm going up to the training school at Bina for two months. If I pass the exam I'll get on as a guard. I'll be getting better money.' 'Is that a plan?' she'd asked him, sleepily. 'Yes,' he'd said, 'that's the plan.' (He said nothing of the rest of the plan – or was it a different plan? – the trials, the Olympics in London, the promoter, the pro–boxing, all the sweet pussy . . . He didn't think about it. His instinct was to make her his. Everything else would have to fit round that. When it's her, Hector had confided to him, disgusted, when it's *her*, brother, you'll know, believe me. And you'd better pray to Christ in Heaven she's not already taken by some bleddy English hotel manager bastard . . .)

The plan held while Kate waited. Ross came home at the end of September with the Inter-Railways Bantamweight Title (he'd had to go to Calcutta for the finals, where he'd beaten the BB&CIR's southpaw Lester Parnell with a knockout; a close fight he came near to losing when Lester's renowned left uppercut caught him at the very end of the first round – white sizzle, cymbal smash, faltering waltz with gravity – but he survived, kept his wits and dropped his man with a right cross a minute into the third), and his centre half's share in the football team's glory; at the Cooperage ground the GIPR's first eleven had beaten the NWR by three goals to one to lift the cup for only the second time in the company's history. He spent Christmas and New Year in Bhusawal before going north in January 1947 to the training school at Bina. According to the plan: three months, sit the exam, pass, come back to start life as a goods guard, on which wages, sooner or later, they could marry.

Then, at the end of February, the day before Ross was due to return, Kate's grandfather died. She found him as she had found her father ten years before, at dawn, with the life gone. Not peacefully, either, the rictus grimace said.

She was past being surprised by her feelings – in this case not the loss of him, personally, but a disorientating shift in the invisible machine weights of her world, as if the old man had been wittingly or otherwise holding some swing or motion in check.

Before Cyril spoke, later that afternoon while Dr Bannergee was writing the death certificate, she knew what he was going to say. 'Well, that settles it. We'll go to England with Sellie and Will.'

We. She was to be included. The Lomaxes were leaving that summer. Tens of thousands of Anglos had already gone. The names of distant countries had become common currency: Australia. Canada. England. People kept talking about Motherlands and Fatherlands. It sounded babyish to her, as if they were talking about fairies and monsters. It first surprised and then irritated her that people attached so much weight to the idea of a country as some living thing to which you were related. She never thought in that way. India was the name of the country she lived in but home was herself, under her own skin. God and men went about their brash business any- and everywhere, like the weather. There was no home. Or every place was home whether you liked it or not. She knew these feelings were peculiar. She knew *she* was peculiar. But she knew, too, that Ross Monroe wanted her, that she was almost sure she wanted him. That, in the first instance, would have to be enough.

'I don't know what you think you're doing,' Cyril said. That evening, after Bannergee had left he'd come to the door of her room and found her packing a small bag. The tinny shouts of children playing in the street came in through the open window.

'Leaving.'

There was a silence (which said he knew she wasn't joking) before he let out a puff of laughter.

'And where the bleddy hell is it you think you're going?'

'That's none of your business.'

'Don't speak to me like that.'

Nothing. She balled two more pairs of white ankle-socks and dropped them into the bag. In the space between her and him it was as if the last of something was being burned away, going quickly in sizzling seconds, astonishing both of them with its friability. Adrenalin murmured in her. She pushed past him in the doorway, felt one last surge of the habit of himself mass, climb, reach out, incinerate. Nothing. Only a shorn quality to the air. At the front door she paused (a miracle she could hold the bag, wrists and hands weak with excitement) and looked back at him. He stood with one hand at his side, the other absently clutching the front of his shirt, as if he was about to try to yank himself off his feet. The rimless glare glasses were pushed up on to his forehead. The monkey mouth had gone small and tight.

'You walk out of that door,' he said, 'don't think about coming back.'

She stood on the threshold and looked out, not from hesitancy but to commit the moment to memory. The children were playing kick-the-can; someone was booting it *tink-tatonk-tank-tonk* while the rest shrieked and cackled and cheered, kicking up a yellow mist of dust. The tops of the banyans at the edge of the front garden were oranged by a shaft of late light. A cloud of frenetic gnats hung between the gateposts. The evening had a soft golden gravity. She had no money and nowhere to go if her instincts were wrong.

'I'm warning you,' he said.

She turned and walked away.

To Sellie's. 'Just for tonight, Aunty. I feel funny sleeping there where grandpa died.' Sellie had been in bed all day, incapacitated ostensibly by grief. 'Yes, yes, Kit, it's all right,' Will said, ushering her into the parlour. 'You bunk up with Lucy or Dalma. We're all sleeping outside, anyway. No point in troubling Aunty now, she doesn't know whether she's coming or going.'

'What are *you* doing sleeping here?' Robbie wanted to know. 'It's a secret,' she said. 'What secret?' 'You'll see.' 'It's the end of the Empire!' Robbie said, jumping up and down inside his mosquito net. 'God save the King!'

She was waiting on the platform when Ross got off the train the next day. 'I've left,' she said. They were her first words to him as he stepped down with his suitcase. The cool season was over; for a week now the middles of the days had been advertising the coming conflagration with yawning white skies and heat like a billion fine needles gently increasing their pressure against you. Kate felt tired and light, standing there with the chaos of passengers and hawkers around her. *Hindi pani, Mussulman pani, pahn biri, tahsa char, garumi garum.* She couldn't remember when she'd last eaten. It occurred to her for the first time that if she'd made a mistake she was going to have to think of what to do. In the seconds that passed before he spoke, while she watched his young face take it in, calculate, she asked herself: What will I do if . . . ? The question diffused into a vague image of herself walking with her bag through empty sunblasted land.

'Will you marry me?' Ross said.

The soonest they could manage was the twentieth of April (in the meantime Ross installed Kate – since Beatrice wouldn't have her at Bazaar Road, to all the world *living in sin* – at his sister Rose's, where she spent six weeks quietly observing the strangely successful, slovenly marriage of Rose and her according to Beatrice goodfornothing husband, Eric), on which day at eleven o'clock in the morning they were married by Father Francis Menezez at the Church of the Blessed Sacrament, Lime Road, Bhusawal. The number of Ross's siblings alarmed Kate, the tribal ease they had with one another. They were all, too, ferociously direct. Well, madam, I hope you're going to sort this harum-scarum bugger out once and for all? Kate nodded, though she had no idea what needed sorting out. At the Limpus Club reception Hector got leadenly drunk and after much indecipherable poisonous talking to himself passed out under the table. Sellie, Will and the kids were Kate's only guests. Eleanor Silvers and her family had left for Australia that year. Cyril was not invited.

Kate had assumed (not without trepidation) that they would move into the Monroe family household, temporarily, immediately after the wedding. But late into the reception Ross ushered her outside and into a waiting ghari. 'Where are we going?'

'Shshsh. It's a surprise.' He put his arm around her and kissed her, a little drunk, the breath said, but manageable. He lost his temper easily, drunk. She'd seen it once or twice at the dances, all the largesse and bonhomie at the stroke of one misinterpreted remark transformed into focused aggression. Not at her. At other men, the perpetual flame of competition. He wasn't, she knew, a hitter of women, though his father, he confessed, had given his mother terrible beltings. It disgusted me, he'd said, head down, standing with her on the banks of the Taptee one evening at dusk. The water had been membranous, the colour of mercury, sliding slowly past, here and there rucked and ruffled by stones. On the bridge half a dozen other couples were silhouetted against the peachy sky. I couldn't look at him in the same way afterwards, the cowardice of it. And yet when he's sober you won't get a better man. Kate had had to sift and weigh all this in the first months. But he'd passed. You knew, she told herself, if a man was dangerous to you: the potential was there like an undisguisable odour. He didn't have it. Seeing his father brutalize his mother had drawn a line in him, sealed dignity at a certain depth. He wouldn't go past it. The commitment to his own idea of himself wouldn't let him.

The ghari stopped outside a small bungalow on Armoury Road and Ross told the driver to wait.

'What?' Kate said.

'Come on,' he said. 'We're here.'

She put her arms out and he swung her down. Fished in his pocket and brought out a key. It glinted in the moonlight.

'You're not serious?' she said.

'I am.'

'How?'

'Never mind how. Come on, have a look inside.'

Fresh from the boxing Inters, bantamweight champion for the second year running, he'd gone straight to the accommodation office. Old Clem and Reggie Hodge had already put in their requisite words. Here's the list of vacant houses, the officer had said. Take your pick. He'd picked the one furthest from her uncle's.

'There's a bed and a table and chairs,' he said. 'The rest we'll have to get bit by bit.' Then after a pause when he didn't know what was going on in her head: 'We don't have to stay here straight away, tonight. There's room at home.'

She crossed from the darkness through a slab of moonlight on the bare floor, put her arms round him. 'I want to stay here tonight,' she said.

At a press conference at the Legislative Assembly in June 1947 Viceroy Mountbatten told journalists – casually, as if mentioning possible future weather conditions he didn't expect anyone to be much interested in – that the transfer of power would be brought forward from the previously proposed date of June 1948 by some months, in fact that it 'could be about the 15th of August'.

News of a ten-month advancement should have had India's hacks in a fever. It didn't, for the simple reason that many of them couldn't believe it. Was the viceroy serious?

But by the third week of August it was apparent that he was.

'Christ, *look* at all these fellows, men.' On Victoria Terminus's platform 5 Ross and Eugene stood side by side on a bench, looking over the heads of the swollen crowd. The station's baked concourse was a deafening mass, barely movable through. Everywhere faces were tight, sweat-sheened, everywhere eyes busy with fear, everywhere someone trying to get past someone else. Families with what they could carry on their backs, in their hands, on their heads. Here and there station staff who looked like they hadn't slept for days. Three locomotives stood like animals trained not to panic in crowds. Two days ago the Frontier Mail had arrived twenty-four unthinkable hours late in Bombay, having been held up, looted, and turned into a mass-murder scene en route. Thousands of Muslims were now to all intents and purposes living on the platforms of VT, waiting for trains to take them north into newly created Pakistan. The violence around Lahore was so bad that railway employees had stayed at home to protect their families. Suddenly Anglo-Indian staff had found themselves in curiously fierce demand, the (so far sound) reasoning being that since they weren't Hindus, Muslims or Sikhs no one would murder them.

'I don't like it,' Ross said to Eugene. 'I don't like it one bit.'

'I know, but what to do? He's a grown man, dammit all, isn't he?'

Hector, this was, who was scheduled to take a train out from Bombay that evening.

'He's not in a fit state to be in the middle of all this bleddy madness,' Ross said.

'Leave it, men. There's nothing you can do.'

'I can't leave it,' Ross said. 'You don't know the state he's in.'

The Inter-Railways season, the Hector–Bernice affair, the transport system, the country (or now countries, since stick-insect Jinnah had got his way), the collective sanity, all were in a state of collapse. Last night Reggie Hodge, the football manager, had called a halt to the GIPR's part in the tournament. Team members were disappearing, from India to Pakistan, or from VT to their homes, or from fixture commitments to sudden demands from their employers. Within the last seven days the squad of twenty-two had been reduced by half. It was the same for all the competitors. 'You can't have a Cup without teams,' Reggie had said, disgusted. 'What a bloody enormous bollocks-up.'

The BB&CIR had pulled out of the tournament the previous week and Hector had gone back to work. Then, three days ago, Bernice had broken it off with him. He'd gone on a two-day drinking binge, got into a fight, ended up in jail and had to be bucksheed out by Ross and Eugene the following morning. Kept his job by the skin of his teeth. If Anglos hadn't been such a precious commodity he'd have been sacked. As it was they'd scheduled him to take a passenger train up to Baroda this evening. They should have sent him to a sanatorium, Ross thought.

'I'm going to get a pass,' Ross told Eugene. 'I'll go up with him in the brake.'

Eugene groaned. 'What *for*?'

'To keep an eye on him. The way things are at the moment, I'm telling you he'll get into trouble on purpose.'

Eugene looked around them at the throng. 'You'll never get a pass with all this madness going on,' he said.

Hector, ravaged by booze and heartbreak, was in a state of thunderous misery.

'Come on, for God's sake,' Eugene said, grabbing him by the back of the neck and giving him a friendly shake. 'Think of all the other women out there. You've got to' – eyes sparkled, fingers of free hand wiggled – 'you've got to get tough with yourself and use them to get her out of your head, yes?' Ross rolled his eyes, secretly touched by Eugene's insistence on coming with them. They were half an hour out of Bombay. 'You've got to *go* at it, you've got to fuck like a bleddy *lunatic* until the memory of her is gone, absolutely bleddy *vanished*. Understand? Like this, you see.' Eugene started to sway and very gradually move his hips in circles while surveying an imaginary horde of available women. 'Oh, yes, what's your name? Lucy? Yes, come on Juicy Lucy that's right, thank you . . . And what's *your* name, my little poodle, eh? Cindy? All right, come on, chalo, Cindy, I can see you're one of the Seven Deadly Cindys, aren't you, eh? Thank you. Now you, you there with the legs, just lift your skirty for the dirty, come on, chalo, don't keep Daddy waiting . . . You're next, Charlotte, then Peggy, then Bernice . . . Oh yeah—'

Hector flung himself at Eugene and got him by the throat.

'Wha—' Eugene squeezed out.

'That's her bleddy *name* you idiot,' Ross said, getting to his feet and grabbing his brother's arms. 'Hector, come on now don't be stupid. He didn't know, he just forgot. Come on, men don't make me—'

With the application of the emergency brake all three men went over. It took a few moments for them to untangle themselves.

'What the hell?' Eugene said. 'Why're we stopping?'

Ross and Hector looked at each other.

'Shit,' Ross said.

In brash light on the veranda at Armoury Road Kate was thinking about England. There had been a letter from Sellie this morning and this was the second time she'd read it. Actually, a letter from Robbie (full of back-to-front consonants and ropy spelling) with a drawing of a house being virtually obliterated by slanted dashes she understood to be rain. '*This is our hows in England.*' Robbie wasn't happy. '*At skool the call me names.*' It touched Kate that he'd written. She'd missed his harmless madness; the thought of him growing up depressed her, all his occult communications with insects and trees and imaginary things gone, the uncomplaining spirit driven out by whatever there must inevitably be, a job, money worries, lost love, the awakening to God's cold experimental interest in the world. '*Cyril's in London with Arthur Cavendish,*' Sellie's cursorily tacked-on paragraph informed her. '*Arthur says he can get him on at Tate & Lyle.*' Sellie, Will and the kids were at Will's mother's house in the north, a town, Bolton.

'Memsahib?'

Kate turned. 'Yes?'

The servant, Dondi, of wizened mahogany-dark face and pickled eyes, stood in the kitchen doorway with a straw bag over his shoulder. (In it, as per Kate's instructions, spices to be taken to the mill for grinding.) Dondi was an alcoholic station beggar Ross had one morning found shivering outside the team carriage in Bombay and taken pity on. Kate was discovering her husband's hodge-podge: a willingness to break the law; emotional honesty; a feeling of entitlement to life's treasure; stabs of empathy; caprice. Ross had taken Dondi under his wing, informally, paid him a pittance to run errands and polish his football boots, then a few weeks into the season brought him home to work at the house in Bhusawal. No drinking during the day, okay? After seven o'clock you can do what you want, but until then no high-jinks, understand? Dondi had wept as if he'd been adopted by royalty – though gratitude proved no match for addiction. Kate knew he knocked back a mug of meths now and then to get him through the day, but she couldn't bring herself to care. He was gentle and devoted. It always seemed to her that the dark brown of his face had tinctured the whites of his eyes. He'd been skeletal when Ross had picked him up. Now, on leftovers that amounted to three square meals a day, he'd acquired a look of surprised wiry health.

'No,' Kate said, 'there's nothing else. When you come back from the chakki you can take the afternoon off if you want.'

Dondi grinned and joined his hands and shook his head slowly as if she'd made an outrageous joke. He was terrified of being given time off in case when he returned they'd changed their minds about him.

'It's all right,' Kate said. 'You can come back, drop off the masalas and do what you want till dinner time.'

Dondi bowed, hands still joined, still grinning and shaking his head and began to reverse out of the kitchen. 'I'll come back, sweep up,' he said. Sweeping up was the default if he felt evidence of his redundancy beginning to show. Kate smiled and waved him away.

When he'd gone the house's baked stillness reasserted itself behind her. The airmail paper's pale-blue delicateness made her hold it up to the light. Liberation from Cyril had given her a new, amoral sensuous curiosity. (She wasn't resolved about sex. It had frightened her and, initially, hurt. There was the mess Cyril had made to be somehow got through, wrongness that clung like dark strands of a stubborn web; but she was patient. Of late once or twice there had been intimations of pleasure, as shocking as if she'd felt a prickling of clairvoyance. They hadn't talked about it; bedroom life was inarticulable. But there were looks, hers saying don't force anything, his wanting to know it was all right. She wasn't sure it *was* all right. Her understanding even of the mechanics of conception and pregnancy remained sketchy. She was shy of asking Ross, though she knew he knew.)

She looked again at the address on the airmail letter. 7 Lever Street, Bolton, Lancs., England. Funny to think it had come all the way from Robbie's hand some morning weeks ago. England. She folded it up and slipped it into the pocket of her skirt.

The compound's copper and bronze red-flecked chickens glowed in the sun. In recent days the town's collective spirit had been pulsed through by trainloads of people making connections for the north and east. When you stopped and attended to it the land was animally alert. Anglo-Indian faces were changing. It was as if the temperature had dropped, unseasonably. She'd asked Ross, one night in the dark after sex (because the silence afterwards did seduce them into speaking from the core of themselves, simply and honestly, even if it wasn't to speak about what they'd just done), What does it mean to us, the British going? Will we be in danger? There'd been a pause before he'd answered and with a crisp thrill of wifely intuition she'd known he was weighing up whether to lie to her about something. She'd known, too, that he wasn't going to lie, that the weighing-up had already been done when he married her. Listen, he said, I want to tell you something.

They'd lain side by side, not even holding hands, while he told her of the plan. The Olympic trials. England. He could turn pro, make money. They could travel. She'd listened staring up at the ceiling, feeling the house and the night listening with her. She didn't say anything. So much new had happened that anything seemed possible. When he touched her hand she got a fright, and they laughed, and he said, And if there are children there'll be more money to give them a good life with.

Kate thought about it now, standing looking out into the afternoon's glare, remembering the dream she'd had, the curious little bud from her thigh, the thing that turned out (by the time she found her mother on the train) to be a baby. She'd lived her life by such things, impulses, dreams, instincts, the knotted logic of the Deal with God. She hadn't told Ross about that. Other people, she knew, didn't make decisions the way she did, instead worked things out through a sort of mathematics of anxiety, with arguing and jabbering and reading the newspapers. To them the world was . . . She couldn't finish the thought. She'd asked him, that night, in pure neutral enquiry, Are you that good? And he'd said, Yes. And it had delighted her that he knew this of himself. She'd said, I want children, and he'd squeezed her hand and said, Well, we'll have them. How many kids in the world have a father who's an Olympic champion?

She smiled, remembering it, but felt with the smile's dissolution a slight resurgence of the depression she'd been feeling on and off all day.

In the confusion it was hard to tell how many people were attacking the train and how many attempting to defend it. It looked initially like a Laurel and Hardy crowd-clash, suitcases and bags flying through the air, exploding on the ground, pots and pans, bed linen, underwear.

'This is my train,' Hector said, quietly but as if by Divine intervention audibly in the clamour of shouts and screams. They were between downpours. Ross looked up and saw dark curds of monsoon cloud ravaged here and there by brash sunlight. The land steamed. He was glad Kate had gone home. For a couple of weeks after the wedding she'd sampled first-class-carriage life with him in the VT sidings. Some bleddy honeymoon, Eugene had said. Ross had watched her around the other wives and men. She was

the great Unknown Quotient as far as they were concerned. They
were all unnerved by her self-containment. The absence of need
for their approval came off her like a subsonic hum. It delighted
him. His instinct, he told himself, had been sound: it would be
the two of them, a flame of private understanding in the world.
Already, this season he'd realized he had to force himself to forget
her in the ring, to focus on the fights. Their love only added to
invincibility, took any strength and made it stronger; the victories
filled him with a new pride in how small they were next to the
mystery of marriage. Stepping in under the ropes he had to
expunge her from himself so that later, when he'd won, he could
enjoy the idea that he'd done it for her. The wins were jewels he
could drop in her lap, casually, enjoyable beautiful things but next
to love, trinkets, trinkets . . .

'My driver's Muslim,' Hector said. The three men leaned out
from the brake (in spite of himself Ross thought of the Three
Stooges) and looked down the length of the train. Hindus and
Sikhs with hatchets, clubs, tools, knives were swarming the carriages.

'That's his bleddy lookout,' Eugene said. 'We sit tight.'

Hector, moving with the weary deliberation of a man who's
been got out of bed in the middle of the night to attend to something, jumped down from the brake. Absurdly, he held in his left
hand his pair of brass-handled signal flags, red and green, as if with
them he might impose a referee's order on the madness. 'I'm
telling you,' Eugene said, 'don't be so bleddy—'

'They won't interfere with us,' Ross said. His limbs felt full of
calm electric strength but when he jumped down after Hector the
pain of impact shot through his ankles.

'You can smell it,' Eugene said, with tender awe and disgust.
Fear, he meant, the passengers' penned stink. The beauty of such
a moment, Ross thought, was that a single clearly felt imperative
was enough to cut through it: I have to go with Hector, he's my
brother. Morality in these moments had to be a kind of idiocy.

You could imagine God laughing and clapping His heavy hands in delight. That's it! That's the spirit!

'Give me that,' he said to Eugene. A crowbar had been rolling around under Hector's box the whole journey as if (it now seemed) advertising its availability should something like this happen. Eugene, pale and sweaty, passed it down. 'You stay put,' Ross told him. 'They're not coming in here.'

'Fuck it,' Eugene said, jumping down with a crunch. 'I'm not staying in there on my own to be murdered.'

It was a dreamlike procession up to the engine. Eugene, unwilling to rely solely on his fair skin and GIPR jacket, yanked out from under his shirt the gold cross and chain he'd been wearing since his wedding (Mitzi had given it to him as a keepsake, and, he'd uncharitably thought, as further endorsement of conservatism in the bedroom, since it glimmered there censoriously between her breasts) and held it up in front of him. As against vampires, Ross thought, past surprise at what thoughts came and went.

Chaos was human movements sometimes unnaturally speeded up (a Sikh with a perspiring tight-lipped look of concentration repeatedly clubbing the head of a man who between blows, incredibly, babbled and blinked), sometimes unnaturally slowed down (a huge silver blade's elastic stretch of time slicing through first air then the neck of a man who already looked unconscious on his feet), and sometimes (a bloody-nosed woman gripping a carpet bag being shoved from behind through a window) at their normal speed. There were bubbles of pure silence. Individual screams surprised you, tore off the mass of sound in unique shreds. Chaos was unassimilable. Only fragments could be allowed in. A man naked below the waist lying with his head face down in an open disgorged suitcase. A woman's severed breast on the track next to a blackened skillet. A man brimful of energy twitchily holding a machete but, paralysed by the wealth of choice, unable to fix on a victim.

'Jesus Christ,' Eugene kept saying. 'Jesus Christ, Jesus Christ . . .'

No one touched them.

Ross was thinking of Kate, imagining her watching him. After two weeks in the carriage she'd said, I'll go back. There's so much we need to get for the house. I want it to be nice for when you're properly home. Properly home. It was how he'd always imagined it would feel when you found the right woman. They weren't there yet. The intensity of his feelings making love to her had shocked him. There had been a struggle to get past his own and her obvious nervousness, the shadow (despite his acceptance of the six sentences like a line of stones) of what the bastard uncle had or hadn't done. But he had crept past it, up (or was it down?) into pleasure, though he knew it had hurt her that first time. After the first time it hadn't hurt, but she'd observed rather than gone with him. Her watching, the quiet, curious intelligence while she gave her body to him, drove him nearly mad with something, a reaching out towards her.

'Oh, dear God,' Eugene said.

Long years ago we made a tryst with destiny. The papers had carried Nehru's speech. These last days the words had made celebratory circles in Ross's head. She'd gone past the window of Ho Fun's and the light had flared off her poppied hip and bare shoulder and he'd got up and gone after her. If he hadn't . . . Again the if this then thatness of the world buzzed like a consciousness in everything. The priests talked about God's plan and the assumption was that if there was one it must be good. But you caught glimpses of it now and then – *while the world sleeps, India will awake to life and freedom* – and saw not that it was good but that it was endlessly, if you were God, entertaining. Ross had overheard Kate talking to a neighbour and caught the words 'my husband' and the thrill of it had made him grin. He'd been shaving; there was his familiar face in the mirror, grinning (the lather's white made your teeth look yellow, a sudden flash of the grave) because she'd affirmed her ownership of him to the public world. The public world was the erotic foil to the private. There was Mrs Vaughn, the front garden, the road, the sunlit town, the words 'my husband', and in here, in the house in the dark, was the wealth to which being her husband entitled him. *A moment comes, which comes but rarely in history, when we step out from the old to the new . . .* They had added their names – it truly astonished him that he could think this way – to the secret scroll of history's lovers all the way back to tenderly sinning Adam and Eve. It had made him reimagine God's last words to the fallen couple as they left Eden: Now you know what there is to know. Go out and see if it was worth it.

It's worth it, he thought, as Hector sprang forward and he found himself (and Eugene, with a moan) following. He was aware of himself smiling. One of the reasons God was there was so that there would be someone other than you to notice incongruities like that.

What happened next happened with a purged clarity, as if the universe had cleared a space to make every detail of the moment precious. Rain began to fall in drops as big as grapes. Even people being murdered noticed. Suddenly a carriage door flew open, revealing a fair-haired man in a pale suit with his back to them struggling to keep hold of something – a bag or suitcase, Ross inferred – which an unseen adversary fought to wrest from his grip. The back of the linen jacket showed a spatter of blood, as if someone had flicked a paintbrush from top to bottom. Silence rushed up and gathered here. Hector had run on ahead but Ross paused; this also was the way of it: lesser tableaux uncannily arrested you. He thought, Any second now the fellow in the train's going to boot this poor bugger clean out of the carriage. Presciently: there was the small, distinct sound of a bone breaking. The suited man doubled up (his hand, Ross suspected) and released a groan as of only very slight complaint before being kicked in the solar plexus hard enough to eject him from the train.

He crashed on to his backside and screamed (tailbone) rolling as if in a hurry before coming to rest on his side, pale face frozen in a silent grimace. There was a moment for Ross of mental scurrying, swirl, check, forward grope — then recognition. Without making it obvious, is anyone looking? Long years ago we made a tryst with. Underneath the released adrenalin was the shock of seeing the Britisher's tight-skinned face without its composure. Two each, yes? It seemed a lifetime ago to Ross. He remembered the queer relief when the Malaysian had pronounced, Common brass. Worthless. The con like a beautiful woman stepping out of her robe. He wasn't, in his current purity, angry, but he would be as soon as the Englishman opened his mouth, as soon as the voice got to work. In the absence of language there was an honourable solidity to the betrayal. He took a few steps towards the prone and now retching figure but was halted by a shout, a scream in fact, Eugene's short falsetto; the Englishman, foetal, finished retching and with tenderness laid his head cheek-down in the mud. His face had lost its grimace to the delicate paralysed beatification of being utterly at the mercy of pain.

'Brother!' Hector bellowed. Ross turned and ran towards him.

Hector's driver (and BB&CIR inside right), Saleem Khan, was struggling with a giant purple-turbaned Sikh in tight brown slacks and a bloodstained white shirt who had one hand round the throat of a Muslim woman backed up against the carriage. She was on her tiptoes, one shoe off, toes as if playfully touch-typing the ground, with both hands locked round her attacker's wrist, bangles tinkling, eyes wide with what looked like cartoon panic. A kirpan lay between two sleepers, its blade being *tang-tang*'d by the rain. Hector grabbed the Sikh's throttling wrist and squeezed. Sikh fingers released, but Sikh knee jabbed upwards into Hector's groin and Hector tenderly genuflected, couldn't get up. Eugene pushed the Muslim woman away and she ran, open-mouthed and silent, stumbled, fell, got up, ran. There seemed to Ross endless time and space for the watching of all this. Hector looked like a supplicant, down on one knee holding the giant's hand. Saleem Khan, having grasped the other Sikh arm, could do nothing with it but hold on, jerking as if with irregular electric current. There was all the time in the world for Ross to consider his options, notice that the Sikh's nose had at some time in the past been broken, that there was a maroon ballpoint pen still clipped to the white shirt's front pocket, that the left trouser leg's knee was stained with mud. He lifted the crowbar. You're going to hit me with that. Yes I am. Where? Not sure yet. You and I know the head, the brain, the centre of operations. Yes but I don't want to kill you. The knee will be a big problem for me. Yes, the knee. I'm glad we're agreed on that.

Someone very distantly said, 'Ross!' But the crowbar was already in motion. Sorry, Ross thought, remembering the humble look of the patella from Basic First Aid at Walton. Then noticed the Sikh's eyes flick left. Just before impact. Again very distantly the voice, Eugene's, surely, saying through the rain's hiss, 'Behind—'

Impact. The Sikh's knee shattered and he tumbled forward with an anti-climactic mewl. Ross found himself on the sodden ground. Saleem Khan leaped over him and rolled away with another attacker Ross hadn't seen. Hector crawled towards him. 'Are you all right?'

'Fucking *hell*,' Eugene was saying, standing with arms slightly out from his sides, as if he was expecting to suddenly inflate. 'Christ have mercy.'

'You're hit,' Hector said.

'What?'

'Your leg, men,' Hector said, still struggling to get his breath.

Ross hesitated, conscious primarily of being on the verge of saturation, now that the last threads restraining the rain had gone. There was, now that he came to think of it, something like a line of fire or ice. It took him a moment to locate it. Then he could, and looked. Left leg. Hector took the crowbar from him, adjusted his grip, then swung it hard against the floundering Sikh's kidneys. Another low mewl. It was as if he was being unfairly put upon.

'It's deep,' Eugene said. 'We've got to get you out of here.'

Thus duper and dupee met again, levelled by injury.

'Why'd you do it?' Skinner, the Englishman, wanted to know. This was the hospital in Chowringhee that evening. Ross, not long out of surgery, was still morphine groggy. Skinner (chipped but not broken coccyx, stab wound in the calf) was lying on his side on a trolley with his smashed wrist in plaster and his broken thumb in a splint. Independence had put hospital beds at a pre-mium. Money was changing hands every minute. Patients were on tables, chairs, the floor. Eugene and Hector, unscathed, had gone down to VT to get a message to the families in Bhusawal.

'I don't know,' Ross slurred, the truth. Get that fellow there, he'd gasped, as Hector and Eugene had carried him back towards the brake. Get him on to the train. Eugene had said, What? are you fucking crazy? he's dead; but Ross had been insistent. Get him, I know him, he's not dead. Hector had gone back and with the help of Saleem Khan lifted the unconscious Skinner on board. The raid had ended as suddenly as it had begun. Rioters melted away. The rain stopped and the sun came out. Half-naked bodies looked not murdered but ecstatically spent, limbs spread, lips parted. Blood-puddles gleamed in the mud. The wounded who could be torn from the corpses of their loved ones struggled back on to the train. It was twelve miles to the next waystation, from where a signal was sent to clear the line; with so many in need of hospitalization there was no choice but to go back to Bombay. Eugene had ridden with Saleem Khan in the engine, Hector, still, incredibly, bearing signal flags, in the brake with Ross, Skinner, and half a dozen walking wounded.

'Your friends said you know me,' Skinner said. An effort, Ross heard, not to make it sound like an accusation. The hospital was hot and murmuring, its dignity wrecked; doctors needed shaves, nurses' eyes were lovely with exhaustion. Ross kept rolling to the edge of unconsciousness then lazily rolling back. Time pooled, spurted, pooled. Skinner had asked him something. It might have been an hour ago.

'You robbed me in Lahore five years back,' Ross said. 'Gold bars. Stiffed me out of my mother's bloodstone ring. It was my fault. I should have gone after my wife.'

Skinner, caught by a twinge in the bashed coccyx, gently jack-knifed. Terrible, Ross thought, to see the confident young face ambushed like that. 'You're drugged-up,' Skinner said, trying a slight adjustment to his position, apparently without improvement. 'They're going to run out of morphine if this carries on. Someone's going to make a pile.'

Save his life and he wants to know why, Ross thought. That's the imperative.

'Christ, I need a cigarette,' Skinner said. Five years hadn't changed him. Still the sharp, waxworkish white face and oiled fair hair, narrow blue eyes, that cleft chin as if God out of creative boredom had nicked him. They'd cut off the left leg of his linen slacks at the knee to get at the wound. The bare leg was blond-haired, thin, here and there bruised. 'Haven't got one on you by any chance, have you, a smoke?'

Ross shook his head. The ward's mumble confused his ears. He'd remembered the voice as classier, suggesting a life of gently exercised entitlement. A layer of that refinement was missing but the aura of up-to-the-minuteness remained, the modernity of the man, the certainty that in his presence you were at the tip of your times.

'If you're staying you'd better get used to all this,' Skinner said. 'People cutting each other's bloody heads off.'

Staying? Ross's eyes closed. Leaden dark-red effort required to open them again. Staying here. In India. Politics. Oh, that. He wanted to sleep. There'd be pain when he woke up, but still, the

deliciousness of going under now. He smiled, laughed; his feebleness was funny to him.

'Yeah, it's hilarious, I know,' Skinner said. 'Well, I don't
remember you, sport, nor any gold bars or bloodstones, nor much
else from five years back, but I'm in your debt for not leaving me
to get fucking scalped.'

'I'm falling asleep,' Ross said. 'Are you supposed to keep me
awake?'

'What?'

'Is it safe for me to fall asleep?'

No reply. With an almighty struggle Ross opened his eyes and
raised his head. Skinner, having beckoned a cigarette-smoking
doctor over, hadn't heard.

The Wound wasn't, as Pasha has subsequently made it in the
telling, 'nothing' (the blade went through the back of his thigh
and chipped the edge of his femur, introduced him to doctors'
Latin: *gluteus minimus, semitendonosus, semimembranosus*) but he
maintained ever after it wouldn't have kept him out of the
Olympic trials. If he hadn't got pneumonia in hospital and gone
with it, as he's fond of saying, to 'death's bleddy threshold', he'd
have made it to London in the summer of 1948 and his whole life,
as he's also fond of saying, would have been different.

Against husbandly instructions Kate (and Mitzi) came in from
Bhusawal the next day. In the general confusion Eugene recom-
mandeered a couple of abandoned team carriages in the sidings at
VT and reported sick, but Hector went back on line, coming
home every evening with fresh horror stories. Children gutted,
women raped, men's penises cut off. Murder. The word was too
small. Murder was an isolated act, intimately done by one person
to another against a background of not-murder. But now murder
was everywhere. Now murder *was* the background. The country
had overnight acquired the ability to assimilate the most hellish
human cruelties. 'Who are all these crazy people?' Eugene asked,

repeatedly. 'I mean, who *are* they to do such massacring?' 'Ordinary people,' Hector told him. (Kate, overhearing and thinking of the machete, said nothing.) 'Up north neighbours are killing each other's children.' 'But they've got bleddy military chaps there, haven't they?' Hector laughed. (Since Bernice had dumped him horror was funny, confirmation, the world going mad in sympathy.) Armed Indian troop carriages had been attached to the rear of refugee trains – until it became apparent that soldiers were Hindus, Sikhs and Muslims first, soldiers second. Reports came back of 'selective firing', Hindu and Sikh soldiers firing on Muslim rioters, Muslim soldiers firing on Hindus and Sikhs. The uniforms meant nothing.

'I remember,' Skinner said, crutches-propelling himself on to the ward three days later. 'Lahore. You were in uniform. Bloody— Oh, excuse me,' to Kate, who sat alongside Ross's bed. Ross introduced them, watched for the ignition of the other man's desire, was surprised by its absence, again wondered if Skinner preferred men. 'I remember,' Skinner said. 'You've got it wrong, you know. They took me for a ride, too. Wristwatch and bloody fountain pen for a couple of bits of what turned out to be brass. You thought I was in on it.' He'd been discharged, on the crutches, since his coccyx screamed every time he stood on his own two feet, but instructed to come back for calf-wound dressing changes.

'You were all in on it,' Ross said. 'I lost my mother's bloodstone ring.'

'Singh and that little bugger Ram. Took me months to get over the embarrassment.'

'You said you knew them.'

'I did know them. Ram was just one of those little chiku boys who ran errands for pice. Singh and I had done a bit of business, and to be honest I came away from it pretty certain he'd stiffed me. Which is why I didn't . . . Well.'

Which is why I didn't mind stealing from him. Quick glance at

Ross, the question of how much Kate knew. *Two each, yes?* The shared molestation. Ross had long ago told Kate the story of the gold (downplaying letting her go in favour of it) and discovered in the telling that no slant disguised the moral kernel: that he was willing to dupe and steal for profit; a child, moreover. Kate hadn't censured, just left a solid silence round it like a paperweight. She disapproved, he knew, but shared his feeling that the two of them together enjoyed moral exemption.

'I'll tell you something else,' Skinner said. 'I saw you fight. Damnedest thing. I was at the Inter-Railways finals in Calcutta last year. The whole time seeing you here it's been niggling me. It came to me last night. It is you, isn't it? You do box?'

'Bantamweight. You were there?'

'I was there. You walked it. Your husband's a class act in the ring, Mrs Monroe.'

'Oh yes,' Kate said. 'I know.'

'Starts to look like there's a higher power at work, doesn't it?' Skinner said.

'Could be,' Ross said. He was aware of Skinner feeling Kate's suspended judgement. 'My mother's a big believer in fate,' Ross added. 'In destiny. That bloodstone ring belonged to her first love.'

'You still think I was in on it.'

'Look I'm not saying—'

'I'm sorry you feel that way.'

'I'm not saying you were in on it. I'm just . . . It's my own bleddy fault, anyway.'

'If you thought I robbed you, why didn't you leave me on the tracks? What were you going to do? Wait till I got better, then beat me up?'

Though he'd asked himself umpteen times, lying in bed with nothing to do but listen to the throb-drone of his stitched-up leg, Ross didn't know the reason. The charm of coincidence, perhaps. God's capricious hand again. Your life was a story.

'I'll tell you something,' Skinner said, looking past them towards the doorway with the calm of a man who'd grown large or tired enough to forgive himself. 'I'm not, as you might put it, the soul of moral scrupulousness. I'm a businessman, and in business, especially in this country, you've got to be prepared to bend the rules. People want something, they come to me because they know I can deliver. You want a pin, you come to me. You want a boat, you come to me. Ask my clients, they'll tell you.'

Ross glanced at Kate. She'd become, without his realizing it, someone he relied on to explain people. Kate merely raised her eyebrows.

Skinner laughed. 'Sorry,' he said. 'It's just the irony. What I'm telling you is that on another day I might well have been in on it. It just so happened that on that particular day I wasn't. On that occasion I was, like yourself, well and truly had.'

'Okay,' Ross said. 'Forget it. It was the bloodstone I was bothered about. If you'd still had it I'd have got it back, that's all.'

Skinner looked out of the window. 'Never had it in the first place, sport. Probably still got the brass bars somewhere, mind you. Most likely kept them as a reminder that you're never too sharp to get caught with your pants down.'

'What business are you in, Mr Skinner?' Kate asked.

'George, please. Negotiation, for want of a better word. I bring buyers and sellers together.'

'Buyers and sellers of what?' Ross asked.

'You name it. Someone wants something, I tell them where and how to get it. Agent, consultant, freelance commercial liaison, you can dress it up however you like but in the end it's just knowing who wants what and how to make everyone feel they got a bargain. You really wouldn't believe the stuff that's flying around here at the moment. Typewriters, armoured cars, rare birds, antiques.'

It bordered the ludicrous, this world-weary nous in a man still only in his mid-twenties. Skinner sensed it. 'I know,' he said. 'I sound like I've been walking the globe for a hundred years. But it's dog years here for my lot. I came out when I was fifteen. Game's up now, pretty much. Can't bear the thought of going home, mind you. It's like you don't speak the language any more. Last time I went I was on hot bricks till I got back here. You make your bed.'

The peculiarity, Ross and Kate agreed later, was that he spoke to them as equals. It was what Ross remembered from the first encounter in Lahore, that manner, as if the haze of colour and class had evaporated. You didn't get that from the British. Risible imitations of it, yes, from the clergy and the progressive well-to-do, but nothing like this clean indifference.

'He's not interested in any of that,' Kate said, later. 'That's not what he . . .'

'What?'

'I'm not sure. It's of no use to him.'

'In his line of work, you mean?'

It was Ross's sixth day in hospital. He had pneumonia. Rioting had upset the movement of medical supplies; the hospital had been waiting for antibiotics for almost a week. Ross dipped in and out of fever and had these surreally casual speculative conversations with Kate when he was lucid. Kate spent all her time at the hospital, an unofficial volunteer, made tea, mopped, fetched and carried. Part of her kept asking, *What if Ross . . . ?* but she silenced it. She must have let it slip that neither she nor Mitzi had brought servants. The next day Skinner had sent a young man, Veejay, beaming, severely hair-oiled and side-parted, very crisp and natty in kurta pyjamas and black plimsoles. 'No wages, memsahib, wages paid by Skinner Sahib in the full particular.' 'Please,' Skinner had said, when Kate had protested, 'it's nothing. It's really absolutely nothing but my pleasure to do it. Not that it repays a fraction of what I owe your husband, obviously, saving my miserable hide.' She was never alone with the Englishman except at the bedside if Ross fell asleep; precaution from habit rather than any suspicion of danger. Skinner didn't seem interested in that, either. She couldn't make up her mind about him. The Englishness, his version of it – quick, modern, smart, no nonsense, hints of complexity, overall a humorous capableness – seduced. The appeal was that he didn't seem to care that he *was* English. Occasionally both she and Ross came to with a start because they knew nothing about him, the entire relationship was absurd. Why *did* you pick him up? Ross remained vague. I couldn't not, he told her. I don't know, it just felt inevitable.

'I'll be leaving Bombay in a day or two,' Skinner said.

'Your back's okay?'

'No, it's killing me, frankly, but I've got business in Jabalpur that doesn't give two hoots about my back.'

Another week had passed. Antibiotics had arrived. (Hmph, the ward sister said, when Ross thanked God aloud, you'd do better to thank your British friend. Ross and Kate gawped at each other, incredulous. Skinner, when they tackled him about it, was dismissive. Bit of chivvying, he said. Nothing, really, if you know who to chivvy.) Ross had been started on the drugs but wasn't, as the doctors kept reminding everyone, out of danger. The pain was a tightening strap round his chest and back. In the febrile throes he listened for his sternum going with a dry crack.

'Anyway, I might not see you again before I go,' Skinner said. The two men were alone. Kate had gone to get a cup of tea from the canteen. 'I wanted to talk to you.' There was no one within earshot but he leaned forward and lowered his voice. 'I know people,' he said. 'You want to go pro in England, I can help with that.'

'I'm not going anywhere like this,' Ross said. 'They've already told me I'm not going to make the trials.' The doctors had given him the same answer no matter how many different ways he'd asked the question. That's all bleddy rubbish, he'd told Kate. They're making it sound worse so they feel like big shots. That was his mantra. But increasingly in his moments of unoccupied consciousness the truth came and lay upon him like a heavy invisible animal. His jaws tightened and his fists clenched, a rage against its leaden simplicity – then off again into the non-logic of sheer will. These bleddy doctors don't know anything. I'll get out of here soon enough. A fellow knows his own body, damn it all.

'I know, I know,' Skinner said, patting the air. 'I'm just saying. There are ways I can help you. I know people. You understand?'

Ross didn't, but nodded anyway. The other man's clipped excitement was contagious – laxative, too; Ross, constipated for days from the antibiotics, felt a promising twinge in his gut.

'I do a lot of business in this country,' Skinner went on. 'I mean a *lot*. You work on the railways, right?'

'Yes.'

Skinner hung on his crutches. He was wearing another of his seemingly inexhaustible collection of pale linen suits. Always a dark paisley tie with a small loosened knot. Creased embassy secretary or weathered attaché. Bit of chivvying.

'The point is we can be useful to each other.'

What Ross wanted to say was: What the bleddy hell are you talking about? But the invitation into a sophisticated scheme of things was hard to resist.

'Look, sport, you know how this country works, don't you?'

'Buckshee?'

'That's the least of it. British out, it's going to be a free-for-all. Lot of gains, lot of losses.'

Ross waited.

Skinner stared at him. Then changed tack. 'I want you to know something,' he said.

'What?'

'I believe in fate.' Invitation again, this time so frankly to intimacy that Ross's embarrassment bordered the sexual. Skinner laughed. 'I know,' he said. 'No excuse for it in a cynical sod like me, but there you have it. Extraordinary business, you and me on the train, don't you think?'

'Yes.'

'I know you've played it down since but I feel I owe you my life.'

'You forget I wanted you alive so I could beat you to death.'

Skinner looked out of the window. Nodded. 'We're men, so we have to joke about it, I know.' He looked back down at Ross in the bed. 'Let's just say I remain in your debt, shall we?'

'You're not in my debt. It's nothing.'

Kate came back with three cups of tea, sensed the arrested current. She thought the Englishman looked exhausted.

'We were just saying goodbye,' Skinner said. 'I've been under your feet here long enough. I wanted to hang on till the antibiotics came through. I can see our friend's going to milk this a while yet.'

'I'm a sick man,' Ross said.

'I'd get a move on if I were you, sport,' Skinner said. 'Even your wife thinks it's starting to look like malingering.'

They gave him their address ('I go through Bhusawal from time to time, if you can bear the idea of me looking you up') and watched him swing himself expertly away. He didn't look back. It occurred to Ross that he'd got used to the visits, come to look forward to them.

'So?' Kate said. 'What was all that about?'

CHAPTER THIRTEEN

suspects

(London, 2004)

AOL News:

23rd October 2004: Charity appeals for hostage's release:
New plea for Margaret Hassan's release after <u>distressing video.</u>
Plus: <u>Nadia lands top soap role.</u>

30th October 2004: Terror fear over Bin Laden tape: Experts
fear new video may signify <u>an impending attack.</u>
Plus: <u>Renée's dirty secret.</u>

31st October 2004: British UN worker in hostage video:
Afghan kidnap <u>victim Anetta Flanigan paraded in video.</u>
Plus: <u>New love for Kerry.</u>

It's my day off and I'm at Heathrow. I'm not flying anywhere or
meeting anyone. I come here to wander around, drink coffee,
watch people. Well, where *do* you feel at home? Vince asked me,

years ago, exasperated, because I'd said no, not Bolton, not
London, not bloody *England*. Airports, I told him. Specifically the
Departures lounge, where you're nowhere, where no one has any
claim on you, where no one expects anything.

A joke, but it wouldn't leave me alone. A week later, forcing
myself past *This is stupid*, I took the Tube to Heathrow. I've been
coming here (and going to Gatwick) ever since.

It's a strange thing to have sex with someone to establish you're not
going to have any more sex with them, but that's what Janet Marsh
and I thought we were doing last Saturday. She rang and left a message: 'Hi, it's Janet.' Long pause. 'Give me a call when you get this.'
(There was another message, from Louisa Wexford at Sheer Pleasure.
'Hi, Owen.' Sigh. 'Look, for the money involved we think the sim-
plest thing is to just draw a line under it. You'll get a letter to that
effect some time next week. Okay? It's all got a bit out of hand and
to be frank we want to just get it behind us. Anyway, it means no
more unpleasant emails and nasty letters, I hope. Let me know if you
haven't heard anything by the end of next week. Bye.') I rang Janet
and arranged to meet her for dinner in Ladbroke Grove. Putti. 'It's
expensive,' she said, 'but don't worry, I'm paying. I'm rich now.'

After dinner we went back to her flat in Holland Park, a basement but a big one, with cream carpet, a lot of white, a sofa of teal
leather slabs and an open-plan kitchen–diner separated by a breakfast bar built of those Seventies blueish glass blocks currently
enjoying a revival. He, the ex, had been interested in decor, she
hadn't. 'It used to look a lot better than this,' she said, noticing the
place again through me. 'I can't be arsed with all that.' There were
spaces where pictures (I imagined original framed film posters,
sub-Miró canvases) had been removed and not replaced. She didn't,
apparently, care about *things*; she'd wanted the money for the power
to control what happened to her. There were round frosted lights
set in the bedroom's eggshell panelling that gave it the snug feel of
a ship's cabin. All evening at Putti the conversation – America; pets;

Rome; *Lost in Translation*; not having children; not being safe on
the streets; *Friends, Sex in the City, Six Feet Under* – had in its avoidance of *us,* the phenomenon we constituted, said there would be
sex later but probably nothing after that, almost certainly no future,
no – when you really got down to it – *us.* She was, as she had been
underlyingly that night at my place, sad and excited. Those two
currents would run off her for a finite time. Then, since she had
money but no faith in the likelihood of love, the excitement stream
would die and only the sadness would remain. There had been
love, I saw. (Our irises in their tired nebulae concede, if we've lost
love, that we at least had it to lose.) Janet's love – not the ex – had
gone bad or been destroyed or perverted or betrayed, had suffered
one of the love fates – but it had been love. The sadness was of
knowing the best of her life was behind her and that there would-
n't be children – not her own, at any rate. Which still, since she
wasn't stupid, left the money. She wasn't ungrateful, in fact was
filled with a sense of her own well-placedness; but there wouldn't
be love again, or her own children, which meant in the end she'd
be dying alone. The spirit of that had already started hanging
around on the edge of everything she did.

'I've made some travel plans,' she said, post-coitally. At the flat
we'd had two whiskies apiece, started kissing, gone to bed. We'd
gone slowly, patiently and with mutual sensitivity made pigs of
ourselves. It was (although we didn't quite mention it) laughable
that we got on so well between the sheets, a mild annoyance
since there was no future. It gave us a sod's law fellowship, as if we
were the combined butt of someone else's joke. Her body was as
I'd remembered it masturbatorily (amped-up by the process) in the
fortnight between. I'd taken a delicate meditative diversion to her
anus, of which she wasn't, eventually, shy. Already playing the
footage back to myself (let her take her own sweet time with the
travel plans) I remembered my mum's birthday at Maude's, Mater's
response to the concept of anal bleaching, and despite my best
efforts laughed out loud.

'What?'

'I was just thinking of my ma. Not Freudianly. Just something funny.'

'What?'

'You had to be there. Sorry, it was rude of me. What travel plans?'

She reached for her Marlboro Lights on the bedside table, lit one, offered. I gave up smoking seven years ago but still have the odd one. I'd had one after dinner at Putti with an espresso. (Served by an Italian waitress with eyes and hair as dark as the coffee, outlined brown lipstick and despite a tidy figure a look of transsexualism.) Took another now. All those hours and days Scarlet and I had spent in bed, smoking, eating, boozing, having sex. We *live* in bed, she'd said, that first summer. Do you realize that?

'Well, I'm going to New York at the end of the month to see a friend. Then I'm coming home for Christmas and New Year, then I'm going to the Caribbean for three weeks. After that I don't know.'

'Whereabouts in the Caribbean?'

'Barbuda. It's a luxury resort. I'm doing it now in case I run out of self-indulgence later.'

'What about your dad?' I asked. We'd established over antipastos that he was willing to see me. There remained, troublingly, since here I was in bed with Janet again, the question of whether Nelson Edwards was in fact George Edward Nelson Skinner. This question, fundamental, remained unanswered.

'He's okay, actually,' Janet said. 'He's got a home help comes in a couple of hours a day and we've got him hooked up to one of these private RapidCare things. He's got a gizmo he can press and they contact the emergency services straight away if it's anything serious. Plus my sister's in Earls Court. She's around if I'm not. He can pretty much do for himself, and besides he's a stubborn old bastard, hates being helped.'

I'd never considered other family. Her interest in herself had made me think of her as an only child, but her childlessness was responsible for that. The effect was always similar. Look at me.

'Is Nelson Edwards his real name?'

Wrong. Should have said, Did he publish under his own name? I hadn't known it was going to come out right then. She paused fractionally (which on its own would have tipped me off) before saying, 'Why d'you ask?'

I yawned for camouflage. Out of the tail end of it said: 'Colleague of mine's doing a paper on pen names.' I stared up at the ceiling. 'You'll love this: *Social Dynamics and Pseudonymity: A Study of the Politics of Literary Identity.*'

'Christ, you're the guys with the catchy titles.'

'Makes mine sound pretty sexy.'

'What was yours again?'

'*Moral Exotica: Race and Pulp Fiction.* I can't believe you've forgotten already.'

'Well, I'm like that, you know.'

Which was all well and good but we'd cul-de-saced. I couldn't ask her directly a second time. She was still calculating. Just habit, I thought. There might have been a time when it mattered, years ago, not any more. My guess was the reflex and its redundancy were reminding her of how old her father was, how much it couldn't at this late stage in the game matter. It released another little pheromone of sadness from her. Mixed in was all that we'd just done. We had – there was no denying it – liked it, been surprised by how at only the second encounter so many of the awkwardnesses had been rubbed smooth. Which made her want to trust me. Made her trust me. Someone does all that to your anus, you've got to trust them. She's going to say, It isn't, actually, and I'm going to say, Isn't what? and she's going to say, His real name, and I'm going to hold my breath and be very delicately ready and she's going to say, His real name's George Skinner.

'I'm going to get that lemon meringue out of the fridge,' she said. 'I hope you think that's as good an idea as I do.'

Or maybe you don't have to trust them.

You can't go into Departures unless you're departing, and the martial frenzy of Check-in has little to offer. There is of course the sprawling pre-departures lounge, with its pub carpet, its fluorescents, its shops, its roped-off smokers who stare out from their zones as from a purgatory of ennui, but of late, these days of suddenly filling up with tears and being unable to stop thinking about death, I come to Arrivals. People in all shades of brown (as Updike says in *Brazil*, as far as skin's concerned, white is a shade of brown) emerge from the gates pushing their trolleys, carrying their bags, blinking, as if they've arrived in the afterlife unsure of what to expect. The lovers' faces are tentative, open, the eyes with that mixed flicker of doubt and hope. In the first look each brimful face asks the other: Do you still love me? Is it all right? Did you fuck someone else? I watch the lovers meet. And make no mistake: if he doesn't still love her, if it isn't all right, if she has fucked someone else, that first look will tell all, will accommodate the poisonous bulk of the truth; he'll know, she'll know. They may smile, kiss, embrace, hold each other, hurry home to fuck, smother it with all the clutter of habit but its information will have gone in anyway, like a solitary quill from a deadly plant, and sooner or later it will start to hurt, will start to take effect. I watch the lovers meet and it makes me feel lonely, paternal, far away from all that, as if I'm their benevolent grandfather finished with sex and passion and blood, thinned or purified by time into a papery chaste guardian. They don't notice me, and that's right and good, I tell myself. It hurts my heart, pleasantly. I think of Vince telling me of Nazi sentimentality, inwardly nod my head, yes, yes, of course, it's come to this, it's bound to come to something like this, without God or love or meaning.

Or rather that's usually the way of it. Now (the thought makes me feel abstractly flirtatious, flirtatious with the world, which is surely being flirty with me) there's Janet Marsh, the surprisingly refined sex, unawkward mutual visibility. Now there's for the second time not quite having closed the door on further carnal trysts. Breakfast at the glass-bricked breakfast bar hadn't been great. She'd taken two phone calls and for both of them walked away with the cordless into the bedroom. I took reassurance from it, that she didn't want me hanging around, that we weren't going to attempt half-dressed ease, newspapers, the always disastrous shared shower, a *day* together. It gave me a glimpse of the formidable force she must have been as a businesswoman. As soon as she registered the call was work (or rather ex-work) her face tightened and her voice moved up into her nose. By the time she'd finished the second conversation I'd laced up my shoes and drunk all but the last mouthful of coffee. I saw the relief – He's going; good – but also lingering puzzlement. In the moments we knew were leading up to saying goodbye we avoided looking at each other. Then when I picked my jacket up off the couch and turned to face her we stopped, looked, conceded . . . what? That it had been too enjoyable not to repeat? In the end I said, This is slightly mad, isn't it? She'd nodded agreement, almost physically bundled me towards the door, saying, We'll arrange something for seeing my dad. Next week. I'll call you.

That afternoon I got on the phone to Pasha.

'What's that?'

'Dad, listen carefully. Is Ma in the room with you? Just say yes or no.'

Two or three seconds of rising heart rate for him to sort this out. He hates talking on the phone.

'No.' Then, quietly, 'She's in the kitchen.'

'Right. If she comes in you say, "George Bush," and I'll start talking to you about the election, okay?'

He had to run all this by himself internally again before replying: 'Okay.' I knew how he'd be sitting: in the armchair by the window, leaning forward, right elbow on right knee, left hand mashing receiver against left ear, the *Sun* open on his lap at something like 'ASYLUM SEEKER BENEFIT CHEAT HAS SECRET YACHT'.

'Now listen, Dad, but stay calm. I think I've found Skinner.'

It was a fraught conversation. He had to George Bush twice, nearly deafening me. He couldn't stop with the questions. 'Dad, for God's sake hush up a minute, will you? Listen. We may only have one shot at this and it means you're going to have to come to see me next week. Can you do that?'

'What'll I tell your mother?'

'Tell her a friend of mine's got comp tickets to an evening of amateur boxing here and I thought it'd be nice for the two of us to go. You know, like I took her to *Les Misérables* that time.'

'When next week? I've got my feet on Thursday.'

'Jesus Christ. Just cancel it. This is *him*, Dad, I'm sure of it.'

'But how did you find him?'

For a moment I completely forgot. Then remembered. Stacks of Books seemed a long time ago. *Raj Rogue*. A fluke, I told him. Just a random bit of luck. Incredible, really.

I've booked him an open return. He'll be here Monday. I woke this morning with the feeling that things are tightening up around me. When that happens, there's only one place to go.

There's a weird atmosphere here today, a vibe of urgency in the wake perhaps of the US presidential elections. It's only days after the return of George W. Bush to a second term of office. The swing states didn't swing, but the main problem was that John Kerry looked like a troubled pre-op transsexual. Or the Republicans spent more money on cable ads in Ohio. Or they rigged the electronic voting machines. Or released hundreds of thousands of artificial persons cultured in underground laboratories and genetically engineered to vote Republican. Some such explanation will follow in Michael Moore's next book, which will be another huge seller, gobbled up by the millions of people like me for whom very occasionally reading a horrifying exposé of political corruption at the highest, most serious, world-wrecking level is a titillating and more than adequate substitute for doing anything about it.

Vince and I are in one of our strange little spells of being interested in the news. We find ourselves buying the *Guardian* every day, the *Observer* or *Independent* on Sundays. We've let various things grab us: Enron, Milošević, the war in Afghanistan, guerrilla atrocities in Zaire, Abu Ghraib, the Sudan crisis. We go through bubbles of time in which, for a week, a fortnight, a month, we're compressedly informed, grown-up, high on appropriate anxiety. 'They're raping the women in Darfur,' Vince said, not long ago, over a Saturday kitchen breakfast where everything was fiercely sunlit, the teapot's languid S of steam, the marmalade jar like a lump of amber; even the hacked-at Lurpak creamily glowed. 'Militia and government forces, together. Blair says the reports are a cause for great concern.' Not without emotion I closed my eyes and squeezed my molars together. Three layers of feeling: first, a gauzy filament of distress and compassion; second, a richer stratum of satisfaction at discharging my duty to know what's going on in the world; third, a fathomless bedrock of boredom and self-disgust, since the deep knowledge, the knowledge of myself is that I'm not going to do anything about it, not even write a letter to my MP. Not even open the email from Oxfam when it comes: Darfur: Humanitarian Disaster, though I'll lack for weeks the integrity to delete it.

'Did you know,' I asked Vince in response, 'that in Berlin the Russian army raped the Jewish women they were liberating before liberating them?' It's not a competition. More like a shuttlecock we're batting back and forth. In an earlier phase, before the war in Iraq, Vince told me that Saddam's goons had murdered a boy, dismembered and beheaded him, then taken all the severed body parts and dumped them outside his mother's house. They told her she must leave them there for a week, and that if she didn't they would come for the rest of her family and do the same to them.

When the Abu Ghraib story broke, both of us resisted the reflex – to respond to the pictures with our usual moral fracture and frowning urgency (as if we know the government will be on the phone any minute asking us what, exactly, should be done) – and plumped instead for jaded irritation: these are soldiers with prisoners, for fuck's sake, of course they're going to torture and sexually humiliate them. Soldiers have been doing this sort of thing to prisoners ever since there have *been* soldiers and prisoners. Now because it's Americans on camera we're supposed to be shocked? Americans are supposed to be better than that? The only amazing thing, we agreed, was that Americans were dumb enough to think that in this day and age you could take photographs and not have them leak out and incriminate you. 'It's in the nature of diaries to be found and read,' Vince said. 'That's why mine's full of lies.' The more interesting discussion, we agreed, with a Radio 4-style self-congratulatory sidestepping of the obvious, was whether the act of photographing yourself committing a crime was really an expression of the desire to be caught and prosecuted, which was the referred desire to be relieved of the burden of your own freedom. Vince said no, he thought it was just that for twenty-first-century Western humans (especially American humans) the validity of an experience, our ability to remember it, to believe we'd had it, resided in its photographability.

Meanwhile, the news will accumulate, circle, repeat its deep structures, and the novelty of following it will wear off. Another experiment in being the sort of people who keep up with current events will be over. We'll stop reading the newspapers we buy, then stop buying them. Like cohabiting women whose menstrual cycles gradually synchronize, Vince and I have lived together long enough to enter and exit these phases at more or less the same time. A blessing. Asymmetry would mean judgement, difficult weekend breakfasts, a flat filled with the dark matter of unhad arguments. It's like something we have to keep trying out, to see if, after all, we are the sort of people who care. So far it's failed to convince either of us. So far our cogs, as Vince would say, haven't bit. But how bad does it have to get before they do? he wants to know. What sort of atrocity has to be perpetrated, what sort of corruption uncovered, before we become political? You know, *do* something. It's hard to imagine. What if it directly affected you and me? he says. What if there was a major political party that was campaigning for the rounding-up of Anglo-Indians and queers and sending them to death camps? No one's *heard* of Anglo-Indians, I tell him. Jesus Christ it's hypothetical, Owen. Sup*pose*. Would you get off your arse? Oppose them? March? Shout slogans? Get involved? It's hard to imagine, I repeat. I'd probably emigrate to Sweden.

However, American marines have begun the taking of Fallujah. Last night on Channel 4 News Vince and I watched footage first of aerial bombardment by attack helicopter, second of apparently indiscriminate mortar bombardment from perimeter positions, and third of penetration of the city's outskirts by ground forces. The reporter went into the city to show us a couple of kaftaned civilians wailingly bemoaning the destruction of their houses. 'What *I* wonder,' Vince said, in the bitter, righteously facetious manner we reserve for this sort of thing, 'is how, when the insurgents decide they've had enough and take their headgear off and chuck their guns away and walk out of the city with all the other civilians, the Americans are going to know that they aren't civilians at all, but insurgents?' We were on a couch each in the living room, eating one of Vince's chilli con carnes off trays in our laps. (It's dark early these nights, and last night raining, too. If Vince and I had partners, romantic partners, sexual partners – or were such partners; the possibility's a threadbare gag between us – this would be a welcome inducement to stay indoors. As it is it just makes the prospect of having to go out and find sex more dismal than it already is. I'm still thinking this way, obviously, though I repeat there is the matter of Janet Marsh, about whom Vince knows. It's all right for you, he's been carping since the first encounter, you've got a *bird*. A *rich* bird, more to the point, you jammy bastard. She hasn't got a rich gay brother has she?) 'Maybe,' I said, equally facetiously, 'they're hoping they'll have forgotten to remove their insurgent T-shirts and badges.'

Rumsfeld had been on earlier, talking at a press conference (the cameraspeak, the film whirr, the shutter click, the flashbulbs that don't go *bish* any more except in your imagination, evoked the red carpet outside a Hollywood premiere) about minimal civilian casualties. 'Yeah, Don,' Vince said, 'sure, Don, absolutely, Don, we trust you, Don.' I was racking my brains to remember in what way, precisely, Donald Rumsfeld is bad. I'd read all about it somewhere, Moore's book, probably. Pharmaceuticals? Or was he in on the Enron thing? Actually, what *was* the Enron scandal again, exactly? I know it was something massive and simple and fundamental, but outside the phases in which we're interested in this sort of thing the facts refuse to stick in my head. Slippage. I accept Rumsfeld's evil in the way I accept that the square on the hypotenuse is equal to the sum of the squares on the other two sides, not because I can remember the proof, but because I can remember that there is one. And still, the man's press-conference look of perplexed outrage and his delivery of plain-idiom common sense impressed: he was saying that you can't have people *cutting off people's heads* as a way of trying to stop democratic elections. Who could argue with that? We've tried everything else, he said. He really looked like he meant it. (He's handsome, in a mannish, liver-spotted American way; you can still see the side-parted headshape of the seven-year-old boy in him, whereas with Bush all you see – though he walks as if holding a tennis ball in each armpit to indicate a superabundance of testosterone – is the two-year-old, specifically, as I think someone in the *Guardian* said, the two-year-old who, after having had his first on-the-potty bowel movement, has been told by his mother that he's a good *boy*.)

The ironic old Channel 4 News producers cut from Rumsfeld to an American marine saying that they, the marines, were going to 'unleash the dogs of hell' on Fallujah. He pitied 'em. 'Cos they didn't know what was comin'. Hell was comin'. He said it all very calmly and reasonably, ending with: 'If there are civilians in there, those people are in the wrong place at the wrong time.' 'You couldn't write it better, could you?' Vince said. I was thinking of the soldier years ago, who with dangling chin-strap had come up to the camera and said, 'That's all, folks.' I smiled in a way meant to indicate beatific horror.

There are many satisfactions higher than being able to sit and eat your dinner and see on television something so obviously wrong and disastrous and know it is such and make facetious comments which reify your own liberal sanity, but this satisfaction is still pretty good. If only it wasn't spoiled by the nag of one's track record. Beyond Jon Snow's birdlike integrity Jeremy Paxman and *University Challenge* twinkled cheerily on the televisual horizon. Beyond that (while safe at home the VCR skips into life to tape *Friends*, *The West Wing*, *Sex in the City*) the step out into the howl of the city, the world, the void, in search of sex. Love and sex, it used to be. It doesn't matter what's going on in the world: one is always going to want sex. One is always going to want love, too, but there comes a time when one stops expecting it.

Thinking this reminds me, as the look on the tanned face of an arriving granny changes from profound anxiety into beaming delight when the first grandchild ducks the barrier, of the only march Scarlet and I went on, in our last year at UCL. That spring Chernobyl had reminded everyone (after Gorbachev had spent two weeks saying nothing about it) that nuclear power was a dangerous thing. A resurgence of anti-nuclear activism – activism generally – followed.

'I can't stand this,' Scarlet said, as we neared Tottenham Court Road. The procession was to take in Trafalgar Square and Westminster, culminating in a rally in Hyde Park. It was early

November, crisp and blue-skied. Flares of blinding tepid sunlight, the buildings' planes of shadow meat-freezer cold. Sometimes the sun shone through the yellow teeth or red nostrils of a shouting or laughing student. People were teary, scarved, ear-muffed, bulky with coats.

'No,' I said.

'It's making me feel ill.'

'It's the slogans.'

'It's everything.'

She was looking at a trio of fat, ugly girls, one of whom, with a bullhorn, was leading this legion's chant: 'Maggie Maggie Maggie! Out out out! Maggie! Out! Maggie! Out! Maggie Maggie Maggie! Out out out!' Her face was red, porcine, frosted with eczema. There was a terrible contrast between the shouting and not-shouting versions of her face, between something bestially enraged and something humanly sulky. She had mesmerized both of us.

'I hate her,' I said.

'So do I, but it's wrong to.'

'I know.'

The protest had been billed as anti-nuclear but the slogans reflected a wide range of causes. Free Mandela Now. Apartheid is Murder. Meat is Murder. Stop Bombing Libya. Israel Out of Palestine Now. One banner sported a caricature of Ronald Reagan with his pants down, shitting on a building marked 'The Hague'.

'I can't stand this,' Scarlet repeated. I knew she was remembering Gary and Wally Da-Da, the consultation in the head's office. They won't believe us. I glanced at her, the high cheekbones, the eyes saying the main object of consciousness was somewhere else, the future, the past, another place. (That look of averted attention combined with her appetite for sex kept me in a state of more or less constant desire. Elsewhereness and availability produced between them a maddening friction. I could imagine mid-coitally belting her across the mouth, throttling her, anything to finally *get* her.)

'Come on,' she said. In the street behind the Astoria (a street which in all seasons at all hours is pungent with spilled booze and old piss) we found a doorway for a joint. After we'd smoked it she kissed me, tongue flicked, intimated in the shorthand that had been ours from the start. Go on. Here. I hesitated, felt her certainty, went on. Under her long coat a V-neck green sweater over a white blouse. A grey woollen skirt, stockings. Schoolish. 'Pull my knickers down.'

It seemed impossible that even in this place someone wouldn't pass by. She didn't say anything about the appositeness, us skulking in alleys, didn't have to. Pulling her knickers down hardened me, which she with her hands already working felt. I clumsily and with her help went with a little exquisite friction inside her, pushed her back against the freezing wall and filled my hands with the cheeks of her bum. Soft. Firm. The cold's force and our little groove of blood heat. All the female life in her concentrated in these pure moments into the sly soft wetness of her cunt. She lifted her legs and wrapped them round me. (Well, where *do* you feel at home? In Scarlet, I should have said.) There was the world in which you scuffed and worried and didn't make the grade, then there was this, the not being able to get any closer, further in, the addictive not-enoughness of going inside her. Before we'd turned off Charing Cross Road I'd had a vision of the march going on not to Embankment, Westminster, Hyde Park, but into a dangerous future, a landscape full of bodies and bomb craters under the same cold blue November sky. I'd watched the long line of dipping banners and thought of the delicacy of all those heads, how easily they could be cracked, drilled, blown to bits. All the eyes, watery with the cold. It was an obscenity, the vulnerability of the human eye. Shrapnel and bits of glass. A scalpel, the torturer with a look of irritable concentration, like a man forced to do an extra shift by the skiving of a colleague.

She drew her breath in and turned her face away, as Melissa had done. Her neck was warm where she'd loosened her scarf. I bit her gently there, felt calmly the gap between doing that and sinking my teeth carnivorously in, ripping her throat out. All these narrow margins crammed with the human effort at morality—

'Excuse me, sir, do you have a few moments to spare?'

I'm flanked – out of nowhere – by two policemen. Airport policemen, with bullet-proof jackets and automatic weapons (*machine-guns* is how my suddenly salient eight-year-old self puts it). My stomach in two seconds fills not with butterflies but with fat-bodied and big-winged moths, not fluttering but hairily battering themselves into a frenzy. Reverie to nausea. Even now a separate inviolable observer in me says, Yes, well, that's the great rich business of being alive, isn't it?

'What?'

'Nothing to be alarmed about, sir. It's a routine set of enquiries we're making at all the London airports as part of the new security initiatives. You're the twenty-fourth person we've done this with today. It'll take five minutes. You're not in trouble, don't worry.'

The reflex thought is that I've been Caught and Found Out. Bound to happen, almost a relief – would be if I could remember what it is I've done. You're not in trouble. This more than the automatic weapons loosens my bowels, the presence of the word 'trouble'. Simultaneously I'm trying to get hold of the phrase 'security initiatives' and use it to calm myself down, tell myself there's a context, police training, post-9/11, it isn't me personally.

'What is this?' I ask. I'm convinced that if I don't make some bodily inclination of co-operation, a step in the indicated direction, one of them, the taller of the two, with short blond hair, wintry blue eyes, aftershave and an air of scrubbed muscular vitality (all that backed-up training desperate for somewhere to go), will put his hand on me, the coercive hand between the shoulder blades. Thought-fragments whizz: ask for ID; demand a phone call; ask them if they're arresting you; *leg it*. I tell myself to stay calm. I tell myself I haven't done anything.

'Are you arresting me?'

'Of course not, sir. It's nothing like that. What time's your party expected?'

I'm so scrambled and terrified I don't understand. Party? What the fuck? Then I get it. My party, the person I'm presumably here to meet. I'm in, after all, Arrivals.

'I'm not here to meet anyone.' I expect them to exchange a look – eh, Steve, eh? – but they don't. The other officer is shorter, round-shouldered, with a moony, moustached face that reminds me of Beau Bridges. Manifestly when in civvies someone's husband, someone's dad, mowing the lawn on a Sunday afternoon, wandering into the kitchen and rubbing his paunch and saying, Is there any of that cold chicken left, love? The shirts under the bullet-proofs are crisp, white, short-sleeved. It amazes me that his freckled and soft-haired arms cradle an absolutely authentic up-to-the-minute automatic weapon.

'If you wouldn't mind, sir, it really will just take five minutes,' he says.

'Let me get this straight. You want me to come and answer a set of routine questions because it's part of new security at airports?'

'We're trying to avoid saying it's a training exercise,' he says, with a wry look that further says to me, bloke to bloke, It's bollocks, but what're we going to do? Fucking idiots in Whitehall. 'Twenty-five punters and that's our quota for the day.'

It nearly works. The hint of English blue-collar solidarity, the suggestion that they're fucking-up by even telling me it's a training exercise, the little collusion in fallibility. I feel myself relaxing, smiling, inanely – but pull up: it's a con, a masculine seduction. Oldest police trick in the book. I must be an imbecile.

'I don't believe you,' I say. Saying it I realize I'm trembling.

You're in trouble. For the umpteenth time my childhood says, Yes, still here, all the feelings. Owen Monroe, you're to go to the headmaster's office immediately. Oh God. Shit. *Fuck.* I haven't done anything. Hold on to that. I haven't done anything.

'Okay, sir, fair enough,' Beau says. 'Have you got any identification on you?'

'Look, what's this about?'

'Do you *have* any identification, sir?' the blond one says.

I exhale, heavily. Tut. This is what you do, take all the shitting yourself and turn it into a grotesquely transparent performance of exasperation. I reach for my inside pocket and am freshly, electrically astonished when Beau says quietly but clearly, '*Very* slowly there, sir, if you don't mind. What is it? A driving licence?'

'Yeah, actually, I do have my driving licence. I don't usually, but as it happens I do today.' This also is what you do, frothily blab irrelevant details, that you're not the sort of anal psychopath who always carries ID (that would be suspicious) but a person so far removed from criminality, with such a heady quantity of mentholated Nothing to Hide that the thought of carrying ID just in case would never normally enter his blameless head. Maude's castoff Fiesta needed a new rear number plate to clear its MOT last month, to buy which, these days, you need your driving licence. It's been in my pocket since then. There's all the usual crap in my wallet: Switch, Visa, Mastercard, stamps, receipts, Blockbuster, Balham Library. All the pertinent plastic says Owen G. Monroe. Who can they possibly think I am?

'Okay, Mr Monroe,' Beau says (the accent's Midlands, maybe ten years' London influence), 'here's the situation. We're speaking to you because you match the description of an individual we're looking for to help us with our enquiries.'

'Hang on a—'

'Now, since you have ID, and since I'm sure it's genuine, I reckon we can have this cleared up in two shakes if you come along and let us run a check on your licence.' His walkie-talkie crackles. Something indecipherable comes out. 'Roger,' Beau says. Then, to me, 'What do you say? Okay?'

'What enquiries?'

'Sir, come on. Let's go and run the licence check and you'll be on your way.'

'But who can you possibly think I am?'

'Let's go,' Blondie says, and there *is* the coercive hand, not between the scapulae but in the small of my back, which on top of everything makes me feel like a woman wearing a backless dress. I'm very aware of my heart, the thuds sounding like gulps or glugs, as if it's being forced as at Caligulan whim to drink until it bursts. Bits of my consciousness not waltzing with terror are busy with things like me saying later to Vince, I was manhandled by an Aryan policeman today. People have noticed, are nudging each other, staring. I look over my shoulder at the gaggle of hire-car drivers with their passenger placards – SABADZE; COOLIDGE; SWEENEY; KIRSCHENBAUM – and think they must be prone to varicose veins, all that standing and driving, automatics, too, those airport cars, not even a clutch to keep your left foot busy. I can't believe I'm walking along with two armed police officers. Floating along. Those television phrases, 'match the description of . . . help with our enquiries', they're supposed to stay on television. They've got no business in my real life.

Off the Arrivals lounge through an alarmed door for which Beau punches in an access code. My armpits push out the week's E numbers. I think how good it'll feel to get home and take my clothes off and have a slow and gently purgative shit in my own bathroom, which from this hell seems like a beautiful ceramic nook of heaven, with its window of frosted glass and stack of out-of-date magazines by the loo. How thoughtlessly we consume pleasures, take for granted great gifts such as being able to sit naked on your own crapper with the door locked and no one home, soothed by the white tiles and friendly toiletries, reading a feature on Cate Blanchet in an ancient Sunday supplement. Down a corridor, left. A door marked IR 07. Beau knocks and enters. I follow. Heinz brings up the rear.

Inside the room there's another (unarmed, older, bald) policeman, the Friendly One, I decide, and two men in the sort of plain clothes I imagine are supposed to fool drugs dealers but never do: leather bomber jackets, jeans, trainers. Furniture is a wooden desk between two orange plastic chairs. There are no windows. This is ridiculous. My assumption is that Beau and the Aryan, having delivered me, will leave, but they don't. The Friendly One (it's based on nothing more than his resemblance to an old maths teacher of mine who despite my numerical dyslexia never lost his patience and always spoke gently to me) steps forward, smiles and says politely, justifying my suspicion, 'If you wouldn't mind just raising your arms for me, sir, so I can check your person . . .'

It occurs to me, with a muscular spasm I just manage to conceal, as I'm being patted down that it's not absolutely impossible that if they go through every pocket in this jacket they might find an old forgotten baggie with a few wisps or nodules of grass in it. I close my eyes. There's that whirling circus of adrenalin. Oh please dear sweet Christ but it's a ridiculously remote possibility but what if Vince for some reason borrowed and or left a spliff half-smoked oh dear sweet Jesus God in Heaven—

'Thank you, sir. All done.'

But what if there's a sniffer dog? Those little bastards—

'Have a seat, Mr Monroe,' one of the plainclothes says. 'I'm Detective Reece. This is my colleague Detective Keogh. Do you know why we wanted to speak to you?'

Reece is late thirties, attractively pock-marked, with an expensive brown and blond haircut which shows blatant application of product. His pale blue eyes are large and almond-shaped, and his mouth in repose looks like it's just about to do a satirical offended-homosexual pout. Keogh's probably the same age but looks younger. Long body and lightbulb-shaped head with receding hairline. There'll be an occipital bald spot soon if there isn't already. Small mouth, weak chin, but the rosy look of a long-distance runner.

'Because you think I'm someone else?'

'Well, there's a resemblance,' Reece says, 'but frankly, face to face it's not compelling. In any case, that's easily dealt with.' He hands the driving licence and wallet to Keogh, who without a word or a glance at me slips out of the door and closes it behind him. 'Won't take long,' Reece says. He sits back in his chair and the leather bomber creaks. Head slightly on one side, he takes a look (meant to express careful weighing up) at me. 'Our guy's bearded,' he says. 'Surprise. We can do a projection of what he'd look like without it, and on the CCTV footage you're close enough. But not in the flesh.'

'So why am I here?'

'You're here, Mr Monroe, because CCTV keeps picking you up. In the last six months alone you've made eight visits to the airport. You're not flying anywhere, you're not meeting anyone, you're not plane-spotting and you're not shopping. We've checked surveillance at Gatwick and you're on their footage, too. So in short we'd like to ask you what you're doing here.'

Ah.

Silence. The silence they resort to with such brutal effect in films when someone goes off the edge of a cliff or tower block, the silence of time purified, not seconds, milliseconds, nanoseconds, but a soundless, seamless continuum that brings your own naked existence right up to you and shoves it under your nose. Now that this has happened, I realize that for months there's been at the back of my mind a small cloud of objectless anxiety attendant on these visits. Objectless no more. The object was something like this happening. I think of the Malaysian's bubble-bursting pronouncement: Brass. My father's feeling of relief. God's making a fool of him proof that God was there. But God *isn't* there, Dad, I said to him, last time round. *No* one's there. He and my mum smiled and shook their heads: Poor Owen, telling himself what he needs to hear.

'I come here . . .' I say. 'I come here to watch people.'

Reece stares. The Friendly One is taking notes. I laugh, and it sounds like a bad actor doing a nervous laugh, badly. 'Look I know this may seem bizarre and tragic but I come here because I like airports, always have. You've heard of people-watching.'

'What's wrong with Oxford Street?'

'Nothing. But I prefer airports, watching people arrive. It may seem stupid to you, but . . .'

'Yes?'

I can't continue. I look down and shake my head, as if we've reached a sexual fetish too embarrassing to discuss.

'What?' Reece insists.

What can I say? That it's the feeling of everyone being from somewhere else? That it's no one knowing I'm here? That in Departures you can see whether a marriage is unravelling? That in Arrivals you can breathe the secondary smoke of love? That in an airport every hello and goodbye marks the beginning or end of a story? That there's always the possibility that one day, instead of saying, wouldn't it be incredible if, you'll actually do it, fuck the whole routine and jump on a flight to somewhere far away where no one knows anything about you?

No. I can't say any of that.

'It's just something I enjoy,' I say at last. 'I'm not altogether sure why. In any case presumably I'm not breaking the law?'

As soon as I've said this I realize there aren't many things more guaranteed to piss a policeman off. Reece blinks once, extra-slowly, shorthand for all his years of idiot people trotting out this idiot line. As if it's ever going to be as simple as that, as if we'd all be sleeping safe in our beds if it was ever as simple as that.

Keogh comes back in and drops my wallet and driving licence on the desk in front of Reece, gives him a look that says legit. Reece slides them over to me.

'Is that it?' I ask.

'Yeah, that's it,' Reece says. He's bored. I'm a ninny. Some people collect thimbles, some people are obsessed with tulips, some people dig airports.

There's a general relaxing of muscles in the room as I put my things back in my pockets and get to my feet. Reece doesn't stand, rocks his chair on to its back legs, shoves his hands into his jeans pockets, yawns.

'You're not breaking any law, Mr Monroe,' he says, through the tail end of the yawn. 'Unless, of course, we decide you're loitering. Point is, you keep hanging round airports looking suspicious, you're going to keep getting questioned. It's that simple. You're visible. These are the times, right?'

'Yeah.'

'I suggest you bear that in mind.'

'Yeah, okay.'

He lets the chair back on to all four legs. I'm thinking, as the panic subsides, that's another simple pleasure gone. Reece's mobile rings. *The Exorcist, Tubular Bells.* He gets up, turns away to answer it, says, 'Yeah? What did she want?' And I find myself hurt that he's forgotten me already, that he's on to the next thing. It's like a prostitute taking a call from her next client while you're still zipping up your pants. Detectives are like that, reveal how small your life is next to theirs of death and evil. They can't help it. To them we're all walking around blind.

'Right we are then, sir,' Beau says, holding the door open for me. 'We'll take you back now.'

Weak-kneed I none the less force myself not to leave the airport straight away. Some tremulous mix of civic indignation and emasculation. I feel as if I might vomit. I buy myself a cold sparkling water and stand, too hot but incapable of taking my jacket off, near the posse of bored drivers. You're visible. These are the times, right? The drivers are a species: pub hair, slacks, Seventies sunglasses; they serve, but they've preserved the little flints of their masculine selves. They have that clipped patience acquired by working-class men who've been dealing with the rich for years. ALBERTINE. FENWICK. MCGREGOR. DUNN. My hands are shaking. I'm thinking of what a meal I'm going to make of telling Vince tonight, how I'll play up my sissyness, how he'll interject every now and then with quiet Withnailian *Bastards!* or Absolute *fuckers.*

Passengers from a New York flight are coming through. My usual game is to decide within their first half-dozen steps through the doors which ones are American. The British, especially those returning from their first visit to the US, give themselves away. They look tranquilly humbled and relieved, as if they've just lost their virginity or given birth or at any rate gone through a basic human rite of passage. Which they have: seeing America. Something of its dazzle or glare remains in their tired faces. They'll slag it off in the pub later, all that plastic politeness and righteous self-absorption, the brash narcissistic optimism, the *dumb*ness – but the showgirl glamour and cowboy heft of the place will, whether they like it or not, have aroused them. For a few days or weeks they'll have been where television comes from, their childhood heaven. Even the globally invariable brands – Coke, McDonald's, Pepsi, Starbucks – will have had over there an extra throb or razzle derived from being in the land of their birth. Those all-night diners and the way your drink comes on a little napkin and the bargirl calls you honey or hon or sugar and the way the dollars make English notes look like pompous, gouty old aristocrats. More than anything the thrilling currentness, the feeling that every nation on the planet is grudgingly or amorously trying to catch up.

A family goes past, two ginger-haired freckled kids who might be twins, nose-ringed mum with maroon hair in a ponytail, plump unshaven dad in bermudas and a faded Nirvana T-shirt. A tall, gaunt American academic with close-cropped silver Greco-Roman curls and two briefcases. A trio of girls in their early twenties who've been on what was supposed to be a spree but one of them, who reminds me of the Cowardly Lion, looks like she's fallen out with the other two, pushing her trolley a couple of yards behind, red-eared, letting her flip-flopped feet slap. A family of American Asians (Sri Lankans, I guess), him with a compact lightly worked-out body in crisp white T-shirt and new Levis, her in khaki army-style trousers and a black crop-top, slim with a child-widened ass and, I imagine, tits of lovely tautness prone to gooseflesh; the five-year-old, in obligatory baseball cap – no, an entire baseball *strip* – sitting on the luggage playing an electronic game, looks like an abstracted raja. Then a light-brown racially tricky woman in slender black velvet flares and what I'm guessing is an extraordinarily expensive white shirt comes out pulling a single suitcase with her sunglasses up on her forehead and it's Scarlet.

CHAPTER FOURTEEN

❧

The Silk Train

(*The Cheechee Papers*: Bhusawal, 1952)

Ross emerged from the illness declaring that he'd missed his chance and would never box again, but by the beginning of 1949 he was back in the ring (and on the pitch) for the GIPR, and by 1952 he was on course for Helsinki. Helsinki wasn't London, but the London promoters would still be watching. He was twenty-seven. Five good years, retire at the top. Rockballs's 'all the sweet pussy' had been dropped. There were the kids to consider, even beyond Kate, beyond love. Melissa, conceived not long after his return from Death's Bleddy Threshold, was three years old; Carl would be a year next month; and they were still only half-heartedly practising the rhythm method. The Armoury Road house had become home, but there was never money left over at the end of the month, which of late had begun to bother Ross. They weren't poor; they ate and drank, kept Dondi and a cook, went to the Institute dances; Kate made all the kids' clothes. But Ross's public conviction that this life was temporary, precursive to the real life of international pro boxing stardom, had a parallel private anxiety; the injury, the accident, the tryst with destiny, the hand of God that had shattered his dream five years ago, had left him with a kernel of doubt which, as the time for the new dream neared, grew into the beginning of paranoia. If he failed at the trials, what then? If they were going to England they'd need money, a lot of it. Where was that going to come from?

Working against this was the throb of peace that simply being a husband and a father gave him. That had come as a shock. Lying awake after Kate had fallen asleep he felt the settled household around him and found himself profanely asking, What else do you need? This is the wealth, all the wealth there ever is. Bugger England. He'd prop himself up on one elbow and watch his wife sleeping.

Kate, it turned out, could sing. She sang at the dances. It had unnerved him the first time he heard her through a microphone. She'd sung 'Girl of My Dreams' and 'Blue Moon' and later 'It Had to Be You'. Panic had started in his chest, the audience suddenly attending to her – but it had blossomed into pride: she was his, would go home with him, would go to bed with him. He was sleeping with Kate Monroe, the singer. She was his wife. Astonishing. 'How did you know you could do that?' he'd asked her. She'd shrugged, laughed. 'I could always carry a tune.' The visiting band had offered her a job, not realizing she was married, had two children, had no desire to sing for anything else. The bandleader wore round rimless spectacles like Glenn Miller, gave her a card with an address to write to if she ever changed her mind. Walking home she'd told Ross, shown him the card when he'd asked to see it. Again the thrill of threat, that she was, to someone else, Someone Else. God, if He felt you becoming complacent in your riches, gave you a hint of how easily they could be taken away. This more than the grander beneficences was His mercy, though since the mercy went hand in glove with viciousness (Ross remembered the severed breast on the lines that day, how his own wife's breasts subsequently had shared in the awful pathos, a challenge his lust needed all its cunning to work through) you couldn't bank on it. 'You could have had a different life,' Ross said to her. She laughed again, seeing him unsure of her. 'I've got the life I want,' she said.

Superficially life in Bhusawal wasn't much changed. Plenty of Anglos had left in the years leading up to the madness of '47, but plenty had stayed. Gandhi was dead, shot by a man Hector said had lived for a while in rooms above the Bazaar Road paan shop. Hector had returned from Bombay and was to Beatrice's delight living back at home and acting as a check on Louis Archibald's drunken rages. The first time the old man raised his hand to wallop Beatrice, Hector grabbed it and twisted his father into a half-nelson. 'Not any more, Puppa. You touch her like that again and I'll bleddy settle you once and for all.'

The events of '47 had savaged Hector. He'd started taking a fatalistic interest in politics, regularly cutting out clippings from newspapers and journals and passing them on to Ross to read. 'Community in Peril', one from the *Anglo-Indian Quarterly* was titled:

Of all the challenges Anglo-Indians are sure to face in newly Independent India the greatest by far is that of overcoming our own false sense of security. How many Anglo-Indian employees of Railways, Post and Telegraphs are aware that the protection of pre-1947 quotas – quotas to which they owe their jobs, their very lives – was recently secured by only the narrowest of margins, thanks almost exclusively to the efforts of All-India Anglo-Indian Association President Frank Anthony? How many of us are aware that even as the new Constitution is likely to stand these quota safeguards will drop by ten per cent every two years and be wasted out by 1960? The answer is: very few. For decades we've lived under the romantic delusion that the Raj would last for ever. Wake up, brothers and sisters! The Raj is no more. Your children and your children's children will be fighting for their lives under the new Indian Imperialism!

Ross wished Hector would stop shoving these things at him. The Englishman had sold the Albion Hotel and taken the fabulous Bernice back to England the year after Independence. The sudden bitter passion for politics, Ross thought, was Hector's reaction as much to that as it was to the attack on the train, something for his misery to get hold of and spend itself on. Politics to him, Ross, was as it had always been, an irritant, a disturbance on the periphery of vision. 'I'm not going to be here in 1960,' he told Hector. 'It's not going to affect me.'

Still, if the Olympic plan failed, if Fate . . .

'Stop worrying,' Kate told him. 'You're going to win. We're going to be fine.'

Eugene and Mitzi, now with two children of their own, had taken a house three doors down from Ross and Kate, where they rowed, continually, about everything except the one thing: the rumour that in Jalgaon Cynthia Merritt had a seven-year-old daughter, fathered by Eugene.

Not rumour, as Ross now knew. 'There's nothing like that going on,' Eugene had confided of his secret visits to Cynthia, meaning sex. 'I had my chance there and I missed it. But I love that child. I can't help it. You should see her, men. She's absolutely a *doll*.' Eugene, now a goods driver, was on Rs 250 a month. He, too, was ceaselessly on the lookout for money, specifically money he wouldn't have to account for to Mitzi. Such money, when it came, was sent to Cynthia for the child, the absolute doll, Dinah.

One Sunday in February 1952 Ross and Eugene sat drinking on the rear veranda of the bungalow in Armoury Road. Kate and Mitzi had taken the kids to the Taptee for a picnic. The heat was a palpable ripple. Bass-droning bees wove in and out of the hanging baskets. Dondi had Sundays off to get plastered with the posse of alcoholics who hung around the southern edge of the market; behind the two men the empty house was attentive. The Munroes' tan bulldog, Punch, lay on his side at their feet, each eye preserving a crescent of consciousness. Ross hadn't intended to get a dog — What's the point if we're leaving? — but then Hector's bitch had had pups and when he'd brought one over Melissa had refused to let him take it away.

'Look,' Eugene said, 'it's a straightforward job. 'We'll come out with four or five hundred apiece, minimum. These buggers are in and out like Robin Hood.'

'It's always a straightforward job,' Ross said. 'It's always *supposed* to be a straightforward job. Don't forget it's me stopping the bleddy train.'

Eugene had been sitting forward in his chair, elbows on knees, rolling the tumbler of Three Barrels rum between his hands. Now he sat back, went limp, began dejectedly patting his pockets for a Pall Mall. Life with Mitzi had etched two short vertical lines at the start of each of his eyebrows. The missed opportunity of Cynthia was a perennial misery. His ravenous love for the child, Dinah, kept him in a state of strained alertness, as if he was expecting her to appear at any moment.

'What is the stuff, anyway?' Ross asked.

Eugene lit up, dragged, exhaled in twin plumes through his nostrils. 'Fabric. Good stuff, Chinese silk.'

'Who's setting it up?'

'Friend of Chick Perkins. Come and *discuss* it, at least.'

Chick Perkins was a retired mail guard who'd achieved legendary status by assisting in the theft of a gold parcel ten years ago. Chick's trial defence rested on his delaying signing the parcel clerk's book till the last possible moment, then hurriedly signing for three parcels instead of four just as the train pulled out of the station. The parcel clerk, who spotted the discrepancy and managed to get the mail train stopped only half a mile out of the station, swore there were four, Chick swore there were three. An Anglo's word against an Indian's. The parcel clerk lost his job, Chick worked on and retired with a decent provident fund. The mystery (that, my friends, goes with me to the grave) was how they managed to get one of the parcels off the train so quickly.

'You better get this straight,' Ross told Eugene that evening, walking out to Chick's bungalow. 'I'm not agreeing to anything unless the job's watertight. I'm not joining any gimcrack operation.' It was always like this. Scepticism, irritation, reluctance, submission. Money.

'It's not gimcrack,' Eugene said. 'Chick says this bugger knows what he's doing and Chick's no fool.'

'Maybe so but I'm telling you: this is to discuss. This is to consider. Keep that in your head.'

'What a skittish bugger you are, men.'

'Listen, I'm not the one with the lovechild to keep in dresses and dolls, am I?'

Eugene flinched, looked over his shoulder. 'Keep your voice down for God's sake. And don't speak about her like that. I'm trying to do my best for the child and you're putting the bleddy spoke in? It's all right for you, you married the woman you love.'

This chastened Ross. He could be made to feel sympathy for anyone if it was pointed out that he, not they, had Kate. When he stopped and thought about it, tender, angelic generosity towards the rest of the world swelled in him. Humble details – doorposts, flowers, cigarette butts – brimmed with beauty.

'All right, all right,' he said. 'Just remember: this doesn't commit me to anything.'

Thin-necked and glowingly bald-headed Chick, in checked slacks and canary-yellow paunch-hugging polo shirt, opened the door with a bottle of Johnnie Walker in one hand and a foully smouldering Senior Service in the other. Now seventy-two he looked, as always, impishly alert and in leathery good health; an Arabian Nights genie, Ross thought, enjoying suburban retirement. 'There they are,' he said, beaming out at them with a gap-between-the-front-teeth grin. 'There they are at the eleventh hour as usual. Come on come on siddown. See what grog y'all want.'

They went out on to the back veranda. Chick's wife had died three years before and since then everyone had been secretly touched by his (initially desperate and counterproductive) devotion to keeping up the garden she'd raised and of which he'd been oblivious when she was alive. No one, including Chick, had realized how much he'd loved her until she wasn't there to love. Chick's mischievous genie face endured, but with a piercing acknowledgement that his wife, Vera, unobtrusively the great sustenance beneath him, had made all the freedom and roll of his adult life possible.

'A simpleton could do it,' Chick said. 'Seriously.' It wasn't the first time he'd set up a job.

'Just as well we've got one, then,' Ross said, looking at Eugene.

'How're the Jalgaon girls?' Chick asked.

Eugene swallowed his mouthful of scotch in a convulsion. 'What the bleddy hell—'

'Oh, come off it, Gene, everyone knows.'

'My *wife* doesn't know, thank you very much. Christ almighty, I'm trying to . . . I'm trying to do the right thing here and y'all are all putting the bleddy spoke in. I mean why don't y'all put a notice in the bleddy papers?'

'Calm down, men,' Chick said. 'I'm on your side. Why else am I looking out for these little jobs? You think *I* need the money?'

'We know *you* don't,' Eugene said. 'Sitting on your pile like a bleddy crab. Don't take your cut, then, if you don't need it.'

They were on to second drinks when someone knocked. Chick (servants strategically dismissed for the evening) shot his eyebrows up as he got with ticking kneecaps to his slippered feet. 'That's our chap.'

Ross and Eugene waited, suddenly nervous, staring at each other. Eugene hurriedly lit a Pall Mall. They heard Chick's hullo hullo hullo come in come in come in and sat up straighter in their chairs. They listened to Chick furnishing the newcomer, whoever he was, with a drink.

'We're out here,' Chick said. 'Siddown siddown.' Despite which Eugene stood up to shake hands.

'Blaardy *hell*,' Ross said.

Skinner, a split second behind, hesitated, then barked a laugh and offered Ross his hand. Eugene, who hadn't recognized him, was left with his hand in mid-air.

'Eh?' Chick said.

Ross, still seated, held on to the handshake as in a mild trance.

'We know each other,' Skinner said. 'My God. I told you. Destiny.'

'From the train, men,' Ross had to remind Eugene. 'From the massacre.'

Eugene, slow-blinking his way into delighted awe, said, eventually, 'Holy shit on a stick. This is a sign, what? Absolutely a bleddy *omen*.'

'I told you there was a higher power at work,' Skinner said.

Ross couldn't get past both the immediacy of recognition and simultaneously how much the Englishman had changed. He'd lost weight, and been left with the kind of haircut that might be a last resort against lice. The linen suit had been replaced by khaki shorts and a white vest, the burgundy brogues by chappals. In spite of which the fiercely alert contemporariness remained. He looked, if anything, wider awake. 'Didn't snuff it, then?' he asked Ross, taking the cane chair Chick drew up for him. Ross couldn't stop looking at the haircut. Skinner saw, ran his hand over it. 'Don't you like it?' he said, laughing. 'Butchered by a chap in Nagpur last week. I was wearing a hat until someone pinched it literally off my head this afternoon.'

If the enterprise had been lacking momentum this

synchronicity provided it. They demolished Chick's scotch and moved on to rum. Eugene slumped in his chair, visibly queasily drunk.

'So this is the business,' Ross said, when Chick had gone inside to urinate.

'This is an aspect of the business,' Skinner said. Then after a pause: 'And presumably, since you're here, one you're familiar with.'

Two each, yes? He hadn't forgotten. 'Easy come, easy go,' Ross said. 'What have you been up to?'

Skinner smiled and spread his hands, radiated the familiar casual capableness; the invitation to mutual transparency was, as before, irresistible, and Ross filled with sly approval of the other man's survival. 'Going hither and thither about the land,' Skinner said. 'You know, in the spirit of my forefathers. Making money. Actually, I think my time's probably up here. Too much home-grown competition. King's English doesn't carry quite the weight it did. Queen's English, I should say. Can't be easy for you, either. "Anglos out" and all that?' The slogan had appeared a week ago, raggedly hand-painted in big white letters on the wall of the Church of the Blessed Sacrament.

'I'm going anyway,' Ross said. 'But I'll do it in my own time.'

'Still fighting?'

'Still fighting.'

'This bugger,' Eugene said, levering himself upright in wincing stages, fishing out another Pall Mall, wagging his finger, 'is going all the way. You watch. Helsinki. Those Eskimo buggers are in for a bleddy shock.'

'It's the Americans you've got to worry about,' Skinner said, 'the Negroes especially. I saw one down in Madras last year, exhibition bout. Fought that fellow Ginger Robbins. Gave him rather a lesson, I'm afraid.'

'I know Ginger Robbins,' Ross said. 'I fought him in school.'

'And?'

'Knocked him out in the third.'

Eugene was ambushed mid-giggle by a belch which knotted in his gullet and forced him to scurry to his feet. He let it out – *beey-ouwr* – then ran his hand from the top of his face to the bottom. He looked close to vomiting.

'Walk it off, for God's sake, will you?' Ross said. Eugene closed his eyes, breathed deeply through his nose, then took half a dozen tottering steps into Chick's garden.

'Look, it's up to you,' Skinner said to Ross. 'But it's pretty low risk. I've worked with a couple of these chaps before.'

'Goondas?'

'Not my chaps. There'll be one or two hired hands, I daresay, but on the whole it's a cakewalk. Still, it's your train. Absolutely understand if you want to pass.'

Nothing had changed between them, Ross saw. The shared sense of themselves as savvy adventurers. Life was the struggle to get away with getting what you wanted. Jack thieved under the dozing giant's nose. For Ross the giant was still God, who might at any moment wake up and mightily swipe. Who was it for the Englishman? He seemed Godless, but in the occasional wry edges of his smile to acknowledge that someone was watching, that at any moment Authority might reach down and pin him and make him pay. He conceded this, Ross thought, but with levity; and underneath the levity a kind of glorious Satanic contempt.

'Okay,' Chick said coming through the door with a tray of Indian sweets. 'Everything settled?'

The plan was to halt the train (destination Badnera) between Bhusawal and the first stop, Varangaon. Six men would be waiting with a truck. They'd carefully break the offside seal on the silk wagon, lessen the shipment by forty bales, then reseal the wagon and the train would be on its way. Eugene reckoned fourteen minutes. 'What do you mean "reseal"?' Ross had asked him. 'You can't reseal a wagon like that.' The seal's integrity was established by an unbroken circular pin which fitted through a lead disc. 'We've *been* through this, for Christ's sake,' Eugene said – which was true. Ross had made small noises of scepticism with Skinner but reserved the full weight for Eugene. 'If you cut it carefully,' Eugene said, 'you can thread it back through when you're finished. It looks sealed.' 'But it isn't,' Ross said. 'No, it isn't,' Eugene for the umpteenth time agreed. 'But it's dark, and it's on the off side, ten feet above the watchman's head. It'll look sealed to him. He's not going to be looking that closely. He'd have to get a bleddy ladder and climb up to inspect it properly, and even then he might be fooled unless he grabs hold of the bleddy thing and tugs it. Trust me, men, I'm telling you.'

Ross remained unconvinced, spent the week in a state of agitation. The more he thought about it the less he liked it. It was a pleasure and a relief to him, therefore, when on the night of the operation – gimcrack or not – they hit a snag at the outset.

'*Fuck* it,' Eugene said, after Ross had pointed out the problem.

'What's the trouble?' the station master asked, when they called him. He was an Englishman, Harry Granger, with a militant ruddy face and black-lashed turquoise eyes. With his looks (under the cap a bristling white short-back-and-sides) he ought to have done everything with martial precision; in fact, he was a highly bribable bodger who slacked on every aspect of the job.

'Look at the gauge,' Ross said. 'We're six units short on vacuum pressure.'

Harry studied the gauge, redundantly rapped it with his index fingernail, exhaled. God or the invisible vague conspiracy did this sort of thing to him, personally. It was an obscene injustice if he had to get up from his desk. 'Oh, Christ,' he said, sleepily. 'Well, if it's a leak it's a leak.'

While the engineer tried to track it down Ross went up to the engine. 'Well, that's that,' he said to Eugene. Now that the job looked scuppered, now that he'd got what he'd told himself he wanted, the lost five hundred hurt him under the ribs.

'We'll be all right,' Eugene said. 'They'll wait. What else have they got to do?'

'This is a bad sign,' Ross said. 'You want omens? This is an omen.'

'Don't be such a sissy, men.'

The engineer spent an hour treating what might be leaks, eventually got the pressure up.

'This is ridiculous,' Ross said to Eugene.

'Relax, will you?'

'The rear hosepipe's only tied, you know.'

'Yeah, well, it won't be the first time. Come on let's get her out of here.'

'They won't be there,' Ross said. 'We're an hour behind time.'

'They'll be there,' Eugene said. 'They want the stuff.'

They were there, and as agreed flashed the truck headlights. Ross gave return flashes with his torch. The silk wagon was halfway down the load, too far to pick out any details, though Ross told himself he could feel it like a sentient presence. He listened. A wagon door on the off side opened with a soft roar. He looked at his watch. They were fifteen minutes out of Bhusawal. Starlight but no moon. Darkness was compelled to serve crime. The signal for All Clear was three flashes from the headlights. Eugene stayed put on the engine and he stayed put in the brake. That way no one saw anyone face to face.

Suddenly Ross saw figures on the near side of the train. There were muffled sounds, then the unmufflable sound of another wagon door sliding open.

'What the hell are you doing?' he hissed, having run up, though he could see what they were doing: a stack of some half-dozen silk bales lay palely glimmering on the ground. The six men, gleaming wiry Indians, four in dhotis only, two in kurta pyjamas, were working in relay pairs at an incredible speed.

'You're not supposed to see us,' the one nearest him said – then leaped up into the wagon like a frog.

'You've broken the bleddy seal on this side, too,' Ross said. The track was quiet and alive, the stars like a slowly passing brilliant swarm. A separate part of Ross's consciousness was busy with the way the land's sensuousness ambushed you when you stopped, whatever else was going on. It was as if this spot, at all other times passed through, must let everything it had — two or three thorn bushes, a sprinkling of open-faced feminine white flowers, a solitary dead tree and a scatter of rusting oil drums — gush out while there was someone to receive it, since it might be a hundred years before anyone stopped precisely here again. 'Why did you do this?' Ross said. 'This seal's going to be—'

'We couldn't get them out of the other side,' one in pyjamas gasped, dropping from the wagon to the ground. 'They're stacked too tight.'

'What?'

'Go and see. Go and see for yourself.'

Ross went between the couplings. The off-side door was open and many bales revealed, but he could see why they hadn't been able to shift them. The wagon had been loaded from the opposite side; here you faced a solid wall of bales, no way of dislodging them. Why, Ross wondered, had no one considered this? He looked at his watch. They'd been stationary for seven minutes. He clambered back through the couplings. There were now at least a dozen long rolls of silk on the ground. The shimmer of the stuff was arresting. He reached down and ran his hand along the nearest. Panic was like that, kept offering you openings into dreamily pretending nothing was happening. You thought, Look at me: here I am in the middle of a dangerous situation and I'm fondling a roll of golden silk. He shook himself out of it. 'In exactly eight minutes I'm signalling my driver to start,' he said. The six men ignored him. They were sheened with sweat. The dignity of the body at work was unimpeachable, no matter the job.

The eight minutes passed. Twenty bales lay on the ground. How big was the truck? 'Come on,' Ross said. 'That's it. Let's go.'

'We've got orders for forty,' one of the men said. Since it was the first utterance not whispered, hissed or gasped, it came out dark and wooden, not quite a threat. Ross, armpits aflame, began making power calculations. They weren't armed, but there were six of them. Even with Eugene (who was no fighter) the odds were impossible. 'Okay,' he said. 'I'm going round to seal the off-side door. You get as many out as you can. But when I come back I'm sealing this fucking door without argument or this whole thing is going in my report as an armed robbery. I've seen all your bleddy faces so don't get smart.' Empty. They knew, recognized an offer of compromise. You get as many out as you can. It was still teamwork. He hadn't delivered that 'fucking' convincingly, either. It wasn't one of his words.

'We'll take thirty,' the not-whispering one said, not pausing in the unloading, just as Ross turned his back to go yet again between the wagons. Something else in the tone: you're not a protected species any more. An exciting vulnerability tingled in his fingertips and scalp. There was an endorsement of the idea even in the land's sensuous assault. We pull out, you buggers are going to be up shit creek wi'out a paddle. I'm not going to be here by 1960, he'd told Hector. Since recovering from pneumonia he'd trained lightly but consistently; his body had given him a shock, that it could be laid low like that. Now the training was a dialogue with his body he must stay engaged in. In the dark Kate, like a child, felt his daily hardening muscles. She liked it, she said. That she said such things disinterestedly, not for his pleasure, made his pride feel like a virtue. We'll take thirty. Statement not request. Threat would be next. The certainty of this made him glad of the strength of his body, that if it came to fighting – if life ever came to fighting – there would never be the regret even in defeat that he hadn't made himself as strong as he could be. At the same time he knew a fight here wouldn't be a fight; it would be him getting uglily beaten up, possibly killed. He couldn't afford it. Boxing season only a month away, the trials, the Olympics, the plan.

He did what he could with the off-side seal. Hastily splashed with an unsuspicious torch it would probably pass. It wasn't the off side he was worried about.

'Okay, come on, that's it.'

They had close enough to thirty bales out. Two of the men had been dispatched for the truck, which came gargling up now with headlights off.

'Two more,' the leader said. Ross pushed past him, grabbed the wagon door and hauled it shut. It was a fine calculation to make, whether turning your back on a man disarmed or empowered him. In the push past he'd smelled curryish sweat, smoker's breath, essential cowardice. No, he hadn't smelled that. That was just what you told yourself to force yourself through your own fear. Ross worked on the seal. He could hear them loading the truck behind him, but could sense – through the back of his head, back, buttocks, thighs, calves, heels – that the leader was standing and watching him, weighing up making trouble.

'What the Christing hell is going on down there?' Eugene's voice called through the darkness.

'Almost done,' Ross called back. It was a relief to shout in full voice.

'We've got to go,' Eugene bellowed. '*Now*.'

'Wait for my bleddy signal,' Ross said. This was good, a conversation which edged the leader out of the frame. He could feel the man sullenly accepting that twenty-eight bales was it. 'Almost there,' he shouted, to keep it going. 'Okay!' The seal wasn't convincing but it was as good as it was going to get. They'd just have to trust to luck. He jumped down from the wagon and crossed a second time through the man's aura. There was a surge – he tightened, felt the frenzy of adrenalin in his knees and hands and scalp – then final acceptance. The leader gave a single quiet laugh and turned away.

The watchman at Malkapur wasn't unknown to Ross but he wasn't familiar enough to bribe. He did a cursory pass of the off side without comment, came round to the near side, stopped at the brake to offer a cigarette. The blueish-white platform lights demystified the train.

'No, thanks, I don't smoke.'

'Everything okay, sahib?' He was a young Indian with a happy beady-eyed and thin-moustached face. His shirt collar was too big for him. Ross knew the type: smiled at his uniform when he hung it up on the wardrobe door.

'Will be if we don't lose the rear hose again. Twenty minutes late since Varangaon.' This was the story Ross had settled on. The rear hosepipe, only tied on to the vacuum seal at Bhusawal in the first place, had come uncoupled and had to be retied. He'd had a raft of other bogus reasons for stopping but the pressure leak had a witness, Harry Granger, station master no less. That was sheer luck, but then so was the wagon being loaded from the near rather than the off side. God made it easy for you with His left hand, difficult with His right.

The young watchman walked back down the platform, slowly, flicking his torch up at the seals. Ross leaned out of the brake. He was starving, incapable of eating. The tiffin box held samosas, a chicken curry, three parathas, biscuits, half a bar of Tarzan chocolate and a flask of coffee. He wouldn't touch any of it until they'd dropped off the load at Badnera and were on their way back to Bhusawal. He wished he did smoke, something you could do to feed your nerves and pass the time. Keep going, keep going, keep going . . .

Something fell from the watchman's pocket. Ross squinted. Cigarettes, the pack of Gold Flake. The watchman stopped, bent to pick them up. Noticed something. The torch flicked low, held its beam steady, then skipped up to the wagon's seal.

'Sahib?'

'What's wrong?'

'Seal on this wagon's broken.'

Ross got down from the brake and walked up to where the

watchman had stopped. A triangle of pink silk was sticking out from beneath the door.

'What happened, sahib?'

'Damned if I know,' Ross said. 'They were sealed at Bhusawal. I signed for them. Let's get it resealed as quick as you can.'

'Very good, sahib.'

Ross jogged up to Eugene on the engine and broke the news. Eugene shook his head, kicked a panel, looked for a moment as if he might break down in tears. 'Nothing,' he said quietly. 'Nothing ever goes smooth for me.'

'You?' Ross said. 'It's me they're going to suspect. I'm the one who stopped the bleddy train. I'm the one those goondas are going to pick out if they get caught. Easy money. Bleddy *hell*.'

'Okay, okay, don't panic,' Eugene said. 'We'll just keep cool and play dumb. They may not even notice.'

'What are you, insane? There's a resealed wagon twenty-eight bales short and they're not going to notice?'

'They'll notice at the destination,' Eugene said. 'But that could be miles away. It's probably going to Hyderabad for the Nizam.'

'It doesn't matter where it's going. That wagon's got a Malkapur seal on it and the paperwork's going to have it all in black and white. How long do you think it's going to take them to figure it out?'

Not long, but the investigation, which began two weeks after the incident, dragged itself with exquisite inconvenience into the boxing season and the Olympic trials. Ross had trouble keeping his weight up. Two flecks of grey hair appeared above his left ear.

To make matters worse, there was no money.

'It's idiotic,' Skinner said at Chick's, the night before the investigation was due to begin. 'I mean, it doesn't make business sense. I've worked with him before. He's never stiffed me for a single cent.' 'He' was Grishma Pilay, a roving Maharashtran fence with whom Skinner had had until now a mutually profitable relationship. There had been a small down payment for the silk information. The rest of the money was supposed to be handed over to Skinner at the rendezvous just outside Varangaon the night of the robbery. Skinner and Chick had turned up as agreed. No one else had. Silk and money had skipped town. 'He's not stupid,' Skinner said. 'He knows I'm going to spread the word and he knows my bloody word counts. He's sawing off the branch he's sitting on. I just don't understand it.' The conspirators had taken to meeting at Chick's after dark to drink and mull over the treachery.

I don't know why you're bothering, Kate had said to Ross. There's nothing you can do about it now. She'd been reluctant for him to go through with the job in the first place, not from fear for its success but because this latest encounter with Skinner had convinced her that the Englishman was competing with her for Ross's intimacy. She, too, saw the Satanic contempt, but felt herself an object of it. She and Ross had had their first real fight. He doesn't think of you as his equal, he thinks of you as his instrument. He's not interested in anything or anyone other than himself. You're just flattered because— She'd gone further than she'd meant to. Because *what*? Ross had demanded. They were in the kitchen at Armoury Road. Dondi had scoured all the pans and hundis the day before and in the room's trapped sunlight they glowed with pointless benevolence. Because he's *English*, she'd said, with a sort of exhausted violence which had started Carl, in her arms, bawling. She was trembling herself.

A detatched, analytical part of her was thinking the longer you left it before having your first fight with your husband the more devastating it was when it happened. Suddenly the explosion into mutual strangeness seemed possible. It was terrible to see him sitting there with his face gone pouchy and all the prideful easy motion of his body stilled because she'd told him the truth and it hurt. It thrilled and wounded her that she had the power to unman him like that. At a stroke she saw how a wife might become addicted to doing it – *and Thy desire shall be unto Thy husband, and he shall rule over Thee* – but knew she never would. The revelation – that she was bigger than him – released both a surge of love and a spasm of disappointment: he was after all only a man, dependent on her. Men were needful. Your softness inexhaustible for them. And afterwards troubled, ashamed of how far from themselves they'd been carried. The penis afterwards was like the man himself, shrunk into itself as if traumatized by the desperateness of its own need.

Ross had been awkwardly gentle through both pregnancies, a bit hurt each time because what were they but confirmation that he, her husband, was no longer the main thing in her life? The man was the little king, Kate thought, until you got pregnant, then his littleness was revealed. He shuffled at the perimeter of the glow you and the child made, became a sorry-for-himself petitioner. (Even God conceded it, she'd thought, stayed off stage, left the Madonna and Child in the spotlight.) But then if he really was a man he drew back, forced himself to stop needing you in the same way, made provision and fierce, cold protection the business of his kingship. Ross had done this, she knew, but the self-containment of her pregnancies had ravaged him. Like all men he'd had the choice between yielding to love and keeping the flint of himself to go after adventure or God. He'd softened for her, given her children, and she'd betrayed him by loving the children more; and after love the flint self could never really be the same. Adventure – maybe even God – could never be enough. Skinner (the thought had seemed ludicrous to Kate, shushing Carl and moving over to Ross to give his face the soft hand-touch she knew he wanted) saw all this. She'd told herself subsequently that she was imagining it. She just didn't like the man.

'Come with me for a minute, will you?' Skinner said. The evening at Chick's had broken up. Eugene had passed out (frowning) and been left to sleep it off. Chick needed hardly any sleep.

He spent hours at night sitting in a canvas chair in the blossom-scented darkness of the garden.

'Where?'

'The Ambassador. Won't take long. There's something I need to give you.' The Ambassador was one of Bhusawal's three small hotels. In the lobby, where an Indian desk clerk dozed at his post, Skinner said: 'Come up. Really it'll just take a moment.' Over his shoulder as Ross followed him up: 'Don't worry, sport, I'm not a fruit.'

Which, since it was precisely what Ross had been thinking (the suspicion had lingered; Skinner never mentioned women), left an oppressive silence until they reached the landing. 'I don't think that,' Ross managed to get out, while Skinner struggled with his door's sticky lock. 'There's no need to—'

'Skip it,' Skinner said, still wiggling the key. 'No need to waste breath.' The door opened. 'Bingo,' he said. 'I really do feel one oughtn't to need burgling skills to get into one's own bloody room, don't you? Close the door behind you, please.'

Skinner crossed the spartan room (one crisply made bed, one dresser, one dark wardrobe, one cane chair, one coir mat), got down on his hands and knees and reached under the bed. Jiggery-pokery with floorboard or skirting followed. Ross stood in the middle of the room quite seriously admitting to himself that were the Englishman to turn around, point a revolver at him and pull the trigger, he wouldn't in fairness be able to justify surprise. Skinner got to his feet, held out an envelope. 'Take this,' he said.

'What?'

'Take it.'

'What is it?'

Ross knew what it was. The envelope wasn't sealed and the edges of the bills were visible. Skinner stepped forward and with a sort of formal care forced it into his hand. Stepped back, put his hands in his pockets, met Ross eye to eye. 'There's five hundred in there,' he said. 'About what your cut would've been. It's yours.'

'I don't understand.'

'Yes you do, sport. You've been wondering if I stiffed you. All of you.'

'Is that what this is?' Ross said.

'That's five hundred of my own. I want you to have it. I didn't stiff anyone. I'm down on the deal myself. The other two are just going to have to take my word for it. But you're different.'

'I don't—'

'Listen to me. I owe you. In my scheme of things I owe you double. I owe you for pulling me out of the shit five years ago and I owe you for getting you *in* the shit now.'

'That's not your fault. I went in voluntarily. This is ridiculous.'

'Tell me you haven't been wondering.'

Ross felt his face warming.

'You'd be a bloody fool not to. It's okay. If I were in your shoes I'd feel exactly the same. And now you've got this tribunal or whatever the hell it is and I can't believe a bit of cash won't come in handy. For Christ's sake don't you see? Grease the buggers.'

You're different. Ross looked down at the envelope. He could smell the bills. Money stank. 'I'm not taking this,' he said. In among the other feelings was painful relief that Kate had been wrong. He tossed the envelope on to the bed.

Skinner picked it up and held it out again. 'Don't be an ass,' he said. 'I don't mind you doubting me. It's all right.'

Ross shook his head.

'Take it, for God's sake.'

'No.'

For a moment the two of them stood like that, Skinner holding out the envelope, Ross with his arms by his sides. There was an attentiveness in the silence, as if the hotel's guests were collectively listening, an effect which in seconds became absurd. They both chuckled. Ross wanted to say something. He didn't know what. Whatever it was he couldn't frame it. Instead, saying nothing, he turned, raised a hand in farewell, opened the door and went out.

The head of the investigation was the divisional transport superintendent, an Englishman, Edmund Hoggarth, who'd been in India thirty years. The first thing he said to Ross, as if opening a casual conversation, was 'Do you by any chance have a passport?' Ross said he hadn't. Hoggarth nodded and gave him a crisp smile; he was in his late fifties, a tall, square-shouldered man with coarse grey hair and a long, good-looking, calm face. His full smile was dazzling but his eyes remained distant. 'That's fine,' he said, then with emphasis, 'That's absolutely *fine.*' Pause. 'Because if this becomes a police matter the first thing they'll do is confiscate it to stop you toddling off.' The interview took place in the assistant traffic superintendent's office in Bhusawal. Ross stood, initially, while Hoggarth, the ATS and another British pen-pusher, whose long neck and head together looked like a slender spring onion, sat in a line behind the scalloped walnut desk. The stewed office's only ornament was a series of framed anatomical drawings of horses. A rotating electric desk fan (the ceiling fan had that morning broken down) hummed ineffectually, turned its face from Hoggarth to Ross, Ross to Hoggarth as if with careful slow observation. Hoggarth spent the first few minutes doctorishly reading various fan-ruffled documents in front of him, from one of which he looked up and said to Ross, 'Please do sit down,' almost (but calculatedly not quite) as if Ross needn't have bothered waiting to be asked.

The passport question put Ross on his guard. He wasn't lying: he didn't have one. But he had applied. He and Kate would need them, obviously. (Filling in the application had been a strange experience: Passport of the United Kingdom of Great Britain and Northern Ireland. To be on the safe side he'd applied to the Indian passport office as well, since technically they were eligible for both.) What was Hoggarth trying to tell him? That he knew how much rode on the outcome of this case?

The Indian Olympic Selection Committee's plan was to use as many as practicable of the national and regional amateur tournaments as a filter for a series of elimination contests, which would be held in Bombay at the end of April. Despite the flecks of grey and the low weight Ross had won the divisional bantamweight title for the third time (but for the Tryst with Destiny it would have been the fourth), and was to fight in the All-India Inter-Railway finals in Calcutta on 1 April. Winning that (for what would also be the third time) would take him to the Olympic eliminators. Victory there, naturally, would take him to Helsinki.

'The mathematics of this don't change, do they?' Edmund Hoggarth said. They'd been in the ATS's office for three hours. The ATS himself and the onion-headed pen-pusher had been dismissed but Ross had been asked to stay.

'Sorry?' Ross said.

Hoggarth was sitting back in the ATS's creaking swivel chair languidly pressing the knuckles of his left hand with the fingers of his right as if to soothe arthritis. The desk fan remained on duty, turning its face to Ross, giving a few moments of interrogative warm breath, then turning to Hoggarth, breathing on him, then back. The motion threatened to drive Ross mad if he attended to it. He hadn't been surprised that Hoggarth wanted to speak to him alone. Throughout the interview there had been an awareness between them. Hoggarth had, as the idiom was, stayed on. There was a plump gold wedding ring – so not alone. There was a wife, assuming she was living. Ross pictured a big house, liveried servants, kids grown or boarding away. Burra Sahib.

'The mathematics,' Hoggarth said. 'The logic, the facts.'

Ross came back to the moment. Christ, these drifts. It was this room, the heat, the hypnotic repetitiveness of the desk fan. Some antechamber of Hell would be like this, the creeping realization that time had stopped, that you were stuck here for ever.

Hoggarth rotated the chair a few degrees, crossed his left leg over his right, took the hot balm of window light on his face. He could do the two things simultaneously, put the fear of God into you and keep a little of himself aside for the world's sensuous flux. 'At Bhusawal you sign the station master's log: "All seals intact." Just short of Varangaon you stop the train for twenty minutes because, you say, the rear hosepipe needed recoupling. By the time the train gets into Malkapur, the seals on both near and offsides of one wagon are broken. The wagon is resealed, and on you go. When you reach your destination at Badnera you again sign the station master's log: "All seals intact." The shipment in the resealed wagon is subsequently found to be short by twenty-eight bales of finest-quality silk, which on the black market would fetch, shall we say, a tidy sum. Correct?'

'Yes.'

'Why didn't you mention that the wagon had been resealed?'

They'd returned to this question several times. Ross wished he had an answer, or at least a better answer than the truth, which was that by the time they got to Badnera he hadn't been able to decide whether it was better to mention the reseal or not. The whole journey his head had buzzed with small electrified loops of thinking. Time and miles had passed, his mouth getting drier. He had one hour left to decide. Forty minutes. Eighteen. Badnera. Ten. The platform. Five. Station master's office. Two minutes . . . one . . . and there he was with the last shreds, the slow-motion seconds as the log was handed to him and he lifted his pen. He didn't know. The pen hovered while he thought: should have tossed a coin. Some fractional tilt towards hoping for the best decided him. He signed: 'All seals intact.'

'It was just one of those things,' he said. He was tired of the whole phantasmagoric business. He kept thinking: Just tell this sonofabitch where he can stick . . . But the thought swerved away from completion. He needed him.

Hoggarth smiled. Closed his eyes for a moment. Opened them. 'We're running a test today,' he said. 'We're duplicating the conditions you say caused the rear hose to uncouple. We're testing the theory with an actual train, reducing the vacuum pressure with a tied-on hose.' Pause. 'My guess is the hose won't come off. Of course, even if it doesn't it's not conclusive. You still have in your favour Mr Granger's testimony. In fact, you have a superabundance of character witnesses, most of whom have been to see myself or my colleagues over the last weeks. No doubt all hoping you can bring a gold medal home to India. I've seen the collection of newspaper clippings in the running room.'

Neither man spoke for a few moments. Hoggarth very gently swivelled the chair back and forth through five degrees.

'You were planning on emigrating, were you?' Hoggarth asked. Quieter. Man to man.

'If I won. If there was interest.'

'Everyone's been telling me what a prospect you are.'

It wasn't a compliment. What does he want? Does he want something?

'Did you try out in '48?'

'I was injured. Got sick.'

'Perhaps it's not your destiny.'

Silence. The fan turned its head towards Ross, softly assaulted him with its breath. With relief he realized he was very close to losing his temper. It would be a liberation to jump up and smash something, all the agony of not knowing his fate gone in an instant. Half the world's murders must be committed that way, to settle some unbearable uncertainty.

'Do you think things have got worse since Independence?' Hoggarth asked.

This was such a non sequitur Ross had to fight the reflex to say, What? even though he'd heard clearly. On the wall by the window to his left there was a pendulum clock of dark wood, the soft *toonk . . . toonk . . . toonk* of which emphasized how long it was taking him to think of how to answer.

'In what way?'

'Slack. Less efficient. Less honourable.'

'I don't know about any of that.'

'Not interested in politics?'

'Not really.'

'Same here. Always seems to me politicians'll do anything rather than tell the truth. Best just to deal with the rights and wrongs that put themselves under your nose. They'll always be there, no matter who's in government, wouldn't you say?'

'I suppose so.'

'The thing is, Monroe, I know you were in on it. Don't say anything. This conversation's off the record but still, it's best if you just hear me out. I know you were in on the robbery. I know Drake was in on it. I know the hose didn't need recoupling, and I know I could make this into a criminal case.'

Ross stared at the polished surface of the desk. The walnut grain was a mesmerizing mix of compressed and languid ripples, here and there irregular concentricities gathered round an angry little knot. God thought big – oceans, skies, mountains – but also doodled in every available inch, even the secret insides of trees. 'You know, the feeling among my countrymen, Monroe, has always been that without them this place would be a shambles. Too many religions, too many languages, too many agendas. Too hot. A friend of mine actually said that to me on the docks at Bombay just before he sailed for England: "It'll get hotter now we're going."' Hoggarth chuckled. 'The feeling among those who left was that those of us who stayed behind would be facing insurmountable odds, you know? I never shared that belief. My belief is in the possibility of honourable actions.'

A vague discomfort had been growing in Ross as Hoggarth had gone on. Suddenly it moved with a spasm of weariness into understanding. Hoggarth had an idea of himself: one of the honourable men who stayed on when the less constant had turned their backs. He would maintain Empire standards without the hope of thanks. This was the myth concocted to rationalize the truth: that in England he'd never be the little demigod India had made him and that nothing less than that would do. The wife would have grasped this in spite of him. The wife was devoted. He was the sort that inspired it. But the truth would be with them in the palatial house like the first whiff of something dead that could only, with time, get worse. Seeing this deflated Ross. The man-to-manness had beguiled him for a moment. He decided to concentrate on the walnut grain, and the option to get up and smash the desk fan over Hoggarth's head.

'You people, now, are uniquely placed, you realize that, don't you?'

'Us people?'

'Anglos. There's going to be a great temptation to forget every-thing we've . . . What I mean is you've got a choice.' Everything we've taught you, he'd been going to say. Ross's scalp prickled. 'You can lower your standards,' Hoggarth continued, 'become more like the natives, you know what I'm talking about . . . Or you can honour your heritage.'

Ross was thinking of a story his Aunt Eliza used to tell, about how, when she was a girl, a young British subaltern had taken her to a dance at his club. He'd only been in the country a month. She was fair-skinned, grey-eyed; he'd assumed she was English. After about twenty minutes, he was called aside by an elderly man, spoken to quietly. He came to me blushing like I *don't* know what, Eliza used to say. Didn't know how to tell it to my face. He tried, poor bugger, Madam, Miss, terribly sorry ur ah oo, pulling all the faces . . . So I said let me say it for you: You had no idea I had a touch of the tar brush but now that pompous old twit has put you in the picture you'd better take me home. My *God* you should have seen the looks. So I said, Thank you very much but if I'm not good enough to dance with I'm not good enough to walk home with, either. And I turned on my heel and walked out of there. She told it beautifully, with relish for the moral disgust and a shameless delight in her own heroism.

And you never saw him again? Ross's sisters would want to know. *Never*, Eliza would say, her mouth snapping shut with mean finality, though according to Beatrice, who in sorority as in everything was viciously competitive, she did see him again, and not just for a walk home.

'Now, I'm not going to make a criminal case out of it,' Hoggarth said, 'because I believe that deep down you're an honourable man and it's not going to do anyone any good if you get sent to jail. But we are going to have to accept that you can't just walk away from what is in fact criminal activity without being made to bear *some* consequences.'

'What are you going to do?' Ross asked the grain.

Hoggarth closed his eyes again. The weight of relished responsibility. Suddenly he leaned forward. 'Monroe, we need honourable men in this country. You know yourself the Indians can't be relied on for anything. Not caring, it's in their damned blood. Continent of Circe and all that, it's no joke. There's no unity — never was until we came and made a country out of it — and where there's no unity there's no order. Do you have any idea the sort of mess the railways are going to be in if the whole lot's left to the Indians?'

Ross remained silent.

'Do you know a George Skinner?' Hoggarth said.

Hearing the name Ross realized he'd been waiting for it. He looked up at Hoggarth. No point in denying it. Any number of people could have seen them together. 'Yes, I know him.'

Hoggarth leaned back in his chair, studied Ross for a moment. You know what I want. Yes I do. 'The point is,' Hoggarth said, swivelling away slightly and looking at the floor, 'we know he's involved.'

Ross said nothing.

'The authorities have had their eye on him for quite some time.'

'If you know he's involved, why are you asking me about it?'

'Don't be obtuse, Monroe. Knowing he's involved is one thing, proving it is another. We need a testimony.'

The last of his tension left Ross in a soft electrical shiver. It passed from him and his muscles and bones were at ease. The mathematics of this don't change. He thought of himself and Skinner in the room at the Ambassador, laughing because there was such a need to say something and simultaneously no need to say anything. Remembering, it was a struggle not to laugh now, Hoggarth's comfortable confidence.

'I know Mr Skinner,' Ross said. 'But not well. We met several years ago, during the Independence riots, as a matter of fact, from which both of us were hospitalized. We swapped addresses, and when he came to Bhusawal recently he looked me up. We've had a few drinks together. That's all. He has, as far as I know, absolutely nothing to do with any of this.'

'Monroe,' Hoggarth said, 'you're not being sensible.'

Ross, now experiencing a peculiar heat of anger and euphoria (laughter bubbled up, his effort to keep it down sent up more bubbles; the deliciousness of knowing that sooner or later he'd give in to it), got to his feet.

'Sit down, there's a good chap,' Hoggarth said.

'That's all I've got to say,' Ross said. He turned his back on the superintendent and headed towards the door.

'I haven't finished with you, Monroe.'

'But I've finished with you,' Ross said, without turning around.

CHAPTER FIFTEEN

revisions

(London, 2004)

What do you do? You laugh. The moment expands fantastically, and in the seconds of fresh space it creates you realize how long it's been since you last tasted innocent joy. Admittedly the expansion's brief, a heartbeat or two, then no matter joy's purity the regular shit collapses back in and what was a giant space shrinks, has to truck with the rest of your life's unspectacular moments. Scarlet and I stopped, opened our mouths, let the shock of surprise expand, then, laughing, slowly came towards each other and with only the very slightest hesitation embraced, loosely then tightly, me still holding in one hand the plastic bottle of sparkling water, her in one hand a woollen coat.

Oh my God.

Holy fucking shit.

Oh. My. God.

Then more laughing, but without innocence, extra-sensory tentacles (mine) already reaching out and probing the invisible lifeshape: alone? married? still loves—

She had, I thought, grown very slightly. She'd felt ribby in the embrace, a nervous, wiry strength in the shoulders that hadn't been there before. No fat, no grey, no yawning pores, no loose skin; only the faintest fine lines at the eye and mouth corners. Her face if anything looked thinner, hollower-cheeked. It was worked for. The tension said exercise, the skin and hair healthy eating. I couldn't imagine her smoking a cigarette.

'What . . . ? Jesus.' One had to keep aborting and starting again. 'First, what's the— Do you have to be somewhere straight away, right now?' We had, not quite able to let go of each other, gracelessly got out of the throng. I'd nearly fallen over her suitcase but we were too busy laughing at the other thing – us, here, now, seventeen years – to laugh at that.

'No I'm just . . . I'm on my own time. Who are you waiting for?'

The only immediate place was a Costa Coffee with a dried-blood colour scheme, but I had to get her sitting down, still, able to answer questions. Our eyes kept meeting and igniting, then flicking away, saying wait, wait, calm down.

I got us coffees, pointlessly.

'Okay. First: how long are you here for?' I said.

'As long as I want. Well, no. I'm on holiday for three months.'

'Three *months*?'

She laughed. I saw the inside of her mouth; tongue and teeth and palate all seventeen years older. Bizarrely, I thought of the thousands of times she must have brushed her teeth since I last saw her. 'It's a long story,' she said. 'Oh my God. *You.*'

We must have looked insufferably pleased with ourselves, even for Arrivals, laughing and grinning and shaking our heads. Around us the maroon café was a mess of uncleared tables and spilled drinks and piled-up luggage. There was her face, the eyes darkly added-to, God only knew by what. The years were on her in the thinnest transluscent layers.

'What are we going to do?' I said. The situation was defeating

us. The unbearable roller-coaster brink moment held, indefi-
nitely. 'I mean are you— Do you have any time?'

'Yes. I mean, I'm in London for a couple of weeks.'

'What are you doing?'

'Honestly, I'm on holiday. This is . . . What about you?'

'I'm here. I live here – still in London, I mean.'

It was going to be like this, dead-ending with the small things
because of the big things.

'Do you live in New York?'

'Yes, but that's a long story, too.'

'I can't believe it. I truly cannot believe it.'

'Neither can I. I was thinking about you on the plane.'

My face emptied of tension. 'Were you?'

She laughed, nodded – but there was a surge or flaring-up of
her life I saw her suppress. Things to hide, apparently. I thought:
She wants to get away and think about this before going any further. I had the same feeling, that if we were going to meet I
didn't want it to be like this, as if a rogue spark had got into the
fireworks box and now they were all going off willy-nilly.

But she was thinking about me on the plane. She had said
that.

'Who are you meeting?' she said. 'Don't you need to . . . ?'

I shook my head. 'I'm not here to meet anyone. I'll tell you
about it later.' I paused, but there was no objection. There was
going to be a later.

We were left with the absurd business of getting the Heathrow
Express into London together, me taking charge of her suitcase
and sorting out the tickets as if I had been there to meet her.
Sharing the train would be a deflation but there was no obvious
way to avoid it since she was going to her hotel and I was . . .
Well, wherever I was going I wasn't hanging around Arrivals any
more. She was tired from the flight. I hadn't shaved for two days
(it only very belatedly struck me how much like shit I looked next
to her) and after the adrenal interview with Reece needed a

shower. We had to pass from the miracle to killing three minutes on the platform. I said, It's so much better with this express now and she said, I know the last fucking thing you want after a flight is the Tube.

'There are too many things,' she said. We'd taken the seats facing each other with the little table between. 'I don't know where to start. Whereabouts in London are you?'

'Balham. Teaching in Wimbledon. Don't laugh. You?'

'Well, until last month I ran a talent agency. Don't laugh.'

Intuitive agreement to stick to the safer material but with whether we liked it or not (*I* liked it) surges if we looked at each other too long. After five minutes of false starts and incredulous silences we hit on the subject of my family with relief. 'Melissa and Ted are still together on the farm, all the boys are grown — Ben's got two boys of his own. Maudy got divorced from Chris ten years back, she's with this other guy now, living together. You should see Elspeth. Jesus.' My navel-pierced niece had been a toddler when Scarlet and I broke up.

'And your mum and dad?'

Tentative, they might be dead.

'They're fine. Usual aches and pains. My mum gets dizzy spells now and again. They're not as . . . You know. They've slowed down a lot over the last few years.' I looked out of the window, thinking of Pasha saying, 'I've got my feet on Thursday.' The last time I was up there I opened the bathroom cabinet for a cotton bud and realized its contents were without exception medicinal.

'I've wanted to write to them so many times,' Scarlet said, but that brought too much with it, made *her* look out of the window. 'This is weird,' she said. 'Holy Mother of God.'

'It'd be lovely to see you, you know, while you're here. I mean if you're not . . . if you want to.'

She leaned back in her seat and looked at me. Suddenly we'd run out of it, whatever it was.

'Are you married?' she said.

'No.'

'Partner? Kids or anything.'

'No. What about you?'

'No.'

I'd assumed she'd want a night to slough the jetlag but when we pulled into Paddington she said, 'This might sound crazy, but do you want to meet this evening?' The station clock said a quarter to four. She looked smaller standing facing me on the platform. Her hair was a way I'd never seen it, straight, shoulder-length, a plump dark shiny curtain with sharp, as they said in America, bangs that swung at her jawline. Her eyes said the surreality of the flight's bent time and annihilated distance was at work: extra-ordinary things happening? Fine. I wondered if she needed to do this, deal with me (whatever dealing with me would mean) in the altered state, was counting on its momentum to carry her through. Carry her through what? The way she'd said, 'This might sound crazy, but do you want to meet this evening?' had made it sound as if an existing plan was being altered ad hoc. She gave me the address and number of the hotel (the Grafton, High Street Kensington – we both laughed, her not quite looking at me) and I wheeled her case all the way to the cab. 'I'll see you at nine, then,' she said, and laughing again (different laughter, conceding delayed shock, awkwardness, proximal complications) we chastely kissed each other on the cheek. I waved her off as the cab pulled away.

There, when the taxi had disappeared entirely from view, was London. With Scarlet in it again. This had been the way of it for hundreds of years, the city going dead and coming alive as love entered and withdrew. Tiring and exhilarating to consider. A nimble journey home I made, smiling at strangers, buying an *Evening Standard*, skipping down the escalators, my London legit-imacy restored after all these fraudulent years.

'Okay,' Janet Marsh's message said when I got home. 'How

about Wednesday afternoon? I'll be there myself from three onwards. He doesn't know what you can possibly want to talk to him for but anyway, you can come and . . . you know. Whatever. The address is 46B Fox Road, Shepherd's Bush. It's off the Uxbridge Road after the Hammersmith and City Tube, going, what? . . . west. I'll see you there if I don't hear otherwise. By-eee.'

I was soaking in the tub when Vince got home at six. He had to go and pee in the back garden.

'You're never seeing her again, are you?' he said, putting his head round my bedroom door. He meant, Janet, whom he's started referring to as the Porcine Richwoman. 'Is she paying you?'

'You're not going to fucking believe what happened to me today.'

I realized, saying it, that I'd forgotten the incident with the police. I told him about Scarlet. I couldn't be bothered telling him about the police now.

'You're joking,' he said.

'I'm not joking.'

'What, she was just *there*?'

'She was just there. There's been a lot of weird shit happening in my life recently.'

'Christ, it's destiny.'

'That's what my dad would say. He's coming to stay next week, by the way, so try not to be too gay, will you?'

'Oh God, great. What if I want to bring someone back?'

'Bring them back, it's fine, this is your home. Just don't bark while having homosexual sex, okay? Just, if you can, refrain from *neighing*.'

I joined him in the kitchen, where he sat with his feet up, drinking a glass of wine and smoking a joint. He took in my sartorial efforts. I'd polished my shoes and ironed a shirt and found it incredible the difference such things made. 'Look at you all ponced up.'

'Yeah, well, you haven't seen her. I felt like bloody Oliver Reed at the airport. I used a whole load of your cosmetics, by the way.'

'I can see that. You look practically newborn. Have a stiffener before you go.'

While I poured he reached into his satchel and pulled out a sheaf of bulldog-clipped papers, slid them over to me. 'Downloaded it. There's a copy for you.'

'What is it?'

'A collection of quotes from various people, mainly in the US administration and the British government. These are all things that people have actually said. I mean they're in print. It's mind-boggling, you know?' Tilted up into a question because the grass was working. I looked at the first page:

'Oh, no, we're not going to have any casualties' – President George W. Bush.

'Every statement I make today is backed up by sources, solid sources. These are not assertions. What we're giving you are the facts' – Colin Powell to the UN.

'With a heavy dose of fear and violence, and a lot of money for projects, I think we can convince these people that we are here to help them' – Lieutenant Colonel Nathan Sassaman.

'It is really wild driving round here, I mean the poverty, and you see there is no money, it is disastrous financially and there is a leadership vacuum, pretty much like California' – Arnold Schwarzenegger to US troops in Baghdad.

I laughed, as was expected of me. 'Yeah, well, I'll have a look at it later.'

'What am I going to do when you kick me out, by the way?' Vince said.

'What?'

'To move your half-caste tart in. It'll be like Paki-Frankenstein and Bride of Paki-Frankenstein.'

'We'll adopt you.'

'And what is the Porcine Richwoman going to say?'

'That's nothing. I'm going. Don't wait up.'

'Take these and read them on the Tube.'

I waved the papers away. 'I can't I can't I've got to prepare myself.'

The Grafton, I'd guess, is about two-fifty a night. Forty rooms, understated contemporary designer furnishings, pleased with itself. The desk duo was a pretty white-bloused spectacled girl with dark blonde hair side-parted and scraped back from a shiny, bulbous forehead, and a black-suited possible queen who looked like Tony Curtis. Tenderness flowed out of me to them. 'I'm here to see Scarlet Reynolds.' How many years since I'd said her name aloud? Ten? Fifteen? Tony (I forgave him the riff-raff here smile) dialled and waited, just long enough for my armpits to start up, looked at me and began to say he was sorry sir but there was no reply from— when Scarlet said, 'Oi, mister,' from the doorway behind me.

She'd booked us a table in the Grafton's bistro, which was dark, winkingly lit with tapering high-backed leather chairs and brushed-steel fittings and in which my guess was that the cheapest bottle of wine wouldn't be less than twenty-five pounds. 'We're not going to talk about the wankery of this place, right?' Scarlet said. 'I just thought it was easiest to eat here. Plus if I fall asleep at the table you won't have so far to carry me.' The English accent had been slightly compromised, required a few days here to revive. She was wearing a charcoal long-sleeved fitted woollen dress with a square neckline you needed her smooth throat to carry off. A single silver fishmail choker and plain silver hoop earrings. The idea was it all sat back and let her eyes and mouth and colouring do the work. Which they did, though she was wearing more make-up than she used to.

'You should get the airline to pay you, looking like that after a red-eye.'

'I take a pill and zonk out. I suppose that means my youth has gone, but . . .'

'Look, I need booze, pronto,' I said. 'Sorry if you've gone all healthy but I'm still happily killing myself.'

'Don't worry, you're not going to be drinking alone.' She picked up the wine list. 'Now, you're going to have to let me choose because I know what I want and I don't care what you want, okay? Plus I'm paying.'

'Can't say fairer than that,' I said – and thanks either to finely tuned ESP or to the wine list's being bugged a waiter of improbable Nordic good looks appeared and took Scarlet's order for a bottle of Liberty School chardonnay, of which I'd never heard. Her mobile rang.

'Oh God,' she said. 'Sorry.'

'Take it, take it—'

'No, no, I'm switching the bastard thing off. I thought I'd left it in the room. Sorry.'

The wine arrived. She tasted, thumbs-upped, white-eyebrowed Lars poured. I drank half mine at one visit. 'Yes,' Scarlet said. 'We'd better get pissed, fast.'

'Quite. George Peppard's just come in, by the way. Your left. Slowly.' Which was a little gift from God or the gods or accident, since it was exactly the ludicrous degree of resemblance – our George had the white hair and piercing eyes and even the cigar but was about five three with manifestly false teeth – to give us a glimpse when she laughed and looked at me of the old collusion.

We were tipsy but not drunk by the time the starters arrived. Enough to concede that trying to unwrap this without tearing the paper was pointless. 'I think the best way,' Scarlet said, 'is to not attempt chronology.'

'Okay. How come you live in New York?'

'Well,' she said, digging into her wild mushroom salad, 'I went there about two years after we split up and started singing in a band—'

'Get the fuck.'

She laughed – at how preposterous her (either of us) doing something like that would have been when we were together. Back then delight in our own complete lack of cool was a luxury affordable because we had each other. Even after the pole-dancing it would have been impossible for me to imagine her – I could barely credit it now – singing in a band.

'I know,' she said. 'But listen, we were good. We supported Dinosaur Jr once.'

'I don't believe you. What were you called?'

'We changed names three times. The last one was Ghost Race.'

'And you sang?'

'There's no need to sound so stunned. I can, you know. You're the one who's tone deaf.'

This wasn't the hoot I was letting it appear. I'd gone in at random and already here was pain. Singing in a band? And what about the two years before that? I topped up our glasses.

'Anyway,' she continued. 'It started as a bit of a laugh, but then things looked like they were going to happen and I had to find a way of staying in America, so I married the bassist's brother's friend.'

'I thought you said you weren't married?'

'Well, I'm not now. It wasn't a real marriage. He was gay. He slept with his boyfriend on our wedding night, which I thought was a bit unnecessary.'

'Christ.' Good-humoured agogness, yes, but I was seeing how this would be: life after me a demonstration of what a crippling restraint life with me had been. The more I asked the worse it would get. I felt tired suddenly, and renewedly annoyed by the snootiness of this place.

'We stayed married for three years, I got my green card, then we got divorced. We were lucky because after '96 they made it so that you had to stay married five years. Also, the band broke up when we'd only been married a year, but he didn't mind. I didn't even pay him, which is what most people do.'

'And then what happened?' Our rejection of chronology notwithstanding, I couldn't think of another way to proceed.

'Then I did the thing on the trains for a year.'

'What thing on the trains?'

'You stow away, but it's on freight trains.'

'You're making this up. Seriously?'

She took a gulp, swallowed. The bistro was full. A soft din of clinking and conversation had been steadily swelling around us. I'd forgotten what my starter was, had to look down at my plate: a minute portion of seared salmon on rosemary-flecked mashed potato with a lemon and dill sauce. I'd ordered an entrecôte steak, medium rare, for the main, couldn't imagine eating it.

'It's a thing,' Scarlet said. 'Have you heard of it?'

'Stowing away on trains?'

'You travel, see how long you can hack it. Skint, obviously. It's like the old hobos.'

I made a flaccid non-judgemental face. She'd wanted it to hurt, of course – *I was right, you were strangling me* – but now that it had she felt petty. 'Anyway, that was a long time ago,' she said, pulling back. 'It feels longer ago than when we were together.'

The change was that her attention had always been elsewhere. Now it had been elsewhere and was back. Now here was elsewhere, or as much elsewhere as anywhere else. Time brought these equalizations, presumably. She was calm, substantial with assimilated experience. The grey dress and uncomplicated adornment testified. But there was something on her mind, beyond even the ridiculous coincidence of the airport. As we talked longer looks crept in, let pulse between us the possibility of something. Sex? I tried to imagine her naked with this older, sadder face, kept getting flashbacks of the younger her naked on the bed in the attic. That's nice what you're doing, just keep doing that.

The Rollicking Adventures of Scarlet after She Left Owen had been established and there was a limit to how many it was decent to recount at one sitting. It was so soon so obvious that next to her life mine was dull that we started taking some of the tangents conversation threw out: the elections; *White Teeth*; the gherkin building; the *Lord of the Rings* films. But it was impossible not to keep coming back to the subtextual essential (was this something? was anything going to happen?) for which, short of asking the questions direct, there was only talk about life since separation.

She was reluctant to expand on the talent agency. 'I went to work for someone, got no thanks, fell out with her and left, by which time several of her clients had got used to me, so I poached them and started up on my own.'

'And now you're loaded.'

'I took advice and made investments. There are people who advise you, you just have to pay them. Let's not talk about that, anyway: it's all shit.'

We'd finished the main course and were now, there was no denying it, drunk. She'd always had to watch it with booze. There was a vicious streak that could emerge and if she carried on drinking become pure evil. She was a long way from that but her eyes had enlarged and her cheeks were flushed. That last 'shit' had had a bitter inflection. She'd registered it, too; I saw her adjust her shoulders, remind herself to slow down. Irritation had crept in. I'd felt my self-ridicule – 'Well, of course, for the real rock-and-rollers there's teaching English Lit in Wimbledon' – not being funny after about the third time. I didn't know what she wanted. We hadn't, beyond the most glancing references, discussed the past, the shared past, *our* past.

'Are you fading?'

'No, just pleasantly tingling.'

The waiter appeared. No we didn't want dessert but yes we did want coffee, which, when it arrived, prompted her to get out cigarettes. I told her she didn't look like a smoker any more.

'I'm not,' she said. 'Very occasionally I'll buy a pack, smoke one or two then leave it somewhere.'

'You've achieved smoking Nirvana,' I said. 'Whereas I,' taking one, lighting, feeling nil respiratory protest at the first drag, 'am fast in danger of starting again if I don't watch it. This is about my fifth in as many days.'

'Tell me what you were doing at the airport,' she said, sitting forward, one hand flat along the table the other holding her cigarette away from her face, a not entirely unselfconscious Mrs Robinsonish pose. Veins showed faintly under the pale skin of her bent wrist and palm. There had been a phase when she'd made me take a long time kissing her wrists and ankles before going anywhere sexual. (Kiss me there. Keep kissing me there. That was part of her pleasure, to keep me doing the thing that made me desperate to do the other thing. She had a tone of gentle instruction that at the time aroused me beyond all reason.) I was drunk enough to have to keep stopping myself saying I've missed you so much you have no fucking clue dying's only ever been a bearable idea if living was with you and how could you have left me you fucking cunt when I loved you in the great old high romantic way of love and now look at us we're full of all the rubbish.

'I was getting interrogated.'

'What?'

I told her.

'And you just go there to watch people?'

'Well, yes, and to plan my next terrorist action.'

'I was there, you know, when the towers were hit.'

'Christ, were you? Where?'

'I was on the roof of a building half a mile away. Watched the whole thing.'

'Holy shit. What were you doing on the roof?'

'It was a friend's roof garden. Actually . . .'

'What?'

'Nothing.' Then she sat back in her chair, let her shoulders sag. This was the same air of having run out of a particular strategy she'd shown on the train. 'Do you want to come up for a drink?'

The room was large, warm, thickly carpeted, decor subdued

neutral contemporary but with a black leather Sixties-style couch and three sub-Rothko panels above the bed. Scarlet having kicked off her shoes went to the minibar, bent, stock-checked, the soft dress pulling tight enough over her backside to show manifest knickerlessness. 'Two Rémys and two Glenlivets,' she said. She was in a bad mood with herself, deep down. Contempt for the coincidence? Something.

'Either. Whatever you want.'

We took the couch, me sitting facing front, her sideways with her back against the arm and her feet up on the cushions. Painted toenails under the nylons' gossamer, a stripe of reflected light down each shin. The smell of leather was a challenging third presence with us. She'd given me the scotch, taken a brandy for herself. This presumably was the quiet the day had been weaving and scribbling for. I stretched my legs, pointed my toes, let my ankles softly crack. She had the option of putting her feet in my lap. Not yet. No point trying to think about any of it through the booze. Easier just to give yourself up. Fate, as Pasha would say. *Destiny.*

'I saw the whole thing,' she said. 'From the first plane hitting to the second tower going down. People jumping, all of it. The thing is, we went in and turned the television on. There it was, happening in front of our eyes, but still, you need to see it on television. I kept going up and down the stairs between the two.'

'I can't imagine what being there must've been like.' No, I couldn't, but I could clearly remember what watching on television had been like for me. Tara Kilcoyne's predecessor, Amy Waterhouse (with whom I'd shared staff-room half-hours in mild, wry, consoling acceptance of the smallness and glamourlessness of our lives) had come into my room between lessons and said, There's something you should see.

'You're probably expecting a story,' Scarlet said.

I turned to look at her. Lighting was the bedside lamps and by the dresser a tall standard in a translucent, papery, ribbed shade that looked like the cocoon stage of a science fiction creature. In its diffuse, warm, buttery light she was dark golden, soft, tired-womanly inviting.

'There isn't one,' she said. 'It was exciting, that's all. Something out of the ordinary was happening. I'm telling you because it came up. It's not my shock-the-guests party piece.'

Courtesy of being drunk I was mildly insulted. 'Well, thank you very much but I'm afraid even I, hick that I am, need a bit more than that to be shocked. I mean it's great you were there and got to see it but the emotional response is hardly news, is it? Something big happens, it's a thrill. I watched them going down on television myself and thought, Fucking *great*. It's nothing, just a relief that all the world's information isn't, as you thought it was, in. All the ethics and emotions come along afterwards because we know we're obliged. It's grim that people died but people die every day. Who gives a fuck, apart from their relatives?'

'Sorry,' Scarlet said. 'I didn't mean to be patronizing.'

'You're a big person,' I said, the genie threatening to come wholly out. 'But even small people watched it on telly and pretty much just went, *Wow*.'

She didn't say anything. I stared at my feet. It was a relief to be shifting into the rawer mode. All the years waiting and then it turns out you're angry because when all's said and done she left you. *She* left *you*. I felt her moving on the couch, tensed – but she was getting up. The cushions gasped; the removal of her weight left me feeling as if I was making the couch, the world, lop-sided. Anger had surged and subsided in the time this took, revealed itself as an option, potentially useful in the business of staying excited; nothing more. She put her drink down on the dressing table. 'Got to pee,' she said. It took two skewed steps and a quiet 'Bollocks' to right herself. I imagined her at a brown-stone's parapet, leaning on the heels of her hands. Who was the friend? I pictured a preposterous James Bondish man, evening dress, bow tie, mid-morning notwithstanding. The hard blue sky and the brilliant buildings with their shared wreath of thudding smoke.

The images on television had reminded us that geological time was still going on, even the biggest things were little.

The bathroom had a low-noise Expelair over which I could hear her stream hitting the water. No amount of time apart would reinstate the bodily privacy those Brewer Street years had blasted. I could walk in there now and pick up the conversation with her on the can and it wouldn't mean anything. She hadn't even closed the door. I couldn't see her but the idea depressed me. The older we get, the sadder we look on the toilet.

She took a few minutes after the flush. I'd finished the first Glenlivet and was into the second when she emerged. I'd framed a jokey apology – Sorry, I appear to have become a twat under the influence of drink and the shock of seeing you – but now that she was there (she'd taken a couple of steps then stopped near the dresser) I knew it was the wrong note. We looked at each other. She came to the couch, stood in front of me. Touched-up lipstick and reapplied perfume. I was thinking: What was the point of slogging through all those years in between if we're going to have this, now? Had she never come back I could have told myself the loneliness was a searing education, an ascent into the grace of accepting being alone. But here she was. What a waste. If I'd missed her by ten seconds.

Scarlet very slowly (filmically, since one's seen it so many times on screen) straddled me and put her hands on my shoulders. Seventeen years. Her face had a slight frown and hot front of urgency that made me expect an intimation of her peculiar absence underneath. Instead I got . . . What? Her unexpected concentration on the here and now. And naturally, since like me she'd been walking the earth the better part of forty years, sadness. Was there an escape from sadness, anywhere? (No. The answer came clear enough. No, there is no escape from sadness because behind all life is death.) It was impossible to tell if she wanted this, any of it, but the momentum was unarguable with. No way of not going ahead now. There would be time later for Oh, fuck, what have we done? I had a very clear perception of the swirling unknown information, fragments of New York and lovers and incarnations and investments and lies, a history which, no matter what we brought into being now, would always have the power to corrupt it. But we'd got to the point of not caring, fizzled into annoyance then past it into letting things play themselves out. My mother had said once: 'For years it was like I was swinging alone on a trapeze, then suddenly one day the other one came towards me with your father on it with his arms out for the catch and I thought, If I miss I'll fall and die, but if I don't try this one chance will never come again. Mind you, I say I thought all this but it was really just a moment of letting go and all that empty space for a split second underneath me.' I remembered the afternoon she said this. She was sitting on the couch braiding Maude's hair. Scarlet and I were lying on our bellies on the floor, colouring. My mother's voice had stolen into our awareness and without realizing we'd become rapt. She rarely talked that way. A moment of holiness in the middle of a nondescript afternoon.

The image of the trapeze flight and catch was in my mind when Scarlet (with dress ridden up to reveal lace tops to the black stockings, the intolerable softness of her upper thighs and the beginning of the firm tendons that with the legs apart reach in and meet at the cunt) leaned towards me, that canvas-dust space just under the striped roof of the big top so remote from the audience and so familiar to the fliers, my mother with the dark hair and distant, clear-eyed look of the India photographs suddenly launched into nothingness, her bare arms out for my father's grasp, the first touch of hands and wrists, the grip, the plait, the swing away into the future.

Afterwards we lay awake side by side with only a ripple of light from the curtains' gap crossing our shins. Half the bedding was off. Sweat cooled. After the bliss of the void the incremental reintroduction of humble finites: fingertips, eyelids, wrists, nipples,

soles. London was beyond the window, seven million anonymous
lives bearable again now that adventure had returned to mine. In
the last months before Scarlet had left me we'd become enam-
oured of a particular position, her on her belly with her hands
between her legs and her arse raised, me astride her thighs entering her from behind. We'd started off just now traditionally, with
me on top, but with sly telepathy had worked our way back to it.

'Like picking up a conversation,' I said. Brave words. The dirty
wave had heaved us up and deposited us. Now here she was lying
next to me with her legs parted and her arms held away from her
sides like a woman tanning. Already life was starting to mutter, the
insistent prosaic substructure.

'I came to London to look for you,' she said. 'It's what I'm
doing here.'

The muttering ceased. Impossible. But not as impossible as the
idea of her saying it for any reason other than that it was true.
Honesty whether we like it or not stabs out brilliantly. 'Imagine
my surprise, then, when there you were at the airport waiting to
meet me.' The tone was deliberate ungenuine levity. Defeat, in
fact.

'I can see I've spoiled something.'

She didn't answer straight away. Thinking of whether what she
had to say was funny or flat or angry. 'Well, I had a quest, didn't
I? You don't often these days undertake a quest, do you?'

'No.'

'And then there you were and I thought there'd been a reality
shift, as in: Whatever you want, there it is.'

That wasn't what she'd said in Arrivals. She'd said she was here
on holiday. Started with a lie. There was a Hot Chocolate song 'It
Started with a Kiss'. Errol Brown could do *anything* to me, she'd
whispered in my ear one day during a lecture on *Mrs Dalloway*.
He could nub me with his head. I panned out from this one
memory and saw with a sort of vertigo the mountain of memories of which it formed a tiny fleck. We'd have to decide what to

do with it. Do you remember that little wooden box you had with that . . . Do you remember that time when you said . . . The potential to sicken each other if we didn't watch it.

'When did you decide to come and find me?' The empty space above our throbbing bodies didn't to me seem quite empty; some just-palpable weight or heat, an angel or devil lying on top of us.

'I don't know. It wasn't a concrete thing. I just realized after a while that I'd been doing things in preparation for coming here. My passport needed renewing beginning of this year.'

'Don't you have an American one?'

'Yeah, but I like to come in on the British one. There's a psychological difference at the airport.'

Between utterances I was busy with the same paradox, that she couldn't possibly be telling the truth and that she couldn't possibly be lying. I came here to find you.

'Must be great knowing you can do the same trick going back the other way.'

'It is. All those losers queuing to be bullied, meanwhile I swan through. There's not much to compare with being entitled to enter America.' She was rubbing the top of her left foot with the ball of her right, an itch. These were the shocking intimacies, not the sex, although I'd been surprised to find she shaved between her legs now. Her cunt had felt meaty and blatant, the shaved lips' frill of flesh arousingly cynical, used to the world. Twenty-first century, I reminded myself. Women follow porn's dictates with a shrug. In the Eighties middle-class feminism was everywhere. Now all the gals are good-time gals; even Germaine Greer's been on the front of a Sunday supplement in the soft-lensed buff, wearing make-up and trinkets. What happened?

'What does it mean?' I said. 'Us. Meeting like this. It's got to mean something. Hasn't it?'

'Well, you'd think so.'

Which turned us up into heightened silence. I was already over the irritation of the wasted past. Seventeen years but here she was again. Fine. No problem. I'll take that. Well, you'd think so. The idiom implied a qualifier.

'To find me for what?' I said. I could feel her thinking that she'd been carried this far without having to ask herself. A few seconds passed. Tiredness radiated from her, a boredom with the complexity of everything. Plus the latest kink of jetlag. I thought she was going to say: I'm not sure.

'To see if I'm still who I think I am,' she said.

Careful what you ask for. I'd been resisting the temptation to take what she'd said about coming to find me at face value. Now I was glad I had resisted and depressed that I'd been right to.

'My life,' she said, but didn't know where to go with it. Reached instead for the cigarettes on the floor on her side, lit one, passed it to me, lit another for herself. The first exhalation was a heavy one. 'I didn't run a talent agency,' she said. 'I ran an escort agency.'

The room, I realized, had a softly humming air conditioner. There was a little digital programming pad on the wall by the door, studded with three frosty green lights and one martial red one. Between couch and bed I'd had to go to the bathroom to pee and when I came out she'd been resetting it. So we wouldn't be cold when we kicked off the bedclothes. In a moment of disinterested sociology I thought how much better everyone's sex lives would be if their bedrooms were warm enough to dispense with bedding. Your mind will go anywhere rather than.

'You heard me correctly,' she said.

The need was to do something: get up, retrieve my drink, look out of the window. All I could manage was to haul myself a few inches higher on the pillows. Every hooker call girl whore prozzie tart escort courtesan from every book film play television programme King's Cross and the trip to Amsterdam and that one woman I saw entering an Arab household in Knightsbridge that time and thought Jesus that's amazing it's really going on and this is what you get if you're loaded and she really was absolutely astonishingly beautiful and at the back of it in the colours of a faded snapshot my old man sitting in Ho Fun's, the egg custards, Eugene's appearance in the blinding band of sun opposite. *Whoreshop.*

'I haven't got anything,' Scarlet said. 'A disease, I mean, assuming that's part of what you're cogitating on.'

'I'm lost for words,' I said. 'I don't think I ever have been before. Are you saying you're a prostitute?'

'Was. Last paying customer ten years ago. Then I set up the agency.'

'You have sex with men for money?'

'Had. Watch those tenses, please.'

'*Why?*'

A pause.

'You're joking, presumably?'

'No, I'm not joking. Jesus *Christ.*'

She got up from the bed, went flat-footed to the minibar, squatted and opened it. Icy light from its interior on her face, breasts, belly, knees. Making love, I had after all found signs of aging, the backs of her hands, her elbows, her feet. It had stirred tenderness into lust, annihilated and simultaneously insisted on the distances between the child, the girl, the woman. Kissing her underarms I'd thought what a fierce, humble, honourable, sad, beautiful business it was having a body, all that silent, invisible, blazing cellular death and renewal. She'd been written on in the years since me, carried time's accrual in the lines of her wrists, eye-corners, the backs of her ankles, even the nipples, erect, seemed more concentratedly puckered as with an effort at holding on to youth; I could love her just for that, her body's honourable testimony to the life lived. Love? Yes, that was the word. It had flashed like a blood-gout in the lamplight with no respect for absurdity, for years, for the logic of estrangement. If I'd stopped for a moment I could have laughed at myself. But I would have laughed and kept the word. Love. I'd wanted to say it.

I still love you. I had had in the languid phases of the long cou-
pling images – imaginings, rather – of her life since me. I'd seen
her (what was this? telepathic insight? fantasy? whatever it was, the
insistence was irresistible) in the high-ceilinged polished main
hall of a Thirties American train station, the one from *Witness*,
Philadelphia, presumably; naked in a field of long-stemmed small-
faced swaying wild flowers; in a deserted alleyway between beach
houses on a hot day; in a rumpled bed alone in the early morning
oranged by curtain-filtered city sunlight. Now, as she rummaged
through clinking miniatures, I thought with a feeling of irreversible subtraction of the men, the Men, who must be
upper-cased when they've paid, unlike lovers who no matter how
many they are retain the innocence of the untransacted. There was
this feeling of her having been to a place which would always
come between us, but a feeling too (let's not be naive) of hector-
ing excitement. Experience. The sly aphrodisiac. All the cocks and
come and surely fascinating psychic fracture. It was one of the
ways open to a woman who wanted to discover America.

'It's not the only thing I did,' she said. 'Do you want one of
these?' Stolichnaya, Blue and Red.

'Either.'

'There's no ice.'

'Never mind. Whatever mixer there is.'

There were several. She poured two vodka and tonics.
Returned to the bed, handed me the drink, sat up with her back
against the headboard, ankles crossed. 'Well, working for someone
else was out of the question. I have to have money and freedom
and I have to be in control. If you don't mind having sex with
strangers it's the obvious choice.'

'You'll have to tell me whether you're being serious.'

'Yes, I'm being serious. There are certain practical matters of
fact. If you're the sort of professional I was, you make more
money in a couple of hours than most people make in a couple of
weeks. Money shapes reality. The richer you are the more you

have to learn who you are. Poverty has a similar effect. It's the great mass of people in the middle, the people with enough but not plenty, who are still flailing about and joining cults and doing Open University degrees in their forties and fifties.'

'Oh, right, there's a philosophy. I didn't realize.'

She waited a moment, sipped her drink, then said: 'Listen, I'm not trying to be difficult but there are certain things you're going to have to abandon if we're going to have this conversation. Sarcasm in the service of some sort of pseudo-moral rectitude. I don't live in that world any more.'

I said nothing.

'You're excited by what I've told you,' she said. 'No doubt depressed and disturbed, but primarily it's just made me more interesting. So, please, let's not have postures.'

'Am I allowed to say I'm glad you're not doing it any more?'

'*I'm* glad I'm not doing it any more.'

'But I mean . . . What . . . Didn't it make you feel bad?'

'Of course, though most of the girls spend a lot of time and energy telling themselves the opposite: it's fun, it makes them feel powerful, they're learning, they're proud of their bodies, they like having sex, all of which from time to time may be true, but the cumulative effect is undeniable. Learning's possible if you abandon the romantic notion that men don't hate women.'

'Oh, great.'

'That's one end of the spectrum. The other is that men go to women for the answer to the question of themselves, the question of what they are and whether what they are is acceptable, manageable, okay.'

'I'm getting unpleasant images, I'm afraid.'

'Well, yes. I've seen unpleasant things. But I have to have money. The first message America gives you, from the second you step off the plane – in fact, while you're still on the plane if it's American – is that you have to have money. You can see it in the cabin crew: there's a particular vividness to their wristwatches and haircuts, there's a look in their eyes, the presence or absence of medical insurance.'

'So you did it to make money. Wasn't there any other way you could have made money?'

'Not fast, no. But I did it, too, because I was interested. In sex. What it was to me.'

'Years ago you said a therapist told you it was to punish your mother.'

'Well, it is that, was that, but it's a lot of other things, too. It's an extreme experience for me. Possibly you never really got that, how much I liked it. The trip out into the void.'

'And you liked it with these men who were paying you?'

'Only very occasionally. But I had men who weren't paying. I had boyfriends when I wanted them. I'm being misleading. Pleasure wasn't primarily the incentive. It was that I was good at becoming things, what they desired. That, believe it or not, is empowering, or at least it creates an illusion of empowerment.'

She was wide awake now, emanating controlled excitement. The excitement was an unavoidable phase, not the end; she was already in possession of conclusions about herself, had been for some time.

'Anyway, the novelty wears off. It becomes impossible to see non-paying men as anything other than furtive or repressed versions of paying ones.'

Which begged the question of what sort of trick I was, in potentia. She raised her hand, pre-emptively. Later, if you really want to know. I said nothing. Turned on my side. Just close enough to her soft flank to feel its warmth. She held the tumbler above her breasts.

'I'd made money. I started my own agency. Particular kind of girl. White, educated, upper-middle-class American. Clients were businessmen, diplomats, brokers, lawyers and celebrities. There were two hundred and ninety lawyers in the Éclat Rolodex when I sold the company.'

'Éclat?'

She laughed, once, through her nose. 'My theory was you could weed out undesirables according to how they pronounced it. But look, I'm not telling you anything right, I'm making a mess of it.'

'Feels like you're telling me quite a lot.'

'Okay, let me go off at another tilt. For the last six years I've been dividing my life into thirds. One third spent making money, one third spent doing good, and the last third spent on myself.'

'Doing good?'

'I look after old people, believe it or not. I visit prisoners, read to the blind, clean toilets and wash clothes at homeless shelters. You name it. If it's conventionally regarded as good works, chances are I've done it.'

'A woman of many parts.'

'In a nutshell, yes. I've given up thinking about it. I have needs and things that I know are good for me. They're hardly ever the same. The unified self is a myth. Leave the myth and you lose the dissonance.'

'Voluntary schizophrenia,' I said – and regretted it immediately.

'I'll overlook the bad tasteness of that,' Scarlet said. 'But you're not far off. My mother kept waiting to arrive at herself. She couldn't help it, she had the illness. I'm not waiting. I'm not waiting for resolution.'

So why are you here? I didn't ask the question. Didn't need to. The old mutual transparency had endured.

'Yes,' she said, as if I had spoken. 'Well.'

Don't say anything. Don't push. Push and she'll run.

She'll run anyway. It's why she's here: to see if she'll still run.

'Let's talk about something else,' she said.

Which, no matter how hard I tried, told me all I needed to know.

'You remember the girl in the photograph?' she said, when it became obvious I couldn't think of a suitable shift. 'The Vietnamese girl?'

Gary had made Wally look at it. I'm keeping this, Scarlet had said. It's mine. Rubbishy theorizing on my part down the years had led me to the conclusion that she'd taken it totemically. The girl looked like she felt. She identified with her. That or she kept it to take out and look at to remind herself that however bad things were they weren't *that* bad.

'Have you still got it?'

'No, I threw it away. Some years back they had this thing, a "ceremony of forgiveness" on Veterans' Day in Washington. She's alive — her name, rather unfortunately, is Kim Phuc — and living in Canada. Anyway, the point is that at the ceremony a US staff officer — now a Methodist minister, incidentally — came forward and took responsibility for what had happened to her. He wasn't the pilot, but he was the guy who allegedly ordered the air strike. So he comes forward and there are tears and the girl — who's obviously a grown woman with kids and everything now — publicly embraces and forgives him. It was a very moving moment, you can imagine.'

'But?'

'But it wasn't him. He *wasn't* the guy who ordered the strike. He'd just got caught up in the need to be forgiven. He was in Vietnam, but he had nothing to do with the strike. Press investigation revealed that not only was this guy an impostor, but the girl, Kim Phuc, knew the whole thing was a set-up. She went along with it.'

'I don't get it,' I said. 'Presumably she was paid off, but what was in it for the impostor? A fee?'

'Apparently not. He just felt lousy about Vietnam, lousy enough to cook up a fiction of responsibility so that he could be forgiven and move on. Amazing, isn't it?'

'There are worse things in the world.'

'Of course. I said amazing, not terrible.'

I got up on one elbow to look at her. 'You're astonishingly beautiful,' I said.

'It's all going, darling.'

'I know, but you've got years.'

'This is work you're looking at here. There's a gym in Manhattan called Crunch where the motto is "No judgment".'

'Sounds like my kind of gym.'

'Yeah, well, I don't go to that one. I go to one called Hell. Their motto is "No mercy". Let's order something. Champagne?'

'Christ, what time is it?'

'It doesn't matter. Champagne and what? Not caviar. Are you hungry?'

'No, dear God.'

'Just champagne. Do you want to make love before it arrives or after?'

We made love after it arrived. Slower the second time. Better. The best. With her, always. But that we'd ordered champagne at all bothered me. A gesture. Wilful celebration in the face of, etc. She'd already made her decision. I probably fucked it up by being at the airport, gave the Quest for Owen no chance to develop momentum, to exhaust her so that when she finally found me she wouldn't have the strength to do anything but stay.

'I gave up,' I told her, meaning my porn sideline as Millicent Nash, having just confessed it. She lay on her back, legs parted, me at right angles to her with my head resting on her thigh. The hotel bed was big enough for a football team. All beds, I thought, should be this big. It should be the law.

'How come?'

I hadn't really known how come until I found myself answering her. 'This is going to sound ridiculous,' I said, 'but it dawned on me that it was something my parents would have thought . . . dishonourable.'

She exhaled smoke, rotating as she did her slim-ankled left foot until she got the tiny click she was after. A while passed before she said, with a discernible closing of something against me: 'Yes, well, that's the beauty of being an orphan. You can be as dishonourable as you like. Not that my mother would have been in any position to pass judgement.'

If I could have reached out in the bedroom's darkness and pulled the words back into my mouth I would have.

'You've got a strange disease,' she said, after a pause. 'The opposite disease to the one everyone else has. You don't want to put any distance between your parents and yourself.'

I'd forgotten the analysis, the insistence. No mercy, as her gym said.

'What were you doing on the roof?' I asked.

'On the roof?'

'When the towers were hit.'

She paused. Just long enough for me to guess.

'Having sex,' she said. I kissed her thigh. Reached up and placed my hand against the warm flesh of her belly. 'Not with a client. With the guy I was seeing at the time.'

'Oh, please,' I said. 'Let me guess: orgasm at impact. The earth moved.'

'It'd be a nice story, wouldn't it? No. We were done, actually, but he was still inside me. We were standing up, me against the parapet looking out over the city, him behind me.'

'I don't like this guy, whoever he is.'

'Was. Owen, your tenses.'

'Was he wearing a dinner jacket and bow tie?'

'No. Why?'

'Never mind. Go on.'

'We froze, naturally. Shock is shock. I saw those buildings virtually every day for years. Some things, a change in their state seems inconceivable. There's no equivalent in London, nothing that dominates the city, claims it, defines it in that way. The thing was I thought: This is . . . This is a world event. This is history being made right in front of my eyes. It still didn't touch me.

What touched me was him inside me, the intimacy of the flesh. I wanted him to stay exactly where he was.'

'But he didn't.'

'No, he freaked out. I wish he hadn't. I couldn't bring myself to see him again after that. It was a betrayal, because I was sure he'd felt it, too.'

I got up for the ice-bucketed bottle. 'And this is *not* your shock-the-guests party piece?'

'I suppose what I mean is that I still felt outside it even though I was in the middle of it.'

'You wouldn't have felt outside it if you were in one of the towers or one of the planes,' I said, topping her glass up.

'No, I wouldn't, you're right. I would have thought: Fuck, I'm going to die. But I would have also thought: I'm glad I lived for myself, the project of myself. I'd have had no regrets about not having lived for the project of the fucking *world*. I couldn't care less about the world.'

Vince, I thought, had a kind of strength. The straight world hurt the gay in a million ways. His parents hadn't exactly disowned him when he came out but they'd never been the same. It had toughened him, forced the recognition that suffering and justice don't know what to do with each other, keep missing each other like two people in a pitch-black arena. He'd had to find sufficiency in himself. Scarlet had strength, monstrous strength, derived from accepting her aloneness. She relied on no one but herself. It was either a triumph or a deformity. It was what had always drawn me to her. The people you need most are the people who need least.

'It's because they never believed us,' I said, lying down alongside her. She put her glass on the bedside table and snuggled against me.

'Who didn't?'

'The school. St Thomas's. When we told them what Gary did to Wally Da-Da.'

She was quiet for a moment, lightly drawing her fingernails around my chest in circles and eights. Then she said: 'What do you mean?'

'I mean,' I said, 'we were witnesses. We testified and they didn't believe us because we were . . . well, beige. Bloody Anglo-Indian. It was the first time in my life I'd ever had to take personal experience and make it count in the political world, the school. And the world, the school, said: It doesn't count. We don't believe you. Your money's no good here. Nor Miss Scarlet's, neither. Ergo, we rejected the political in favour of the personal, tragically or otherwise, for the rest of our lives. That's what you're talking about on the roof, isn't it? Not caring because you're not part of it? I think all Anglo-Indians feel like that, actually.'

Her hand didn't stop, but there was something different.

'By the way,' I said, 'that "Da-Da" must have come from Idi Amin. He was in the news at the time – for, among other things, sending Christ knows how many Ugandan Asians with British passports back to Blighty. Idi Amin Dada Oumee. Wally Da-Da. Gary must've absorbed it from somewhere. Incredible, isn't it?'

Her hand came to a standstill, rested flat against me. 'How serious are you?' she said.

'About Idi Amin?'

'About the not-being-believed theory.'

'Not very,' I said. 'Well . . . No. I mean, I'm being flip, obviously, but there's something in it, don't you think? If you have no voice in the arena, then fuck the arena, right?'

'Owen, that's not what happened.'

'What do you mean?'

'I mean we didn't tell them. We didn't testify. Gary cornered us and told us if we said anything he'd break our legs. We were terrified. We told Tyrell we hadn't seen anything. Don't you remember? *That's* what we agreed.'

★

I didn't sleep much during what was left of the night, and when I did drop off woke an hour later, whimpering the scream of another things-speeded-up dream. A birthday party, mine, with strangers seated round a long, festooned table. Suddenly their hair falling out, the B-movie quick shrivelling and flaking away of teeth and flesh. Scarlet sleepily held me, said shshsh, wrapped her fingers in my hair and fell asleep again. I thought about my flat, all the nights there would be without her, without anyone. The golden crumb of comfort having Vince snoring down the hall – and who knew how long he'd be around?

There was love again when the windows greyed with first light (love? Yes, with our limbs wrapped tight and our faces close, the inarticulate admission that at death our last thoughts would most likely be of each other, the one connection life had given), but afterwards silent sadness and the struggle to accommodate in the small business of getting up and showering and dressing the big business of having failed, of Scarlet's having tested the water and pulled back. My mind ran its loop. Why can't she . . . ? Because she's . . . But why doesn't she . . . ? Because you're . . .

'This isn't it, is it?' I said. Rhetorical question. She stood at one end of the window, looking out over dully lit Kensington, I stood at the other, looking at her. Traffic was drearily up and running, affirming the world's indifference to the rest of my life without her. Last night's woollen dress had been stuffed into the case. Now she wore faded Levis and a black vest. Her feet were bare. I wished she'd put shoes on; then when I left I could imagine her leaving straight after me. The alternative image, her sitting on the couch or lying on the bed contemplating her next move, made it impossible not to think of coming back, seeing her again, convincing her to stay.

'Isn't what?' she asked, resting her forehead against the window pane.

'The time when we meet and you know that it's always going to be me. The time when you accept it and stay.'

'I'm not ready,' she said. 'I might never be.'

'Because I love you and want to marry you and have children and live happily ever after with you.'

'Something like that.'

'I know, it's disgusting. I should be ashamed of myself.'

'I thought I might be able to,' she said. 'But seeing you, I can still feel it. I'd hurt you. You know that.'

'I'm not the sap I used to be,' I said.

She turned, gave me a look. Yes you are.

'We could have breakfast,' I said.

She came to me, put her arms round me.

'I'll come round again,' she said.

'Like a comet.'

'Yeah, like a comet.'

'You know you're killing me, don't you?'

She kissed me and said: 'You'll live.'

CHAPTER SIXTEEN

※

The Sucker Punch

(*The Cheechee Papers*: Bhusawal and Calcutta, 1952)

The letter was waiting when they got back from the fight in Bombay. Ross's shoulders ached. A cramping tension had driven him nearly mad for the first round. Every additional day the investigation had remained unresolved had wound him tighter. The other man had been good, the worst combination: fast hands and a hard hitter. The first three minutes all Ross's energy had gone on keeping out of trouble. When he sat down Old Clem had said, 'What's wrong?' Ross rolled his neck, felt threads of tension snapping and immediately re-forming. 'Can't get loose,' he gasped. Clem massaged demonically, saying, 'Come on, he's an old woman.' 'He's a *fast* old woman,' Ross said. Clem had said, just before the bell for the second, 'I don't know if this bugger's going to drop. You'd better start hitting him. He thinks you're scared so that's good. Hell-for-leather first thirty, dodge, then hell-for-leather last sixty. Listen for the shout. Go!'

It went against the grain to throw that many punches. Ross had won almost all his fights with knockouts because he did easily the two things so many fighters found difficult: he watched and he waited. The other man was a system, a pattern, a flawed machine. Time other fighters spent trying to weaken the machine by hitting it he spent learning its moves, finding the gap. There was always a gap. The guard always, without exception, came down. Then you unloaded. Easy as pressing a button. By the end of the second Ross had evened up on points but he still felt tired and tight. 'Just keep doing it,' Clem said, again ferociously massaging. 'You're scoring, heavily.' 'So's he,' Ross wheezed. 'Taps,' Clem said. 'Pit-pats.' Ross looked over to where Kate sat in the second row with the kids. Carl was more or less oblivious to the ring, pointed at and burbled about faces closest to him in the crowd, but Melissa was rapt, standing in the aisle, mouth open. She'd inherited Beatrice's green eyes, but unlike her grandmother's the child's were big and long-lashed. (She was a wilful little thing, tokenly shy with strangers for a few minutes, then off into the unre-strained performance of herself. No amount of adult attention filled the well. He took her to the station running room to be teased and adored by the men, of whom she catastrophically spoke the truth: 'Uncle Benny, your cap smells.' 'Yes, darling, that's the leather smell you're getting.' 'No, it's sweat.' They loved her impe-riousness because it went with beauty; laughing, they prostrated themselves before her judgements. Ross enjoyed it, too, let it go right up to the point beyond which it would have soured, started harming her character, then scooped her up and took her away on his shoulders.) He winked at her, but it was too small a detail in the whole by which she was transfixed. She'd remember it later – you winked at me! – but for now there was no penetrating the dream. He wanted the knockout for her. Kate, wiping Carl's mouth, missed his glance. The bell rang.

The gap revealed itself halfway through the third. Ross's guard (perversely helped by the tension) was tight and for the last minute of the previous round his opponent had started throwing body shots with his right. Kidneys and ribs. Pain, yes, but prosaic, cumulative, nothing to worry about. Ross watched. Let him keep throwing them. It was tough to keep watching with the kidneys detonating like that, sending those big signals for attention, took an appalling heave of the will. Clem was screaming: 'Move! *Move!*' But if he moved he wouldn't be able to confirm his suspicion. His suspicion was that the right hooks low to the body were taking his man's left on a little drift out of position. There it was again. A shade further each time. Getting complacent. How criminals eventually got caught. His corner should have warned him. Two more, Ross thought. Third time, that left's going to have drifted six inches. That's the gap.

It was always the same. You weren't aware of the decision to throw the punch, but suddenly it was in flight and all the sound got sucked out of the world. It seemed to take such a long time that you couldn't believe the other man wasn't seeing it coming. The space between the two of you had been waiting for this, the sweet single parabola. It rang a little bell in the universe, one of the infinite harmonics.

Then sound rushed back in and you had to sort it into meaningful bits: the ref's inhuman count; Clem's shouts; the crowd's stirred hive. Afterwards, with everyone making such a fuss, you felt humble, fraudulent, embarrassed by how easy it had been, how at the core of the moment something else seemed to do it for you.

'What does it say?' Kate asked. She'd shooed Melissa out into the compound, where Dondi was feeding the half-dozen chickens. Carl, asleep in her arms when they'd arrived, had been put down in his cot.

'It's bad,' Ross said. He handed her the letter and sat down on the couch. The doors were open. Outside the veranda's stirred-up dust was in sunlit suspension. There was a fresh blue sky, occupied here and there by soft masses of brilliant white cloud, a sort of urgent optimism. Kate read not linearly but in a flicking search for salient phrases. '. . . *and whilst we are satisfied that no knowing part was*

taken in the crime it is the investigators' view that the incident exemplifies the consequences of slack standards . . . Without negligence on the part of Mr Monroe the crime could not have been effectively perpetrated . . . It is therefore incumbent on us to recommend that Mr Monroe be suspended from duty for a period of one month without pay and be denied any promotion for a period of three years, effective from the date of this letter . . .'
She looked at him. His face had gone little-boyish around the mouth, smacked but too old to cry.

'That's not so bad, is it?' Kate said. 'A month's suspension? What's a month?'

Ross shook his head, held out another, smaller note which had also been in the envelope. Kate took it. Handwritten. '. . . *failure to inform the Passport Office would, I'm afraid, constitute negligence on my part. Therefore I have apprised them of the situation, which may bear on your recent application. Naturally, a copy of my report has also been forwarded to the Indian Olympic Selection Committee . . .'*

The terrible weight of the effort she'd need to get him through this for a moment pressed on Kate, the weeks and months and years ahead of treating the poison this would set to work in him. The question was whether love would be enough. Asking it excited and exhausted her, the unknown difficult space into which this would force them to move.

'The selectors won't care, will they?' she said. 'I mean what do they care? They want you.'

'They won't care,' Ross said. He'd got up and gone to stand in the open doorway, looking out. At the other end of the compound Dondi stood languidly broadcasting feed to the chickens. Ross and Kate had avoided talking of leaving in front of their servant. Kate thought how happy he'd be to know that now he could stay with them for the rest of his days. It gave her a small, sweet pain of the relativeness of things.

'They won't care but it won't make any difference,' Ross said. 'It's the passport. It's the *passport.*'

'But surely if the selectors—'

'You weren't there. If he wants to stop me leaving, he can. It's as simple as that. Rat on your friends or else.'

The day dragged them in and out of the same conversation, Ross oscillating between clipped disgust and maudlin fatalism. The blinding white clouds moved off, leaving a monotonously burning milky blue. Kate struggled with resentment: wasn't love enough? He had her, the children, friends, a home, comfort. The moments in the dark. Didn't he know what all that was worth?

'I love you,' she said to him, 'if that helps.' He was sitting on the veranda with a scotch (the third large one; one more and he'd be drunk). She stood behind his chair with her hands gently pressing his shoulders. His body felt different after a fight, simplified into peace, like an exhausted child's. She knew he loved her touch on him then. Knew, too, that three scotches could make it an irritant, though he'd take it out on someone else, shout at Dondi or Melissa, go out and savage Eugene, ridicule Hector. It was a risk, the *I love you, if that helps*, an implicit insistence that it ought to help, ought to be enough. She'd said it partly to provoke the confrontation, get it out of the way so they could move on.

'It's not about me,' Ross said, with a sobriety that surprised her. She waited. He looked down into his drink. 'What kind of a future do you think there'll be for these kids?'

'What do you mean?'

'I mean there aren't going to be any jobs. Not for Anglos. What's Carl going to do when he grows up? Do you know how much boarding fees have gone up since we were at school?'

Kate didn't know what to say. These things weren't part of her thinking.

'He'll work on the railways like his father,' she said.

'There won't *be* any work on the railways by the time he's a man, not for Anglos. Nor in the police, nor in Post and Telegraphs. You think Nehru cares about a handful of bleddy cheechees? India for the Indians. Hector's right.' It was a revelation to him as he said it. For years the facts had been impinging,

the old disturbance on the periphery of his vision. Gandhi's
Untouchables who were now Children of God. They wanted,
and the government said they would be given, jobs. Our jobs,
Ross framed it, knowing even as he did that they were only his
and Eugene's and Hector's and Chick's because people like
Hoggarth had made it so. He thought of all the orders he'd given
to Indians, servants, subordinates, coolies, box boys. We're taking
these donkeys. His whole life had been a casual exercise of entitlement. We pull out, you buggers are going to be up shit creek
wi'out a paddle. A whole life of imperfectly ignoring the future.
Now the future had arrived. 'If we stay here,' he said, 'we're
doomed.'

'All right,' Kate said, 'then we'll go. They can't stop you getting
a passport for ever. And if we can't go to England via Helsinki,
we'll just have to save up until we've got enough to go there on
our own steam.'

'They can stop me getting a passport as long as they like,' Ross
said, still with the unsettling calm quiet voice. 'But even if I get
one, do you have any idea how long it's going to take to save that
kind of money? Read the letter: "denied any promotion for a
period of three years". We could be here for another ten years. By
that time they won't even be letting us *in* to England. There's no
point in me going to the finals. It's a waste of time.'

'You'll win,' Kate said. 'That's not a waste of time. We'll find a
way round this.'

'How?'

'I don't know.'

That evening Ross, not drunk but sour and saturated with booze,
went with Eugene over to Chick's. Skinner was already there.
Rum and ginger beer, choora, lamb samosas, half a dozen sambals.
Chick had been laying on hospitality ever since the job had gone
wrong, and would go on doing so, Ross and Eugene rather
shamefully knew, until they made a big effort to let him know

they didn't hold him to blame. I can't keep coming here, Ross thought. It's just wound-licking. Does no good to anyone. With a struggle he'd managed to say nothing about Hoggarth's quid pro quo offer. It was a jewel-like pleasure to have done what he'd done for the Englishman, but the temptation to cash it in had been almost overwhelming. He'd flirted with the idea of telling Eugene, in confidence, knowing Eugene wouldn't be able to keep his mouth shut. He'd blab to Skinner and the great act of manly selflessness would shine. Ross was ashamed of how much he wanted this credit. Ashamed enough, thus far, to rise above it.

He showed them the letters from Hoggarth.

'Madhar *choth*,' Eugene said.

Chick shook his head. 'Bleddy *hell*, men. See the bastards, no?'

'Christ knows what I'm going to do,' Ross said. 'There's no point in going to the finals. The whole bleddy thing's . . . Cheh.'

In the heads-down silence that followed, each of them realized they were all waiting for Skinner's reaction. Impossible quite to shake the old conviction that an Englishman could do something.

Skinner lit a cigarette, inhaled, exhaled with a shake of his head. 'I can help you,' he said. 'But it's not going to be easy.'

It would cost, he estimated, somewhere in the region of two and a half thousand rupees. 'Now, first,' he told Ross as they walked back from Chick's, 'you can knock off five hundred. I don't want any argument. I'm putting that in. You gave me the slip with it the other night but destiny is destiny. The whole thing's my fault anyway so I'm not taking no for an answer. Now, do we under-stand each other?'

'What difference does it make?' Ross said. 'That still leaves two thousand. Where the hell am I going to get two thousand rupees from?'

The sun had gone down ('Gets dark here like someone falling off a bloody cliff,' Skinner had observed. 'Doesn't matter how long you've been in this country, you never get used to it');

constellations were in the first phase of their frozen ferocity. They were passing the deserted market where beggars – among them a few of Dondi's brothers-in-meths – huddled over a fire. Somewhere in the darkness a dog was barking, repeatedly, like a stuck record. Men were out on the streets, idling, smoking, paan-spitting, gossiping or staring into the night. 'Chick's in for five hundred, too,' Skinner said. 'I've spoken to him about it. He feels bad about the whole thing, you must know that.'

'I'm not taking money from Chick. It's not his fault. It's not anyone's fault.'

'Which leaves,' Skinner said, ignoring him, 'fifteen hundred. And I don't know how you're going to get it, but you're going to have to get it and get it fast because these things move bloody slowly. I want to go down to Bombay within the next couple of days.'

'A couple of days?'

'Look the finals are on the tenth, right? You need to tell the selectors you've already got a passport. They're not going to ask questions, because they want the medals. Fuck Hoggarth. He's been after me for years. I know he probably tried to get you to give him my name and I know you didn't give it to him.'

Ross felt the jewel melt into something more precious, which filled and enlarged him.

'If I had the money I'd foot the whole bill myself. I owe you more than I can ever repay as it is. But the fact is the five hundred's pretty much the last five hundred until I can . . . Look, the point is: for Christ's sake take this chance, because another one's not going to come.'

Ross, still suffused with the pleasure of knowing that Skinner knew what he'd done (the ancient nobility of honour among thieves), said nothing, walked with his head down, relishing.

'You come to the Ambassador two days from now. Get the money from the baniyas if you have to. I mean, why not? What are they going to do? Come looking for you in England? I don't think so. You'll be long gone. Although if I were you I'd still haggle hard over the interest for the sake of appearances; these chaps aren't stupid.'

'They'll think I'll need it because of the investigation,' Ross said, surrendering himself to the plan's flow. 'Word will have got around, and if it hasn't I'll get Dondi to spread it.'

'Better and better,' Skinner said. 'Monroe sahib in big trouble, one month no pay, etc. It's right up their street. Christ, man, we should've gone into partnership years ago.'

'But I mean . . .' Ross hesitated.

'What?'

'The passport. What about my wife, the kids?'

Skinner stopped to toe-crush his cigarette butt. Cogitated. 'I know,' he said. 'I know.' The barking dog had stopped. Up ahead of them the Ambassador's doors were wide open. The lit lobby revealed a different, sprucely awake desk clerk sharpening a pencil with martial concentration. 'This is hard,' Skinner said, looking not at Ross but into the hotel doorway. 'You might have to go on ahead of her. She follows later with the kids. I mean, *her* passport application could go through legitimately, right?'

'Well, yes, I suppose it could.'

'Alternatively, you get another thousand together and I'll try'n get a deal for two. It's usually cheaper that way but these bastards are whimsical.'

They stopped and shook hands at the edge of the Ambassador's radius of light. A pariah dog nosed something in a blocked drain nearby.

'It still seems . . .' Ross said. There had been flurries of hope as they'd talked, but his feeling of stagnant fate had endured.

'What?' Skinner said.

'I don't know. Impossible.'

Skinner grinned. 'One thing my years here have taught me,' he said. 'In this country, nothing's impossible.'

★

Considering what was at stake it wasn't a big crowd. The hall at the Calcutta YMCA in any case only held three hundred. The space inside was filled with pliable heat against which you could lean. Cigarette smoke, fried snacks, sweat; the odour of the canvas drew you, said here you can forget everything else and settle your fate. Ross's heart lifted and hovered in its cavern, netted in nervous currents.

'Well,' Eugene said. 'You made it. Now don't bugger it up at the last hurdle. I've got bleddy money on you, men.'

'Cheh,' Chick Perkins said, face contracting with irritation, 'you don't talk to a man like that just before he goes into the ring. What's the matter with you?'

Ross had come out, hands taped but not gloved, to get a final look at the ring from the outside. The last two weeks' training had been a hard, lovely poetry; he'd fashioned an ultimate version of his physical self, seen people noticing it. Even now Eugene was registering the deltoids like smooth oval stones and finding it hard not to laugh. Perfection was funny, the great human improbability of it. If you laughed it was from delight that someone, even if not you, was doing the job of achieving it. Ross had felt it himself, watching gymnasts; once a sax-player from Madras at the Institute.

'How are you feeling?' Chick said. 'Nice and loose?'

'I'm okay,' Ross said. An agreement had evolved between the men not to talk about Skinner. There had been three letters from him since he'd left for Bombay, euphemistically reporting on 'the business plan' ('our partners', 'our intitial outlay', 'the necessary paperwork'), all of which was going ahead, but slowly and unpredictably. Skinner's tone was one of weary determination in the face of ceaseless setbacks. 'Please, for God's sake, don't worry. This is still our best option. Things have changed since the last time I had to do anything like this, and more than a few of my contacts have left twitchy successors. They still speak the same language (money talks!) but I've had to start with some of them from scratch. I know you're worried but you have to concentrate on the job in hand. I'm moving things forward as fast as is humanly possible. I'm promised completion in two weeks. At the very latest I'll be at the finals in Calcutta. Keep training!' That had been more than three weeks ago. Since then nothing.

With a blank superhuman effort Ross had pushed the question of what was going on aside and sunk himself into training. His inner voice had said, once, early in Skinner's absence: He's not coming back. Ross had allowed it this single utterance, a heart's entitlement in exchange for which he would have the right not to hear it again until the fight was over. Through all the sit-ups and pull-ups and push-ups, the roadwork, the skipping, the hours with the heavy bag, the shadow-boxing, the sparring, he kept everything out except the growing awareness that he was taking himself to a level of fitness and strength he'd never known before. When he wasn't training he sat on the veranda staring into the bleached dust of the compound, or studying the sky. Evenings he went down to the Taptee and floated on his back. He made love to Kate in silence, as if his mind had been freed of consciousness altogether, as if the boundary separating him from his experience had burned away. Contemplating either the past or the future led to Skinner, the inner voice, the annihilating doubt. Therefore he lived, as the Buddhists claimed one could, entirely in the now, sipping water from a tin cup; walking from bedroom to veranda; hitting the heavy bag; floating in the river face up to the starred sky.

He'd borrowed from his father, Hector, Agnes and the baniyas.

'Better not to have the wife and kids this time,' Chick said.

Ross shrugged. 'Little fellow's not well.' This was true; Carl was teething, miserably, but it had been a relief to have the question of whether Ross should go without family settled extraneously. Kate knew the ferocity with which he wanted this. It was better he went to it alone, not just for the idea of himself solitarily facing combat (this business of destiny, he'd made it) but also so there would be no one else to blame if he failed. The desperateness of

his need would tempt him to look for explanations outside himself if he lost. That was what they'd conceded back in Bhusawal,
without words, in looks and the lucid telepathy of post-coital
darkness. He was ashamed that she'd sensed it. But when he kissed
her goodbye she'd said, 'I love you,' and so that he knew she
meant it had held his face and made him look at her. Grinned, to
contain his weaknesses. I love you, *including* that.

'No, no, of course,' Chick said. He had to shout. The crowd's
murmur had swelled. Eugene's fixed smile was nerves, a look of
inane mild bliss. 'You can feel it, men,' he said. 'The bleddy
thisthing. Atmosphere.'

Old Clem the trainer appeared, a towel draped over his shoulder, in the doorway to the dressing rooms. 'Monroe!' he barked.
'Get in here, will you, for Christ's sake?'

Much of the crowd was on its feet now, milling about around
the ring and in the aisles. Some pitch of expectation had been
passed and not fulfilled. The collective mind had been counting
down to action; the countdown had zeroed and no action had
begun. Now they were irritated, absurd. The right man could
seize them with a shout and make a mob.

'Monroe!' Clem screamed over the din. 'Now!' Ross smiled at
him. The man's little face was tomato red with the heat and the
terror of losing and the anger at his fighter gone off for a fucking
stroll. The red face and the snow-white brush of moustache. You
look like Father Christmas, Clem, he'd say to him, walking up.

'Right then,' Eugene said. 'No half-larks now. Get in there and
hammer that sonofa—'

'There he is,' Chick said, face suddenly unpinching into the
genie smile. He was looking past them into a ringside knot of
people. Ross and Eugene turned.

'What?'

'He's . . . I just *saw* the bugger,' Chick said.

Clem, with thickened forehead veins, had come up. 'Are you
fighting today or not?' he said.

'Which bugger?' Eugene said.

'Skinner. I'm sure it was him.'

'Monroe,' Clem said, trying to shove Ross away. 'I swear on my mother's grave if you don't—'

'Where?'

'I just saw him there in the crowd.'

'Are you sure?' Ross said, over his shoulder, as Clem used all his weight to get him moving.

Ross's opponent on 10 April 1952 was the East Bengal ABA bantamweight champion, Ahmed Ibrahim, a stocky, aggressive fighter with a murderous left hook but whose right shoulder was prone to dislocation. 'Make him miss with a big shot,' Clem had said, half seriously, 'and you won't need to knock him out.'

One round in Ross knew he *was* going to knock him out. He'd already found the gap. At five foot seven, Ibrahim was a difficult man to hit on the chin. Taller opponents (and even most bantamweights were taller than five seven) found themselves punching out of their natural plane. Instinctively or from smart training Ibrahim ducked low, pulling the strike zone further south still. It took the sting out of a punch to have to throw it downwards like that, betrayed your shoulder, made you feel you were flailing. It needed only one small obstacle to your fight geometry for the suspicion of futility to creep in. It was a terrible thing to know the full force of a blow wasn't landing, was getting burned up in the weird line of its flight. Exacerbated by this bobbing bastard whumping you in the guts and when you'd got used to him working you downstairs suddenly popping up and hitting you with that hook the size of a football. Ibrahim had won a lot of his fights with knockouts precisely because the big upward-climbing left hook was always such a surprise.

But Ross had found the gap. An idiot could have found it. Coming in low, head down, Ibrahim was wide open to an uppercut. The right body shots were thrown from wide and the left guard was angled high, forearm across forehead, as if there was an invisible desk he was resting on. It left an empty lift-shaft straight up the middle. The problem was that the uppercut wasn't, typically, a knockout punch. You couldn't see the man's chin, for one thing, and for another it was tough to get the power of a cross or a hook coming up from below like that. To turn an uppercut into a knockout punch you had to roundhouse, make a cartoon-like golf swing out of it, momentum as much as muscle. Hit a man on the point with that, and he'd go down, no argument.

Therefore, halfway through the second, that's exactly what Ross did. 'You looked like bleddy *Pop*eye, men,' Eugene said afterwards. 'Nearly lifted the bugger off his *feet*.'

It was a lovely connection. Ross felt the truth of it. There was time to note the expression on Ibrahim's face (he had taurine good looks under the short fringe of close-cropped curls) of mild complaint, as if some negligible but disappointing injustice had been done to him, before he, Ibrahim, with two hesitant backward steps in slow motion sat down on the canvas.

As the sound rolled back in, Ross in the neutral corner looked down into the crowd and saw Eugene jumping up and down. You've got him! You've bleddy got him! Ross smiled, looked up at the ceiling lights high above like a ring of angels, then with a smile again back at Eugene. Time was trying to push its way through the knockdown's blockage. The referee screamed 'Four!' as Ibrahim got to his knees. Ross could feel his lungs labouring, his body's blood-crowd packed tight. Skinner, he saw, was seven or eight rows deep, with his back to the ring. He was talking to someone behind him, but the slicked-back blond hair and slim shoulders were unmistakable. He'd gone back to the pale linen suit (the jacket was slung over his shoulder), which almost as much as the repaid trust gave Ross a feeling of poetic satisfaction.

'Five!'

Ross's lungs would have to be ready. The fight demanded things, specifics of the legs and shoulders and chest, told you that they must be so, therefore you made them so. Ibrahim had got one foot flat and was wobblingly pushing himself into a stand. Whatever Skinner was talking about to whomever he was talking to he was animated, emphatically pointing a finger. Any moment he would turn. Ross's mind moved like a girl dreamily following a riverside path. Wouldn't have come if the plan had failed. You're different. Destiny is destiny . . .

'Seven!' Skinner was here and Ross felt a gentle benevolence towards the world. He forgave Eugene and Chick the overheard doubts and shifty looks and loud avoidance of the subject after the first suspicion had begun creeping in, and the detonation of forgiveness was, despite the already fiery armour of heat on his limbs, a more intimate and urgent inflagration. Gold bars that were brass. Two each, yes? It went like a woof of burned fuel in his chest, as the referee said, 'Box on!' and Ibrahim, with a flatfooted dogged shuffle and a face showing consciousness pared to the single goal of staying on his feet, came towards him. We'll play again, Monroe, God had said rippling past him like a windblown ribbon as he'd left the Malaysian's shop in Lahore, but for now . . .

Now thinking was an enormous weight he had to get out of his way. Rockballs's words were live again: 'Start thinking about anything else and you might as well tie one hand behind your back.' You could slip into a cold palsy, numbed by the *if*s and *how*s. Skinner with ducked head had turned and was making his way closer to the ring. Ross had a brief mental image of the Englishman ringside holding up two passports with the Satanic grin of contempt. There had been Skinner and there had been Kate and God had between them let his, Ross's, will go free into the gold and the relief of being righteously chastised. If he hadn't let Kate go that day, would he have her now? God doodled baroquely in wood grain and stone lode but there was room in creation for amusing little circles, too, ten years in your life but a split-second whim in His. Not what was fair but what was entertaining. And on the *if*s went (Ibrahim's body shots were coming again, the same urgent dumb argument that wouldn't, would *not* be contradicted, so Ross would keep throwing the gruelling down-tilted jabs and short left hooks until he got his mind wholly back, then—): if Robbie hadn't broken his arm, if Eugene hadn't told him to get a sick note, if Agnes hadn't made a show of Carruthers's clap, if he hadn't been hacked at and pneumonia'd in '47 which was if Hector hadn't gone to Bombay after Bernice, if they'd loaded the bales from the off side instead of the near . . . Were the *ifs* a line or a swarm? Could you go all the way back? Was one *if* the starting point or was every *if*? What about Kate's? But if you allowed Kate's you allowed everyone's, even, now, Ibrahim's.

And while all this was going on he was waiting (which pleased him, in a corner of himself) with tugged-at concentration for that lift-shaft up the middle to open wide. If you get a man with a right cross once, Rockballs used to say, don't think he'll have learned his lesson. If he gets up, give him another right cross exactly the same and watch the idiotic bastard go down again. Somewhere in the back of his right shoulder Ross was winding up the Popeye roundhouse. Some punches, Rockballs had said, have been packed away since the beginning of time. They find their way into fighters now and then, and believe me, boys, you'll know when you've got one in you.

Ahmed Ibrahim wrapped his arms round Ross. Resting. It was a delight to Ross, as if his opponent had very gently thrown himself on his mercy, knowing it was right and proper that there would be none given. It was often like this, gestures with love's tenderness. In the ring the two of you fashioned gentleness with violence. Clem was screaming indecipherably from his corner. Ross knew what: the left. Watch for the left. With Ibrahim's warm weight on him he smiled, because even with the mess of thinking in his way, the *ifs* like an infinitely receding line of barbs or a vast cloud of flies, he knew to watch for the left, was watching for it, would, in a moment when the ref stepped between them and relieved him of the loverish weight, be watching for it still, because even this resting might be a ruse.

Ibrahim took three paces backwards from the referee's push. Looked at Ross with a face of tired surprise, as if the world was ending and how curious and touching it was for the two of them, strangers, to be witnessing it together. Ross smiled at him and in the moment before the referee's command to box on glanced down to his right, where the Englishman who was not Skinner, but a much older man with the hair and the white shirt and paisley tie but with also a plump moustache had at last made it to the ring and was looking up at the fighters, one of whom (himself, Ross thought) he had money on, without recognition of anything other than the possibility of gain. Ross's legs emptied but his will held him up. Not Skinner but something like an emissary carrying, if there was any remaining doubt, the message that Eugene and Chick and Kate, in their silent suspicion, had been right all along.

'Box on!' the ref shouted. Ross turned, had two or three seconds to begin the struggle with the desire to see the mind of God at work (would it be more entertaining if, because of—) before the left hook, which by the rhythm Ross had learned wasn't due yet (and which had been waiting for its release into the world since the beginning of time), came early.

CHAPTER SEVENTEEN

options

(London, 2004)

I find a pay-and-display bay two streets from Skinner's in Shepherd's Bush. It's a dull, cold afternoon of measly wind-whisked rain. Pasha, in a black trilby and a charcoal woollen overcoat he's had for twenty years, insists on paying for the parking, and today I haven't got what it takes to argue. I'm a state of electrified weakness which reminds me of nothing so much as my first day at school; fear and inevitability, my rank negligibility in the face of the implacable occult powers that be. In a matter of minutes the quest, my father's quest – my father's past, I suppose – one way or another, will be over. Even if this isn't the man we're looking for, somehow I know the last of the momentum will be spent today.

'But the daughter,' Pasha said last night. 'What the hell are we going to do with *her* there?' I wasn't sure what he was planning to do without the daughter there. Knock Skinner out? Kick his zimmer from under him? Overload his hearing aid? None the less, I'd arranged things.

'She's not going to be there, Dad,' I told him. We were halfway through a bottle of Bushmills (old times' sake); I'd committed the mortal gastro-sin of giving the old man his Main Meal in the evening, rather than at his sacrosanct noon, and now according to his singular logic there must be a few wets 'to help us digest'. 'She said three o'clock, right? So we get there at two. Gives us an hour alone with him. I don't know what you want to say to him, but an hour's going to have to be enough.' He contemplated his scotch. 'What *are* you going to say to him?'

Not the first time I'd asked. He wouldn't be drawn. Instead he lifted his chin and closed his eyes for a second. 'That's between me and him. You don't get involved.' He'd been shocked at the state of my room. The papers. Everywhere. 'What kind of bleddy *organization* is this, son?' he wanted to know, peeping in. 'I mean how are you going to . . . ?'

'It's on computer,' I told him. 'It's all on computer. I've got my own system, Dad, trust me.'

'Looks like someone's *burgled* in here, men.'

'Yeah, yeah,' I said. 'You worry about Skinner, let me worry about The Book.'

'But how can you keep track with this sort of chaos?' I swung the bedroom door shut and hustled him back into the lounge.

Vince phoned earlier to say he was staying out. Thanks to 'a delicious entanglement', I haven't seen him since the day before yesterday. Pasha knows Vince is gay, or rather in his parlance is a 'gay bugger', and has lived long enough to respond to homosexuality with a vaguely perplexed live-and-let-live shrug. He went through a period of anxiety when Vince first moved in, in case via cohabitational contagion I became a gay bugger myself, but that's all passed. Vince is fond of him, and of my mother, who rather likes the modern sophistication her son's sharing his home with a homosexual confers on her.

Hands in pockets and collars up against the rain, Pasha and I leave the car and walk the two blocks back to Uxbridge Road. He's unnaturally quiet. London's perceptual cacophony – takeaway whiffs, sodden litter, car honks, siren whoops, hoardings, a wino, a jogger — might as well be blank silence for all it's penetrating his mood. I keep trying to make small talk — this is where that wait-ress I was seeing used to live; I come through here driving out to the M4 to go to Melissa's; traffic's always a nightmare — but there's no reaching him. He looks small and out of place. I forget how old he is. When I went to meet him off the coach at Victoria, his face peering out from the tinted window, looking for me — what if I wasn't there to meet him? My son I'd've been absolutely bleddy *confused* in this city — hurt my heart with its need, his relief when he spotted me, his wave and scurry to get his bag. Mater had put him up sandwiches and a flask of coffee. He'd done the *Sun* crossword on his own, not the same pleasure with-out her. What he really loves is to pick it up after she's left two or three clues unsolved, solve them, then toss it back to her, saying, 'There you are, I've done it,' and have her say, facetiously, 'Oh yes, well, obviously I had to wait for Mastermind to come and put the finishing touches,' while he chuckles and rubs his paunch.

'Fox Road,' I say. 'This is the one. 46B we want.' Two rows of Victorian three-storey terraced houses face each other across Fox Road's seen-better-days tarmac, rain-speckled cars parked nose to tail along both kerbs. Our pace has slowed. I glance at the house number over Pasha's shoulder: 22. Not far.

'Dad?'

As if with telepathic agreement we come to a halt. The old man is looking not at me but down at the pavement. There's a soaked and trodden newspaper page stuck there, advertising a microelectronics sale at Currys, but he isn't seeing it. This is a new look on his face, a sort of depressed, introspective nervousness. Suddenly I feel sad as hell. 'Dad? Are you okay?'

'Yeah, I'm all right.'

'You sure?'

He clears his throat. 'Funny thing, eh?' he says. 'After all these years.'

I fish in my pockets, pull out a pack of Marlboro (seems I'm smoking again, officially, what with Janet Marsh, what with Scarlet, what with the fucking *Cheechee Papers*) and light up from a Putti matchbook. It has the desired distraction effect.

'What the hell? You're smoking again now?'

'I've been under a lot of stress, Dad.'

'What stress?'

He needs this little stall for time. So do I. It won't be long enough. How could it be? Fifty years remembering and now here we are. Here he is.

'Don't tell Mum,' I say.

He doesn't respond, has in a moment drifted back into himself, looks down at the pavement again.

'Come on, Dad. Let's get this over with.'

We hear him before we see him. The shocking sound of someone too old to be making sounds like a child. 46B is the basement flat. Six stone steps with an old man in a raincoat lying at the bottom of them. He's on his front, one arm up by his head with a bunch of keys clutched, the other trapped underneath him. One leg of his trousers has ridden up, revealing a thin, varicosed calf, a quality old-man sock, a slip-on old-man shoe. His face is pressed against the wet stone, an upper set of jolted-out dentures inches from the mewling mouth. His eyes are pinched shut. They're like babies, you see, my son, my mother said to me, years ago, of the old people she looked after in the nursing home. When people get that old, they go like they were when they were tiny. They can't do these things for themselves. Because of a clash of shifts (my dad on nights at Goodyear, Maude away on a school trip, no babysitter she trusted) my mother had taken me with her for her night shift at Westfield. I was supposed to be asleep in the staff room but I'd heard her going off to make her rounds, followed her and seen through an open bedroom door her wiping the copiously beshitted backside of a lint-haired, frail-skulled old man. It's all right, Ernest, she was saying. It's really all right. There's no need to upset your-self. I've seen it all before. Ernest had been lying on his side with his pyjama bottoms down, whimpering. When she came back to the staff room I crawled into her lap and said I don't like it, Mummy, I don't *like* it. The place stank of urine and medicine, but I pushed my face up close to her neck and wrapped my arms round her and there was Nivea and L'Air du Temps. But these poor people are alone, sweetheart. They can't help themselves, that's all. They're like little babies, you see? It happens to us all when we get old.

Pasha and I stand for what feels like a long time in paralysed silence looking down from the top of the steps. Skinner's aware of us but I can tell he doesn't know what's real. We could be phan-toms, Martians, anything, the ground could open up and swallow him, he could wake up and find he's five years old in bed with fever. However this happened, it's exploded his mental order. His face, momentarily opened by the shift we've made in his periph-eral light, pinches again, and with eyes closed he releases a moan.

'Jesus Christ,' I say, hurrying down the steps. My shadow falls over his face. 'Listen. I'll call you an ambulance. Just lie still. Don't try to move.'

He does move, however. The key-clutching hand grabs my arm. 'Please,' he says, upper-toothlessly distorted. 'No ambulance. I'm all right. No ambulance. Just help me up.'

'You should lie still,' I tell him, thinking of Gilliam's Baron Munchausen saying, 'No doctors, no *doctors*.' Broken hip? Knee? Arm? Thinking, too: Christ, this is when you need a fucking mobile phone (I've resisted, all these years with heroic anachro-nism; even Pasha's making noises about getting one these days) but I'll buzz one of the other flats or next door or—

'I'm all right. I'm all *right*.'

With an ugly twist and shudder and grimace he gets the trapped arm out and pushes himself up on to one elbow. Reaches for and with disgust clasps the dentures. 'Get me inside. It's the red key, the red one.'

Between us, since he continues to protest ferociously against the ambulance, we get him up and, after I've located the red-tabbed front door key, into the flat's surprisingly spruce hallway. The geography of the place chimes: it's the same as mine. The hallway goes all the way back to the kitchen, three rooms to the right, living and two bedrooms. The bathroom will be off the kitchen, a little yard or garden at the rear.

'Kitchen,' he says, disentangling his arm from where, since I've seen the manoeuvre on telly, I've wrapped it over my shoulder – probably threatening dislocation. 'In the kitchen. I'm all *right*, for Christ's sake.' He leans on my father's trembling forearm and limps forward. Pasha himself hasn't said a word, has barely looked at the man.

The whole place smells professionally clean. Janet's money. A grey and black striped cat comes *tink-tink*ing from one of the rooms to watch us getting him settled. The kitchen's big enough for not just a small oak dining table and four chairs (the floors are stripped but with lengths of dark-green non-slip covering laid across the primary routes) but also a new-looking two-seater leather couch facing the window, on to which we lower him. He shoves his dentures back in with a muffled clack.

'You need that disinfecting,' my dad says. The left knee of Skinner's trousers is torn, revealing a cut and a bloody graze just below the kneecap. The rain has stopped. A pleasant dull, rinsed light fills the kitchen. I imagine the Englishman in here with his steaming morning coffee and toast and *Times*, the cat in an oblong of sun licking its paw. Noise is scarce, the place says, layers of afternoon and nighttime silence have been laid down and absorbed.

'Don't *fuss*,' Skinner snaps. Then softens. 'Sorry. It's that bloody third step. I'm not senile. I'll be fine. My daughter's coming soon.'

'You get an infection, it'll be no joke,' my dad says, standing looking down at the bloody knee. 'Might need a couple of stitches even.'

My body tingles with my inability to think of a single useful thing to say or do. I stand in the middle of the kitchen floor, observed by the cat. The crockery from breakfast is in the sink. A calendar on the wall opposite me is a month behind current time. Skinner, shaking, breathing heavily with a slight wheeze, peels the trouser tear apart and examines. The graze is deep and raw, the cut sullen with blood. I keep thinking of the desolation of his face, lying there in the rain. Underneath the tingling uselessness another feeling, an intimation of emptiness. Endings.

'My daughter'll be here soon,' Skinner says, sitting back. 'No need to trouble yourselves now.'

'We were coming to see you,' I blurt. 'I'm the person your daughter told you about? I was coming to talk to you about your book?' Statements as questions because I irrationally believe they've a better chance of restarting a stalled memory.

For a moment all three of us are silent, as if I've said something obscene.

'I'm sorry,' I say. 'My name's Owen Monroe. Your daughter, Janet, said you wouldn't mind talking to me about your book, *Raj Rogue*. For my thesis?' The name's out before I realize. Monroe. I look at Skinner for signs of detonation. Nothing. My father, still in trilby and overcoat, stands with his hands in his pockets, scrutinizing not his old adversary but the cat, who has jumped up on to the couch and is pushing his head against Skinner's absently fondling hand. 'This is my father,' I say. 'I hope you don't mind him coming along. We were early, you see, then we saw you. We were going to go and get a cup of tea.'

It's too much for the old man, the *other* old man, Skinner. His face crinkles with the effort of piecing all this together. I don't know what state I'd imagined Pasha would be in, but whatever I'd imagined it wasn't this deflated version of himself. Then I realize: Skinner looks old. *Ancient.* All but the faintest wispy half-tonsure of hair's gone. The eyes live waterily in deep thin-skinned orbitals behind the magnifying lenses of his spectacles, which miraculously have stayed on through fall and rescue. The cleft, if it's there, is lost among countless other lines. The skin of his long jowls is translucent and finely fractured. This was a delicately masculine face once. Those cheekbones would have been something; now they advertise the skull, say bone, *bone* outlasts all this surface nonsense. That's what my father wasn't expecting. The most obvious thing. He blinks, taking it all in, now that he's had the courage to really look.

'Janet?' Skinner says, struggling. Then something connects. 'Oh, right, yes, yes, she said . . . she did say . . . That's you, is it?'

'Yes, that's me. And this is my father.'

'Is she not coming, then?'

'Oh yes, she's coming, of course. At three, though. You see, we were early, as I said. I'm sorry, this is all very confusing.'

'It's lucky we *were* early,' Pasha says. 'You could've been lying there, some bugger could've *robbed* you, done all sorts.' This isn't, despite the emphasis, irony, just his world view. They − youths, muggers, thieves, thugs, bleddy criminals and delinquent buggers of every stripe − are always there, waiting for their chance.

Skinner looks at him. Still no recognition. 'That's true,' he says. 'These days you're not safe. I've been burgled you know. *Twice.*' This with the quivering pride the elderly take in such things, the credit demanded for still − in spite of what Nowadays tries to do to them − being here.

'Look, I'll tell you what,' I say, glancing at my watch. 'If you've got a plaster or something I think we really should see to your leg there. At least get it cleaned up a bit − otherwise I suspect there'll be hell to pay when Janet arrives. What do you think?'

Skinner makes a dismissive face to hide the embarrassment of having to agree, but after a little puffing and blowing directs me to search the bathroom cabinet, where I'm told 'Janet keeps some first-aid rubbish just in case, though God only knows what's in there because *I* never use the blessed thing . . .' As I leave the room I hear him telling my dad to 'sit down, sit down. Sorry, bit shaken up by that. Is that front door still open?'

The fierce cleanliness continues in the bathroom, all white, with a wicker laundry basket in one corner. No bathtub, but a new-looking shower cubicle with a specially installed handrail and seat for octogenarian utility. All surprisingly natty and well equipped; there are Body Shop toiletries, a couple of potted ivies, a loofah, a few shells and pebbles strategically dotted. Again I feel Janet's hand at work, Skinner carping – What the bloody hell do I want with *shells*? – but secretly loving it, the attention, the fuss, the nice smellies. There is, of course, the other sister in Earls Court, but Janet's got these kindnesses in her, I believe, takes satisfaction in furnishing people with small pleasures. Believe based on what? I ask myself, opening the bathroom cabinet, hands shaking. Two nights together? Pushing forty I don't need much more than that. It's one of the consolations of age: you see a person's kindness in the way they get out of bed and put on a dressing gown, someone else's meanness in the way they hold their knife and fork. Fuck how I know. I just know. Another consolation of age.

The cabinet, mirror-fronted, is, however, rather full. Old spectacle cases, a battalion of pill bottles, contact lens paraphernalia that must be Janet's when she stays over, and a little blue plastic dish of miscellaneous items which, reaching for the first-aid box, I narrowly avoid toppling. I damp what looks like a clean hand towel and return to the kitchen.

'Do you want to do it yourself?' I ask Skinner. My father's taken his hat off and put it on the table, though despite our host's insistence remains standing, hands in pockets. I've got down on one knee to attend to Skinner's injury – thinking knights and squires, idiotically – and have been ambushed by the prospect of touching him, the intimacy.

'Eh?' Skinner says. 'Oh, just stick a ruddy plaster on it, that'll do. Christ, I've had worse. It's just a—'

Interrupted by a quiet *oh* from Pasha, a strange tender noise of gentle revulsion. I look at him, follow his eye back to Skinner, whose nose is bleeding.

'Oh, blimey,' I say. 'Your nose . . .'

Skinner puts his hand up, fingers come away wet with blood. The three of us freeze. I've always had a disproportionate horror of nosebleeds. My supporting knee wobbles.

'Here,' Pasha says, reaching into his trouser pocket and coming out with a pale-blue hanky, still neatly folded. 'It's clean. Take it. Put your head back.'

'Is it back or forward?' I ask.

'No no back, *back*,' Pasha says. He passes me the hanky (I recognize it; my mother – embroidery unsurpassed on planet Earth – monogrammed a whole set for him years ago, *RDM*), which I pass to Skinner, who sits staring at his fingertips with a look of dismay.

'Hold it against your—'

Skinner's mouth quivers, rights itself, quivers again, then horribly downturns. A sob. Three drops of blood fall and spot the hanky, audibly, *putt, putt-putt*. I look at my father. Pasha observes. It's as if we're all inhabiting entirely separate realities.

I take Skinner's hand (cold, phthisic, thin-nailed, the texture reminds me of a frozen chicken foot) and guide it with the hanky up to his nose, very gently recline his head. Language refuses. The forced intimacies are unspeakable.

The cat, having decided that the situation offers him nothing, abandons the couch and avails himself of the cat-flap into the garden. The sound of his exit releases us.

'I get these,' Skinner says, pulling himself together, sniffing. 'Janet makes a fuss. They're just nosebleeds.'

'I was in India,' Pasha says. 'I knew you there.'

Skinner slowly rights his head, keeps the hanky pressed, looks at my father.

'I'm going to clean this up,' I say. 'Tell me if it hurts.'

And so, while I dab, disinfect and dress Skinner's wound, Pasha begins. Lahore, gold bars, Sikh, Ram, bloodstone ring. It comes out like a favourite bedtime story stripped of emotion. It *is* a favourite bedtime story, mine, I grew up with it. Now it's reduced to facts, places, dates. My father sounds depressed.

'Is that right?' Skinner says from under the hanky in a long pause after the Malaysian's *plain brass* diagnosis. 'Can't say I remember you. Nineteen forty . . . I was in and out of Lahore for years. All over the country. I can't just now think . . .' My father stares at him, trains on him the full force of his insistence. Skinner, belatedly registering the morality of the anecdote, tightens. I feel it in his big-boned knee. 'What do you want?' he says.

'You don't remember me?'

'I don't. No.'

'We met again,' Pasha says, 'in '47. You don't remember the riots? The massacre outside Bombay? I picked you up and got you to hospital. You don't remember any of that?'

I've done what I can with the dressing. It doesn't look good. Janet's going to turn up, take one look and redo the whole thing. Thinking of which, I check the time. If she's punctual we've got maybe twenty minutes. If she's early . . .

The two old men are staring at each other. Pasha's aura of disgust (not with Skinner, not with himself – with what? Me?) is palpable. As is Skinner's of rising excitement, fear. What do you want? We want *some*thing.

A chair scrapes in the flat above. Muffled sound of a cutlery drawer being opened and closed. Someone else's life.

'You're the boxer,' Skinner says, in a dead voice, after what feels like a long time.

Pasha continues to stare for a moment, then turns his face away. 'Yes,' he says.

The silence this engenders lasts long enough for my knee's ache to register. I get to my feet.

'Bloody hell,' Skinner says. 'What, from . . . ? You live here now?' He's half smiling; the reflex reaction is pleasure, the satisfaction of making the connection, his past momentarily revivified, endorsed. But my father gives only the slightest affirmatory nod.

It's beneath him, now, all of it. Having led the Englishman to recognition, it seems there's nothing else he wants.

'I *do* remember you. Bloody *hell*. I can't believe it. Christ that must be sixty years . . . You look well.' Anxiety into pleasure. I can see it: the older he's got, the less interested in him everyone's become. The daughters, the cleaner, the home help, the button-holed bystander at the bus stop: he talks of his past and no one wants to hear. Janet *et soeur* barely believe in the place, India, his youth, Dad's off again . . . It gets to the point where you begin to wonder if any of it really happened, since there's no one to cor-roborate it. You're like the last child who still believes in Father Christmas, everyone else has moved on. Now here is the past, his youth, his corroborating witness. I'm wondering how long it's going to take, the synaptic connection between the memory of the person, my father, and the memory of what happened. His face is glassily awake, flooded; manifestly he hasn't put two and two together.

'Dad?' This isn't working for Pasha. Skinner isn't supposed to be glad to see him.

'How did you find me?' Skinner says, tremulous. Then – making the connection – to me: 'How do you know Jan?'

'It's a long story, Mr Skinner. I'm sorry. How's the knee feel-ing?'

'Eh? Oh, that's all right

'Dad?'

Pasha exhales, heavily, slowly shakes his head. This is what you get for building the bridge between then and now. The length and brevity of the years. Time, yes, has passed, tells you what you knew already, tells you what you don't want to hear.

'I think my father just wanted to . . . I think he feels you owe him an explanation.'

'Never mind,' my dad says. 'I don't need anything.'

Skinner takes his glasses off, rubs his eyes, squints. Wonders, I suspect, if this isn't all a hallucination.

'Looks like the bleeding's stopped,' I tell him.

He doesn't know what to do. Too much has happened. I can see from his face that he's trying and failing to get a handle on this. When Janet arrives I'll tell her she needs to take him to hospital. He should have an X-ray. There's the possibility of concussion. I wish we hadn't done this. I wish I wasn't going to have to explain it to her. I wish I wasn't going to have to see her face, angry, disappointed, betrayed — especially now I've got used to seeing it vaguely desirous and sad.

'What's he on about?' Skinner asks my dad.

'You took my money and skedaddled,' Pasha says, not looking at him. 'You said passports. You don't remember?'

Skinner's face creases, the effort. It's the look a face gets on the brink of an almighty sneeze.

'Cheh,' Pasha says — to me, emphatically excluding the Englishman. 'He doesn't remember. Come on, let's go.'

'Dad, Jesus . . .'

Another hiatus.

'I got arrested,' Skinner says.

My father looks at him.

Skinner lets out one dry laugh. Goes quiet again. Frowns. Is this the right story? His hands are trembling. That fall was no joke; it's jolted the accrued undifferentiated days, the backwards stretch of what had become a white noise existence.

The clouds are breaking; the kitchen brightens and dims by turns.

'In Bombay,' Skinner says. 'The police picked me up. I did six months in the bloody clink, then they deported me.'

My father says nothing. A twitch in his jaw indicates molars being squeezed together.

'Is that what you're talking about? I sent you a letter with a cheque.'

'Rubbish. What letter? I never got any letter.'

'I sent you the money.'

'Lies,' Pasha says. 'I never got any bleddy letter and I never got any bleddy money.'

'Look here,' Skinner says, trying and failing to extricate himself from the couch. 'You can't just come in here and call me a liar. Who do you think you are?'

'Take it easy,' I say, tidying up the first-aid stuff. 'There's no need to get agitated, either of you.'

'You can't come in here,' Skinner says, lower lip quivering again, hanky raised. 'You come into my house and make accusations . . . This is my *home*.'

It's not right that he's so teary. *I'm not senile.* The possibility's been in the air, then. Overheard daughters, perhaps, or an eavesdropped confab between Janet and GP. *You'll find he won't remember things. Once it starts, I'm afraid it's irreversible. We'll just have to keep an eye on him.* I'm not senile. Maybe not, but precarious. No match for Pasha after all. That's Ross's deflation. This is a feeble old man struggling to get out of his own couch. He feels cheapened, cheated, tired, embarrassed. Sad. It's never what you want, when you get it.

'I'll put this stuff back,' I say, picking up the first-aid box. 'And then we can . . . Dad?'

A reverie. He and Skinner have dropped back into themselves, Skinner with a frown, as if he's lost his thread.

'Eh?'

'Don't you think we should leave Mr Skinner in peace?'

'Did you win?' Skinner says.

'What?'

'The boxing. It was boxing, wasn't it?'

'I lost.'

'Did you?'

'Sucker punch. Muslim bugger.'

'You got knocked out?'

'I got knocked out because I was looking for you in the crowd with the bleddy passports. I lost *focus*. Cheh. What's the point?'

Pasha, after this brief engagement, returns his head to profile. Skinner shuffles to the edge of the couch and tries to stand – again unsuccessfully. Weight on the knee makes him wince, with a flash of the formidable dentures. He remains seated. 'My daughter'll be here any minute,' he says. Part self-reassurance, part threat. He's worked it out and will keep hold of it now: the man's got something against him.

'You seriously expect me to believe you sent me the money?' my dad says. 'That the whole thing wasn't just another bleddy scam?'

'That's what happened, I'm telling you. I don't care what you . . . I can't believe that after all these years you come in here and you're—'

Key in front door, front door opening. 'Dad?' Janet's voice calls. 'It's Jan.'

Pasha looks at me, doesn't want this, reaches for his hat.

'Now listen, Dad – where are you? – I couldn't get the Greggs pasties because they were—oh!'

Well, here we all are.

'Oh,' she says again, this time without surprise, when I've given her the bare bones. We're out in the little back garden. The two old men, left to get on with it, are chunnering in the kitchen. Skinner has been re-doctored and equipped with a fresh pair of trousers, but has thus far stood fast in the matter of not going to hospital. (He'll go, Janet said. I'll take him in a minute when he's calmed down.) The garden's well kept, small patio, oval lawn, trim borders, a couple of eucalyptus trees, a cherry, a dozen waxy green shrubs I can't identify. She's brought shopping for him and the Caribbean brochures to show him where she's going. Three chocolate eclairs (one for me), a bottle of Glenmorangie, an *Options* magazine for herself, no doubt, to flip through while I 'interviewed' her aged dad.

The 'Oh' is shorthand for: so that's why you slept with me.

'So that's why you slept with me,' she says, lest I'm in any doubt.

'No. Not that there's any point in my saying this now, but no, that's not why I slept with you. I slept with you because I was attracted to you, very attracted to you, and because you seemed to want to sleep with me. You don't have to tell me what a disgusting mess I've made of all this, how badly I've behaved.'

'What a bizarre thing.'

'What?'

'All of it. Your *dad*.'

Emphasis shifted to this not because I'm forgiven but because now isn't the time. Or possibly because she assumes it's clear enough I won't ever be forgiven, therefore it won't ever be the time.

'Look, please,' I say. I'm still holding the goddamned first-aid box in my hands, like an offering. 'I know what I've done. Lying's no way to get anything started. I know I can't—'

'We got something started, did we?'

She's standing with her weight on one leg, arms loosely self-hugging. Dark maroon blouse, black corduroys and a dark green long woollen cardigan-coat. Her make-up's precise and lovely; I wonder what she thought this afternoon was going to be like, me meeting her father, the faint boyfriend connotation. Dad, this is Owen. I wonder if she was construing it as a Third Date. However she was construing it, I've fucked it up. I'll come round again, Scarlet said. Like a comet.

'Is there any way on earth I can apologize enough?'

'Probably not.'

'Will I see you again?'

'Probably not.'

'But not definitely not?'

'I don't know. At this stage I'd say it was definitely more definitely not than probably not. At this stage I'd say don't hold your fucking breath.'

Back in the kitchen Pasha is seated in one of the dining chairs, turned round to face Skinner. The cat sits on the floor between them, gives a yawn when I come in behind Janet.

'No, no, *Walton*,' my father's saying. 'I was up there for basic training. IAF. I didn't go back to Bhusawal till the war was over in forty-five.'

'Your wife,' Skinner says. 'I remember her in the hospital.'

'Kate, yes. She doesn't know about any of this.'

'I'll put the kettle on, shall I, Dad?' Janet says. The two men look up, sheepish. Can they drink tea together?

'Bugger the kettle,' Skinner says, deciding something. 'Let's have a drink. Don't open that new bottle, Jan, there's one in the cupboard already open. You'll have a drink, won't you?' This is to me, initially, but veers to my father when I hesitate.

'We should probably . . .'

'Put that back, will you, for God's sake,' Janet says to me, meaning the first-aid box. 'You look like you've lost the other two Wise Men, standing there holding it like that.'

'Did you do my tapes, Jan?' Skinner says.

'What do you think?' She fishes in her bag and pulls out a VHS cassette. '*America's Wildest Police Videos*,' she announces, for me, eyebrow raised. 'Trevor's coming on Saturday with a new recorder for you so you won't have to rely on me. You shouldn't be watching that rubbish, anyway. I've told you. You give yourself nightmares.'

'Those fellows are crazy,' my dad says. 'Whatall *stunts* they get up to.'

'Oh, they don't care in America,' Skinner says. 'D'you watch that *CSI* thing?'

'That's another good show,' Pasha admits. He's got a thing for Marg Helgenberger. I don't blame him. I've got a thing for her myself, the American high backside and those fitted slacks; if Janet dropped a couple of stone she'd look a bit like her – but all of us realize we've slipped, rather, from the point.

'Owen says you two knew each other in India,' Janet says. 'Is that right?'

Awkward silence.

'He thinks I diddled him,' Skinner says. 'Tell him: wasn't I arrested and sent home from Bombay in fifty-two?'

Pasha looks at his shoes. This is vulgar, he thinks, involving the daughter, saying 'he' and 'him' like that, as if he wasn't in the room. Janet, pouring the third of four scotches, doesn't look up. 'Well, that's what you've always told me,' she says. 'In and out of the nicks of the world. I've told you, Dad, it's nothing to boast about.'

This isn't the point, I'm tempted to interject. No one's disputing he was arrested. They're disputing his *honour*.

'Just a very small one for me,' I tell Janet. 'I'm driving.'

I take the box back to the bathroom and replace it in the cabinet, not, this time, without upsetting the little blue plastic dish, which drops into the wash basin below with a crash.

'What are you doing in there?' Janet calls.

'Sorry. I just knocked something over. It's all right I'm putting it back.'

Picking up the bits and pieces I worry there might have been things small enough to go down the plug-hole. I'll keep my mouth shut about that. Tweezers, hairpins, a pencil sharpener, an old watch without its strap, paper clips, tiepins, a broken silver belcher chain, two ancient fluffy Anadin.

A ring with an unusual stone set in what may or may not be gold.

For a few moments I stand with it clasped in my hand while I replace all the other oddments and put the dish back on its shelf. Digoxin, I see among the pill labels. Co-dydramol. Simrastatin. Paracetamol. This is what the cleanliness and small luxuries are up against, Janet knows. It'll be in her mind the whole time she's in the Caribbean. He's an old man. There are things wrong with him. How much time? Never enough.

BLOODSTONE: A green chalcedony with blood-like spots of jasper; haematite.

Somewhere in the file marked '*The Cheechee Papers*' is a pink Post-it with this definition scribbled on it.

It's an oval stone. Dirtyish green with here and there flecks of presumably jasper that look like not spots of blood but membranous strands of it. Menstrual, almost. The whole effect is gory, unlovely, but spectacular. Heavy, too, for such a small thing. I'll take that one ring also, Ram said.

This is the *Raj Rogue* moment in the Wimbledon bookshop all over again, the psyche or soul or spirit or whatever (some incorporeal place) experiencing the psychic or soulful or spiritual equivalent of the salivary glands at the thought of a lemon. You believe in destiny, Scarlet had said, as the conversation had woven through the hotel's small hours. That's your trouble. All the old scams, God, purpose, fate, design – you're desperate for them. It's why you've never got out from under your parents' shadow. *That's* the death you're terrified of, that you dream about: not yours, theirs. Without them, where's the story?

I don't know what to do, laugh, squeeze my jaws together, start believing in God. Whether I like it or not I have a new respect for Skinner. Eighty-odd and still thinking on his feet. Because of course this is my grandmother's ring, which means he was lying to Ross in the hospital in Bombay, which means he was lying to Ross in Bhusawal about being stiffed on the silk theft, which means he was lying to Ross about being able to get passports for money. Which means that in spite of having fallen down the steps and been picked up by two complete strangers, one of whom turns out to be not a stranger but a forgotten a victim armed with a memory, in spite of being so suddenly shoved on to the back foot, he's lying to Ross again, now.

I examine the ring's inner band for an inscription. (Ought there to be one? Pasha's never said. *To my own Beatrice*? *RV&BN*? What would the fabled Raymond Varney have written?) There's nothing, only the ghost of a hallmark. I slip it into my pocket.

'Our eldest girl Melissa's in Devon,' Pasha's saying, back in the kitchen. Skinner's disappeared. There are sounds of rootling from one of the rooms down the hall. 'Then there's Carl, he's in Arizona, computers and banking and whatnot. Our other daughter, Maude, she's still in Bolton, legal secretary, close to home—' He looks up as I reach with trembling hands for the (not small) Glenmorangie. 'Then there's our friend here in London living the bachelor life.'

Which presumably wouldn't have been his choice of words if he knew I was banging Janet – although at the best of times delicacy doesn't come naturally to him. 'The others all have families of their own,' I say. 'There's only me still fighting the good fight.'

Skinner returns with – Jesus Christ, is there no end to absurdity? – a photograph album. Janet rolls her eyes. 'They don't want to see that, Dad.'

Skinner magnificently ignores her and flips the album open on the table for my dad to see. 'I can't find the proper India album,' he says. 'What've you *done* in that bloody cupboard, Jan? I had a system there.' Then to Pasha: 'That's me just off the boat, Bombay, 1936. Gateway to India; I don't know who that fellow is in the picture. And that's me and Frank Sykes at the old Cooperage ground.'

'I played there,' Pasha says, reaching into his coat for spectacles. 'Lot of the Inter-Railway matches were played there.'

'What, football?'

'I played football for the GIPR from forty-five to fifty-three. We used to stay in first-class carriages at VT.'

'I don't know what she's done with the proper album. There's only a few from India in here.'

'Dad,' Janet says. 'All the albums are in there, I've told you. You never *look* for anything properly. Anyway, I thought Mr Monroe junior wanted to talk to you about your book?'

I take this as a good sign, that she's bothering with punishment.

If she was never going to see me again there wouldn't be any point. When she comes back from the Caribbean, I tell myself. Until the Scarlet comet comes round again.

'Have you been?' Janet asks me. Skinner and Pater are discussing Bombay geography. 'India, I mean.'

'No, I never have.'

'You're kidding?'

'Haven't got round to it. I grew up hearing about it, obviously. Don't know why I never made the trip. Some sort of perverseness, no doubt.'

'Christ, even I went in ninety-four. On a street near Victoria Station there was a bloke with an Elvis quiff and a stall selling pirate videos of Hollywood blockbusters. *Alien Resurrection*, I remember. There was an old woman lying on the ground nearby. Turned out she was dead. Maybe you thought it'd never live up to the stories.'

'You must've had them, too.'

'I did, though half the time I thought he was making it up.'

The ring in my jeans pocket is pressing against my thigh.

'It doesn't live up, actually,' she says (she's going through her Glenmorangie fast; my subterfuge has hurt, those hours in the sack, me with the huge lie making a fool out of her). 'If you've had all the stories, the real thing's bound to disappoint.'

'Stories require imagination,' I say. 'Real life just happens. That's the downer with real life.'

'Do you tell that to your students? Or aren't you really a teacher, either?'

'No, I am really a teacher. A crap one, as you'll have worked out by now.'

'I wish you'd been straight with me.'

'So do I. I fucked it up. I always do. There aren't any excuses. I just didn't realize how much it would matter.' A declaration, surely she must see?

'Don't give me any lines,' she says. 'I've heard them all.'

★

I'm wondering, by the time we get to the door (there's been another big scotch for the two old men, Janet showing *me* the brochures, since Skinner manifestly doesn't care; subtext of muscular Caribbean boys and a forty-two-year-old wealthy Englishwoman with money to spend and an ego to heal), how exactly we're going to conclude this utterly ridiculous encounter. Janet hangs back. Pasha and Skinner in wordless intensity shake hands on the doorstep. What can they possibly say to each other?

Nothing, is the answer. The handshake is a strange, silent mutual appraisal. Mistrust? Rapprochement? Enmity? Complicity? It's impossible to tell. I'll write Janet a letter, I think. I'm better on paper.

'Recognize this?'

I've waited till we're back in the Fiesta. Another sudden shower plays humble calypso on bonnet, boot and roof. The windows are already steaming up. Pasha takes the ring from me.

'What's this?'

'You tell me. Is it Nanna's bloodstone?'

He draws breath. Hadn't made the connection until the word. 'My God,' he says.

'It was in Skinner's medicine cabinet,' I tell him. 'Pretty incredible, right?'

'In the *medicine* cabinet?'

'In the medicine cabinet. When I put the stuff back, the first aid. I looked for an inscription but there isn't one. Was there one?'

'My God,' he says again. 'That's the ring?'

Definitely a question. 'Well, Jesus, Dad, *I* don't know. Is it?'

He turns it in his hands, examines it, shaking his head in disbelief. For what feels like an extraordinarily long time. 'Blaardy *hell*,' he says. 'It is Nanna's ring. I think. I'm sure of it.'

'You know what this means? It means he was in on the Lahore

scam, and the silk scam, and the passport scam. The guy's a liar, Dad.'

'You stole this?' He looks at me.

'Stole it? It's *yours*. Bloody hell.'

He gets his glasses out, puts them on, examines again. 'I can't believe it. After all these years, eh? What a *thing* to find it there like that.'

'Yeah, well, that's destiny for you.'

For perhaps a minute we sit without speaking, him turning the jewel in the light, me studying his face. The two big whiskies have loosened him. He looks exhausted. I'm thinking of the pleasure I'll take in telling Vince about all this, the great resolution, the fulfilment of the Quest. Then it occurs to me that after this there's nothing left to add to the file, the notes, the collations, the Post-its, the memoranda, the goddamned *Cheechee Papers*. It's over. The Skinner File is closed. And the Scarlet File?

I'll come round again. Like a comet.

'The only thing is . . .' He places the ring in the centre of his left palm, bends his head over it. Then looks up and stares through the windscreen.

'What?'

'Wait.' He looks at the ring again. 'No,' he says. 'Mumma's ring . . . It had a kind of a . . . I don't think it was an oval shape like this. I think it was more of a rectangular thing.'

'You're not serious?'

'I'm sure Mumma's stone wasn't like this.'

'You were sure it was a minute ago.'

He shakes his head again, tutting. In amazement? In disappointment? Buying time?

'My son, it's bleddy *yurs* ago,' he says.

'You don't think it's a bit of a goddamned coincidence, Dad? You lost a bloodstone ring—'

'I didn't lose it, I traded it.'

'You traded a bloodstone ring sixty-two years ago, *here*'s a bloodstone ring right now, today, the only connection to both is the man we've just met, a self-confessed criminal and by the looks of things a pathological liar – and you don't think it's the same ring?'

'I can't be sure.'

He hands the ring back to me, can't quite look me in the eye. Now *I* sit staring at the trinket in my palm.

I'm not waiting for resolution, Scarlet said.

In the evening, in a spirit of I don't quite know what I cook a huge chicken Madras. The celebratory – the conclusive dinner, it was meant to be. Pasha furnished with a giant tinkling Chivas sits in the softly lit lounge chatting with Vince, who's opened and got two-thirds of the way through a bottle of Banrock Station Shiraz Mataro by the time I join them. Vince has put Lena Horne on, since he knows my father loves her. The delicious entanglement, I'm shamefully relieved to hear, has dead-ended on day three.

'You see, Vince,' the old man's saying, 'the difference is, you people today have got nothing . . . How shall I say? To *steer* by. D'you follow me?'

Vince, judging by his face, booze-crimped into essential incomprehension, doesn't, but nods anyway. This will have started with something innocuous – Vince will have mentioned he's thinking of changing careers, which he is indeed thinking of doing, vacuously, the smart money says – but will have been dragged by the old man into philosophy.

'There's no point in attempting intelligent conversation with him, Dad,' I say. 'He's not properly educated.'

'Ignore him, Mr M,' Vince says. 'He's only the cook. Go on.'

'What I mean is,' Pasha says, sitting forward, opening his left hand with vast reasonableness, 'it's all thisthing, *life*styles. You want to be an atheist, it's a lifestyle, you want to be a communist, it's a lifestyle, you want to be a' – for a terrible moment of folicle constriction I think he's going to say gay bugger – 'murderer, it's a lifestyle. Y'all make choices about these things and it's like choosing a bleddy *hat*.'

'That's me and you, Vincent, that "y'all", in case you were wondering. That's me and you who choose ethics like hats. Or in your case skin toners.'

'In my young days,' my father continues, 'we didn't have so much . . . I mean, things were simpler then. You got married, it was for good. You believed in God, it was for good. The big things *meant* something to us, you know? We didn't know any different, but we weren't miserable like you buggers today.'

'We've got options, Dad,' I say, thinking of Janet's magazine, not really sure whether I'm objecting.

'But y'all are all bleddy un*happy*, aren't you?'

'I'm unhappy, Mr M,' Vince says. 'But it's mainly about the rent.'

Pasha laughs. He's developed this role over the years with Vince, with many of the family's friends and in-laws, fruity straight-shooter, stirrer. He doesn't mean half of what he says.

'Anyway,' I announce, 'grub's ready. Drink up.'

Since my father's bunking on the couch Vince retires early after dinner with a concealed spliff. I wash the dishes, the old man dries. There's a small reservoir of adventure in these London trips for him, then he starts missing my mum. I can see it, the drift of his inner attention back up north. They've been husband and wife for fifty-seven years. They still hold hands, he still sneaks up behind her and wraps her in his arms, nuzzles her neck, gooses her. Outside marriage and family, neither of them has ever seemed to want or need anything else. By the time the crockery's put away, bottles gathered, ashtrays emptied and worktops wiped, he's yawning. The day's most likely worn him out. Skinner. The ring. The not being sure. The whiskies. The options. While he changes into his Man from Del Monte pyjamas I fold out the futon and make up his bed. I'll take him to Tooting tomorrow for Indian sweets, barfi, jelabies, ludoos, doot peras, rasgoola. He can get them in Bolton, but it's something we like to do together.

'You're going to have to give it back, you know,' he says, sitting on the edge of his bed. 'That ring.'

This has occurred to me, though since I've discovered it fits the second finger of my right hand I've been wearing it all day.

'Yeah, I know,' I say. 'I'll do it through the daughter.'

'Something going on between you two or what?'

'I like her.'

'She seems nice.'

'Yeah, well, I'm not in her good books after today. I can't see it getting much better when I tell her I thieved her dad's ring.'

He yawns again, Stan Laurelishly scratches his head. 'How's the book coming?' It's the first time he's mentioned it since this afternoon.

'Don't ask,' I say. 'Goodnight, Dad.'

'Goodnight, my son.'

It's three in the morning. Vince has fallen asleep (I suspect) with his CD player still on. *Mezzanine*, looped. I don't mind the murmur, and Pasha, a bantamweight with heavyweight sleeping habits, won't be disturbed. I sit on the floor of my room surrounded by papers. *The* papers.

'You know the story,' the old man said. 'So what is there to telling it? You start at the beginning, go through the middle, then get to the end.'

It's always been the ending that's bothered me. These days, even the sound of the word . . .

Scarlet, the ether tells me, has flown, and now once again there's life to get through without her, only the dim prospect of the comet's return.

You'll live.

Two hundred miles north, my mother sleeps for once without the risk of nocturnal disturbance. Seeing the old man here on his own has made me miss her, her small face and the tick of her knees. When are you coming to see us again? Soon, Ma, soon.

Skinner, I imagine, has long nights of busy dreams. Wakes to relief, irritation, the tedious wait for the next daughter visit. Asks himself as the shadows revolve through the quiet afternoons: How much time?

Janet may well be awake. Weighing up pros and cons, I hope. If there's only sadness waiting you might as well have fun in the meantime. I wish you'd been straight with me. The wishing itself proves something.

I've been searching for a long time for an arresting opening. *The gods and goddesses of romance make their inaugural demands. So do certain matters of fact.* That was a front runner for a while. Others have come and gone. *Unlike my father, my mother, Katherine Marie Millicent Lyle – Kathy, Katie, Kit, Kitty, but most often Kate – has kept the mystery of her past.* For a while I toyed with *London is no longer interested in me*, but what's the point in starting on a downer? *You write what you want, Sweetheart. None of that can touch me now.*

It's no good. *The Cheechee Papers*, I'm forced to admit, are adrift, beginningless, endless, a fucking mess.

I finish my umpteenth glass of rioja, pour another to kill the bottle, light a cigarette, and without any care for order start to gather up the pages.

When I'm finished the stack weighs as much as a newborn baby. I take it over to the desk and set it down next to the computer.

I remember everything, the first line of the top sheet says. *That's the problem.*

I pick up a red pen, and by monitor light (surprised again by the presence of the bloodstone ring on my finger), carefully cross it out.

Which, in the gently perverse way of these things, feels like a beginning.